Stalin's War: Volume One

A Novel of Alternative History

The World in Flames Trilogy

Written by Jack Strain

Preface

Volume One of this series, *Stalin's War,* was inspired by real historical events centered on a controversial OSS operation named Sunrise. It was an attempt by a senior SS General to surrender German forces to the American and British forces fighting in Italy with the goal of preventing the Russians from capturing Berlin and overrunning Germany. When word of this leaked to Stalin and coupled with the surprising news that American forces captured intact the Ludendorff Bridge over the Rhine River, the Soviet leader saw the two events as nothing less than backstabbing from the Western Allies, causing a near break in relations. An angry series of cables from the Kremlin caught the FDR White House by surprise. They were shocked by the furious allegations from Stalin. This story begins here.

All the historical figures are present, as well as some fictional characters created to help tell the story of how the two greatest powers in world history could have very easily come to blows and changed our world forever.

Prologue

For seven long days and nights in February 1945, three modern day warlords, in command of the greatest collection of military resources in the history of mankind, met to decide the collective fate of two and a half billion people. Together, these erstwhile Allies waged a world war for six years against the combined might of the Empire of Japan and the German Reich. With victory in their grasp, the battle for the peace had only just begun. Each was determined to advance their own national interests, but only one would be able to dictate the terms. When they were finished, the word Yalta threatened to haunt a generation.

The British Bulldog, Prime Minister Winston Churchill, came to the meeting in an attempt to preserve a frail British Empire and stand as an equal between the two emerging superpowers. Frail and dying, President Franklin Delano Roosevelt sought to gain assurances that the Red Army would intervene against the Japanese in Manchuria. More importantly, the American President was desperate to create a world body, a United Nations, under the leadership of the Great

Powers. This was to be his legacy, to succeed where Wilson had failed.

The last national leader, and host of the conference, was General Secretary Josef Stalin. He came to the Yalta conference with his own agenda, one very different than either Churchill or Roosevelt. Stalin had led his great nation from the brink of utter defeat to commanding the greatest army in history. The heroic sacrifice of millions of workers and peasants secured his position and would allow him to dictate his terms. From the beginning it was obvious the Soviet leader hadn't come to Yalta to talk as an ally, but to rule.

With the advancing Red Army in possession of Eastern Europe, land that encompassed most of Imperial Russia's age-old dreams of empire, the Kremlin had no intention of giving them back. Even before the American President had spoken a single word, the cynical master of the Kremlin had decided to enter the war in Asia against the Japanese. The Russian people would exact a terrible revenge for the humiliating loss suffered in 1905. For Stalin, it had been a good war and would become an even better peace.

After nearly a week of banquets, meetings, and toasts, the Big Three ended their conference and went their separate ways. The American leader obtained his commitment from the Soviets to intervene against the Japanese and to participate in his cherished United Nations. As a parting gift to his host, F.D.R. announced that the American people were tired of war and wanted no part in Europe's long-term problems. He openly declared he would withdraw American forces from Europe within two years and raised no serious objections to Soviet demands in Eastern Europe. Even the fate of the Poles was no given a moment's thought.

Throughout the conference, Churchill failed to convince the American President of the need for a united front against the emerging Soviet menace and left bitterly disappointed. He knew the six million man Red Army and a weak American President all but guaranteed Europe would once again be threatened by the evil specter of a more powerful enemy than Nazi Germany. Worn down and feeling powerless, Churchill felt quite alone as the conference came to a close.

As he watched his old friend being wheeled away, he glanced at the gloating Soviet leader. The victor of this conference was clear for all to see. The gallant leader of the British Empire felt like a man standing on the gallows waiting for the hangman's noose, knowing it was too late to change his fate. Europe could only hold its breath and hope against hope for a miracle that would probably not come in their lifetimes.

With head hung low, Churchill whispered to himself, "What shall become of Europe?"

Chapter One

February 24, 1945

London

    Even though the hour was late for most Londoners, Sir Anthony Eden, Great Britain's wartime Foreign Minister, felt deeply troubled when the Prime Minister missed his second cabinet meeting in as many days and decided that he must speak to the man in person regardless of the hour. Usually not one to drop by unannounced, Secretary Eden felt it was his duty to impose himself on the Prime Minister. Something was definitely out of sorts, and Eden felt compelled to find out exactly what was troubling his friend and longtime mentor.

Since the cursed meeting at Yalta, the Prime Minister had fallen into a rather nasty funk. Eden originally assumed it was just the trip, considering the PM began the journey to Yalta while still battling a nasty case of pneumonia. God knew the accommodations were utterly wretched. President Roosevelt's special envoy, Harry Hopkins, said it best, "…that a worse place on the planet couldn't have been found without purposely trying."

The old Czarist summer palace smelled awful and the clumsy cleanup job made matters all the worse. Eden could hardly forget about the pack of oversized rodents poking their disease ridden snouts everywhere. Eden couldn't speak for the Prime Minister but he barely slept all week. *Bloody nightmare, even the Iranians back in '43 knew how to host a conference better than the Russians, the bloody savages.*

Eden knew it was more than the accommodations that had the PM down. Churchill seemed diminished since Yalta. After more than five years of war, no matter the crisis, Churchill always stood ready with his jaw jutting out, prepared to lead the fight, no matter the odds. If he sensed anything less than complete faith in ultimate victory, he'd light up the room with one of his never-ending torrents of fighting words and belief in the English people. Those who served with him during the dark days, when defeat not only seemed possible, but likely, would never forget what he meant to his proud, island nation.

Eden thought Churchill acted guilty, as if he had failed to measure up. Perhaps the Polish business or seeing the American President so near the end was taking its toll. The American leader looked like a decaying corpse being wheeled around from meeting to meeting, simply horrid.

Regardless, the PM needed to deal with whatever was troubling him and quickly. He must address the House of Commons in two days to defend the government's actions at the Yalta conference, plus outline the final direction of the war. The country still needs the Churchill of old, so tonight Eden's job was to remind him of his promise to see this through to the bitter end. Besides, he missed the old bugger and wanted him back.

Meanwhile, alone in his office, Winston Churchill sat in his leather lounge chair and stared at a painting of his famous ancestor, the Duke of Marlborough. He wondered how civilized it must have been back in the Eighteenth Century. War had its rules, peace treaties were negotiated by gentlemen, and, in the end, the balance of power was restored and all set right. How he longed for such days.

Sitting in his darkened office with scotch in hand, the Prime Minister replayed the meetings in his mind. *What did I miss? What could I have said to make the Americans understand? There must have been something he could have used against that murdering bastard Stalin to force him to negotiate on an equal basis.* The futility of the Yalta meetings haunted him by the hour. He hadn't slept properly in days and was starting to feel the effects.

Churchill noticed the way the moonlight filtered through the thick blackout curtains and came to reflect on the face of the victor of Blenheim. In that instant the accusing eyes of the great Duke seemed to light up in consternation and sent a shudder up his spine causing Churchill to feel shame for the first time in his entire life. He had failed and there was truly nothing that could be done. Softly to himself, Churchill said, "Dear God, but I feel old."

Shortly thereafter the effect of the scotch began to tell, and the Prime Minister closed his eyes for what he thought would be the briefest of moments and became lost in dream. His eyes fluttered back into focus, but to his utter shock, he found himself in another lifetime.

He was outside that much he could see as he looked up into the clear blue skies. He knew he wasn't in England anymore. There was activity all around him. As he looked around, he stopped a young man in uniform and hesitantly asked, "Where am I, lad?"

The young man was surprised at the strange question and meekly answered, "Sir, this is your command post."

Within seconds, Winston recognized the khaki colored, mud splattered uniform of a World War One British Tommy and realized he had returned to the trenches of Flanders. In a flash all became clear as Churchill's senses came alive and everything fell into place. The smell of cordite in the air, the sound of whistling artillery rounds soaring high above their heads as they traveled towards the Huns trenches, and the sound of men marching in a sea of mud triggered recognition and brought him back.

He was no longer an old and ailing Prime Minister. He had been transformed back into a young and vibrant Lt. Colonel serving the Crown in the field of battle. He was on the front lines commanding his battalion of the 6th Royal Scots Fusiliers in the bloody fields and trenches of Belgium in 1916. It all seemed so real but it couldn't be. Had he truly gone off the deep end?

Within moments, he felt familiar sensations. He found himself standing tall, walking with a sense of purpose. Lt. Colonel Churchill watched his men go about their business, cleaning their weapons, writing letters back home, and performing the never ending chores to make trench life bearable. How did he ever forget how much he loved his men?

Churchill turned his head as he heard a series of shrill whistles signaling the men for the next push against the German trench line. Gripped with fear, Churchill began to panic. Knowing the outcome, he screamed, "it's all a bloody waste," but no one responded. His men formed up to go over the top. His men being cut down for nothing was more than he could bear, so Winston closed his eyes and screamed at them to halt. But before he realizes what he is doing, Churchill finds himself blowing a whistle.

In that instant, his brave boys moved as a single unit up and over the trench. To Winston's horror, a thunderous roar erupts all around him as explosives and machinegun fire lands on top of their position and tears through his men. His boys scream in fear and their shrieks mix with the sound of the German shells as Churchill becomes covered with mud and the blood of men hit by shell splinters. All around him, his men lay in bloody heaps, begging him to help, to make it stop.

In a moment of clarity amidst the chaos, Churchill wonders, *Why haven't I been hit? Why am I not wounded?* Churchill began to panic and yelled at his men, "Fall back! Fall back!"

But no one listened and his brave troops were mowed down before his eyes. Soon the fields of Flanders were covered with hundreds of dead and dying British soldiers. He had led them to their slaughter and had no one to blame but himself.

Trembling, Churchill tried to tell himself it must be a dream. *It wasn't like this, this God awful nightmare.* Then, as if a switch had been hit, all went quiet. Relieved, Winston began to relax felt a small tug on his trousers' leg. Looking down, he saw a young soldier by his feet, curled up in a ball in obvious pain. The soldier began making horrible sounds, a retching, subdued shriek. Winston pat the boy's head and told him to have faith, it would be all right.

But the sounds kept growing louder until Winston couldn't take it any longer. He turned the boy over and pulled the boys' hands apart, away from his face. To his horror he sees why the soldier couldn't speak. The boy had no mouth, no eyes, no face, just a bloody mass of torn flesh. He stared at the hollowed out crevices where eyes should have been. Churchill's hands trembled as it became clear the boy was begging him to do something.

Bloody hell, I have to do something. I am his commanding officer, but how can I give him back his face? Churchill noticed more of his men around him making the same horrible sound. They lay in clumps, twitching and slithering towards him. *How is this possible? Why don't they have faces? Why are they blaming me?*

Unable to take it anymore, tears streaming down his cheeks, Churchill screamed, "It's not my fault! It's not my Fault! Dear God, believe me, it's not my fault!"

Eden rounded the corner to the Prime Minister's office and heard a scream inside. Alarmed, he flung the door open as Churchill snapped out of it. Eden rushed to Churchill's side, "Winston, calm yourself. It's all right, everything's all right."

Breathing heavy, Churchill stared back at Eden, but said nothing. Eden noticed the half-finished bottle of scotch on the desk and asked, "Come now, Winston, are you having some sort of attack?"

Churchill slowly regained his color, but instead of responding to Eden, he reached for the bottle of scotch. Thinking more alcohol was the last thing he needed, Eden spoke sharply, "Winston, for God's sake, man, what's wrong? Answer me damn it."

Finally, still dazed, Churchill poured himself a drink and downed its contents. He looked directly at Eden and said, "Anthony, what will they say?"

Eden looked back perplexed and asked, "What will who say? Really, this has gone on long enough. You're beginning to make me think you have gone ahead and suffered a bloody stroke."

Stung by his young protégé's reply, the Prime Minister rose unsteadily from his chair and faced his Foreign Minister, "I was referring to those who gave their lives during this terrible war."

By the way Eden looked back at him, Churchill realized he had best explain what had been on his mind for the past two weeks or people would begin to think he had gone off the deep end. Anthony, above all others, must understand.

So Churchill began, "Anthony, do you know what it feels like to truly believe the deaths of so many of our lads may, in the end, mean nothing when this great conflict has ended? Do you fully grasp that it is now a certainty that the Bolsheviks will sweep into Germany, capture Berlin, and dictate the remaining terms of surrender?"

Becoming more agitated, Churchill's voice grew increasingly louder as he continued, "Anthony, do you appreciate the implications for Europe of having that brute Stalin's Red Army control all of Eastern and Central Europe?" Then he roared, "All of the Empire's subjects have died for nothing! Europe will be forever changed and there isn't a damn thing we can do about it."

Eden began to say something, but the Prime Minister looked him directly in the eye and continued, "We have failed the Crown and let down the British people. Because of those ghastly agreements at Yalta, the citizens of these Isles should hold us in contempt. We are no better than Chamberlain and his "peace in our time" babble."

"Now, that's enough!" Eden shouted back, his pride now stung. . "What would you have us do? Roosevelt is gone, he's done, and he's not half the man he was just six months ago. With all that power, the Americans are led by a man who could die at any moment. For God's sake, Winston, Roosevelt announced he was pulling all U.S. forces out of Europe in two years…two bloody years. Did you see the smug smiles on Molotov and Stalin's faces when the American President made his grand announcement?"

Trying to regain some control of himself, Eden spoke more calmly and said, "We have no choice but to make the best arrangements with the Russians as we can, somehow secure the Empire, and hope that DeGaulle can rebuild France into a great power again."

Churchill shot right back, "How can you stand there and glibly defend that despicable document as if this was a question on the Foreign Service exam? Anthony, for God's sake man, we are talking about why we went to war. We are talking about Great Britain's historic mission on the continent that dates back to the Thirty Years War."

Before Eden could get a word in edgewise, Churchill sternly addressed him, "The mission of the British people is to ensure that no single power dominates the continent. That's why we fought against Louis XIV, Napoleon, the Kaiser, and now Hitler. But even as we speak, the Bolsheviks are occupying Warsaw, Bucharest, and will soon enough reach Berlin, Prague, and probably Vienna.

"I am the Prime Minister of His Majesty's Government and must live with the burden knowing we failed in our historic mission, and I can barely live with the shame! How many have died in this war and for what? I guarantee you that Yalta will be talked about for the next generation, and they will say that we wrote off entire peoples because we were afraid."

Eden took a step back and listened as Churchill poured out his heart and soul. Knowing the old romantic warrior in Churchill was too aroused to simply dismiss his demons, Eden chose his tone and words carefully, "Winston, however much I find your words compelling, sometimes one must secure the best arrangement that one is able. I don't see any other way short of negotiating a separate peace with the Germans to prevent Stalin from having his way on the continent."

At the mention of a separate peace, Churchill looked up at Eden and his guilty expression gave away the unthinkable. Eden saw his mentor's eyes and knew this was why Churchill had been so depressed.

Eden quickly ran through the PM's calculations. One, accept the distasteful fact that the Soviets had no intention of following the terms of the Yalta agreement, and consent to the de facto subjugation of most of Europe, or attempt to convince the Americans to deal with anti-Nazi forces, preferably the Wehrmacht, and turn against the Soviet allies before the Red Army controls the better part of Europe.

Eden began to understand. It wasn't in the man to sit back and do nothing. No other political figure on the planet had led the fight against the Nazi menace for so long, but he actually seemed prepared to join forces to stop an even greater danger from emerging. The implications hit home and the normally cool and collected Foreign Secretary said, "Bloody hell Winston, I do believe that I'll be joining you for one of those drinks."

The British Foreign Secretary shuffled over to the Prime Minister's desk, poured himself a drink, and slumped into the couch to think. A disconcerting quiet swept through the room, as both men allowed the other time to consider what would be said next.

Finally, the Prime Minister walked over to the couch, sat down, looked Eden in the eye and calmly said, "Anthony, for the first time in my entire life, I truly don't know what to do. The only thing I do know is that to do nothing condemns millions to life under the rule of that tyrant."

Deeply shaken, Eden looked over at Churchill and said in a solemn voice, "I fear we shall be equally damned, whatever choice we make."

Churchill felt slightly relieved to have unburdened himself, but he could tell his Foreign Secretary was no more prepared to do anything at the moment then he was. Maybe that was for the best. Dark days were approaching and deep down, Churchill prayed that when the time came, he would be able to act, somehow restore England's honor and make a stand against the Russian bear before all was lost. He hoped it wouldn't be too late.

Chapter Two

February 24, 1945

U.S. Embassy, Moscow

Deep within the cramped confines of the US embassy in Moscow, Ambassador Averell Harriman, heir to one of the richest families in America, struggled to complete a cable he desperately hoped would rattle some cages back in Washington. Yalta. Just saying the word brought a grimace to the normally calm and reserved face of the former Wall Street corporate attorney. He couldn't believe how everything had gone so goddamned bad. He tried to warn them ahead of time, but to little avail, and it might be too late.

Worn down, Harriman drained his glass of vodka, which was

about the only damn thing the Russians did well those days besides building tanks and killing Germans. Shaking his head, he sadly recalled the moment he saw Roosevelt and he knew the American position would be in jeopardy. Franklin's appalling physical condition was apparent to everyone. Shaken by memories of Franklin's tired, vacant eyes, Averell searched for any hint of vitality, but all he saw was a sick old man on the verge of death.

Sadly, Roosevelt really seemed to think he could convince Uncle Joe one last time, that somehow the old FDR charm would convert that hardhearted son of bitch and make everything right in the world. But what was truly inexcusable was the way Secretary of State Stettinus actually appeared to believe the meetings were a grand success because Stalin agreed to join the United Nations idea, so dear to some in the White House.

God, how he loathed Stettinus for arrogantly believing he alone secured President Roosevelt's legacy because of this damn treaty. *Though I have to admit, it wasn't all that long ago I was one of Stalin's greatest American admirers.* Realizing what a fool he had been, Harriman felt duty bound to convince the administration that the so-called great ally in the Kremlin forced us to pay too high a price. The vain Secretary of State would hear none of it and, as a result, millions would fall into the Soviet orbit.

What really stung Harriman was the empty feeling, that he utterly failed both a longtime friend and the nation. Maybe the Moscow Embassy's number two man, George F. Kennan, was right. The Byzantine-like practices of Old World diplomacy really were lost on a Wall Street lawyer and a child of American privilege. Though he knew George would never say it to his face, deep down, that was exactly what Kennan thought, and maybe he was right. He had been too proud to take the advice of some mere academic sent by the State Department to watch over him and it took the tragedy of the Warsaw uprising to finally see the Soviets for what they were, pure, cold-blooded murderers.

He almost had Kennan recalled back to Washington last year. Kennan had tried for months to warn his boss and others back in Washington that relations with the Soviets was about to dramatically change since the Germans were on the run. Harriman had to swallow back the bile as he recalled the self-righteous lecture he delivered to his subordinate. To his credit, Kennan remained respectful and continually tried to educate his boss, until finally Harriman saw the light, but it was too late.

Feeling a little drunk as he worked his way through a third vodka martini, Harriman jumped when he heard a knock at his door. *Oh Christ*, he thought, all he wanted to do was drink himself into a stupor and pass out for the night. Was that really too much to ask?

Moving a bit unsteadily towards the door, Averell tripped and banged his into a table in the foyer and limped towards the door. Through the peephole saw the young, dark-haired Kennan, who looked a bit harried, himself.

Kennan greeted his boss warmly, "Good evening Mr. Ambassador, sorry for the late hour but I just received your message. I've been gone most of the evening, and the message did say it was urgent. So, here I am."

Forgetting he had even asked George to stop by, Averell tried to shake away the cobwebs and replied, "Come on in, George. Perhaps I should be the one apologizing, considering the time. Can I at least offer you a drink?"

Taking careful note of Harriman's appearance and official documents all over the desk, Kennan was curious, so he loosened his tie and answered, "Since we both seem to be up Mr. Ambassador, I think a drink would be a fine idea."

"Excellent, George. You know how I hate to drink alone."

As Harriman filled a second glass with vodka, Kennan cautiously asked," May I assume sir that this is about Yalta?"

Wincing at the mere mention of the word, Harriman mumbled, "Just hearing that word makes me feel downright nauseous. Earlier today I pulled that cable you sent to Washington back in September and made myself read it again. It was uncanny reading it, "Russia, Seven Years Later." To think I actually gave you hell about it. What a fool I was, but no longer."

Kennan stiffened a bit at the memory. He, nearly resigned after Harriman's brutal rebuke, but decided to stick things out and was glad he did. The two men were not friends and probably never would be, but the ambassador was learning and that was a start. Far too many back in Washington continued to ignore that Soviet power was growing by the day and soon would be in position to dominate post-war Europe. And, unlike Nazi Germany whose maniacal leadership doomed the Third Reich, the Soviets were led by a man devoid of sentiment or emotion. Stalin possessed enough power to turn Lenin's dream of a world revolution into reality.

Sensing Harriman was being genuine, Kennan respectfully replied, "Please, sir, there's no need to revisit the past."

Harriman hesitated for a second, looking for some hint of "I told you so" from Kennan, but quickly put such thoughts aside and responded, "Excellent George. I want you to take a look at a cable I'm preparing for Washington. It's time to make the administration face some cold, hard facts. This charade must come to an end."

Still trying to absorb his boss's change of heart, Kennan was relieved Harriman finally seemed ready to put that famous name of his on the line. Thinking he had better take advantage of the situation, Kennan got right to it. "It's not the administration that worries me. All this talk that the war is over and it's time to bring the boys back home, then, all of the sudden, the American people find out the Soviets are as bad or worse than the Nazis and maybe we can't bring everyone home right away. It'll get ugly and fast."

Shaking his head, Harriman asked, "What do you mean George? Ugly how?"

Disappointed Harriman was missing the obvious, "Mr. Ambassador, think about it. The American people actually believe all of that Hollywood inspired nonsense about Old Uncle Joe wanting the same thing as us. They forget that in an extraordinarily short period of time, we went from treating the Soviets like an enemy, after teaming up with the Nazis to stab the Poles in the back, to all of a sudden becoming Russian patriots overnight. It was as absurd as it was necessary. But now the American people will be forced to see them as the thugs they truly are."

Still unsure where Kennan was going, Harriman interjected, "But George, doesn't that actually work in our favor. Hell, most Americans didn't like the Commie bastards in the first place."

Frustrated he had to spell it out for the man, Kennan replied, "That's just it, sir, American public opinion will change back again, with Congress probably leading the way. You and I both know how paranoid Stalin is and if they think we may be turning on them, it will likely drive them into more desperate actions in the name of security."

While handing the martini to Kennan, the ambassador replied, "If I understand you correctly, rather than forcing Stalin to pull back, you feel he will press us even further?"

Kennan stirred his martini and reflected on the question. Casually, Kennan answered, "The issue before us is not how to prevent it, but instead, how to control it. We really have to start thinking about American interests in the post-war world. Eventually, the administration will understand that a policy of appeasement will be no more effective with the Soviets than it was with the Nazis."

Kennan thought, *this is where it gets tricky*. He would see how far his boss was willing to go. Taking a quick breath, Kennan said, "I propose to immediately begin contacting like-minded, key people in the State and War departments by diplomatic pouch to begin leaking information to the Press. That will force the administration to publically address the brutality of our erstwhile ally in the Kremlin. Further, we must hold the Soviets accountable to every detail of the Yalta accord, exactly as written, while at the same time begin pushing them on a host of smaller issues we have neglected for two years."

Suddenly feeling all too sober, Harriman paced the room, trying to absorb what Kennan asked him to undertake. Finally, he replied, "Fine. We push hard on everything from the promised Polish elections to treatment of refugees and repatriation of Allied airmen. For two years we've played nursemaid to them because we were so damned afraid of collapse or worse, a separate peace, that we let them literally get away with murder. It's going to feel pretty goddamned good to sit with Molotov and try to make him enforce agreements he crafted in Yalta, figuring the whole time we wouldn't bother on enforcement."

Cautiously, Kennan wanted to offer one last piece of advice, "Please, Averell, do not underestimate them. Stalin believes he's won already. The moment we begin challenging him, expect them to push hard in Eastern Europe, especially with the Poles. America loves an underdog, almost as much as it hates a cheat. What happens when we start leaking what the Soviets do in Poland? It's going to change everything."

The gravity of what Kennan described washed over him like a winter chill. Harriman answered in a whisper, "George, I feel worse now than I did before you came over tonight. The more we talk, I don't know, I have a bad feeling where this is all heading. Once this begins, where will it end?"

February 24, 1945, 7:30 p.m.

Office of Strategic Services, Washington D.C.

Major General *Wild Bill* Donovan, head of the Office of Strategic Services, sat in his office and stared at his typewriter as he contemplated the major change in policy he was about to order. Earlier in the day, Donovan had lunch with Secretary of the Navy, James Forrestal, and the only real topic was Yalta. Forrestal raged against the weak-minded advisors around President Roosevelt. In between mouthfuls of lamb chops he cursed everyone from Hopkins to Stettinus. Forrestal was perhaps the most vocal and openly anti-Soviet political figure in the American government. He argued that Yalta allow the Russians to dictate terms after Germany had been defeated.

The Navy Secretary asked, "Why in the hell did we fight the goddamn Nazis if it meant turning Europe over to Stalin? Christ, when I think of all the men who fought and died on D-Day and at the Bulge, it just makes me want to scream at Roosevelt and get it through his thick skull."

Donovan replied, "Mr. Secretary, we need to begin developing several contingencies for U.S. policy in post-war Europe. This report will include the likelihood of a significant break in relations in the immediate aftermath of the war. It will likely generate a significant reaction among the pro-Soviet forces that dominate the cabinet. I was hoping I could expect your support with the President on these matters?"

Unsure himself if he could convince the President, Secretary Forrestal finally answered, "Look Bill, if you can put together some official report to sell this then you can damn well count on my support."

The head of the OSS responded, "Until we can begin building a real political consensus on how to handle the Russians, my people will treat this as an operational O.S.S. matter. I just worry about what could happen in the meantime."

Later in the day, Donovan thought to himself that the moment the OSS begins gathering intelligence on the Russians and make contact with anti-Soviet movements in Eastern Europe there will be hell to pay. This memo would get the ball rolling.

To: Eyes Only, All OSS Station Chiefs

From: Head of OSS

Re: Operation Fortitude

Effective immediately, each O.S.S. station is to begin targeting the Soviet Union and developing hard intel concerning political, diplomatic, economic, and military intelligence, with special emphasis on identifying opposition groups in the newly liberated countries of Eastern and Central Europe. Whereas your main intelligence duties remain aimed against the Germans, this new initiative will be given high priority. Every Soviet general, diplomat, suspected NKVD agent, etc. are to be logged and dossiers begun to be compiled and a plan to track movements and intentions of Soviet leaders. This new directive requires a level two clearance, and is not to be shared with any other member of the alliance at this time. Report any contact by an outside agency or foreign power in regards to this mission.

Further instructions will be forthcoming.

With this memo, Donovan knew he had committed the members of his agency to an entirely new role. *Well, that's what Roosevelt gets for making a bastard like me a Major General.* Even though the memo specifically ruled out discussing the matter with anyone, even the Brits, Donovan knew that really wasn't realistic. So he picked up the phone, and dialed a dedicated phone connection to a number in New York City, set up for calls like this one. After three rings, a cheery voice answered, "My dear William, bucking for yet another undeserved promotion?"

Donovan answered in a serious tone, "Actually, I was calling to see if you had a moment."

The man on the other line was William Stevenson, also known by his code-name Intrepid. He was the British Secret Service's senior agent in the United States, responsible for coordinating intelligence operations between the Allies. In a few short years the two men had become friends and knew when something was not quite right. Stevenson sensing the tension in Donovan's voice, asked, "Bill, I take it that you didn't call merely to hear my voice, what can I do for you tonight?"

Donovan very carefully chose his words. "I need to know the unofficial version of your government's reaction to Yalta. In particular, how does His Majesty's Government intend to deal with the implications of the Yalta agreements?"

Stevenson had been ordered to be on the lookout for any changes in the American view of their mutual Russian ally. Obviously, President Roosevelt's actions in Yalta pushed the conservative elements within the American government too far, and Donovan was reaching out. Stevenson replied, "I can say with some assurance that more than a few have raised an eyebrow and some have written this off as another amateur like move by the Americans. For Christ's sake man, why didn't you tell us you were leaving the bloody continent in two years?"

Donovan somewhat embarrassed said, "Hell, I didn't know we were leaving that soon. Hopkins and Stettinus have Roosevelt's ear, and you know how they are. What I am looking to get from your end is to establish the official British government' reaction to the Russians."

The British MI6 man was poker straight when he answered, "Any open British policy change at this time would be a waste considering the recent decisions by your American government. You and I both know that without American support, the bloody Soviets will have us on the run. Okay old man, quid pro quo, what's happening in Washington?"

After an uncomfortable pause, Donovan responded, "Some are quite angry and have begun whispering the word appeasement in certain circles and want Franklin to reconsider. It won't happen overnight, but many are starting to think that we have allowed the Soviets to push us too far. But let's cut right to it, you know what I am proposing. Effective immediately, I want to begin sharing intelligence on the Russians and coordinate our assets, obviously unofficially of course."

Stevenson knowing all along what Donovan was hinting at, laughed, "Well, it took you bloody well long enough to get that off your chest. You're only talking about basically advocating the fundamental change in the official foreign policies of both of our governments."

Donovan replied, "Now this has to be kept low key for right now, you know as well as I do that the Soviets have no intention on following through with Yalta's terms, especially with the Poles, so this thing could go bad fast."

Stevenson closed the conversation in a serious tone, "I hope you are wrong Bill, but they pushed too hard at Yalta. I believe that old Uncle Joe feels that since the Germans couldn't stop them, then the Americans and Brits don't stand a chance." Both went silent as the implications spoke volumes for both countries.

Chapter Three

February 24, 1945, 10:30 p.m.

SS Headquarters in Italy

Desenzano, Northern Italy

SS General Karl Wolff, the second ranking officer in the entire SS, sat at his command post and thought time was rapidly running out. Official broadcasts out of Berlin continue to speak of victory even with the hated Bolsheviks fast approaching. Propaganda Minister Joseph Goebbels continued to demand faith in the Fuhrer, but with the Russians only fifty miles from Berlin, the Allies preparing to cross the Rhine River and the front in Italy hanging on by sheer willpower and the virtues of geography, how much longer before the whole dirty thing collapsed?

Wolff's mood turned particularly dark as he thought of the reports coming from the East about the murderous wake of the Russian advance. From sources within the SS High Command in Berlin, Wolff received hard evidence of unspeakable horrors taking place against the German people, far worse than was originally thought. It was one thing to shoot partisans, God knew Wolff had more than a few shot himself, but to allow troops to systematically rape entire villages? Young girls and old women alike were being taken as spoils of war. What those animals didn't steal, they burned. What they didn't rape, they murdered.

How had it come to this? For weeks, if not months, he had been contemplating some form of action, but time was clearly running out. Wolff knew he needed to take more active measures, whatever the consequences. Knowing it was not a time for half measures, he picked up the phone and made a long overdue call.

As he waited for his visitor, Wolff thought about the days prior to the war, before Hitler, before he was anyone. He wondered how a successful advertising salesman in the 1920's could somehow, twenty years later, be in command of one million German soldiers in Northern Ital. Laughing to himself as he drank his schnapps, *no wonder we're losing the war.*

Wolff was a realist, perhaps the last high-ranking Nazi who harbored no illusions about himself or the so-called cause of Greater Germany and the superiority of the Aryan race. He knew he gotten where he was for the same reason he was a successful salesman. Always the same two rules, tell the bastards what they want to hear and know when to be in the right place at the right time with the right person. After his business collapsed in the Depression of 1929, joining the Nazi party seemed natural, so easy. The only thing people were buying in those days, the only thing people could afford, was ideas, especially of the extreme variety.

Whether it was the communists, the Nazi's, or the various center-right parties, Germans were desperate to believe in something. The Nazi party wanted believers, and when he joined the SS in 1930, he easily convinced them of his undying belief in Germanic superiority, hatred of Jews, and other such nonsense. Wolff knew he could go far with these people, he just never dreamed how far. Christ, he never saw so many people who were desperate to believe, who were waiting for someone to say the right thing, in the right way. By 1933, Wolff was promoted to be a personal adjutant of Himmler, the head of the emerging SS, and from that point, he met everyone whom mattered.

His most important ally outside of Himmler was Rudolf Hess, then Hitler's right hand man. As the number two in the Party, Hess helped introduce Wolff to every top Party, military, and industrialist in the Reich, including Hitler. Even still, Wolff had to admit the man was completely hypnotizing to meet in person, at least back in the old days. Everyone knew he was not a military man, so he cultivated a persona as a diplomatic and personnel expert. Himmler had enough knuckle dragging muscle men on the payroll, so Wolff portrayed himself as the man who could get things done without bashing in skulls. If one had to deal with the SS in the early days, most would rather deal with the reasonable and urbane Wolff, who took full advantage of his newfound importance.

He traveled throughout the Reich as Himmler's personal representative. Nothing brought more pleasure than to walk into a factory or a local Party office and watch as proud, highborn Germans turn into kiss ass bootlickers. All he had to do was walk around in his black uniform with the ever present skull and crossbones insignia, look fierce, and lay down the Party line. These same people wouldn't have taken notice of some ad salesman five years before, feared him, knowing one word whispered in Himmler's ear would mean life or death. Since the majority of Hitler's Nazi Party hierarchy didn't really belong in the world they were creating, it was so easy to rise up through simple cunning and balls.

The insanity of it all still defied explanation. By 1945, Wolff found himself the number two man in the SS hierarchy, and nominally in charge of nearly one million soldiers fighting a desperate and hopeless battle against the Americans and British in Northern Italy. He wondered if cunning and balls would be enough to get Germany out of the mess it was in or whether all was lost. Regardless, something had to be attempted.

At ten in the evening, Wolff's personal adjutant, Colonel Eugen Dollmann, knocked on his office door and entered, "Good evening, Herr General."

Wolff waived him in and asked him to sit by the wood-burning stove. As Dollmann took his coat off and sat, Wolff shook his head, *here's another one who had no business wearing a uniform.*

Eugen Dollmann ran away to Italy in 1937, hoping to escape the coming war. His love of Italian artwork and desire to remain a simple scholar was thwarted in 1938 when he was drafted to interpret for Hitler during a State visit to Italy. Both Hitler and Himmler were so impressed with Dollmann that he was immediately commissioned into the SS and assigned to Rome as Himmler's personal diplomat to the Italian government. At the late stage in the war, "Eugenio" as Dollmann was called jokingly behind his back because of his love of Italian culture, found himself waiting for the end. Dollmann was as scared for Germany's future as Wolff, but prepared to wait for the Western allies to capture the whole lot of them and hope for the best.

Wolff began by saying, "Eugen have you read the reports coming out of the East lately?"

Dollmann replied in an academic monotone, "Yes, Herr General, but surely, the Americans and British won't let the Soviets do what they're doing in East Prussia to the rest of Germany, will they?" Dollmann looked like a wounded child as he allowed himself to think about what was happening to German women and children.

With a piercing glare, Wolff looked directly at Dollmann, and asked in an icy tone, "What are you prepared to do?"

Looking confused, Dollmann asked, "Excuse me sir, but what exactly do you mean? Seven years later, I still don't know why Himmler put me in this ridiculous uniform. I just want to wait this thing out and hope for the best."

Smiling a rather evil grin that frightened Dollmann a bit, Wolff answered, "My dear Colonel, I do believe it is time you took a little trip. In fact, we can call it a diplomatic mission. However, I am afraid this little mission will be a bit more dangerous than what you have experienced so far in the war." Wolff watched as Dollman's face displayed first bewilderment and then fear, and thought he shouldn't be enjoying this so much. Dollmann was such a fool.

Confused, Colonel Dollmann finally asked, "What type of diplomatic mission? Where could I possibly be going to that would accept a parley an SS officer?"

The SS General decided he was being unfair to Dollmann and realized it was too damn important to leave anything to chance. Softening his tone, Wolff began, "Eugen, you are going to Bern, Switzerland and will make contact with the American OSS station chief, Allen Dulles. The recently completed talks of the Americans, British, and Russians have just finished in Yalta. I believe this alliance that came together to defeat Germany is an unnatural one, and Germany's only chance is to come to terms with the Americans or even the British. The only way to end this war without completely destroying Germany is to either convince the Americans to join with us or at least enable the whole German war effort to focus on the Eastern Front."

Realizing just what type of danger he faced, Dollmann asked, "Why me?"

Eugenio's child-like responses were starting to really grate on Wolff who spat out, "If you would stop shaking in your fucking boots for one moment and think about the possibilities. Do you really think the Americans know what the Russians are doing in the East?"

Dollmann stared back, not comprehending what he was being asked to do.

Wolff tried another tack, "Have you ever read the Atlantic Charter or President Wilson's Fourteen Points from the First World War?

The Americans go to war for ideals, they believe in universal rights and freedom, and other such fantasies. Do you think they would want to be allied with the goddamn Russians if they knew what was going on in the East? I want you to talk with Dulles and set up a meeting between him and myself for early March, the sooner the better. I am going to propose to Dulles cease-fire terms between our two countries to end the war on the Western Front, or at least I can offer him the surrender of all German forces in Northern Italy. The former I probably can't deliver, but the latter I most certainly can and will."

Finally, Dollmann understood the implications. If suddenly one million German soldiers laid down their arms, the Allies would have a clear line of march into Austria and Bavaria. Maybe, it would force the whole Nazi government to collapse and then the Western Front would do the same thing. Both Berlin and Vienna would be open to the Allies instead of the Red Army and that could spare most of the German people from further devastation.

Colonel Dollmann smiled for the first time that evening, and said, "Herr General, when do you wish me to leave?"

Pleased, Wolff replied, "You are to leave at first light and make contact with this Dulles character as soon as humanly possible. I think you now understand the importance of what I am asking, but I also want you to understand the risks. If you are caught in this attempt, both of us will be shot for treason. Do not trust anyone else other than myself or whomever I appoint to assist you in this mission. Is that understood? At this point, neither your life nor mine mean anything, but if we fail, then countless millions will suffer for our mistakes."

Dollmann answered, "General, I will perform my duty for the Fatherland, plus I have relatives in Berlin and I fear for them."

Nodding to himself that the first move was made, Wolff hoped the American would be willing to *play ball,* as they say.

February 25, 1945, 12:30 a.m.

The Kremlin, Moscow

Even before the war, Stalin kept strange hours, often not going to bed before three or four in the morning. With the advent of the war, late nights for his aides were even worse. Often times Stalin would call important staff meetings as late as ten or eleven o'clock at night, and rarely would these meetings end before the coming of the dawn. Tonight was no different.

Lavrenti Beria, the dreaded head of the NKVD's vast secret police empire, could barely contain his excitement. He was about to give a report to Comrade Stalin about their so-called Allies. The Yalta Accords offered so many delicious possibilities for mischief that part of him still refused to believe the imperialists would ever honor them.

The short, balding, bespectacled, dark skinned Georgian was perhaps the most sinister man in the entire Soviet Union, except of course for the man he served with such sycophantic devotion. Beria had seen his power grow enormously over the course of the war. His kingdom had grown from command of the secret police to control of vast numbers of heavily armed NKVD divisions to oversight of the massive expansion of Soviet armaments, including the Soviet atomic bomb project.

Sitting in the back of his chauffeured car as he was whisked to the Kremlin, a sick smile came across his face thinking *who would have thought how much practical experience we learned during the time of the purges.* During the Great Terror, Beria personally ordered the deaths of hundreds of thousands of people, deported untold millions, and created the Gulag system of work camps in Siberia to re-educate political criminals. He knew the mere mention of his name was enough to scare grown men and make people tremble at his approach.

As he contemplated the re-education of the newly liberated peoples of Eastern Europe, his power would continue to grow. *Who knows maybe I'll become more powerful than the great man himself.* The swarthy Georgian didn't want to get too far ahead of himself, all good things in time. Even Lenin wasn't exactly ushered out of power right away. A well-timed stroke could be just as effective under the right circumstances, but he knew it was not the time for such adventures.

The master of the NKVD was someone who took true pleasure in his position. For all of the cruelty inherent in the Soviet system, the Russian people needed a firm hand. Russian history was clear on this. Only an Ivan the Terrible, Peter the Great, or a Stalin could force the Russian people to rise above all of their many weaknesses. Deep in his soul, Beria thanked the gods for a system which demanded men like himself, devoid of sentiment and without mercy, to force the children of Mother Russia to become a great nation.

Even in his exalted position, nothing made him feel the power he possessed more than to personally participate in an interrogation. To walk into a prisoner's cell and watch the victim as their eyes grew large because they understood the devil himself had entered the room. Secretly, it gave him a degree of satisfaction that not even sex with a fresh faced virgin could approach. His body would flutter as the adrenaline coursed through his veins when the fear and cries filled the room. He never grew tired of the screams.

Beria reveled in the court politics that existed within the Kremlin, and after eight years of control, he knew how best to maintain his power. Always provide his master, Comrade Stalin, with what he wanted to hear. Nothing else mattered. Experience taught him the best way to maintain favor with Stalin was to provide a never-ending list of suspects to be watched and then liquidated. It didn't really matter if they were kulaks, Red Army officers, Trotskyites, or Western imperialists. It made little difference if a threat truly existed, but the mere possibility or potential was enough to justify direct action against individuals, wives, children, or whole peoples. The NKVD was the Sword of the Party, and Beria was the man who wielded that terrible sword without mercy.

The Soviet Union had all but won the war, and with the German threat crushed for a generation, new enemies were needed. Beria had already decided the Red Army would have to be taken down a notch or two. In many respects, the Red Army had done too well, so another purge would have to be arranged, but that would come later. Beria shook his head, the greatest threat to Stalin and Mother Russia was none other than his erstwhile allies, especially the Americans. It was always invigorating to present a new threat to Comrade Stalin's attention. The man was so predictable in some things, whereas in others, even Beria couldn't keep up with his paranoid fantasies.

Only Comrade Stalin's inner circle, Foreign Minister Molotov, Moscow Part Chief Nikita Khrushchev, and Marshal Voroshilov were present for the meeting. After a fairly typical dinner, Stalin waived at Beria to begin. Beria first passed out an abridged version of the NKVD policy report and then began to speak.

"First, the amazing victory of the Soviet people would not have been possible without the great leadership of Comrade Stalin. The Nazi's and their mongrel allies have been defeated one after another and shortly the Red Army, under Comrade Stalin's direction, shall capture Berlin. The Yalta talks clearly indicated that the Western powers intend to return to their pre-war policies of opposition to the peace loving peoples of the Soviet Union. The imperialist Churchill and his sickly ally Roosevelt already seek to deny the fruits of victory. The Soviet people bled by the millions to stop the Hitlerite invasion, now what are these so-called allies prepared to give us? Nothing!"

As was custom, several of Stalin's cronies banged on the table and cursed the Imperialists. Stalin waved for them to be quiet and so Beria continued, "They opposed us at every turn at the Yalta conference. We, who have sacrificed millions and suffered untold billions in damage, are made to feel as if we must beg for our just spoils of war. Comrades, the imperialists fear our power and this new League of Nations is nothing but an attempt to limit the natural progression of communism throughout the world under Comrade Stalin's benevolent guidance." Beria watched as Stalin's facial expressions changed from pride to anger.

Stalin interrupted, "Comrade Beria, we always knew the imperialists feared us, so why should we be concerned with such things now?"

Beria happily responded, "Comrade Stalin, we have information that certain reactionary elements in the American and British governments plan to deny us our great victory and are reaching out to the Germans to make a separate peace to oppose our peace-loving policies in the liberated countries in Eastern Europe."

Stalin's twitching eyes betrayed him. Beria knew Stalin's greatest fear throughout the war was the possibility of the West turning against the Soviet Union by making a deal with Hitler.

Sensing Beria was planning some mischief, Molotov's monotone voice countered, "Comrade Beria is right to be concerned with the Imperialist powers, but I think it is unlikely they would do the unthinkable and negotiate with the fascists. Comrade Stalin, I propose we continue to use the power of the Red Army to first achieve victory as soon as possible and then plan to do as we choose in our zone, as we see fit. Comrades, the Americans have no heart and are looking to leave Europe while the British are too weak to matter. They will have their hands full just trying to hang on to their dying empire in Asia and Africa."

Sensing Molotov saw through his attempt, Beria looked directly at Comrade Stalin and stated, "Comrade Stalin, Foreign Minister Molotov makes some valid points, but I believe he underestimates the lengths in which the imperialists will oppose us. For example, Churchill insists on calling for free elections, so those Polish stooges in London can create mischief for us."

With his mouth half filled with bread and venison, Khrushchev blurted out, "Comrades why are we even talking about the fucking

Chapter Four

February 25, 1945, 7:00 a.m.

Bern, Switzerland

Moving slowly out of bed, Allen Dulles, OSS Station Chief in Switzerland, began his day early. He shivered as the Swiss winter chill enveloped him. When *Wood* material was due to arrive by special courier, time was always of the essence.

After a quick change, he sat in the library of his comfortable, eighteenth century, Swiss home, and reflected upon the man behind the *Wood* intelligence. Dulles' prize agent, code named George Wood, came knocking at his front door in August of 1943. The funny thing was Dulles wasn't even the first one *Wood* asked to come to the dance.

No, Wood went first to the British, but was turned down. The British agent in charge of the Swiss mission thought the shabby German walk-in was certainly a double agent, and described him as being too "bloody obvious."

Two years later, the disheveled, gray haired, middle aged clerk who fell into the Americans' lap had emerged as the single most important American intelligence resource in the war. His reports proved frighteningly accurate and valuable.

Dulles wondered what type of man could face his fears and do what this man did month after month. In front of the fireplace, Allen admitted he was having a rather comfortable war. He was too old for a line commission and too easily bored for some innocuous position on one of Washington's numerous War Production Boards or other political service. But, he wanted to play a significant role, so when Wild Bill Donovan called him to serve in the new American intelligence service, Dulles jumped at the chance.

He served in a similar capacity for a short time during the First World War and relished the chance to be back in the Spy Business. He knew his modest contributions to the war effort were because of

Wood. The agent risked his life every day, without fail, while Dulles went to bed safe and secure.

George Wood, a.k.a. Fritz Kolbe, did not fit the Hollywood casting call of a wartime spy. The forty-three year old Kolbe came from an undistinguished German family. He put himself through night school to reach the lofty rank of a simple, mid-level clerk working in the Foreign Ministry. He was the type of man that one could pass going down the street and make not the least impression. After twenty years of undistinguished service, he had become a personal assistant to a ranking officer in the Foreign Ministry.

Fritz Kolbe was special because he worked directly for Karl von Ritter, head of the Foreign Office liaison with the Wehrmacht, the German Army. Ritter reported directly to the German Foreign Minister von Ribbentrop on all military and intelligence matters that could impact the Reich's diplomatic policies. This gave Kolbe access to all forms of military traffic, everything from reports on damage from Allied bombing efforts to military deployments on the Eastern Front. Kolbe even stumbled on to specific intelligence operations being conducted against the Allies in embassies around the world.

When Dulles first met Kolbe, he asked the clerk why he was doing this.

Kolbe replied, "I am anti-Nazi and anti-Communist." Kolbe was a religious man who believed neither ideology represented the real German people.

As Dulles finished his coffee, Mary Bancroft, his personal assistant, came into his office with some paperwork. Mary greeted her boss and lover, "Good morning, Allen. You're up early, expecting something from Washington?"

Shaking his head, Dulles responded, "Good morning yourself. Actually, I was expecting the next courier from Wood, not Washington. Why?"

Shrugging her shoulders, Mary handed him the cable from Washington which had come overnight.

Seeing the code in the upper-right section indicated level one clearance, Dulles knew it was important. "Mary, do me a favor by bringing over my cipher booklet and call Gero and tell him to report early today. I suspect we will find ourselves occupied for the better part of the morning."

Gero Schulze-Gavernitz was a German national living in Switzerland. Dulles recruited him in Bern. The German national had since become indispensable to the Swiss OSS station. Dulles knew Gero's father who was an economist and politician who befriended Allen in the confusing post-war days when Germany needed

American Wall Street money to pay the reparations from the Versailles Treaty.

Dulles had maintained informal ties over the years and knew the family was anti-Nazi, but very circumspect about it. As it turned out, young Gero not only wanted to avoid service in the German Wehrmacht, but also wanted to work with the Allies to help overthrow the Hitler regime.

Dulles had come to rely heavily upon Gero's instincts and his uncanny ability to make contact with anti-Nazi elements still within Germany. Being an unrepentant playboy made his cover as hiding out in Switzerland pretty easy to be believed and the Gestapo never really suspected what he did and basically left him alone. Gero became Dulles most successful talent scout, sniffing out who could be useful and who would waste their time. Dulles never could have put his network together without him, and therefore he gave Gero allowances he never would have with another agent.

While Allen waited for his younger associate to arrive, he began to decipher the coded message from Washington. It wasn't often that Donavon saw fit to send a high level memo himself, so Dulles was curious. Deciphering the message was tedious. After thirty-five minutes, Allen completed the memo and sat back to read it.

Dulles whistled aloud and uttered, "Jesus Christ, no wonder Bill made this a level one." Dulles knew he held political dynamite. The former Wall Street lawyer was no friend of the Communists and couldn't have agreed more with his friend's initiative, but the timing was dangerous. What would happen if the Germans or the Soviets got a hold of this information? There would be hell to pay from Franklin and his people.

Gero strolled Allen's his office. "Good morning. What is so earth shattering that requires my presence before noon?"

Too absorbed in the implications from the new cable that Dulles just motioned for him to sit down and Gero sensed that something more than the cat had gotten his boss' tongue, so he asked, "What the devil put that look on your face?"

Dulles was barely paying attention as his mind raced a mile a minute wondering what propelled Donovan to push this memo through, especially timed so close to the conclusion of the Yalta summit. Dulles knew that Donovan was much more of an open anti-Communist, like his brother, John Foster Dulles, but he was a team player. The idea he would unilaterally institute a major change in seemed extreme.

Finally, Dulles turned to Gero, "It seems we've received new marching orders. As of this moment, the Bern OSS station just went into the anti-Communist business."

Gero felt glum as he realized his country would turn into a different type of battlefield. Not usually one to take things seriously, Gero turned to Dulles and in a light hearted tone said, "It could be worse. I thought you were going to cut my expense account." Dulles' vacant stare and lack of a response hardly boded well for the future.

Later that evening a local Swiss intelligence officer, Major Max Waibal, who was aware of Dulles' wartime role in his neutral country, contacted him. Dulles and Gero met Major Waibal for dinner to discuss an interesting request by two Italians living in occupied Northern Italy. The two men claimed to speak for ranking SS officers from the German High Command in the Italian theater. The Swiss officer's instinct told him something about the two Italians was genuine. He recommended Dulles take them seriously.

After dinner Dulles sent Gero to investigate matters. Gero came to Allen's home the next day to report on the mysterious visitors. The two men, Parilli and Max Husmann, claimed the SS leadership in Italy wanted to speak directly to members of the American mission in Switzerland to discuss military and diplomatic matters.

Gero was intrigued by the offer and told Parilli if the Germans were interested in making contact, they would be conducted to a safe house just over the Italian border. Gero thought it was strange that these two men seemed relieved to being pushed out of the picture. Usually cutouts like Parilli thrived on the excitement of being involved in matters like this. Not these two. They clearly wanted to leave quickly to report back to their German bosses.

Dulles asked Gero, "Well, what do you think? Himmler is sending out peace feelers all over the place, but no one really takes him seriously. What did you tell these two?"

Gero replied, "I told them to head back to Italy and send over these SS officers but tell them not to waste our time. If they are serious, we may be on to something. If not, then we really didn't waste much time on them."

February 27, 1945, 4:30 p.m.

London

Prime Minister Winston Churchill took a deep breath as he prepared to deliver his closing comments about the Yalta agreements to the House of Commons. He felt certain all in attendance saw right through him, and he shuddered inwardly when his own Conservative bench members hit him hard on Poland, as he knew they would. He made the high sounding pronouncement that Stalin had agreed to full cooperation with Allied governments to oversee free and fair elections in Poland within one month, but was met with shouts and abuse.

One member asked if the NKVD would be acting as official election monitors. That one bothered Churchill though he did quickly retort this particular MP didn't have room to talk considering a member from his family occupied the same seat in the Commons since the days of George III.

Churchill ended his speech with simple language spoken from the heart. "No one in this room more deeply understands the importance to the English people to have fought the good fight and to know that their sacrifices have some deeper meaning. No other people on the planet have sacrificed so much for so long as have the citizens of these great Isles. The Yalta agreements signify the high water mark of this difficult, yet grand alliance against the unbridled aggressions of the Nazis. To undo all of the harm and tremendous suffering of the peoples of Europe is a task almost as daunting as the war itself.

"I ask this House to offer support and lend themselves to promoting these agreements as the last, best hope for peace and prosperity for all of the peoples of Europe. These accords, if implemented as agreed upon, will enable the Great Powers to work together with the same determination that has allowed us to achieve so many glorious victories on the battlefield. So to, with God's good graces, we will cooperate together to create a lasting peace. I ask you all to support this agreement and this Government in the challenging days ahead. Rest assured that whatever your doubts, this Government and the English people would never stand for a peace that did not bring honor to our people and our traditions. Trust me, as I trust you to do your duty. God bless the King."

As Churchill hurriedly left the House of Commons and immediately returned to his residence at 10 Downing Street. Feeling drained, it took every once of strength to deliver a speech he knew to be patently false. He wanted to sit for a while and read or maybe do a little painting later to calm his nerves, but as he walked through the hall towards his office, a familiar face leapt at his approach and demanded an immediate audience. The one man Churchill least wished to look in the eye cast a penetrating gaze that made him feel like a thief caught red handed in the dead of night. The man giving that look was none other than the leader of the London Poles, Stanislaw Mikolajczyk.

The Polish leader was cordial but insistent when he asked, "Mr. Prime Minister, please pardon my timing, but my Government must speak directly with you to discuss the recent Yalta accords."

Sensing Churchill's unease, Mikolajczyk politely added, "You know this is something neither of us can avoid, so please, may I have a moment of your time this evening?"

Churchill acquiesced to his sense of duty and ushered Mikolajczyk into his office. Taking off his jacket, Churchill motioned to the couch so the two men could face one another as friends, not adversaries.

Clearly anxious, the Polish leader took a deep breath and began, "Mr. Prime Minister, you and I have come to know one another over the years, and I need to ask why you have betrayed my countrymen to the Russians and condemned the Polish people to a fate of servitude?"

Mikolajczyk tried to maintain the proper decorum, but he began to lose control of his emotions. The strain and guilt that consumed him after fleeing his poor country more than five years ago, then the indignity of living as exiles, and worse, the guilt of knowing the hardships his people suffered under the Nazis occupiers while he spent the war in relative comfort threatened to overwhelm him. All of that could be dealt with, but to have been used as a mere bargaining chip to appease the Russians was too much, the final straw. The dream of living in a free Poland was to be extinguished forever.

He abruptly stood up and glared down at the British Prime Minister with a look of disdain, "Have we not shed enough blood?

Our cities are destroyed, our fields have been fought over, and my brave Home Army nearly destroyed during the uprising. Damn you, and all of your sentiment. My God, your country went to war to protect the Polish people. You do not know the Russian bear as we do. Have you no sense of our history or dot you and the Americans not care enough to make a stand?"

In a calmer, yet more chilling tone, the Polish leader asked, "Do you so fear the Russians that you won't dare stand up to them?"

Churchill winced and turned away from the glaring Pole but before he could speak, Mikolajczyk's eyes ablaze declared, "That's it. Admit it, you have lost heart. Well, guess what, Mr. Prime Minister, Stalin will not stop until Germany and all of Europe is at his heels. Then what? How much blood will flow in the decades ahead?"

With disgust, Mikolajczyk mocked Churchill, "Stalin knows that you and the Americans don't have heart anymore. Europe is about to enter a dark age and, Mr. Churchill, this time you signed the papers yourself. It isn't Chamberlain they will be writing about with disgust years from now. They will say that Churchill became weak and then scared and that he bargained away the people of Eastern Europe to save the final breathes of a dying Empire."

The British Prime Minister doubled over in shame. Every word rang true. Only the Americans could possibly stand up to them, and they were too blind to see the dangers ahead. Churchill understood that without the raw power of the Americans, the British Empire would crumble if the Russians forced a show down.

He looked up at the Polish leader and said, "Stanislaw, I will do you the honor and courtesy of at least giving you an answer in my study that I could never give you in public. Everything you have accused me of this evening is correct, but you tell me, what I should have done? If you know, then please, tell me because I haven't slept in two weeks trying to figure out what I should have done."

Walking over to the bar, Churchill poured two drinks and said, "Please, sit and let's do this as friends, not enemies."

The Polish leader was flushed with anger, but he took the offered seat.

Churchill started, "The Americans just want to ignore Europe's problems while they prepare to invade the Japanese homeland. To be fair to them, they will probably lose more than a half a million or more and were prepared to trade anything to get Russian support in Asia.

"As for the British government, I knew we could never stand up to the Russians without the Americans, they are just too powerful. As a result of this disastrous war, Stalin will emerge more powerful than any Czar would have dreamed for Mother Russia. My God, man, if he is willing to shoot millions of his own people, what do you think the lives of Poles or even Englishmen mean to Him? He has no soul. He is a man of absolute resolute purpose and cares nothing for sentiment, only power. He has it, we don't. End of story."

With that said, Churchill looked across the table hoping to find some hint that the Polish leader understood. His eyes pleaded to the leader of the London Poles to tell Churchill that there was nothing that could be done, that he could sleep again. Silence greeted his gaze.

Mikolajczyk stared at Churchill, shook his head, and stood up to leave, realizing it was a wasted visit. The dynamic man who stood up to Hitler and all of the power of the Third Reich had departed from the scene. It was clear Prime Minister Churchill and England's day in the sun had faded to night, and the people of Poland had but two choices: either, allow itself to be completely subjugated under Stalin's boot or prepare to fight the Russians to the death.

On his way out, the Polish leader abruptly turned to face the Prime Minister and said, "Mr. Churchill, I will always remember the way the British people came to the defense of my poor country six years ago. It's for that reason I feel so alone at this moment of even greater need for my nation. The Polish people have suffered for as long as any people on the planet and we have fought Germans, Swedes, and Austrians but always the Russian bear was ever present and hungry to devour us. From 1919 to 1939, the Polish people lived free. That memory will not simply fade into the night. I swear to you, on the souls of my children, we are prepared to fight them and any Pole who becomes a traitor and serves their new master. This is not the end, Mr. Prime Minister, but the beginning. Remember it was Poland that ushered in the Second World War, and perhaps, it will be Poland that shall ignite a third. Good evening, Mr. Churchill."

A speechless Churchill sat shamed into silence and watched as the proud Pole exited his study.

February 28, 1945, 10:30 a.m.

US Embassy, Moscow

A knock at the door forced U.S Ambassador Averell Harriman to look up from his desk for the first time in two hours. Since the Yalta conference, Harriman and his staff had been reviewing all of the agreements signed a short two weeks ago. George Kennan believed that by examining the documents carefully, the US delegation could exert pressure on the Soviets. Clearly, the Russians had no intention to implement most of the provisions, like free elections in Poland, joint oversight of election committees, or the disclosure and repatriation of Allied investments in the former countries occupied by the Germans. *George was right. He needed to start thinking like a lawyer again.*

Stalin and his cronies must be held accountable for their actions. Washington and the American public would see the Russians as an aggressive, totalitarian power that could not be trusted.

As his door opened, George Kennan entered along with General Deane, the head of the military mission to Moscow. The three men had developed a strong working relationship, especially since Harriman had come around towards a more realistic view of things. General Deane almost smiled every now and again.

The first words out of Kennan's mouth were, "We have problems. The Romanian government just found out who was calling the shots about twelve hours ago."

General Deane looked grim faced and added, "Mark my words, this is just the beginning. The Soviets played a fast one down in Bucharest and if you think they are going to stop there, you're crazy. We have to tell those sons of bitches that the ink hasn't even dried yet, and they already broke the goddamned treaty."

Averell couldn't believe Stalin was so contemptuous of his Allies he would start that soon. He wanted clarification, so he asked Kennan to further explain the situation.

Kennan described the basic issues, but cautioned that more information was still coming into the embassy. "Apparently, the Romanian government was forced to capitulate to Soviet demands or face direct military intervention. Yesterday, Foreign Secretary Molotov ordered his special envoy, André Vyshinski, to address King Michael of Romania concerning the current prime minister." Kennan reminded everyone this was the same Vyshinski that was the lead prosecutor for many of Stalin's show trials in the Thirties.

King Michael was a constitutional monarch until overthrown by the previous fascist regime. The newly installed king had nominated General Radescu to head a moderate government until general elections could be organized after the war. King Michael wanted to maintain strong relations with his new Allies and even included the small communist party that had survived underground since 1941.

"The Russians demanded King Michael depose General Radescu in favor of the head of the Romanian communist party, Peru Groza. Vyshinski made it clear to King Michael that he had little choice in this matter and would be held personally responsible for whatever consequences that would be forced upon his country. The excuse being used is that General Radescu was connected to the former fascist regime and is openly anti-Communist and opposes the dominant presence of Soviet occupation forces in Romania. The bottom line is that Romania has been told, in no uncertain terms, that the Soviet Union liberated them and that the Soviet Union would dictate the terms of their liberation."

Kennan noted that his superior looked very serious and a bit unsure of what to say next so he added, "Quite frankly, I am taken aback by this aggressive move from Stalin. He clearly believes he has a free hand in his occupation zones. Either way, this reaffirms our conversation the other night."

General Deane added, "George is right. This Mickey Mouse bullshit stuff of let's play nice with the Russians was one thing when we needed them to bleed the Germans, but now it's time to start facing facts. We need to set up a meeting with that cold blooded bastard, Molotov, and soon. Let's hit the bastard hard on this stuff, and maybe shake him up a bit."

Harriman listened carefully to both men and knew if the Russians pulled this in Romania, Poland was definitely next. If Poland was forced to roll over without diplomatic protest from the Western governments, then issues in Germany and Austria at the end of the war would probably go Stalin's way as well. George was right Diplomacy was really nothing more than a series of chess moves, all progressing towards a single goal. Checkmate. "Okay, you two sold me. I will call the Foreign Ministry today and see if we can't set up something soon, tomorrow if possible, with Molotov. I really thought they would wait until Germany had surrendered before attempting to intimidate everyone."

Deane cut in, "Ambassador, they are making one hell of a mistake. Stalin had better be careful because Americans don't like to stand by as a weaker country gets bullied and watch it happen."

Harriman shook his head in agreement and picked up the phone to make that call.

Chapter Five

March 1, 1945, 9:15 a.m.

Kutno, Poland

The small Polish town of Kutno was about one hundred miles west of the capital city of Warsaw. Kutno was just another Polish village surrounded by farmland and possessed little in the way of factories or most things of the modern world. The only significance the village possessed was that it sat astride a key highway heading west towards the huge Soviet armies of Zhukov and Konev. The crossroads of Kutno had been designated as the route for the huge resupply effort by the Red Army as it prepared for the final attacks against Nazi Germany.

Most of the men from the town were long gone. Many had died as part of the valiant little Polish army of 1939 while others served with either the Western powers in Germany or with the Polish armies under the Soviet Union. Most citizens of the village had managed to stay alive under the brutal German occupation. A select few brave souls fought with the Polish Home Army. Most of these men however were either dead already or hiding out in the forests and surrounding countryside.

Although everyone was happy to see the Nazi's leave, most were unhappy to see Russians strutting about and giving orders. The one fortunate thing that the people of Kutno could say was that at least their town had seen little fighting and almost no damage. In a world of turmoil, suffering, and hunger, if the war passed them by then they thanked God for His blessings and looked forward to the day when at least some of the sons and fathers of the town might return.

At nine o'clock in the morning, a rumbling of tracked vehicles could be heard rolling through town. The sight of tanks and armored cars was so common by this time that no one gave the appearance of Soviet units rolling through town a second thought. Some villagers became concerned as these tanks moved to the town square. Other tanks parked at the crossroads running through town, bringing all traffic in and out to a halt. Then trucks full of Russian troops began entering the village and before anyone realized what was happening, the small town of Kutno was effectively sealed off. Polish speaking men with loudspeakers drove through town demanding everyone was needed in the town square.

The people of Kutno remembered the sounds of other loudspeakers and sharp barking orders in German back in September of 1939. Most began collecting their children and walked nervously to the center of town, hoping the Russians wanted to make an important announcement. In half an hour, about 475 people had gathered, 125 families clustered around one another trying to stay warm in the early morning winter chill. Many looked a bit relieved when the mayor of the town emerged from the crowd of townspeople to search out someone to talk to from the Soviet authorities. He was led to a small command post around a cluster of Red Army tanks to wait.

Mayor Kasimierz Skulski nervously stood for ten minutes until a tall, light haired officer in his late thirties approached him. The Russian officer was wearing a heavy black, leather trench coat and possessed a sinister look, no different than the Gestapo bastards he had had to deal with under the Germans. The Russian stopped about two feet away and looked down at the Pole with disdain.

The Russian officer finally motioned for one his Polish interpreters to come over and translate, "Let me first introduce myself. My name is Colonel Boris Gudonov of the NKVD. I have been chosen to administer the surrounding area, which includes your small town, on behalf of the Soviet Union and the Red Army. I have been handpicked by comrade Beria, himself, to bring order to this miserable and ungrateful country. I have a few questions before I go over your new responsibilities as liberated subjects of the Soviet people. I expect your complete cooperation in these regards. I am afraid that failure to comply satisfactory will be dealt with most harshly. This entire region is under martial law and thus completely under my jurisdiction."

The Polish mayor seemed to lose the color in his face as he heard the words NKVD and Beria. The NKVD was Stalin's secret police. The mayor felt real fear for the first time since the Nazi's left. The Russian standing in front of him looked like a man without pity.

Obviously scared, Mayor Skulski stuttered as he responded, "Colonel, welcome to my small town. We thank the Soviet people for liberating us from the Germans. Whatever I can help you with, I would be glad to be of service."

The mayor held his breath as he hoped he could just say what the man wanted to hear and hopefully he would leave and go to another town.

The NKVD officer's smile was even more unnerving as he spoke, "Two days ago, a convoy of Red Army supply trucks was attacked by Polish criminals. Many brave Soviet comrades died for no good reason and valuable property of the State, supplies meant to kill Germans, was stolen or destroyed. Are you familiar with what happened? Which of these criminals live in your town?"

The mayor began to protest, "No, Colonel I heard some explosions but I just assumed it was some type of air attack, certainly not the work of citizens of this town. No, we are a peaceful people who just want to go back and tend our fields and pray for the war to end."

Gudonov waved his hand in anger and declared, "No! Trucks just do not blow up in the dead of night. This was an act of sabotage and a direct attack on the good nature of the Soviet people. We have sacrificed too much and for too long at the hands of the Germans, my Polish comrade. I will not allow a single Soviet soldier to die needlessly at the hands of Polish bandits, so I will ask again which members of your town belong to the Home Army and any other criminal organizations. I want an answer in three seconds or else I will be forced to resort to cruder methods to get my information."

The Mayor began to experience true fear because he honestly didn't know about any Home Army men that were left alive. Some he had heard were living in the forests fifteen miles south of the town, but who could say? The look in Gudonov's eyes was that of an animal about to devour his prey. The mayor grew cold as he feared where this would lead.

He didn't know what else to say so he began to plead for mercy, "I swear on the lives of my children that I and no one else in this town had anything to do with those attacks. I swear to you."

Gudonov cut in and said, "So you have children. Are you really ready to sacrifice their lives to pay for your sins? I want to know immediately, I am tiring of this exercise."

The mention of his children nearly caused the mayor to faint as he pictured this animal butchering his three young children. His hands shook uncontrollably as he struggled to speak. The frightened Pole finally said, "Colonel it is said that there are remnants of the Home Army about fifteen or twenty miles away in the forests and hills south of the town. I will show you myself, just please show mercy to my family and the town. Please, I beg of you."

Gudonov broke into a half smile again and said, "Now Mr. Mayor was that so hard for a peace loving partner of the Soviet people to do? You see, I already know about that band of thieves and bandits south of here, but I needed to see if you were willing to cooperate. That is all I am looking for, simple cooperation. Soon we can put this nasty business behind us, you will see shortly."

Colonel Boris Gudonov had served in the NKVD for more than fifteen years. He had joined enthusiastically in 1930 as part of Comrade Stalin's call for dedicated young communists to go to the countryside to free the peasants of the dreaded kulaks. Once the land had been redistributed and collectives set up, the Soviet people would be more equal and the path towards true Communism in their time would be possible. During this early service, Gudonov was noticed as an up and comer. He soon developed a reputation for efficiency and a taste for personally taking care. It was a dirty business, but the Soviet Union needed to be purified. He was part of a new breed of man, remorseless and dedicated to the ideals of Marxist-Leninist thought. Admittedly, Gudonov was not an intellectual, but the war with the Germans allowed men like Gudonov to rise to the top because it was only in war that Gudonov's talents came to the fore.

In 1943 he was ordered to organize NKVD armed task forces to eliminate partisan activity in zones recently liberated by the Red Army. Gudonov was shocked and disgusted by the thousands of Soviet citizens who collaborated with the Nazis. He became driven to hunt and exterminate any hint of fascist sympathy or cooperation with the invaders of the Soviet Union.

He came to the attention of Beria in mid-1944, in the Ukraine, then a hotbed of anti-Soviet sentiment. Using a variety of tactics, from torture to reprisals, Gudonov secured an important stretch of the Ukraine for the follow-on forces of the Red Army as they pushed the Germans out and into Poland. Without a secure rear area, the Red Army could not turn all of its energy towards the final destruction of the German army. His job was to secure the countryside by whatever means necessary.

Gudonov not only knew his job, but also took special pleasure and pride in being responsible for cleansing the liberated lands of any hint of fascists or enemies of the State. His posting to a key region in Poland reflected the faith of his superiors. He knew the Poles were a stubborn and proud people who would not be easily intimidated. He decided that only terror could sufficiently pacify the region. He would teach the Poles a lesson they would not soon forget.

Colonel Gudonov said to the trembling Pole, "You are to choose those fascist families from the town who have exhibited anti-Soviet attitudes in the past. I would choose myself, but I am a fair man, and would not want to choose at a random. We are not animals."

The mayor immediately began to tear up and fell to his knees, begging for the lives of his neighbors. The NKVD man bent over and whispered, "Either stand and make your choices or else I will assume everyone is guilty and put a torch to the whole town. Is that understood? Have I made myself clear?"

With a vacant stare on his face, the mayor picked himself up and began to compose himself and prepare to make the most difficult choices of his life. No matter what he did at this moment, he would forever be hated for the choices he made and haunted by the memory of being forced to play God. He looked up at the Russian Colonel and nervously nodded his head acknowledging what he had to do.

As he walked over to the people standing in the square, he decided that if he had to make such decisions then he would choose the worst of the village and pray for God's forgiveness. He pointed out neighbors who shirked their duties, some who hoarded food, and others who collaborated with the Germans, plus the very oldest in the village. Each family chosen began to cry or protest, but were quickly subdued by NKVD guards who forced the lot of them into the middle of the square. Armed NKVD guards ringed the town square and looked on with complete indifference to the mass of wailing families begging for their lives.

The rest of the families of the town were forced into the Church, which overlooked the square. The mayor and his family were directed off to the side and forced to watch the consequences of his decisions. The mayor kept saying to himself, *Merciful God forgive me, but I had no choice. I tried to save the best of us. Please forgive me.*

Russian troops surrounded the condemned families and made sure that none could escape. Those in the church were forced to watch through the windows while the others kneeled and prayed. Gudonov watched the scene play out almost with a sense of delight in his eyes. Once he saw all of the pieces in place, he spoke into his radio and gave the orders. At his command, the soldiers surrounding the condemned in the square peeled away and moved towards the church. Within two minutes, the exits were sealed shut and the sound of tanks could be heard moving down a side street towards the back entrance of the church. The people in the church began screaming.

Two tanks opened fire on the roof causing debris to rain down on the trapped people. Soldiers began throwing grenades and then set off a couple of incendiary charges that immediately started a fire. More high-explosive tank rounds ripped through the large, beautiful glass windows, sending deadly shards of colored glass into the mass of trapped Poles packed inside. Hysterical screams resounded from within the burning pyre as smoke and flames began to spread.

The Mayor Skulski looked on in absolute horror and screamed as if he were going mad. What had he done? His neighbors and friends were being burned alive by that evil bastard. Machine gun fire struck those few who successfully escaped the inferno. Gudonov walked towards the mayor who had fallen to knees begging for God's forgiveness.

Gudonov bent over and said, "Let this be a lesson, my little Polish comrade, I knew that you would never have chosen the best members of your little village as examples. Go collect those that remain in your village and wait for my orders. Kutno has now officially been pacified. I hope my services will not be required again."

Colonel Gudonov mounted his staff car and turned to survey his handiwork. An hour later as he pulled out of town, he felt his actions should get Comrade Beria's attention. With a little more luck, he'd make general yet.

March 2, 1945,

Desenzano, Northern Italy

SS Headquarters

SS General Karl Wolff felt stretched well past the breaking point. It had been more than a week since he sent Dollmann and Zimmer, along with those two Italian idiots, to contact the Americans. He told them not to contact him, but the delay was starting to drive him mad. Reports from the other fighting fronts were getting worse by the day. What was happening to German civilians in Prussia and Silesia was sometimes too much to bear.

Wolff knew deep down that maybe Europe would be better off without Hitler and his insane regime, but these animals from Russia will devour us all. Wolff shook his head as he looked up towards the ceiling. The almost constant drone of American bombers moved overhead. *It is truly the end.* The Americans seemed to have gotten their act together and appeared to be making a serious drive towards the Rhine. No doubt they would be too late. All of the bridges would be blown, but who knew, perhaps if he could convince Dulles, then maybe the Americans could move up from Italy, *and end this thing before anymore of Germany is overrun by those Mongols from the East.*

At a quarter to twelve in the evening, Wolff had finally put himself down to sleep, hoping by the morning he would have heard something. Just as he closed his eyes, a sharp wrap at the door caused him to roll over in one fluid motion, grabbing his Luger pistol in case the Gestapo had found out about his plans. He barked through the door, "Who the hell is it? State your business."

If he was going to be arrested in the dead of night, he had nothing to lose at this point, so he released the safety and readied himself. If it were the Gestapo, he would have only one chance to make good his escape. As his heart beat louder and pulse quickened, he heard the halting, nervous voice of Eugenio.

Colonel Dollmann whispered through the door, "Sorry to bother you sir, but you said to come immediately, as soon as we returned."

Wolff hesitated, and then asked, "Is there anyone with you or are you alone?"

"Just Zimmer. Please sir, can we come in?"

Wolff calmed himself deciding if it were the Gestapo, they would have barged in.

With his Luger pistol in his waistband, he opened the door. He growled, "Dollmann, it's about goddamn time. What the hell took so long? I thought that either the Gestapo grabbed you or the Americans decided to keep you in Bern for the duration of the war, and I am sure you would have just hated for that to happen. Anyway, grab a drink and sit down. Captain Zimmer, you too, this is no time for formalities. I wouldn't have picked you unless I knew you could be trusted."

In fact, SS Captain Guido Zimmer was chosen because he was a real soldier, unlike Dollmann. Young Zimmer would not only take a bullet for Wolff, but he was someone who would do whatever was necessary to complete his mission

"Okay, begin and don't leave anything out. I want details."

Dollmann described how the Italian cutouts successfully reached out to Dulles through the Swiss intelligence officer, Max Waibal "A German national interviewed the Italians that same night on the twenty fifth of February and made it clear to our two friends that they would not take our approach seriously until they actually meet with men from the SS."

Dollman expressed concern about direct contact on Swiss territory, but Captain Zimmer assured him that it was the only way. Zimmer knew Wolff wanted to meet Dulles himself and this was just the first step.

"So, four days later, we crossed into Switzerland and were taken to an American OSS safe house and met with one of Dulles' agents. The OSS man was named Paul Blum, and he acted unimpressed at first. In fact, I think the fact that Dulles sent a Jew to meet with a couple of SS men was intended to send a message. Anyway, this Blum obviously had no love for us, but he acted in a professional manner, except when he occasionally smiled whenever I mentioned that the war was lost for Germany."

Zimmer tired of the halting manner this Dollmann recounted the events and cut in, "I answered numerous inane questions from this OSS man and came right to the point. I told him we were directly representing the commander of the Italian theater of operations and the second ranking officer in the SS, General Karl Wolff. I expressed your desire to discuss terms to either strike a formal truce between our two countries or at least a cessation of hostilities on the Italian front."

Dollmann grinned as when he said, "This Blum was drinking coffee and started to gag in mid-sentence, but quickly got control of himself and said that we were making quite an offer."

Wolff eagerly wanted to hear what happened next and nervously began pacing and said, "Then what happened, what did the little Jew say next?"

Dollmann tried to remember everything but his nerves made it difficult. "The OSS man then left the room for about ten minutes, I had assumed at the time, to speak to Dulles or someone else higher in authority. Upon his return, Blum was much more cordial yet still a bit guarded. He then said that if we were serious General Wolff would have to demonstrate this by offering something to the Americans as proof. I said we were putting all of our lives, including our families, in danger. The OSS man seemed to enjoy my obvious nervousness and didn't say a word for about a minute or so. Finally, he told us they wanted the anti-Communist partisan leader, Ferrucicio Parri released immediately.

Wolff immediately sneered and said, "Parri, we should have shot that worthless dago whore months ago. What do they want with him?"

Zimmer cut in again and said, "The American said if we did this, then Dulles will meet you in Switzerland as soon as possible. We ended things there and raced back here. It would have been sooner except for American bombing raids that disrupted train service."

General Wolff listened intently to Dollmann and Zimmer's adventure and saw that the American was a crafty customer. No one in the entire theater could release Parri because neither Mussolini's people nor the German military command wanted him on the loose again. Wolff thought it would take a bit of doing, but Parri could be released or stage a breakout of some kind and then sent back to Switzerland. Would it be enough, he wondered. He turned to Captain Zimmer and asked, "Guido, what do you think the Americans will do if we release Parri? Do you think Dulles will believe we are serious and act quickly?"

Zimmer thought for a moment. The only reason he had agreed to play a role in this desperate ploy was because the Bolsheviks were practically at the gates of Berlin, but General Wolff was a dangerous man, and his answer had to be framed carefully. "Herr General, I believe releasing Parri would have been effective six months ago, but I am afraid the Fatherland does not have the time. What if it takes too long for Dulles to believe you are serious? What if the Americans move too slow or want more proof from you? Won't it be too late?"

Wolff saw the look of despair in the young SS man's face. As brave as Zimmer was, he knew the boy was dying inside. His mother and sisters lived in Potsdam, just to the west of Berlin, and the boy was likely frightened for them.

Zimmer was right though. Six months ago, they would have had the luxury of time but it was too late for long, drawn out negotiations. *Think!* Wolff became agitated and walking in circles trying to think of something. The goddamn Russians were practically at the Oder River, fifty or sixty miles from Berlin. The Americans were more than two hundred miles away and stopped cold at the Rhine. Even if the Americans or British organized themselves for a formal assault over the river, the bridgehead could be contained at least for a while, certainly too long for a dash to Berlin.

He stopped short and looked at the map of Greater Germany on the wall in his bedroom. He remembered a report he had read two days before about the recent decision by Himmler to use roving inspectors from the SS to ensure all key bridges over the Rhine were properly wired for demolition. Since the Army had attempted to kill Hitler in July of 1944, he didn't trust the Wehrmacht. Reports of Army officers looking to arrange terms with the Western Allies were driving Hitler insane with rage. Hitler appeared worried that weak-willed Army officers would make some attempt at the last minute to sabotage German defenses along the Rhine River. The roving teams of SS inspectors were intended to prevent such treachery.

All of a sudden it hit him. General Wolff punched the wall and declared, "Son of a bitch! That's it. I will give those Americans a present that will make their heads spin." Excitedly, he called out, "Look the both of you, the Americans are about here, south of

Cologne. If they could cross the Rhine at this point, they would have a straight shot at the Ruhr and then Berlin."

Captain Zimmer offered an uncomfortable look almost as if he was embarrassed for the man and politely asked, "Excuse me, General but I do not understand. What does it matter where the Americans are now, once our forces pull back and the bridges blown, what else can be done?"

Wolff grabbed the young captain by the shoulders and said, "What if the Americans find a bridge? They would move fast. The whole American army will push through. We both know that no matter how close the Russians are right now, every division in the Waffen-SS is rushing to the defenses of Berlin and will hold until the last man. No, the Russians won't take Berlin for a while yet, and maybe we can hold long enough to allow the Americans to get there first."

Zimmer thought the General sounded as giddy as a child. *How could it be this simple.* Someone had to say something to get him back to his senses.

Poor Colonel Dollman openly wondered, "Excuse me, General, but it would seem that you need a bridge for this, ah plan to be put into effect. How do we hand over a bridge in Germany, while we are in Italy?"

Wolff understood that both thought him to be mad. With a smile on his face, Wolff said, "All it takes is one man in the right place with the proper motivation, my friends, and I know just the man for the job. Captain Zimmer, you are about to take a trip and deliver a message to an old friend."

Chapter Six

March 4, 1945

Moscow, Soviet Foreign Ministry Building

Vyacheslav Molotov, the Soviet Union's Foreign Minister and key advisor in Stalin's inner circle, waited impatiently for the Americans to show up. Ambassador Harriman had insisted meeting to discuss the situation in Romania and, of course, the Americans would want to talk about Poland. Molotov allowed himself a bit of a smile as he thought about what must be going through the American minds, those who actually understood what transpired at Yalta. As he stirred his steaming tea, the Foreign Minister couldn't understand himself just how easy it was for Stalin to secure nearly everything they wanted prior to the meeting.

To watch that old man Churchill turn beet red as if he was about to have a stroke when Roosevelt declared that some new League of Nations would guarantee the future peace in the world. Only a people who had never really bled in more than three generations could be that absurd. The League couldn't stop Mussolini in 1935 when he invaded Ethiopia, let alone Hitler and his Nazi's. No, Comrade Stalin saw right through the man. He knew all along that Americans, even with all of their potential power, were not to be feared.

No, the West must be taught a lesson and soon. Comrade Stalin had long ago decided that wherever the Red Army had shed blood, no power on this earth would tell it what to do. The Poles, the Romanians, and everyone else would have to accept the fact that the Soviet Union will never be allow itself to become vulnerable and open to invasion again. The Americans could talk until they were blue in the face, but the issue had already been decided. It was Molotov's duty to make it so.

As the Foreign Minister drank his tea and reviewed documents on the consolidation of the new Romanian leadership, his door opened and an aide announced the American delegation had arrived. Molotov instructed his aide to hold Harriman off for about ten minutes and then see him into the office. Molotov figured that if the Americans had come to annoy him and waste his valuable time, then perhaps he could return the measure in kind.

Harriman had always disliked Molotov and believed him a very small man. Even Kennan referred to Molotov as a man not without some talents, but really nothing more than one of Stalin's many servile henchmen. Harriman looked over at General Deane and knew he was the one to watch. The military attaché certainly looked the part of a real professional, military soldier. Serving the administration as head of the embassy's military mission was not exactly what a professional soldier wanted in the middle of the biggest war of his generation, but the Moscow embassy would never have been as effective without him.

The wait was not sitting well with Deane, who fidgeted and kept straightening his uniform as it became a bit wrinkled while sitting. Harriman wished he had forced Kennan to come along instead of sending Deane, who George thought would send a more appropriate message Molotov's man motioned for them to enter the Foreign Minister's office.

Ambassador Harriman took a deep breath and walked into lion's den, knowing it would be the beginning of the mini diplomatic offensive recommended by Kennan. Molotov hesitated before getting up to greet the Americans. After several moments had passed,

Molotov finally looked up from his papers as though he were doing the Americans a favor by allowing them an audience.

The Soviet Foreign Minister spoke first, "Good morning, Mr. Ambassador, I trust I didn't keep you long. Issues from the front unfortunately demanded my attention. I expect you understand such things."

Molotov intentionally directed his remarks at Harriman and initially ignored General Deane, who usually dealt with his counterparts in the Defense. Seeing right through the American demonstration, Molotov smiled to himself as he thought; *you amateurish Americans, none of you would have lasted two months living in the Kremlin under Stalin.* Finally, he nodded at General Deane and motioned for everyone to sit down.

Molotov began, "Our regular meeting was scheduled for next Tuesday, but since you were most insistent upon moving the meeting up, I assume this is urgent."

Steely-eyed, Harriman refused to show any trace of emotion after the various slights accorded the U.S. delegation. Russians liked to be blunt when they wanted to send a message, so he got right to the point. "Foreign Minister Molotov, I appreciate you have taken the time to see us at such short notice. I would not have asked for this meeting if I did not believe there were issues emerging in the past several days that could have direct consequences on relations between our two countries. My government is very concerned over your unilateral actions in Romania. We have confirmed your direct representative, Vyshinski, personally threatened Romania's King Michael and is attempting to force him to accept a new government headed by the Communist Petru Groza. We believe this is a direct violation of the Yalta accords, which specifically demand joint-Allied cooperation and consideration in all newly liberated countries."

General Deane watched Molotov who usually never gave a single hint of emotion. However, Molotov reacted a bit different; first a sense of surprise was given off and then shifted to a bit of anger.

After listening to Harriman's accusation, Foreign Minister Molotov coolly responded, "Mr. Ambassador, if this is the tone you are going to take for this meeting then we had better discontinue, because I believe this will become quite counterproductive and should be added to the agenda of next week's regularly scheduled meeting. As for your incorrect and insulting accusation, the Soviet Government does not have to discuss the specifics of state-to-state diplomatic discussions as part of the military alliance against the Germans. All I will say at this juncture is that whatever help the Foreign Ministry can provide our military leadership in organizing secure rear areas, then that is an internal matter and not the concern of the American government."

Molotov wondered how the Americans found out so fast about the details of securing Romania against revamped fascism under that King and General Radescu. The way he turned right back on the Americans should be enough to buy a bit of time.

Not this time. Instead of allowing the Russian to make patently false statements and leave for the next meeting, Harriman went right back at him. Harriman leaned towards Molotov in a fashion that seemed to surprise the Russian a bit and said, "The United States did not come into this war to see another nation intimidated by tanks in the streets. It appears to my government that this is no different than the stab in the back the people of Poland experienced when they were bravely attempting to fight the Germans in 1939."

Molotov's eyes became large at the stinging reference to its actions taken in conjunction with Nazi Germany to eliminate the Polish nation. The American's had never once mentioned the old Non-Aggression Pact in any of its dealings with the Soviet government.

Molotov immediately leapt to his feet in obvious anger and pointed his finger at the two Americans, "How dare you compare the two events. The Romanians are a pack of fascists who were part of the invaders of my country and only now that the Red Army has nearly destroyed the Nazi's, they want to be friends again. Do you think we are children and should just meekly sit back and allow another anti-Soviet government to be organized to threaten our border again? You are sadly mistaken. Your government will not be allowed to interfere with legitimate security issues facing the people of the Soviet Union. Comrade Stalin will not allow you to help establish governments that openly yearn for our destruction."

The normally unflappable Molotov couldn't figure out their real agenda, who could tell with these Americans? *We could practically treated them like a second class power in Yalta and they didn't even blink, yet here they could lose their temper over a country that means nothing to them.*

Harriman said, "Mr. Foreign Minister, we are not ignoring your legitimate security concerns, however we signed an agreement and intend to ensure all provisions will be implemented fully. We will not allow your heavy-handed actions in Romania to be repeated in Poland. We will support the legitimate interests of the Polish people and look to ensure complete fairness in any election. I am sure that by acting together, all of Europe's security can be enhanced by our cooperation. Good day."

Harriman gave Molotov a look of determination and hoped his words about Poland sunk into the Foreign Minister's mind. As Harriman walked out the door with General Deane to his side, he turned and said," Well, if George doesn't think I sent a strong enough message, then next time I will send him in with a Louisville Slugger."

Chapter Seven

March 5, 1945

Bonn, Germany

It was nearly midnight and SS Colonel of Engineers, Friedrich Hoppe, sat in his field billet just to the south of the city of Bonn wondering, *how did that bastard find me?* The letter from his past had long since been destroyed, but its words still chilled him. After somehow surviving more than four years of combat on three different fronts, now he would meet his maker as a result of this insane request. *Some request, that son of bitch Wolff just signed his death warrant.*

He could barely comprehend what the madman was asking of him, let alone the consequences if he failed. The words would not go away. The end of the letter read,

> *"If you fail Germany in this task, the records that I expunged for you eight years ago will suddenly be corrected. Even at this stage, my old friend, the Gestapo would not take kindly your actions to hide the Jewish bloodlines of your wife and daughter. It would be a tragedy for you to lose your wife but an even greater tragedy for your daughter. How would one carry on after such a loss? The choice is yours."*

The words haunted him ever since they were delivered that morning. The messenger stayed until he read the letter and arrogantly demanded an answer so he could return it to the Italian Front Headquarters. Wolff was forcing him into an act of treason by threatening all that he loved

He never really trusted Wolff, but when the Nazi's came to power and the entire anti-Jewish furor began to take hold, he knew he had to make the necessary arrangements and Wolff was the man who could take care of things. He met Wolff back in the late Twenties when he tried to sell advertising space at his father's construction company. Hoppe had worked for his father since he could pick up a hammer but didn't have his father's good business sense.

Wolff was an effective salesman and convinced him to purchase some ad space in a local political magazine. His father was angry, but Hoppe liked the smooth talking Wolff. The two became friendly and helped one another in the difficult years ahead.

After losing the construction company and suffering like everyone else in Germany, Karl convinced him to join the Nazi Party and later got him into the SS. At the time, it was a guarantee of employment and with a friend that looked to be rising through the Party ranks fast. Hoppe couldn't lose. All he had to do was to salute the right people and look fierce occasionally to scare the communists and later the Brownshirts of the SA. It all came crashing to end in 1937 when a series of racial laws began to be actively enforced.

In 1937, his wife had told him that her maternal grandmother was Jewish and was worried that the authorities would find out and take her away from her family. Hoppe had never thought to ask, but after the Party began actively persecuting Jews, even those that were not full-blooded Jews, she became scared. Hoppe told his good friend Wolff who since getting the attention of Rudolph Hess, the number two man in the Nazi Party, was well on his way to the top rungs of Nazi society. Wolff listened to Hoppe but this time was far less friendly because with the Nazis, blood meant something and he obviously didn't want anything to upset his long term plans.

The deal made to the Hoppe family was that he would have to transfer to the emerging combat formations being formed by the SS and that the family would move to another town in southern Bavaria. Wolff had somehow changed the birth records of both the grandmother and his wife and wiped clean the sin of possessing Jewish blood, even blood twice removed over two generations.

Wolff said that they would have to part company at this stage and never mention to anyone ever what had transpired because both would suffer as a result. So Hoppe thanked Wolff and went on to serve the Fatherland faithfully throughout the war and never made contact again with his former friend.

Deep down he knew that Germany had lost the war and that the Americans would offer at least a civilized peace while the Russians were seeking to destroy Germany for its sins. Regardless, this request to sabotage one of the Rhine bridges to allow the Americans to cross unhindered would probably result in his getting shot anyway, even if he didn't get caught by the Gestapo. Did Wolff really think that Hitler would fail to punish those responsible for failing to destroy one of the few Rhine bridges remaining?

After a moment's reflection, Hoppe kept coming back to the same conclusion. The Gestapo would almost certainly arrest his wife no matter what happened and would probably send her away to some camp or perhaps dispense with such charades at this point in the war.

The mere thought of his dear Beatrice being awakened in the dead of night by those animals in the Gestapo was enough to bring him to his senses. He had no choice. He had to find a bridge and deliver it for the Americans.

For the first two or three years of the war, Hoppe had made a name for himself for building pontoon bridges and clearing minefields under fire for the fast moving panzer divisions to cross as they advanced. However, the past two years had been spent blowing up bridges and building obstacles trying to prevent the Russians and then the Americans in France from trying to cross them. Not only did he know the best ways to wire bridges for destruction, he had a reputation for setting charges in such way that made it difficult for someone to easily disable one of his targets. No simple infantryman could get onto one of his bridges and simply rip a few wires and capture a bridge wired by Hoppe.

It was this reputation that led to his promotion to full Colonel and his position as one of the inspectors of the Rhine bridges. He almost laughed to himself, but right now he would rather be on the Eastern Front clearing minefields. At least there he had some semblance of control.

Reading by flashlight in the underground bombproof shelter, Hoppe looked for the best bridge to make this insanity go away. It had to be a heavy duty, high traffic bridge, and one that the

Americans would need to move a lot of troops over. Unfortunately there weren't too many of those left along the main lines of the American approach. The best bridges were in Cologne because they would allow the Americans to race to the Ruhr and then Berlin. Too obvious, plus he had already inspected the bridges and re-wired them a week ago. A second inspection would not only look bad but would probably get him killed before he had a chance to do anything.

No, what was needed was for the bridge to be off the most direct route and one least likely for the main effort of the Americans to be heading. *Dammit, not only do I have to find this bridge, but also I have got to figure a way to make it look right.*

For the next hour, Hoppe stared at the map using his fingers to trace likely American march routes and bridges and highways leading to Berlin. The only time Hoppe missed an assignment was a small bridge over the Dnieper River in the Southern Ukraine. He had set everything right but the bridge only partially exploded. When the Russians were beaten back and the bridgehead contained, he tried to figure out how the hell that bridge didn't go under, then it hit him.

Instead of firing high-explosive artillery shells, the Russians fired shrapnel shells at the bridge, trying to kill Germans manning defenses along the river line. The shrapnel shells sent thousands of razor sharp shards of metal every which way. The shrapnel shells exploded all around the bridge and damaged wire and TNT bundles that caused the firing package to fail when he hit the plunger. The shrapnel didn't make just one nick, but dozens.

The SS engineer thought to himself that the key was to make it look like an accident. Even the madmen in charge today couldn't possibly fault an engineer for something completely out of his hands. However, all of Hoppe's experience and skill would be needed to figure out just where to rearrange the TNT bundles and determine which spans could take how much punishment. If the bridge sustains partial damage, then perhaps he could somehow get away with this crazy scheme. If the bridge suffers too much damage and the Americans can't use the bridge then his wife dies and if the bridge fails to explode at all, then he would be held responsible as inspector of the span.

All in all, Hoppe figured that no matter what happened, his life was probably forfeited anyway. The only thing that mattered was saving his wife. If he could accomplish that goal, then nothing else mattered. Not the Americans, not Wolff, not even Germany. So long as he knew that his darling wife and daughter were safe, then he could meet his fate without fear. One way or another it shall be done.

March 7 1945

Remagen, Germany

The 9th Armored Division was part of the general advance of the American First Army and was tasked with spearheading the U.S. III Corps attack along the approaches to the Rhine River. The 9th Armored Division's objective for the day was the riverfront town of Remagen about ten miles from its current position The Germans were offering token delay tactics and preparing to pull back their main forces for defense of the expected combat crossing of the Rhine. The Rhine River had been Germany's great western barrier and believed capable of holding up the Allied advance for several months.

Due to the relatively flat terrain and shorter distance to Berlin, the main effort of the Allied Army was made up north by Monty's Twenty First Army Group. The British Field Marshal was accumulating enough supplies and men for the biggest Allied attack since Normandy. The Americans were tasked by General Eisenhower to support Montgomery's right flank and wait for him to cross with the British Second Army and the Canadian First Army.

Since most Americans commanders, especially Bradley and Patton, seriously objected to Ike's decision, everyone was trying like hell to get at a bridge and by some miracle make the crossing before Monty grabbed the headlines again. So, Major General Millikin, commander of the U.S. III Corps, ordered the 9th Armored to send a task force to try to capture the Ludendorff Railway Bridge at

Remagen. The chances were small the Americans would catch the Germans unaware, but the American task force was ordered to get that bridge if it was still standing, no matter the cost.

Lieutenant Colonel Leonard Engeman was ordered to take the bulk of the 27th Armored Infantry battalion and part of the 14th Tank battalion and move out at first light. Engeman drove the task force hard and managed to reach the edge of the city limits by noon. That was when a recon detachment raced back with the incredible news. The Ludendorff Bridge was still standing. The American commander could hardly believe his luck. Lt. Colonel Engeman immediately ordered his infantry and tank units to clear the light German opposition guarding the town. When out of nowhere the commander of Combat Command B, Brigadier General Hoge arrived to oversee the operation.

After seeing it with his own eyes, General Hoge said to Engeman, "I don't know what the Krauts are thinking, but I want that goddamn bridge!"

Engeman agreed, but was nervous the Germans were trying to sucker play them and blow the bridge while his whole battalion was half way across.

Hoge grabbed his binoculars and observed the German units still fleeing across the bridge, retreating from the American attack moving through the center of town. He shook his head and turned to Engeman, "No way Len, they waited too long. Maybe the demolition charges are fouled up or something because they know we are here and getting ready to make a go of it. No. We can't wait. It's now or never. Understood?"

Lt. Colonel Engeman was not nearly as thrilled as his boss, but he knew all he could do was nod his head and get ready.

Hoge pointed towards the town and said, "Good. Now deploy that platoon of new heavy M26 Pershing tanks on the ridge overlooking the bridge entrance and give some direct suppressing fire on anything that moves on the other end. Then deploy two companies of infantry as close to the bridge as we can without drawing fire from the Germans. Once we get the men in position, I will get Division to start popping as many smoke rounds as they have on hand to give you some cover. If they haven't blown the bridge by then, send a couple of half-tracks and M8's to start clearing the far end and shoot the rest of the task force through the bridge. Got it?"

The task force commander nodded his head, still nervous at the prospect of sending his men across without knowing if they were walking into a German trap.

The Ludendorff Bridge was a double-tracked railway bridge with footpaths for walking and covers on the tracks so vehicles could use it as a motorway. The structure was built in 1916 at the height of the Great War and named for the famous Army Quartermaster General. The bridge was solid and anchored on both ends by a huge stone, castle-like structure for support and defense. Three arches on four stout stone piers on the water supported the bridge. The German engineer detachment was becoming nervous as reports that more German units were on the other side still defending the town of Remagen. They didn't want to blow the bridge and risk trapping their fellow soldiers on the other side. The German Army engineer, Hauptman Karl Friesenhan, in charge of the bridge thanked his good fortunes that the bridge had been rewired less than twenty-four hours ago by a Colonel from the SS. The SS engineer ranted for a half hour about the improper wiring his team had done and that they had jeopardized the Reich through their stupidity.

He watched as the SS Colonel skillfully hid the primer cords himself and reworked the wire to several of the main explosive clusters around the main spans. Friesenhan was not one to argue, let alone with a Colonel of the SS and prepared to blow the bridge. He wanted to do it an hour ago when word of the American attack was first confirmed, but some damn shakeup up in command structure delayed the orders. Looking at his watch, it was time. He quickly checked the final connections and pulled the plunger up and then quickly pushed down. A tremendous roar exploded seconds later, forcing the German commander down in his bunker.

Meanwhile, Captain Ernie Fox led company B of the 27th Armored Infantry and was given the order to prepare to capture the bridge. Fox was a combat veteran who took one look at the objective and thought the Lieutenant Colonel was out of his mind. The damn Jerries were still raking the west side of the bridge with machine gun fire and had started dropping mortar rounds across the approaches to the bridge. Positioning himself with a platoon of his men behind a stone wall in someone's backyard, he could clearly see the two block approach to the west side of the bridge. He didn't like what he saw. The whole avenue of approach was open on three sides once he cleared the last building along the block and then he would have to run like hell across the whole bridge. Fox didn't give a shit if it was the Rhine or whatever river, his men's asses were hanging out in the open and were about to catch hell.

Fox radioed his weapons platoon to begin laying it on and then contacted Lt. Colonel Engeman. The Colonel ordered Fox to move fast once the smoke rounds hit. Covered in sweat and breathing heavy, Fox said, "I don't know, sir, it's pretty damn quiet right now. I think maybe the Germans are about to...."

A tremendous roar went off in front of the company's position. The air was forced out of Fox's lungs and sent him flying for cover as a wave of concussion washed over everyone. Before anyone had a chance to react, the men stared at the bridge as a series of explosions went off. The bridge seemed to lift up in the air momentarily and then fall back down into place. A huge rolling black cloud of smoke and debris swept over the company position as everyone hit the deck behind an earthen mound.

Fox was coming to his sense when the smoke began to clear and then he saw a sight he would never forget. Somehow that big, son of a bitch of a bridge was still there. The main spans were definitely damaged but the footpaths looked in pretty good shape, maybe not strong enough for armor to cross but definitely could hold men.

Sensing one of those moments that couldn't be wasted, Fox jumped up and yelled, "Everybody form up. Move, move, move. First platoon lead off followed by third and then second cover the middle of the walkway. The Germans are probably every bit as shocked as we are, so let's hit them hard and fast."

Many of the men were still shook up by the explosion and nervous about moving out to cross the bridge. Then they heard the fearsome voice of Sergeant Williams, "Goddamnit, what the fuck are you ladies waiting for? Do you want the Germans to have enough time to get their shit together and blow this bitch one more time? That's it, Jacob's move. Davis, if I have to carry you myself you will cross that bridge, understood?" One by one the men formed up. It was not just any bridge. It was a bridge over the Rhine River, the last hurdle they needed to cross so they could get to Berlin and then get the hell home.

Captain Fox shouted over the roar of artillery to his men, "We get this bridge, we win the war. It's that simple. No more bullshit. I want everyone to get ready, move in thirty seconds. We are going to move as one whole unit. The Krauts must be scared shitless knowing we can get this thing and will hit us with everything they can once they come to their senses. Sergeant William's, you grab five men and follow behind and pull whatever wires you see. I don't think we'll get this lucky again. Let's move."

With that, Captain Fox led his men and in fifteen frantic moments Company C successfully captured the bridge and held long enough for General Hoge to get a considerable force to the far side. The Americans had just captured the most important piece of real estate in all of Germany, except for Berlin. It wasn't in the best area and the terrain was situated in a way that would make it difficult to cross too many men at once, but it didn't really matter. It came down to logistics, and no army was better than Americans at moving men and supplies in huge numbers when needed. The American Army had just upstaged Monty and got themselves a bridge.

Twenty miles away in Bonn, a certain SS Colonel heard over the BBC radio that the Americans had just gotten a scratch force over the Rhine and captured the Ludendorff Bridge. Hoppe allowed himself to smile for the first time in three days. He only hoped that he would live to see the end of the war.

Chapter Eight

March 8, 1945

Bern, Switzerland

Allen Dulles sat grim faced in his office disgusted as he viewed the pictures sent by Wood that lay on his desk. The normally detached and balanced Dulles stared in shock at one image after other depicting unspeakable scenes of death and torture. The special packet with the latest Wood intelligence had been eagerly opened, but instead of reading Foreign Ministry documents, Kolbe sent him a letter and an envelope filled with pictures of absolute barbarism. Fritz Kolbe wrote,

Dear Mr. Dulles,

When I approached you two years ago and offered my services to the Allies as a German citizen of conscience, I did so to help Germany's enemies to remove the ugly scourge of Nazism from the German volk. I feared for my nation's soul, as I now fear for our very existence. These photos were taken from villages in East Prussia that were recaptured by German forces after being forced out by the Russians. In three days, the Communists carried out a drunken orgy of violence and rape. More than half of the women of the village were raped and then sadistically murdered, many in front of their husbands or fathers who were then in turn murdered. Mr. Dulles, to think that my treason may have in some small way contributed to the destruction of the German people is more than I can bear.

Now, I beg of you to look at these pictures and ask yourself how your country can ally yourselves with those animals. Please, let those in your government see these terrible snapshots of the terror now being inflicted upon innocent German women and children. Do they truly deserve to suffer for the sins of the Nazis? Have we not suffered enough from the constant bombing and near starvation? I beg of you. You are a righteous and God fearing people, just tell them the true nature of your ally, and they will understand that the Bolsheviks are like a scourge from the Old Testament. I will be sending you a report in a week or two that the Foreign Ministry is compiling that details the murderous advance of the Russians. That report will document the savage excesses from the Soviet offensive and prove it was encouraged from the highest circles. I pray you will take mercy on the German people and know that for all of our sins, ask yourself, do we truly deserve the wholesale systemic rape of a nation. Tell them, please.

Yours Truly,

Wood.

Dulles read and reread Kolbe's letter several times and each time he felt a range of emotions. Above all things, Dulles was a moral and upright man whose whole being was utterly disgusted by the scenes of near naked women, lying dead in grotesque positions. To see the look of fear forever etched on the face of a girl of about ten as her mutilated corpse lay in the open for all to see generated a sense of revulsion and anger Allen never thought possible. The pictures of veteran German soldiers kneeling in the street beside themselves in tears as they tried to comprehend the suffering of the poor village leapt off the page. Dulles had always been able to avoid many of the more grisly aspects in both world wars. He had seen dead men and known of agents that were blown and arrested and suffered for it. He often read accounts of German reprisals at villages known to be supporting the underground anti-Nazi movement, but never in his whole life had he considered a civilized people could, as a matter of policy, sin against so many innocent women and children.

Kolbe's letter and pictures generated a resolve in Dulles he had never felt in his entire life. Kolbe was right; there was no way the American people would continue to support the Soviets if they knew what they were doing to German civilians. It was one thing to drop impersonal, yet deadly bombs each night, but it was another for a group of soldiers to rape a daughter in front of her father. Such personal brutality was beyond the ability of Americans to imagine, let alone justify. Dulles felt he had to help Donavon convince FDR that this alliance with the Russians was simply immoral.

Later that same day, Mary Bancroft, his personal assistant and lover, found Allen sitting at the back of the Swiss villa in the gardens looking utterly depressed. Mary walked up to him and lightly touched his cheek and said, "I don't know what was in those documents from Wood, and I know you can't tell me, but whatever it is, you have to let it go for now. I just got off the phone with Gero and he said he got a call from Major Waibel, and it was urgent. He would be here in about fifteen minutes. I never heard Gero quite so excited."

Not really listening, Dulles turned to his companion and almost in a whisper, said "Those pictures from Wood were awful. I never saw pure evil until now." He paused and looked her in the face and said, "I don't know if we're strong enough to stop them."

Mary moved closer and lightly touched the back of his neck and tried to calm Allen. She had never witnessed such emotion from the man in the two years they had been together. Usually, it was all she could do to try to get anything out of him. It was most upsetting to see him like this. Mary took his hand and said, "I don't know what you saw in those photos, but too many of our people are counting on you to lead them. Whatever anger or fear you feel right now, trust it and use it in the months ahead."

Dulles squeezed her hand as her words gave him strength. His decision was made. Allen knew it would probably take every effort his nation was capable of offering to prevent the Soviets from spreading their evil system throughout the globe. The fight had to begin somewhere, *might as well begin here.*

Meanwhile, Gero drove his car as fast as he could without getting stopped by Swiss police for a speeding violation. The emotional German OSS agent reached Dulles' block, parked around the corner and entered the house from the rear in case anyone, including the British, was observing the front entrance. This was too big for even the American's cousins, the British, to find out. Flying through the back door and right into Allen's office, Gero saw his boss at his desk as usual and exclaimed, "They're here."

Still not quite himself, Dulles answered rather gruffly, "Who's here?"

Gero smiled and said, "Remember those two Germans that Blum met a week or so ago and he told them to release Parri if they were serious, well Paul just had his bluff called. Parri and that Major Antonio Usmiani just arrived at the safe house across the border from Italy about two hours ago."

Dulles was floored. Both men thought the two SS officers were merely trying to cause a bit of mischief and nothing more. Dulles started running the possibilities through his head and only came up with one answer. Only the very highest ranking German could have released the two men. Both of whom were considered dangerous to the present fascist regime surviving under Mussolini in Northern Italy. It must be genuine and maybe it signaled a real opportunity to send some important back channel communication to the German High Command in Italy or maybe even to Himmler in the Germany.

Dulles slapped his leg and said, "That's excellent. When can we begin to debrief them? They must have an unbelievable story."

Gero kept on smiling, holding something back and said, "Why don't we begin the debrief by asking who drove them to the border?"

Dulles pointed at Gero and shook his head and announced, "Okay, enough guessing out with it. What the hell has happened for you to still have that goddamn smirk on your face, number one, and number two, who drove them across the border?"

Gero grabbed a chair and faced his boss and whispered, "Remember the SS men, Zimmer and Dollmann, well they drove our two Italian friends over the border themselves. They also brought their boss, none other than SS General Karl Wolff, second in command of the entire SS, who is now currently sitting in front of the fireplace at the safe house drinking schnapps. I do believe that in the intelligence community, we call this an important development."

A flabbergasted, Dulles, didn't know what to do first. Part of him knew it was too big for his little part of the war, but didn't want Washington involved just yet, even if Donavon was his friend. If Wolff was serious and could deliver, it may not only stop the fighting on the Italian Front, but if handled correctly and quick enough, could alter the endgame in Germany. Quickly he outlined a blue print for moving forward and decided to call the operation Sunrise, it seemed appropriate, considering.

About an hour later, Gero was driving the two men to the Zurich apartment Dulles kept whenever he was in town on official duties. Gero was very quiet during the drive and didn't say anything other than to answer some operational questions concerning the Wolff interview. Dulles gave his number two man some time to absorb the pictures from Wood. Dulles and Gero had agreed Wolff needed to demonstrate several things, but most importantly, to determine if he had the power to act and not just talk.

As Gero continued driving down the road, his mind rushed a hundred miles a minute. Those horrible pictures from the Russian front made him seethe with anger. The war in the East always seemed so far away, completely removed from his immediate concerns. Now that the Russians have not only recaptured all of Poland but now have started to overrun parts of East Prussia and Silesia, his personal war against the Nazis seemed far less important considering the Russians were racing towards Berlin.

Working for the Americans had been good and he believed service against the Nazis was an honorable pursuit considering the evils of the Nazi regime. But, as a German, service to the Americans was far less important than his sense of duty to the Fatherland of his youth.

After following the OSS agent's orders, General Wolff found the Zurich apartment was a modest building overlooking the Lake of Zurich. The SS General dressed in an unassuming suit coat and was greeted by Dulles' German aide de camp. Wolff barely hid his feelings of utter disdain at his fellow German. Wolff thought, *I may be in the SS, but at least I fought the enemies of Germany, not like this traitor working for the Americans. This young pup probably sold his soul to the Americans to escape the rigors of war like the rest of his generation.*

He was led into a dark room and saw the back of a man facing the fireplace and stoking the embers to warm the room up a bit. Wolff did not move to offer his hand and the OSS man similarly withheld a hand offered in friendship. After a formal greeting, Dulles' aide supplied chairs and left the room. Dulles looked right into the German's eyes, looking for any hint of weakness or even fear, something that could be used to possibly shake the man.

With a rather awkward fifteen-second silence hanging in the air, ever bold, Wolff began the discussion. Trying not to look as nervous as he felt, Wolff studied Dulles and noted the serious eyes and the impression he exuded, a sense of being someone of means. Wolff hoped that Dulles' confidence was not an act, but that he was a man who could move the necessary levers of power and quickly. *Well, I think to shake him, I will hit him up front with the gift.*

Wolff stood up and said, "Herr Dulles, I first want to thank you for both taking the time to meet with me and displaying the proper level of discretion. I am afraid if word was to leak of my proposal, then the Gestapo would probably make short work of me and my staff."

Dulles responded, "General Wolff, the fact that you are here meeting with American intelligence agents says much about our current situation. The release of the two Italian underground commanders was much appreciated and I am sure their families are beside themselves in joy at their good fortune. Too many good and brave men have failed to return from their activities down South. Please let us both sit and discuss the exact nature of this meeting."

Wolff noted Dulles' passing remark about German anti-partisan reprisals, but decided to let it pass. He instead sat down again, but leaned closer to Dulles and began "Mr. Dulles, our two people have been fighting one another for several years now, but the war clearly is unwinnable for Germany and has instead caused wide scale suffering and privation for not just Germany, but most of Europe. I am not here to offer apologies or explanations about the causes of this war. Who is right or wrong really doesn't matter. What does matter is that the unnatural and unholy alliance of the Western powers and the Soviet Union has succeeded in destroying Germany.

"However, I believe that neither you Americans nor the English are really thrilled the Communists are in the process of absorbing all of Eastern Europe and are looking to annihilate the German people. I want to appeal to America's good nature and mutual interest and attempt to find some way to prevent such an ending to my country."

Wolff watched Dulles listening intently to what he said and noticed the way he shook his head as if he knew about what was happening during the Russian advance.

Dulles listened to Wolff's opening speech and believed it to be a bit rehearsed, but noted that Wolff was not asking for anything yet. Dulles answered "General Wolff, you command more than one million German soldiers defending the entire Italian Front. It would seem to me that if you were looking to sue for an armistice on your front, I would say the Allies would be very interested in such a proposal, but the first thing my superiors in Washington are going to expect is some type of assurance that you are capable of delivering on your proposal."

Wolff thought to himself, *Bingo.*

A smile similar to that of a predator crossed his lips, "Mr. Dulles, I have already provided concrete evidence of my intentions and willingness to use my influence to effect an offering of good intent."

It was Dulles' turn to offer a condescending smile as he said, "General, as much as Washington will appreciate the release of two Resistance leaders, I am afraid that we will be looking for something a little more concrete along military lines."

Wolff sat back in his chair and crossed his leg as if following a script of his making and said, "Mr. Dulles, you must be aware of a certain bridge in the vicinity of the small German town of Remagen. I believe that it is the only bridge seized by the Allies over the Rhine River and has offered some small measure of military advantage, I would think."

It was Dulles' turn to lean forward and in an excited voice said, "You don't mean what I think you mean? No, it's too convenient."

The SS man opened up his hands and spread them before the American and said, "Yes, my new friend, provided to you on a silver fucking platter. Do you really believe the German Army would somehow destroy every bridge over the entire Rhine River and conveniently leave one mysteriously standing? Not only did I arrange to sabotage the demolition placed at the bridge, but I chose the bridge myself and would be glad to offer up the name of the individual who carried out the assignment. Unfortunately, I will be unable to present him as a witness because our dear leader, Hitler, has had anyone connected with the bridge shot by now, but why quibble over details."

Letting the information to sink in let Dulles know how serious he was. Wolff continued, "Herr Dulles, I am prepared to do anything and sacrifice anyone to somehow save Germany. That is why I am here, and that is why I knew I had to perform some tremendous act to grab your attention. I do hope Washington will be sufficiently impressed." The SS General smiled as he watched Allen Dulles face turn away in a bit of shock, clearly not knowing what to say.

Dulles quickly composed himself and tried to get back some semblance of control over the situation. He had assumed he would be the one holding the cards, but this SS General seemed to have come prepared to show his full hand and right away. For Wolff to have risked so much, he must want something more than just to save his own skin, as he already made clear. Dulles said, "General Wolff, Americans are not known for their diplomatic niceties, so perhaps it would be best if we got right down to it. You wouldn't have exposed yourself in such an adventure if you were looking to surrender troops in Italy. What do you expect of my government to repay such a gift?"

The SS General took a deep breath and exhaled, as he knew it was time to begin reeling the American into the boat. Wolff answered "Mr. Dulles, I believe the only thing that may save my people is for the Western Allies to capture Berlin before the Russians. If Americans and the English troops along with my command occupy most of Germany up to Berlin, then perhaps Vienna and hopefully even Prague may be saved."

Dulled didn't like to be lectured upon but before he could cut in, General Wolff continued, "There is no question the final endgame of the war depends on who captures Berlin. The Russians understand this, but I wonder if you Americans understand the gravity of the situation. The war now is a matter of politics, not military strategy. So, while I arrange surrender on the Italian Front, American tanks can be racing towards Berlin. More than ninety percent of the German Armed Forces are facing the Russians. We will hold them for two months at best. If we do, then the only thing that could stop you from reaching Berlin is a lack of gas, nothing more. If you can commit to me that American forces will make a dash on Berlin, I will arrange for a complete ceasefire on the entire Italian Front and open the southern approaches to Germany."

Dulles listened intently to the wily German and sensed he possessed a healthy degree of self- preservation, but that he was also telling the truth. The Russians would never stop until they finished the war on their terms and enforced the peace they chose. Yalta all but guaranteed Soviet domination in Eastern Europe, capturing Berlin would allow Stalin to dominate all of Central Europe and intimidate the rest of Western Europe. Wolff was right, either the United States stepped up to the plate and prevented it from happening or prepare to come back some time in the near future. Thinking back to the images Wood had sent him, Dulles remembered his disgust and anger and what he had vowed to do if the opportunity presented itself. Wolff may not be an altar boy, but he spoke the truth.

Dulles said, "There are many in Washington who have spoken up against the Soviet actions and believe them to be no better than Nazis. No offense."

Wolff laughed and said, "None taken, I assure you. Remember, I rose through their ranks, I know what swine are left in the Party."

Dulles ignored his comments and continued, "I intend to contact Washington and recommend someone go to Eisenhower and convince him to accelerate his movement towards Berlin."

For the first time in about three weeks, Wolff felt a sense of hope. He knew Germany east of the Oder River may have to be written off, but maybe if Berlin was secured in the rear, the Americans could turn the nightmare around.

Dulles noticed the smile on the German's face and rose from his chair and said, "I want you to stay the night and be debriefed in much more detail by my aide, Gero. All I can say is that this meeting is without a doubt the most extraordinary conversation I have ever participated in. I will do everything in my power to help save Germany from destruction, but by the same token, I will do everything I can on behalf of my government to help remove every vestige of Nazi influence."

Wolff stood up, came to attention, and saluted Allen Dulles as befitting a German officer. Then he moved closer to Dulles, offered his hand to shake, and smiled as he said, "You don't know the half of it. Germany will wake up from this nightmare someday, shake its head, and pray that the likes of me never puts on a uniform of any kind, ever again."

Then Wolff started laughing as if he looked the reaper in the face and escaped his lethal grip yet again. Dulles released his grip, and thought, *if this doesn't make it to the history books someday, at least it will make one hell of a story at the club.*

Chapter Nine

March 10, 1945, 9:00 a.m.

Washington DC, OSS Headquarters

Major General *Wild Bill* Donavon, head of the Office of Strategic Services, felt exhausted and his age catching up with him. Normally, he was in by eight sharp, but after another long evening reviewing initial reports from his various station chiefs on his new Soviet initiative, he could barely get out of bed that morning. Things had been moving non-stop since the Yalta trip. From opening Soviet moves in Romania to reports of atrocities filtering in from Poland to General Bradley's 12th Army Group crossing the Rhine. Donovan's head was swimming and he wondered if it was getting time to look for a younger man to head the OSS.

Donavon promised to take it easy that day, maybe even try to read the morning paper, take a long lunch, and make it an early day. What the hell, rank should have its privileges every now and again.

As he moved towards his office, his secretary, Rose, handed him a manila folder marked with the purple seal, indicating a priority one flash message, eyes only for Donavon. *Wonderful, I haven't even had my coffee yet and Rose hands me this hot potato.* Even before he tore the seal, he knew no one sent a memo out like this unless something big happened, and it damn well better be big or someone would have their ass handed to them.

Rose, entered his office with a steaming cup of coffee and said, "I could tell by that cranky look on your face you wouldn't be able to get through that report without this, so here you go. Remember, be nice today. Remember we're winning, so cheer up."

Donavon smiled at his dependable secretary and responded, "Thanks for the coffee, Rose. Hold all calls and any appointment until I am through with this. Thanks." He opened the folder and began reading.

To: Eyes Only, Major General William Donavon

From: Allen Dulles, Switzerland Station Chief

Re: Summary of Operation Sunrise

On the evening of March 9th, I personally met with SS General Karl Wolff, second in command of the entire SS and group commander of all SS forces facing Allied armies on the Italian Front. This meeting was the culmination of more than two weeks of increasingly higher levels of contact, until Wolff crossed the Swiss border. At this meeting, General Wolff indicated he wanted to come to terms with the Americans so as to allow us to reach Berlin before the Russians.

General Wolff claimed that he arranged for the bridge at Remagen to be sabotaged to allow American forces a direct crossing route. The details provided to my assistant have been confirmed and appear consistent with SHAEF headquarters account of the crossing operation. Apparently, General Wolff possessed enough influence to sabotage the bridge and most importantly, did so in a way which protects himself and gives us plausible denial. Further, he wants to come to an agreement quickly to allow him to withdraw German forces along the Italian Front and deploy his forces against the Russians.

Wolff claims his justification is based upon reports the Red Army is systematically raping and engaging in mass killings throughout occupied Germany. This has been confirmed through recent Wood material. These items need to be addressed separately and at a later time, but the documents and pictures of the atrocities are on the way to you by diplomatic pouch. Suffice to say, they are the most disturbing images I have ever viewed. Wolff at no time asked for personal clemency or special treatment for Nazi hierarchy or SS units after the surrender.

With American forces now over the Rhine, General Wolff is correct in his belief that nothing can stop Ike from making an end run and capturing Berlin and perhaps secure Vienna and Prague from the South, if he acts now. Operation Sunrise has grown far out of proportion to this station and, therefore, I am formally asking for orders as to how to direct the next phase of negotiations. At a minimum, we should treat this as a military opportunity but inform General Eisenhower of the full political issues arising from Sunrise and order him to act accordingly. If Wolff feels we are dragging our heels or using him somehow, please note he is a dangerous and ruthless man and there is no telling what he would do. Bill, make them understand, show them the pictures.

Respectfully,

Allen Dulles

Feeling barely able to contain his disbelief, Donavon's sweating hands placed the flash traffic memo from Dulles down and pushed his coffee to the side of his desk. Reaching into his bottom drawer, he pulled out a bottle of Jamison Irish Whiskey and poured three fingers worth. Wild Bill's mind was still lightning quick and the myriad of possibilities that arose as a result of the meeting with General Wolff were endless.

As he downed a glass of Irish medicine, as his father used to put it, Donavon knew he could not make the decision alone. Everyone from State to War, not to mention the President would be outraged if he moved without informing them of the situation. The bottom line: the Soviets were bound to find out. Soviet intelligence was too damn good and the Germans might decide to leak the thing anyway if they thought it would cause the Allies to start fighting amongst themselves. *However this goes, no way we can keep it under wraps forever.*

Scribbling notes as fast as he could run the various scenarios that could play out, Bill knew the Russians would be furious and at a minimum would probably threaten to pull out of the United Nations, maybe even make the U.S. fight the Japs alone. No matter how he wrote and re-wrote the various scenarios, relations with the Russians ended in the toilet. With their huge army facing the outnumbered Allied forces in the West, Stalin might be tempted to pressure the

United States and demand the concessions of Yalta be followed to the letter.

Pouring another shot, Dulles decided to contact the President and call an emergency meeting of the wartime principals and their staffs for the following morning. Whatever his feeling about the Soviets, his main job was to collect intelligence and deliver reports to the President. Hopefully Allen was right, once they saw the images of Soviet atrocities, maybe he could prevent State and War from overreacting. As Donavon picked up the phone to contact the President, he thought, *I hope we can control this orit will spin out of control. God knows what will happen.*

March 11, 1945, 10:30 a.m.

The White House

The previous day's conversation with the President did not go well. Franklin seemed so near the end. In the impromptu meeting with the President, his Chief of Staff, Admiral Leahy, and his closest advisor, Harry Hopkins, Donavon laid out the issues arising from Allen Dulles' Operation Sunrise. The OSS man watched as President Roosevelt struggled to absorb everything he was told, but by the end of his briefing, he understood relations with the Soviets would be forever changed. Leahy grasped the military implications more readily than the political end, but that was why Hopkins was in the room.

Hopkins had not only met all of the key Russian leaders, many believed he was considered by the Kremlin as their man on the inside of the FDR White House. Donavon didn't take that statement literally, unlike some people in town. In reality, Hopkins was a true idealist who believed the wartime relationship would be the foundation of a long lasting alliance that could go a long way to stabilize the post-war world.

Hopkins took the news hard. He understood if word leaked about the Remagen bridge, Stalin's paranoia would forever doom the alliance. The President listened intently and ordered Leahy to chair a meeting of all the key members from State and War, to figure out what to do with *this damn "Sunrise" business*. FDR knew the nation was so close to the end in Europe and he was willing himself to stay in control until then. Whenever he seemed about to lose focus his shaking hands reached for a new cigarette to put in his famous holder and lit one.

As Donavon prepared to gather his things to leave, the President grabbed his arm at the end of the meeting and looked him in the eyes and said, "Now Bill, I know how you really feel about the Russians, just don't go ahead and let that cloud your thoughts. Remember, we need them. We still have another war to win. Let's save a couple hundred thousand American mothers and wives from receiving those terrible telegrams."

FDR paused, as if trying to collect his thoughts again, and then squeezed his wartime spymaster's arm a little tighter and spoke in a whisper, "You will understand what I mean someday when you are near the end. If I can save American lives this way, that's what we have to do, above all else. That a boy."

The President looked up and flashed the intoxicating smile that had charmed the nation for so many years and made Donavon smile back and think, *how the hell can I make him understand that this time he is just plain wrong? I respect the hell out of the man, but how many mothers and wives will get "We regret to inform you..." cables in some future war because we weren't strong enough in the current one?*

An hour later, the men seated around the table were beginning to stifle the small talk and waited for Leahy to bring the meeting to order. All the players were present, Secretary of State John Stettinius along with two key deputies, Chip Bohlen and Alger Hiss, Secretary of War Stimson, the " Assistant President" James Byrnes, General of the Army George Marshall, Secretary of the Navy James Forrestal, and Harry Hopkins. Admiral Leahy motioned to Donavon to begin the meeting.

Donavon nodded and began to explain the events of the past week. "Gentlemen, the President asked me to convene this meeting to discuss the ramifications of an operation called *Sunrise*. In short, Operation Sunrise began in Italy when the seconding ranking general in the SS, General Karl Wolff, initiated contact with OSS agents in Switzerland. In his military capacity, General Wolff ultimately controls more than one million Axis troops in Northern Italy, under the operational field command of Field Marshall Kesselring.

General Wolff met with our station chief, Allen Dulles, two days ago and offered to arrange the surrender of the entire Italian front. He claims he is motivated by the atrocities of Russian forces committed against German women and children and wants German forces to be allowed to shift to the Eastern Front and enable Allied forces a direct avenue to enter Germany and Austria unopposed from the South."

Donavon looked intently at his audience, a group of serious men who had worked diligently in their various capacities to bring the war to a close. The idea that an entire front costing so many American lives might suddenly surrender, brought the whole room to the edge of their seats. General Marshall, in particular, seemed pleased the war might end sooner and with less bloodshed. Everyone looked pretty pleased with his briefing, *in about ten seconds that will change.*

He let the murmur die down and then hit them with the real reason the meeting was convened.

Donavon cleared his throat and let the murmuring die down and continued, "Even more extraordinary than the meeting itself was what General Wolff referred to as the *gift*. At this meeting, Wolff told Dulles he secretly arranged to have the bridge at Remagen rewired to prevent its destruction over the Rhine River, in hopes this would allow American forces a direct shot at Berlin. Our new Nazi friend apparently wanted to get our attention."

Donavon thought, *if that doesn't grab their attention, nothing will.* Leahy stood up and motioned for everyone to allow the OSS chief to complete the briefing. Donavon tried his best to not to smile at the looks on their faces as he scanned the room. *Well, it's about to get worse.*

Donavon began again, "We have been able to confirm the explosive charges placed throughout the Ludendorff Bridge were compromised. In fact, one First Army engineer explained that whoever wired the bridge either was an idiot or a fucking genius, his words not mine. Apparently, to wire a bridge in such a way as to give the appearance of a misfire and inflict just enough damage as what resulted a week ago could not have been done without the direction of someone of considerable expertise.

"Regardless of the details, Wolff's claim has been confirmed and this leads us to the political implications of Sunrise. For all intents and purposes, Wolff has provided American forces with an avenue for a direct movement upon Berlin. Taken in conjunction with his claimed intention to surrender on the Italian Front, it would seem, from a military standpoint, that the Western Allies are in a position to end the war quicker, at less cost, and potentially in a much stronger political position than anyone would have dreamed, considering the serious political implications as a result of the Yalta accords.

The bottom line is that this situation upsets everything set in motion since the Yalta meeting and potentially relations with the Soviets will never be the same, even if they never find out about the bridge. God help us if they do. OSS views this situation as critical and timing is of the utmost importance. Decisions must be made and quickly or the moment will be lost. I will now open the floor to the rest of the group, Admiral Leahy, thank you."

With a barely concealed disgust, Secretary of State Stettinius rose from his seat and responded forcefully, "I take serious exception to Major General Donavon's narrow minded description of the Yalta accords. Let me make this clear for everyone in this room, the accords signed by the President are now a matter of national policy and therefore not open for discussion. These agreements obtained after such difficult and deliberate consultations with our allies cannot be allowed to be wiped away on behalf of some SS Nazi general. The prestige and honor of this country are at stake. I refuse to be a part of anything that means getting in bed with the Germans while our ally on the Eastern Front is bleeding on the battlefield."

General Marshall concurred with the State Department and added, "As much as I am taken aback by the claims of this SS general, I don't see how this fundamentally changes our strategic concerns or erases obligations signed less than a month ago. I believe we must treat this approach by Wolff purely as a military matter and turn it over to an Allied military commission that can work out the surrender details in Italy. Anything else, including the allegation concerning the Remagen Bridge, should not deter our military strategy. Let us not forget the Soviet commitment to enter the war against the Japanese after Germany has been defeated. Failure to obtain Soviet cooperation could lead to countless thousands of unnecessary deaths, not to mention the likely high causalities required to capture Berlin."

General Marshall was as respected a man as any in the nation and many around the table felt compelled to shake their heads in agreement. State said we gave our word, and Marshall explained why we had to give it in the first place. Donavon saw where this was headed and just shook his head in disbelief.

At that point, Secretary Forrestal slammed his fist on the table and stood up with anger in his voice, and said "Oh Bullshit!!"

The Navy Secretary slammed a handful of papers on the table and stood from his seat and thundered, "General Marshall, with all due respect, how can we sit here and ignore that General Wolff has provided this country with an opportunity to end this war sooner and, more importantly, stop the Russians from making all of Europe go communist? For Christ sakes, Stalin has already broken the Yalta accords that you all think so highly of when he threatened Romania and refused free elections in Poland. Doesn't anyone in this room remember why we are fighting? I sure as hell do."

Turning to the Secretary of State, Forrestal sneered, "You call Yalta a victory for democracy? Well I call it nothing but a damn sellout."

Embarrassed for his boss, Alger Hiss stood up and pointed a finger at the silver hair Forrestal and said, "And some wonder why the Russians are so paranoid. Need I remind everyone here that the Soviet Union has tied down more divisions and inflicted more casualties than the British and American armies combined? Why shouldn't they be entitled to additional security considerations? We should be thanking them, not looking to create an enemy. No wonder they don't trust us."

Admiral Leahy pointed at both men and asked for everyone in the room to conduct themselves more respectfully. Stimson supported the war even before Pearl Harbor because he was offended by the aggressive nationalistic policies of Hitler. The idea of treating with a high-ranking member of the SS was something that would have been unimaginable even a year ago, but things had changed. As unhappy as he was about cooperating with Nazis, Stimson viewed the Soviet allies as little different than Hitler's crowd.

Stimson's calm voice spoke next, "Major General Donavon and his organization have put together an interesting operation that holds a great deal of opportunity, but also many what ifs? This Wolff's claim that he can arrange for the Italian Front to lay down its arms seems to be much more important than his claim about the bridge and racing to Berlin. However, I also believe the Secretary of State is correct that we cannot simply choose to ignore stated policy agreed to by the President at Yalta."

Secretary of the Navy Forrestal responded derisively, "Henry, it seems to me you basically agree with everything said by everyone so far. Someone has to be right, and a policy has to be enacted. Don't we have an obligation to those poor people in Poland and Czechoslovakia? Hell, even the average German doesn't deserve to live under those godless bastards. How can I be the only one in this room to see this?"

Stimson shook his head and thought about the poor people who had suffered the evils of war for so long now. Forrestal might be a bit narrow-minded when it came to communists, but he was right that millions would suffer under the Russian boot.

Donavon listened to everyone and held back his own feelings to properly gauge the attitudes in the room. Feeling it was time to make his play, he spoke, "Secretary Stimson is absolutely correct that the United States cannot easily break its word and General Marshall is also correct, but the strategic situation changed with the capture of an intact bridge over the Rhine River. If I am not mistaken, the Red Army is less than seventy miles away from Berlin and preparing to launch a major attack.

In the interim, I suggest we follow General Marshall's lead and direct Dulles to contact Wolff and inform him to begin formal military discussions concerning the mechanics of a formal cessation of hostilities on the Italian Front. If Wolff can deliver on his end, we invite the Russians to the surrender ceremonies, but keep them out of the negotiations so as not to spook the Germans. We weren't involved in Romania's military capitulation, so Stalin can't expect to participate in a purely military negotiation.

"Berlin itself is a political decision, and one I believe is in our absolute best interest. I might add that the British concur absolutely on this matter. If Italy surrenders tomorrow, then I would say the entire political framework of Yalta falls apart anyway."

The others around the table began shaking their heads, forced to acknowledge that too many things needed to happen before any policy changes. General Marshall, in particular, viewed Donavon's recommendation with satisfaction. The Army Chief of Staff was a cautious man who did not believe in jeopardizing his troop's lives for purely political goals. If the Italian Front collapsed, then taking Berlin from the South and West made sense. Forcing Ike to attack pell-mell from the West against still tough German opposition would not happen.

No one in the room needed to know General Eisenhower was under strict guidelines to minimize causalities. Men of the American First Army were already earmarked for landing operations against the Japanese main island of Honshu, tentatively scheduled for early 1946. In Marshall's mind, his soldiers' lives would be better spent fighting against a still very dangerous enemy, not wasted trying to obtain a political objective already ceded to the Soviets at Yalta.

Donavon slowly gathered his papers and watched as the others cleared the room. Everyone left either a little pissed or a little relieved. Stettinius and his people were a bit annoyed with, but he probably wasn't long for the position. The one interesting aspect of the meeting came from the one person who didn't say anything, James Byrnes. Byrnes was a cagey, political animal, but very well respected. When he walked out of the room, he looked at Donavon and winked. *Maybe he knows what's going on, or thinks he does, at least.*

Clearly, what is needed is the re-education of the American public. Once the public becomes aware of the atrocities conducted against innocent women and children by the Red Army, and most importantly, officially condoned by the Kremlin. Then tack on the bullying in Romania and threats to the London Poles, you will begin to see a whole different political response. Whatever happens with "Sunrise", in another two weeks, the Russians will find out that a free press blitzkrieg can be as dangerous as an armored blitz. The next time we meet, the President's advisers will be saying the hell with Berlin, and on to Moscow.

March 11, 1945: 10:35 p.m.

Washington DC

After one hell of a long day at the office, Donavon finally made it home and was relaxing on his favorite lounge chair listening to Beethoven's Fifth. Music by German composers might not be the most popular, *but what the hell, I'll listen to whomever I goddamn well please in my own home,* the OSS chief thought. After sitting for about fifteen minutes and well into his second tumbler of single malt scotch, the secure phone rang. Once, twice, three times the ringer sounded, each time followed by a loud groan by Donavon, until finally he moved reluctantly off the chair.

Picking up the phone with a gruff, "Yes," Donavon was greeted by a cheery English accent. "What a vulgar way to answer a phone William, certainly not dignified enough coming from one Washington's most powerful men. What if it was the Queen calling?"

Not expecting his British counterpart, Donavon chuckled to himself and said, "Well, at least the Queen would have had enough manners not to call at this god awful hour. Some public servants actually rise before eleven in the morning." Stevenson laughed at that last quip, knowing his reputation in New York had been built upon exaggerated stories of his nightlife.

Deciding to get right to it, the British MI6 agent said, "I was actually calling about the reasons behind your rather long day. It would appear a certain number of high-ranking chaps in your government were noticeably absent for several hours today. In fact, one of your up and comers in the State Department, that Hiss fellow, canceled a regularly scheduled meeting with one of his counterparts at the embassy. Being rather curious, I thought perhaps it had something to do with our conversation a couple of weeks ago about our Russian friends. Care to elaborate, my dear Bill?"

While Stevenson playfully got to the point, the OSS chief was thinking the English son of a bitch had some pretty good sources, too good even for an ally. Taking a deep breath, Donavon responded, "Look William, I would have gotten into this sooner or later, so now is probably as good as any. The whole thing revolves around an operation we've designated *Sunrise*. General Karl Wolff reached out to our station chief in Switzerland about surrendering his forces and allowing the Allied Armies a direct avenue to get to Berlin before the Red Army hits it."

The British agent cut in, "You mean *the* bloody General Wolff, second in command of the whole SS? He just walked in off the street and into your lap offering to surrender an entire front? That's bloody wonderful news. Wait a second, by your voice I can tell something else is about."

With a bit more difficulty, Donavon led into the real issue, "Getting to know my voice, Christ you're starting to sound like my wife. The real problem is that Wolff apparently arranged to sabotage the demolition setup with the bridge at Remagen that we captured intact a couple of days ago. You may have heard about that little operation, although Field Marshall Montgomery was apparently less than thrilled. Wolff claims to have done this to prove his good intentions and to allow American forces a more direct route to Berlin.

"Now the dicey part. If we get to Berlin before the Russians without a real fight, Stalin will go off the deep end, or worse, what happens if Stalin gets word of this wonderful little gift? Forget about any post-war cooperation and God knows what else he would be prepared to do. Either scenario could end very badly."

Still trying to absorb the impact of General Wolff's offer, Stevenson was floored by the second half of the American's disclosure that evening. Something was never entirely correct about the American capture of an intact Rhine bridge, but no one could have possibly have divined it was part of an organized attempt by underground elements in Germany, let alone the bloody SS. Most at the Imperial General Staff in London wrote the whole affair off as some individual German suffering from a bout of conscience, certainly not the result of a brilliant operation by the Americans.

Stevenson possessed a much higher opinion of Americans than many of Britain's upper crust, including Montgomery and Field Marshal Alan Brooke. Both believed the Americans to be nothing but sad amateurs who would serve the war effort better if they simply provided the men and the material and let the English direct the war.

Regardless, if this Wolff could effect the surrender of German forces in Italy, then Field Marshall Alexander, commander of all Allied forces in the Mediterranean Theater could move directly through Austria and possibly secure Trieste, and then deep into

Bavaria and beyond. Donavon was right about one thing, the Soviets would cry bloody murder. *What does Donavon want from me? He must want something or else he wouldn't feed this through the underground channel. He either wants my read on things or to give a hint on how this will play in certain circles in London.*

His tone becoming serious, Stevenson responded, "Well, Bill, I must say you have caught me at a bit of a disadvantage. Between Wolff and his gift, I would say the western alliance had better put its collective head together and come up with a joint policy. I think you know London would not be pleased if your people ran with this without consulting your ally. Considering your decision to pull forces out of Europe within two years, His Majesty's forces will be at a particular disadvantage against the mad Russians once this thing gets out, and we both bloody well know the Sovs will find out. How did this play out in the White House?"

Donavon figured the British had a right to know some of the background reasoning behind official policy and so went into detail about the meeting. "Following General Marshall's lead, it was decided that the proper thing to do was to begin formal military discussions with Wolff under the auspices of cease fire talks. This way everything is done above board, as we say, and the Russians can't claim we are going behind their back. Even better, we can reap the rewards from the surrender in Italy and push our way out from the Rhine bridgehead, all without breaking any treaty agreements.

Marshall thinks the whole operation is premature until we see if this Wolff character can actually make good on his offer. You have to admit, it makes a lot of sense."

Nodding to himself, Stevenson saw the logic, but also the dangers. "Look Bill, I think you are underestimating how the Soviets will take this, even if it takes longer for them to find out about the bridge, Stalin will react and likely push us into some level of confrontation. I guess your people are making the necessary contact through the Imperial General Staff in London on the military terms. I will forward our conversation through the backdoor to Churchill and see what he wants to do about it. Not that I don't already suspect what that will be."

Donavon spoke with a deadly tone, "William, I can't impress upon you enough the danger of disclosure about the bridge. If word leaks out on your side of the pond, it will severely impact our relations, and I don't want that. If Churchill or anyone else purposelessly leaks this to the Russians and creates a scandal, there are some who just might say to let your people deal with the Russians on your own. Tell Churchill don't push us on this until we are ready to deal with the Russians on our terms. Americans will resent British interference and end up blaming you guys instead of directing their attention on the goddamn communists."

Hearing the words he was looking for, Stevenson smiled and said, "Rest assured my friend, I appreciate your candor and I will make it clear to the PM what is at stake and that America stands strong as always with her English cousins."

Intrepid hung up the phone and took out paper and pen to begin *composing a cable. The important thing that Bill told me was there are increasingly active elements in the American government who are flexing their proverbial muscles and trying to focus more on the long-term threat posed by the Russians. But, and a very big but, Donavon made clear that the Americans would not allow the United Kingdom to unnecessarily upset the relationship at this stage because they still want Russian help during the invasion of Japan. One can't blame the American President for wanting to minimize casualties in a campaign that will likely prove to be far deadlier than the one currently underway in Europe.*

Perhaps I have been over on this side too long, but I have to admit there is much to admire about Americans. The can-do spirit of most the American people and their belief that anything can be accomplished if they put their minds to it is the most refreshing of attitudes. They may be innocent but perhaps it's a spirit that England could use a bit of these days. Donavon was good enough not to say it, but he made clear that we need the Americans more than they need us. Without America, the post-war world will be a lonely place except for the French, and who likes them anyway?

"The Americans will stay the course if we allow them to evolve on their own. They will not admit it, but the war has already changed them more than they think. I will formally recommend that we cooperate with General Marshall's directive and then only seek to change tack on Berlin if the opportunity presents itself. In the end, Europe and the world will be the stronger with an engaged America. Failing that, I'm afraid the Soviet Union will have her way for a very long time, indeed. I do hope the PM doesn't try anything foolhardy because Bill was quite right, if Stalin figures things out, God help us all.

March 12, 1945, 9:30 a.m.

Washington DC, British Embassy

To begin facilitating the decisions made at the previous day's meeting, Assistant Secretary of State, Alger Hiss, made arrangements to meet with the First Secretary of the British legation in Washington, Donald MacLean. Hiss came from a distinguished, East Coast, old money family. He went to all of the right prep schools and completed his studies at Harvard Law School. He rose rapidly through the ranks, starting in the Department of Agriculture in the early days of the New Deal, then moved to an important supporting role on the Special Senate Committee Investigation of the Munitions Industry, followed by a position over at Justice, but made a real name for himself in the State Department.

Alger Hiss emerged as one of Secretary of State Edward Stettinius' key men and accompanied the President during the recent trip to Yalta. He was brought along for his expertise on international organizations. Many believed he would be the key man in the coming United Nations. His function at State was to augment America's role in the new endeavor and devise a charter to enhance the effectiveness of the United Nations and succeed where the League of Nations had failed. They were compelling motivations, however Alger Hiss's ultimate allegiance was to something very different than God and country.

Pulling up to the British Embassy, Hiss considered the important information he possessed and thought how best to make use of it. Yesterday's meeting confirmed many of Hiss' worst views of the American government. How typical they would rather deal with a German war criminal rather than be honest with a wartime ally. Americans in general didn't seem to realize it was not Patton's tanks defeating Germany, but the sacrifices of millions of peasants and workers flying the hammer and sickle of the Red Army.

Remembering his student days at Harvard when he was first exposed to the teachings of Lenin and Marx, he believed that the capitalists were near the end as the Great Depression ravaged the

Western world. Many of his best friends agreed the world war was nothing more than a plot by Germany to prevent the vision of a socialist society from emerging throughout the world. All of the theories he read about and listened to in various secret meetings over the years about the evils of colonialism and weakness of the West powers and their scheming ways were all true. Now he sat in an important position, walking in the halls of power and confirmed that all that he had learned had been correct.

Hiss decided a long time ago that if ever an opportunity presented itself, he would do what is necessary to promote the interests of all men, not just the wealthy in American society. His modest contributions throughout the war to keep Moscow informed of the real thinking in the American government were motivated by the very highest of ideals. Hiss believed that the information he provided the network merely helped to level the playing field. Yesterday was just another confirmation of the wicked back stabbing views so prevalent in American society. He refused to be party to such a disgraceful lack of honesty and candor.

First Secretary Donald MacLean had much in common with Alger Hiss. Both came from well to do families and MacLean was educated at Cambridge. They both had worked hard and advanced rapidly during the wartime expansion of government. MacLean's posting to Washington in March 1944 reflected his growing reputation as a man to be watched in the Foreign Office. The position of First Secretary was tasked with undertaking much of the real work done at the embassy while the ambassador performed a more ceremonial function.

As First Secretary, MacLean was responsible for coordinating diplomatic and military cooperation between the two English-speaking allies. Everything from Lend-Lease requests to normal diplomatic cables to top-secret updates about the Manhattan Project passed through his desk. The meeting was apparently of some importance because Alger Hiss was coming to the embassy to discuss serious matters of state. Although MacLean had worked with Hiss at a several conferences, for a number of reasons, the two had never met one on one to discuss policy. Knowing Hiss' reputation, MacLean assumed something very important indeed was in the works.

Right on time, Alger Hiss confidently walked into MacLean's office to begin the meeting. Dressed smartly in a charcoal gray suit and crimson tie, Hiss greeted his British counterpart, "Good morning, Mr. Secretary. I appreciate you making time on rather short notice."

"Nonsense", MacLean responded, "I understand this is some rather pressing business, so please sit down. Would you like some tea or would coffee better suit your needs this morning?"

"It's very rare to drink decent tea in this country, so if you would be kind enough to provide some authentic, English tea, I would be most pleased"

While waiting for the tea to arrive, Hiss still wondered what he should feed back to the British. Knowing that no one hated or feared the Soviets more than that old reactionary, Churchill, perhaps leaking the information through the embassy would be for the best. The problem was how to avoid the leak coming back to haunt him. If word got out that he purposely informed the British, then he was putting his own career on the line. He had made contact the previous night to initiate a dead drop with the vital intelligence discussed. Maybe providing Moscow with information wasn't enough, perhaps if the British found out about the bridge incident, Churchill would open his mouth and offer a diplomatic opportunity for the Soviet Union to take advantage. The key was could the First Secretary be trusted to play ball? *We'll see.*

Hiss started his briefing, "Thank you for the tea. I would like to discuss the decisions made at a high level meeting held at the White House yesterday. The commander of German forces in Italy, SS General Wolff, has contacted American OSS agents in Switzerland and offered to begin negotiations to surrender his forces on the Italian Front. General Marshall wants to avoid additional casualties if possible but does not want to give our Soviet ally any cause for concern about American intentions."

MacLean nodded, too true. The Russians were so bloody paranoid and always on the lookout for treachery from their wartime allies. MacLean was no military man, but he knew eliminating German forces in Italy would enable Alexander's forces to move almost unopposed through Austria and into Vienna. Outwardly smiling, the British First Secretary said, "Outstanding. What course of action has your government decided upon?"

Hiss thought, *just another British imperialist. The man didn't blink an eye when I mentioned we were doing this at the behest of a goddamn SS general. Not once did he mention informing our mutual ally. Probably another one who wants to abrogate the Yalta accords and watch as British and Americans waltz into Berlin.*

Trying to hide his disgust, Hiss smiled, "We named the operation *Sunrise*. The Joint Chiefs have already begun with their counterparts in London. I believe General Clark's Fifteenth Army Group, along with Field Marshall Alexander, are being briefed as we speak. We are hoping to treat this purely as a military matter and whatever political fruits that emerge at a later date will appear quite innocent in nature."

MacLean finished his thought for him and said, "Quite right, we can explain things away by saying we are attempting to relieve pressure on the Eastern Front by forcing the Germans to defend their rear. Ivan can't argue against that, now can he?"

Hiss knew Churchill and his government would never let the opportunity slip away. Something had to be done politically, something that would force Churchill to put his foot in his mouth again. Speaking almost in a whisper, Hiss leaned towards MacLean and said, "I'm afraid there is one potential complication. I probably shouldn't be the one to discuss this matter, but I have been assured of your absolute discretion."

MacLean had kept perfect control throughout the whole meeting, desperate for a drink from the outset though Hiss unnerved him a bit. *Maybe I'm getting paranoid but he hadn't felt this nervous since meeting that dreadful chap Hoover at the FBI. Hiss is testing me on some level, but I'm not just sure on what level and for what reason.*

MacLean stood and walked around his desk and sat down next to Hiss, "I can assure you that your trust in me is well founded. We both crave the same thing, for this bloody awful war to end. Whatever you convey will be handled with the utmost of discretion."

Nodding his head, Hiss took a deep breath and said, "We have just been able to confirm that General Wolff arranged to secure the Remagen Bridge over the Rhine as a confirmation of his good intentions. The bridge was basically given to American forces to allow our army a direct shot at capturing Berlin before the Russians storm the gates. If this were to ever get out, Stalin would rightly accuse the American and British governments of collaborating with the Nazis against their ally. The alliance with the Soviets would be shattered, ending any hope for post war cooperation."

Hiss studied the British Secretary's reaction and watched his eyes grow wide the moment he saw recognition. MacLean extended his hand, shook firmly, and said, "Secretary Hiss, rest assured this information you have seen fit to offer my government will be used in the most responsible and discreet fashion. You have my word, as a gentlemen and an ally. I will personally contact you in the near future to describe how my government received your extraordinary news. I share your obvious sentiments that the post-war world shall be best served by a continuation of the Big Three alliance. Anything that could jeopardize this relationship must be dealt with in an honest and direct manner. Good day."

The British First Secretary closed the door and locked it. Rushing to his desk, he reached into the bottom drawer and pulled out a flask of warm gin. Sweating and panting with anticipation because he knew he would have to do it again. The moment Hiss pulled him close and whispered his secret, he knew he couldn't escape his duty. Each time the moment came to shoulder the burden again took more and more out of him. Part of him desperately wanted to forget about his commitments to them, to just be left alone, but after the third tug at the flask, MacLean began to breathe a little easier.

Rocking back and forth in his chair, things came back into perspective. He remembered why he made the promises in the first. Ten minutes later, after one last shot, he emerged from his demons, picked up the phone, and dialed. A sense of calm washed over him once the decision had been made to do his duty. It gave MacLean the strength he needed to say the right words. He spoke into the phone, "Hello, sorry to be a bother, but a rather important engagement has popped up. I need to know how fast I could get a tuxedo cleaned and pressed. It's rather urgent."

A heavy German accent answered, "We are very busy but could work something out after lunch. I will do my best."

The British diplomat responded, "That soon? Excellent. Be right over."

The call placed by the First Secretary rang at a nearby Dry Cleaning store owned by a pair of German, Jewish émigrés. They had a wonderful reputation with the embassy crowd. As the order came in, another individual listening to the same line took the order as well. When this individual heard the coded phrase, "cleaned and pressed," he knew a situation had emerged and immediate contact was necessary.

He walked outside to a pay phone three blocks away, and placed call, to the Soviet Embassy. Anatoli Gorsky, the NKVD illegal resident head of Soviet intelligence in America answered the phone and within three minutes a quick intelligence operation was under way. The former cipher clerk was all business and took a special bit of pride in what just took place.

Gorsky already made preparations to run into MacLean on the way to the cleaners. What MacLean didn't know was that the information he was about to give his control, Gorsky, had already been delivered late yesterday evening by none other than Alger Hiss. Two highly placed agents meeting face to face, neither suspecting that the other is a dedicated Communist was a remarkable feat in the dark world of espionage.

With agents likes these two, how can the West hope to survive? When Comrades Beria and Stalin read about what happened between the German and Americans, the West better start praying to their God for mercy, for Comrade Stalin shall have none.

Chapter Ten

March 13, 1945

The Polish Embassy, London

The former Prime Minister of the exiled Polish government, Stanislaw Mikolajczyk, called a general meeting of the London Poles to discuss his meeting with the British Prime Minister and to decide on a course of action. Although Tomasz Arciszewski had been the official head of the exiled government since late 1944, most of the old guard of exiles still followed Mikolajczyk's lead. Stanislaw stared in the bathroom mirror, at the face of a man who had aged twenty years. Sadly shaking his head, there had been so much pride and hope living as a free Polish citizen in our own homeland, free of Germans and especially from Russians. Splashing cold water on his face, Stanislaw ached for those heady days and wished that this madness were but a dream.

Slowly Stanislaw dried his face and thought, *Today a decision must be made to either accept the Yalta accords or to fight. It's really that simple. Fighting the Soviets will mean the deaths of many thousands of my countrymen, while the alternative means a return to serfdom. What choice do we have?* Closing his eyes, oh how he wished they would all burn in hell for their sins.

At about ten o'clock in the morning, the ten key members of the Polish government-in-exile arrived and took their seats. All appeared grave. This day would be remembered as either the death of the nation or the beginning of the rebirth of the Polish people. Much of Polish history was based upon heroic and often futile struggles against her enemies. What they faced was no different, same struggle, same enemies.

With little time to waste, Mikolajczyk stood up and brought the meeting to order. As a courtesy, he nodded to the current Prime Minister who waved at him to begin. Still unsure of where he stood, he moved his lips to pray for God's divine intervention and guidance. Knowing full well they looked to him for leadership, Mikolajczyk struck a defiant pose and began with a strong and deliberate voice.

"Gentlemen, we are here today to decide if it is possible to prevent the Russians from forever destroying any hope of a restored Poland. No other people in this war have fought as long or have suffered as much as have the Polish people. Worse, we have seen our friends turn their backs on us. When Stalin recognized those traitorous Lublin Poles in January, the British and Americans barely put up a struggle. We are about to become a mere footnote in history if we do not act together to save our people. My friends, I see only two possibilities. We either accept our fate and surrender or we fight."

Pausing a moment to look into the eyes of the men around the table, the former Prime Minister saw the range of emotions from anger to sorrow to sheer exhaustion. *Has the Almighty abandoned our people to those godless Bolsheviks and ended the dream?* Stanislaw closed his eyes and took a deep breath to gather his strength and continued his speech. "After my discussion with Mr. Churchill several nights ago, one thing is clear. The British are weak and, more significant, scared of the Russians. I was taken aback by Churchill. He seemed so weak. He knows without the Americans, Europe will have to bend to the wishes of the Soviets. Poland is but the first offering to quell the hunger of the Russian bear. He doesn't know them as the men in this room know them. Stalin will demand more and more until they dominate all of Europe. All of us are old enough to remember what it was like to have lived under the Czars; can we possibly imagine what our lives will be like under the Communists?

Stalin and Beria and their NKVD make the Czar's secret police, the Okhrana, seem like nuns."

Several men in the room remembered their days in parochial school and began to stifle a laugh which then became a bit infectious as several others joined them in laughter. Stanislaw grinned and added, "Okay, perhaps *nuns* are a rather poor comparison. I still bear the scars on my knuckles with some pride. Regardless, what I am trying to say is that any who lived in a free Poland could not possibly give up without a fight. So, my brothers, I ask of you, what are we to do? Now is not the time to hold back."

The Polish Minister of War, Sosnkowski, wanted to speak next. The War Minister possessed a noble and regal bearing though he had a fearsome reputation on the battlefield, having fought against the Germans in the First World War and later the Russians in the 1920 Russo-Polish War. Sosnkowski believed Poland had been abandoned by the Allies and had no chance of defeating the Soviets, but the culture and the history of the Polish people demanded armed resistance until the very end.

With a quiet determination, he stood to address his fellow exiles. "Stanislaw is correct in declaring that we have but two choices. I do not underestimate the power arrayed against the brave men of the Home Army, but the former Prime Minister left out one very important point. Let us be clear that what we are talking about is not just a declaration of war against the Russians, but we are in fact launching a civil war. As much as it pains me to admit, if we take up arms, it will be against both the armed communist forces of the Provisional Government and the Red Army."

The War Minister hesitated to allow everyone a chance to appreciate how serious the implications of Pole versus Pole would be for their people. He continued, "Since our defeat at Warsaw, the remnants of the Home Army have moved underground. We have been dispersing weapons and establishing cells throughout the country. A partisan war will be messy and many civilians will assuredly die in reprisal operations. We have already witnessed a devastating attack against the town of Kutno about a week ago. More than eighty percent of the village was massacred in the town church. In the end, many sons and daughters of Poland will die, but without open and direct support from the Americans, it will only be a matter of time.

"I was there at the beginning so long ago with Marshall Pilsudski, and I know what he would have demanded of the Polish people and of himself. The Marshall would send out a call to arms and fight until either victory or death. So, my friends, regardless what is decided here today, I intend to resign my position, return home, and fight them in whatever capacity an old man can. I will die, of course, but my death will be of my own choosing. Perhaps our example will fire the minds of our children, and their deaths will enable their children to throw out the beast. But I swear to all in this room, I will draw blood before it's my turn to face my maker."

No one had really thought about the war in terms of becoming a full-scale civil war, and many in the room were moved by Sosnkowski's vow and echoed his sentiment for war. Only President Raczkiewicz courageously spoke out against the horrors that were going to be unleashed yet again on their people.

His voice trembled as he said, "I can scarcely believe the men in this room who know of our people's suffering could so willingly add to it. The Russians have agreed to the Western demands that some of us be included in the new provisional Government. We can then use our positions to protect the people and hopefully vote the communists out of office someday. I strongly urge all of us to reconsider what is being contemplated. I despise all Russians, but if we take up arms against them in open rebellion, Stalin and his Red Army will destroy Poland like Germany is in the process of being annihilated. Do we really want that visited upon what is left of our country?"

Several heads in the room nodded in agreement at the prospect of even more suffering and bloodshed. Mikolajczyk was moved by the words of both men, but felt they were somehow missing something. Going to war in the faint hopes of American intervention was madness and yet how could they stand up to the evil bastard in the

Kremlin? Then it hit him and he blurted out, for all to hear, "That's it! That's how we can do it."

He cut off one of the lesser speakers in the room and spoke nearly in a whisper, "Gentlemen, if we rise up in rebellion now, we will lose and lose everything. Killing truck drivers and blowing up supply dumps and the occasional tank column will not matter in the end and do you want to know why? Because that madman in the Kremlin is prepared to slaughter as many of his own men as long as they are massacring Poles. It's not the generals and it's not the soldiers. No, we must target the puppeteers themselves. The only real target whose deaths matters is the one who pulls the strings."

Prime Minister Tomasz Arciszewski blurted out, "Are you mad? How in the hell are we supposed to kill Stalin or anyone of any consequence? Who the hell wouldn't want to shoot that bastard Stalin or that cold fish Molotov? But wanting it and doing it are two different things. Do you think they will just drop by Warsaw and announce a meeting in what's left of the City Hall? I think not."

Mikolajczyk's eyes opened in stunned amazement as the answer came to him. Turning to the current Prime Minister, he proclaimed, "That's it exactly. We will target them at a meeting, but not in Warsaw."

Arciszewski cut him off and sneered, "For Christ's sake, Stanislaw, we need to be discussing national strategy, not some half-baked scheme to kill the Soviet leadership, no matter how pleasing it would be to read about in the paper. Please focus yourself on the task before us."

The former leader of the Polish Peasant Party stood his ground and pointed at the War Minister, and asked, "General Sosnkowski, what do you think would happen to the Russians if Stalin was suddenly eliminated? I tell you, their whole system of command, both civilian and military, is through the power of one man. Take off the head and the whole dirty system crashes to a stop. Maybe just long enough to enable the Home Army to rise up and overthrow the Provisional Government in Warsaw."

The War Minister stroked his mustache as he seemed to ponder what was said, then he spoke, "Stanislaw is correct in the strictly military sense. I would expect the Communists to maintain viable local defenses, but any real military actions are really extensions of political decisions. Still, we are talking about this as if it is a real possibility. How could we take out Stalin? Are you going to borrow a B-17 Flying Fortress from the Americans and bomb the Kremlin? Unless, we knew exactly where and when the Soviet leadership, especially Stalin will be weeks in advance, I don't see how it could be contemplated for a moment. Let us get back to what we were discussing."

Mikolajczyk barked, "No. We will finish this discussion because I will tell you that there will be an opportunity and only one chance to do this. These so-called Allies have met twice so far and already there are rumblings of a new meeting. If I know that sick Georgian mind as well as I think I do, Stalin will agree to this final meeting. The meeting can be held in no other place but Germany. All of the warlords will wish to see the evidence of the destruction of Nazi Germany. At this meeting, Stalin will wish to claim the spoils of war. Somehow, we must do the unthinkable, we must kill the monster and at the very same moment rise up against the Russian occupiers. Brothers if we do this, our people may have a chance."

The old War Minister rose from the table, poured a glass of vodka, placed it in front of Mikolajczyk and said, "Drink up my friend, since you are probably the only Pole who can get that close. We all wish you the best of luck." The General slapped him on the back and the tension in the room broke as the exiled Polish government broke into the first hearty laughter in a long time.

Prime Minister Arciszewski came to attention and waved for everyone to quiet down. He grew serious and said, "Gentlemen, clearly desperate times require desperate measures, but this is no doubt the craziest idea I have heard so far in the war. However, Stanislaw is right. As long as Stalin is willing to slaughter his own men, our cause is lost. So, we will wait to hear about the next conference and then figure out some way to get to the bastard, even if it means shooting him at the conference table. Until that time comes, we will direct our Home Army to stay underground, recruit more men, and begin stockpiling more arms and material. Hopefully, we can find a suitable candidate other than our dear Stanislaw. Now, let us raise a glass and drink to the craziest and most desperate plan any Pole has dared to utter. Drink, my friends, to a free Poland."

March 14, 1945, 11:15 P.M.

Prime Minister Churchill's Private Residence, London

It was not entirely unusual for the respective heads of both the MI5 and MI6 to meet the Prime Minister at such a late hour, but neither man could get used to Churchill's desire to hold such high level meetings in his bedroom. Sir David Petrie, Director of MI5, Great Britain's domestic intelligence service, called the meeting and insisted only the three men attend. Although a natural rivalry existed between the two sister services, Petrie thought the Prime Minister would have to be carefully handled that night or God knew what the old bugger might be tempted to do with their new information. General Sir Stewart Menzies commanded the wartime MI6, also known as the SIS or Secret Intelligence Service. General Menzies was a decorated WWI veteran and rumored to be an illegitimate son of King Edward VII. Menzies exchanged a nervous glance with his counterpart, nodded, and then entered the PM's sprawling bedroom.

Wearing navy blue, silk pajamas, the Prime Minister was propped up by nearly a dozen pillows. His entire bed was covered with State papers in a series of piles along with the odd book opened and placed haphazardly around him. The PM's reading glasses were tilted at the bridge of his nose and in his left hand he held a tumbler of brandy, in his other hand was his ever-present cigar. He waved both men into the room and pointed to two chairs set out in preparation for the meeting.

Finishing what he was reading, Churchill's tired eyes looked up and greeted them, "Gentlemen, sorry to keep you but I was re-reading some dispatches from my first book about my adventures during the Boer. Those were the days, lads. Oh, to be young and vigorous and possessing no fear. Service for Queen and country was a joy to be held."

Regretfully, Churchill snapped the book shut and tossed it to the side.

"Sorry for the ruminations of an old man, let's get to it. What was so bloody important that the two heads of my intelligence service felt the need to call an impromptu meeting? Have the Germans surrendered? Or better yet, did Stalin have a bloody stroke?"

Sir David Petrie had to laugh. Even while depressed, Winston tried to make light of things. *Too bad though, the old boy looks on his last legs, that fire in his eyes seems pretty well run down. Pity.*

Petrie called the meeting, thus he began. "Good evening, Mr. Prime Minister. I wish to discuss with you a rather serious piece of intelligence that has just been obtained. Yesterday morning, a rather ticklish operation, picked up a conversation on tape of a momentous meeting held in the Polish Embassy by the Polish government in exile."

Pausing for effect, Petrie wanted to impress upon the Prime Minister the importance of the revelation without getting him too excited about the likely success of such a venture. General Menzie's rather dour and often less than optimistic personality should help ground the PM's certain attitude towards the Polish intentions. Menzies found such guerilla operations and partisan fighting to be untidy affairs, very un-British in a way. As a rule he looked down on such ventures and Petrie hoped his views could dampen Churchill's sense of adventure.

When Churchill in 1940 spoke of using the SOE, or Special Operations Executive, to set Europe aflame with subversion and action against the Germans, he truly believed it. Those types of operations got the PM's juices flowing, but he rarely saw the reports of how few successes the SOE had and ignored the terrible loss rate of agents and the reprisal operations that often ensued.

The head of MI5 continued, "Quite simply, the exiled Polish government, led by the former Prime Minister, Mikolajczyk, conducted a rather spirited meeting which focused on their current plight. In summary, the Poles believe their country has been effectively bargained away by both the American and British governments and that unless drastic action is taken, Poland would effectively lose their independence to the Soviets. As a result, it appears they are seriously considering and, in fact, have begun active preparations for a widespread campaign of resistance by their Home Army. They believe their history demands such a sacrifice even though most believe that without massive support from America, the revolt is doomed to fail."

Churchill knew the omission of Great Britain was no accident. Mikolajczyk looked into his eyes and felt he could not lead the British people into yet another war over Poland, especially one that could not be won. Listening to his domestic intelligence chief, Churchill swirled the brandy in his glass and downed the last mouthful. Savoring for a moment, the pride and honor of the brave Polish people, wishing he were younger and could somehow gallop into battle alongside the famed horse cavalry of the Poles against the Russians. Sadly, the romanticism of the mounted cavalry charge died with the Poles in 1939 when they sent beautifully trained and equipped cavalry against the cold steel of the German panzer force. It was no contest in 1939 and Churchill knew any revolt against the conquering Red Army was foolhardy and should be avoided at any cost. Poland would pay a terrible price.

Petrie sensed he was losing the PM, so he said, "Sir, I feel that I should fill your glass before I continue any further. The next part of the transcript is rather dicey."

Churchill smiled, thinking it was a polite way of telling the boss to pay attention. Turning to General Menzies, who hadn't said a word and looked tense, obviously impatient to get to the point, Churchill emerged from his fog and asked, "General, you have allowed your domestic counterpart the floor far longer than I have ever witnessed, he must be leading up to something. Out with it."

Menzies motioned with his eyes to Petrie to get on with it, so he leaned towards the Prime Minister and spoke in a whisper, "There's more, I am afraid, sir. You see the former Prime Minister couldn't accept such a likely loss of life without some possible chance of success. Therefore, he boldly proposed to undertake a major nationwide uprising against Russian occupation forces, as well as the leadership of the Polish Provisional Government. More significantly, sir, it was decided to make an attempt on the life of Stalin at the next Allied conference."

Winston looked as if the MI5 chief was a bit daft, *he couldn't possibly have said what I think he just said. Stalin? Those brave, glorious, mad bastards.*

Before the look of shock wore off, Petrie added, "They believe their only hope for independence is to create enough chaos the Home Army can seize control and pray for Western forces to intervene."

Menzies finally spoke, "Sir, you have got to hand it to them, they aren't looking to pull any bloody punches. It seems they have as much sense as a drunken Paddy on St. Patrick's Day, but unfortunately, about as much smarts. Not too bloody likely for such a scheme to work but makes one hell of an interesting tale."

The tired and defeated old man who had greeted the two intelligence quickly found himself rejuvenated. He leapt off the bed and began pacing. The very idea of seeing that bastard shot, maybe even in front of his eyes in the middle of a conference, was really too much to contemplate. *Just think of it, old Uncle Joe demanding the Germans for dinner and the Poles for dessert and then suddenly, BOOM. In one grand moment, one heroic Pole could change history in an instant.* Bringing himself back to reality, Churchill conceded it couldn't be done.

My God, that Mikolajczyk had some real bollocks to even think of such a thing? They are right about one thing; the Kremlin would be torn apart fighting amongst themselves. If this lunacy became reality, by God, I bet the Home Army could strike a blow for freedom so fast maybe the Americans would actually intervene after all. His two service chiefs came here tonight to hold my hand and make sure that I didn't say anything to blow their little intelligence operation, let alone encourage the Poles. The buggers think they can keep me under wraps do they. Well bugger them.

Becoming increasingly uncomfortable by the excited schoolboy look in the PM's face, General Menzies waited a few more moments before asking, "Mr. Prime Minister, now that you know the severity of the crisis, we were hoping to discuss some options to try to keep this situation from getting out of control. His Majesty's government certainly cannot allow itself to encourage such criminal behavior, even from an ally. In fact, not only do the Poles have no real chance to pull something like this off, but if this taints us in any way, the Soviets are likely to exact far greater concessions at the bargaining table. Sir, we strongly recommend that we quietly speak to the Poles and dissuade them from this lunacy.

In fact, any attempt to encourage what will almost certainly be a tragic waste of life would, in the end, reflect poorly on this Government. We shouldn't be seen as openly encouraging people to march off to get slaughtered, and that's exactly what the Red Army will do. The Poles are about to sign their own death warrant."

Churchill quietly listened to his conservative foreign intelligence chief finish his summary. He knew before he opened his mouth exactly what the General would have to say. Untidy and messy affairs were not really part of the spymasters' version of acceptable strategies. The British Prime Minister suppressed a yawn and said, "I fear that you are correct, General Menzies. After my last unfortunate discussion with the Poles, I was afraid they would be motivated to try something quite desperate, but I never for a moment thought they would try something fraught with so much danger. In principle, I accept your recommendations and intend to keep out of this one, perhaps even stop it if I can. Now, unless you have anything else that can't wait until morning, let's adjourn for the night. Good operation, Sir David. I'll try not to spill the beans to the Polish help in the kitchen. You can count on me. Good evening, gentlemen. I will call on you tomorrow."

As both men were walking out, Petrie said to his counterpart, "The PM seemed to take that pretty well, don't you think? Why?"

Menzies felt too tired to worry how Churchill took the news. If anything, the MI6 chief expected a spirited row with the Prime Minister, one which might last into the night. In a tired voice, he answered, "I really wouldn't read too much into this, David. I think he's not just tired, but worn down."

Notoriously suspicious, Petrie stopped in his tracks and held out his right arm to his colleague and said, "I think not, Stewart. Did you see the old man's face after I said whom the Poles were looking to off. You saw him, jumping out of bed all excited, and then calming himself. No, something's not right here. He's holding something back, trust me. We both need to keep a keen watch on him. I assure you that I will be shadowing the movement of any and all Polish exiles who come within a hundred yards of 10 Downing Street and perhaps, you could use your contacts in the Home Army to keep tabs on what's brewing up over the Channel. Agreed?"

Walking down the steps to their prospective vehicles, General Menzies turned and said, "You don't really believe they could pull it off, do you?"

Sir David Petrie had a feeling of trepidation that perhaps the night's meeting was not the end. Petrie shook his head and with a grimace said, "I don't know, old boy, but why do I feel the old man is going to get his nose into something, maybe for the last time?"

Chapter Eleven

March 15, 1945

Desenzano, Italy

SS Headquarters in Italy

Colonel Eugen Dollmann tried to maintain his composure while ignoring the ranting coming from his boss and leader of this insane plot. General Wolff has been cursing and insulting the weak stomachs of the Americans after finally receiving the long overdue memo from that OSS man, Dulles. It would seem that Dulles wasn't able convince his superiors to act even with the Russians practically at the gates of Berlin.

From the moment that General Wolff informed him that he was to be a player in this conspiracy, Dollman's nerves began to fray. He was a dilettante not some spy let alone anything resembling a real military officer. Beauty was his calling not this hideous uniform.

Shaking his head, what did Wolff think the Americans were going to do? Get on their hands and knees and kiss his arse for giving them that bridge. They hate us as much as the British. These Americans, they obviously don't want to sully their hands with any backdoor deals. I think that the General forgot that he wears the black uniform with the skull and cross bones insignia for a reason. It would be like Germans making a side deal with some Soviet commissar, madness to expect anything else.

General Wolff looked at his co-conspirator disgusted. Scanning the American memo again, he couldn't believe they were so blind, so short sighted.

Dulles wrote,

> *"My government has carefully reviewed our discussions and is evaluating your proposals, as well as your claim about the Ludendorff Bridge. At this time, we feel it best to undertake direct military negotiations by both American and British officers from Field Marshall Alexander's*

headquarters. The Western Allies understand your reluctance to treat directly with the Soviet government, but they want to make clear that negotiating the surrender of German forces in Italy does not mean the betrayal of an ally. We will discuss a ceasefire in good faith, but my government categorically refuses to allow the release of German forces so you can further delay the Russians.

President Roosevelt wants to bring this war to a speedy end and promises that if these talks bear fruit, everything that can be done, will be done to protect all peoples under American occupation. I will send follow on instructions so you can cross again into Switzerland to conduct direct armistice talks with Allied military officers and establish a timetable for the occupation of the Italian peninsula. You are encouraged to facilitate this arrangement as soon as possible for therein lies Germany's best hope for a just peace. The sooner Allied forces can enter southern Germany and Austria, the sooner we can protect German citizens from the danger of occupation by Russian units...."

The letter continued for another page, but the meaning was unmistakable. When the Americans brought in their British cousins, the likelihood of a quick deal was probably lost. *The British are more scared of the Russians than the Americans, and only because they are smarter and the Americans will probably pull another disappearing act like after the First World War.* Exhausted and angry, Wolff thought what more he could have done. *I arranged the gift of an intact bridge over the fucking Rhine River. Are those sanctimonious bastards in Washington so obsessed with fair play they can justify raining bombs on civilians for three years, but can't justify breaking a treaty with a mass murderer? Are they truly that blind?*

It wasn't easy to pretend his life wasn't in jeopardy, let alone the others he brought into venture. The pressure began to take its toll. Wolff needed a bottle of schnapps to sleep at night and found himself in a constant rage, screaming at subordinates. The news from the front in Germany grew grimmer, especially concerning the fates of innocent citizens who lived in Prussia trying to escape the Red Army's grasp. *Must not lose a grasp of why I am doing this or else I could be getting together my fake identification and passport for South America, like half of the SS officer corps right now.*

Trying to regain some measure of focus, he knew it still came down to figuring a way to manipulate the Americans into an open split with the Russians. Of course, it all depended on his ability to avoid getting shot, but so much for details. *I have no real choice, I will return to Switzerland, and convince these military men what needs to be done. If that doesn't work, I will leak everything to the Communists. Maybe I can cause a split in the alliance and get the Americans to make a dash for Berlin after all.*

These thoughts brought a sense of clarity and calm again and so he looked at poor sad Dollmann, and finally said, "Time to back your bags again Eugenio, we're about to take another trip."

Chapter Twelve

March 15, 1945

London

Great Britain's young and dapper Foreign Minister, Anthony Eden, hurried to the Prime Minister's office for what felt like the millionth time to date in the war. It seemed no different than the others. Winston called on the telephone and assured him it was positively an urgent matter of State.

Truth be told, Eden thought, *Winston sounds about as good as he has in weeks.* Maybe he put some of this nasty business with the Poles and Yalta behind. Entering the Prime Minister's offices moments later, Churchill leapt off his chair and met the startled Eden at the door. Anthony, come in man, come in. Terribly damp today, I will ring for some tea right away. Sit, now, sit." Noting the quizzical look on his Foreign Minister's face, Churchill grinned like a school boy and said, "Now Anthony, don't look at me like that. I am perfectly all right... Really."

Stopped in his tracks, Eden raised his eyebrow and said, "Mr. Prime Minister, when you say you are perfectly all right and that I have nothing to worry about, that's exactly when I know I bloody will have something to worry about. What, may I ask, has you all worked up? It must be pretty big, for I don't believe I have seen you this excited since you heard Hitler's generals tried to blow him up. That kept you in stitches for a week."

Taking a deep breath, Churchill thought, *I must convince this man, my protégée, or else no one will understand.* No doubt the idea was fraught with more danger than anything else he had come up with so far. Anthony had to understand it was a matter of national honor, not just policy at stake. *It's bigger than even my ego, and God knows that's pretty bloody big.* Even so, the words from the Pole had kept him up at night for weeks. Everything he had said was true. *I am tired, even scared not just for the Empire, but for Europe, but the instant Petrie informed me of the Poles' decision, I knew what I had to be done...what I must do.*

Taking a moment to light his cigar, Churchill turned serious, "Anthony, yesterday evening at about eleven, Petrie and Menzies called an emergency meeting and came to my bed chamber to discuss something of the highest importance. Apparently, some intrepid fellows at MI5 managed to place several listening devices inside the Polish embassy and recorded a remarkable meeting chaired by none other than the former Polish Prime Minister, Mikolajczyk. After much argument, they agreed to initiate a full-scale rebellion against the Polish Provisional Government and the occupying forces of the Red Army."

Shaking his head in disapproval, Eden responded, "They will be bloody well slaughtered, and then expect us to help them. Please don't tell me you want to support them. Winston, it would be foolish and only make things worse with Stalin."

Upon hearing the key word, Churchill smiled and slapped the shoulder of Eden and said, "Well, you just mentioned the second part of their plan. If things go well for our Polish friends, we may not have to deal with Stalin any longer."

Immediately understanding, Eden angrily pushed the Prime Minister's hand away, "Dear God, Winston, are you mad? It's sheer bloody madness to involve this Government in some insane plot doomed to failure."

Receiving the exact response from Eden he knew Eden would argue, Churchill stood and towered over his longtime political ally and friend, determined to argue all day until Eden understood. "Dear God man, don't speak to me of your high bred sensibilities, we are talking about the lives of millions. All of whom are at risk because of the insane desires of one man. Do you know what Mikolajczyk said the other day that hit home? If Stalin met an early demise the whole disgusting system would convulse, they would feast upon one another trying to fill the vacuum.

"Use your damn head for a moment, it's not as if I am asking you grab a snipers rifle and shoot the bastard yourself. See the big picture. If the Poles can time an assassination to coincide with a major uprising, then who knows where it will end? Think man, if the honor and bravery of the Poles are broadcast to the world, how many other subject peoples may also rise up? Who knows how far this may move and how fast, but it all must start with the First Act. Stalin must die, and we are honor bound to help them."

Horrified at the notion of openly talking about the assassination of a world leader, Eden could not simply commit himself to such a frightful act. Winston didn't understand, no matter how distasteful Stalin may be, matters of State couldn't be handled in this fashion by a civilized society. However, his Oxford educated mind argued, *how is this any different than ordering mass conscription armies into battle or bombing raids of civilian targets at night?* Shaking his head, trying to come to grips with the whole thing, *it's just too much, it feels dirty,* he told himself.

I can't give up this easily, so he lashed back in tone full of sarcasm, "Tell me something Winston, what if they fail? How do you suppose Stalin will react to a failed attempt on his life? How many tens of thousands will die in reaction to his certain fury? You know someone will talk. We both know you're not that clever."

Changing his tone, the Prime Minister calmly pointed out, "Keep in mind several points. First and most importantly, the Poles have already made the decision to make the attempt. Now ask yourself, do they stand a better chance if we provide them with some form of assistance? The Poles are giving us a chance, albeit a small one, of saving Europe's grim future. We both know the key will be to engage the Americans, but I fear it will take a bloodbath in Poland to get their attention. If the Poles are willing to risk the lives of tens of thousands of their countrymen, then I am willing to risk our nation's honor in this grand venture. My duty and conscience is clear, as should be yours."

Feeling he couldn't keep up the argument any longer, Eden slumped in his chair and stared at the painting of Nelson's great victory at Trafalgar. Eden looked at the vivid battle portrait, seeing the hulk of Nelson's ship, Victory, in the foreground grappling with two French men-of-war. Such courage and determination to so brazenly sail into the middle of hell, drop anchor and fire at one another until one side was dead or surrendered.

The man sitting across from Eden would have sailed HMS Victory into the middle of battle without any fear and done so with the same reckless abandon Nelson was often credited with possessing. *It's such a British trait. Single-mindedness. I wish it were that easy for me.*

Eden could see in Winston's eyes that the decision was made and he realized he had no choice but to stand by the PM, even if it was pure madness. He would follow the old man forward and bring everyone else along as well. God help me, but the day this man lets down the British people, I fear his fall from grace will take all of us with him.

With a look of resignation, Eden clenched his fists, moved towards the Prime Minister and spoke in a calm voice, "Well, I hope you haven't gotten me riled up without some bloody plan. How do you intend to help those poor bastards?"

Grasping Eden's shoulder, Churchill broke into one of his winning smiles and said, "I thought I bloody well lost you on this one. Took you long enough to jump on board. I was beginning to have doubts myself for a second or so."

Eden broke the ice. He laughed and blurted out, "Don't be going overboard, Winston, you old bugger. I am filled with doubts, so don't push your luck. So have out with it, how are you planning to pull this off?"

Good, Churchill thought to himself, *back to the nuts and bolts of the matter*. The Prime Minister returned to a more businesslike approach and started talking off the cuff. "I am taking the cue from Mikolajczyk again because he brilliantly suggested the only way to get to Stalin would be at the next, and most likely last, meeting of the Big Three. He knows that nothing else could possibly get Stalin out of the Kremlin. I will insist on a meeting to clear up all of the unanswered questions left over from Yalta and ensure it's held in Germany, preferably near Berlin.

"To be honest, I want to see what's left of that city and see for myself that the war is truly over. He will want to do the same, I assure you. At this meeting, I will insist all three governments work closely on security matters to protect everyone from the marauding bands of die-hard Nazis that are sure to be on the loose. The Poles will be given everything from the dates of the meeting, the travel route Stalin will take, the location of everyone's living quarters, and, most importantly, a blueprint of the security arrangements defending the meeting place. There is little doubt there will be security unlike the world has ever seen for this event, but if one knows the where and the when, the how becomes easier to figure out."

Eden listened intently to the PM's sales pitch and found it tight. In fact, Winston really could make it happen, at least the setting of the scene, and then it would be up to the Poles. Still suspicious Winston was holding something back, Eden retorted, "Winston, we both know there is more to this plan of yours so out with it."

Winston reluctantly added, "Well, there is something else. You see, I am afraid the Poles however brave, may muck it up. So, I pulled the service record of every active Polish operative in the SOE. From what I can see in their service jackets, about three dozen Poles have served behind lines in this capacity and are currently active with the SOE. I've ordered them released from service and given immediate transit back home to Poland to start raising hell against Ivan once the war against the Jerries ends.

Further, I have directed the SOE to start smuggling captured Wehrmacht weapons, explosives, and high end communication equipment to our Home Army friends. They will be happy to get the support and the London Poles will think we are acting out of guilt, but actually, we will be providing the necessary infrastructure to help organize the rebellion. All of this will be closely monitored by both MI5 and MI6 sources."

Exhausted, all Eden could add was, "On paper it seems so neat and tidy. But Winston, just know, if this thing blows up in our faces, there will be bloody hell to pay."

Chapter Thirteen

March 16, 1945

The Kremlin, Moscow

The Kremlin, the very word meant fortress. Many of the men who served Comrade Stalin knew what it was to feel besieged, knowing at any given moment the Boss could turn his deadly stare and suddenly places at the table became empty. The list of forgotten souls was long and infamous. Stalin's march to absolute power claimed the lives of so many, great and small, and the names of Kirov, Kamenov, Yagoda, Tuchavosky, numerous others, yet the story remained the same.

For reasons that even Stalin may not completely understand men, families, and sometimes-whole peoples just had to disappear, as if they never existed. For some it was too much success, others failure, and some for no other reason than they somehow displeased Stalin and they all ended in a one way trip to the Lubyanka.

Molotov's bald forehead openly began to perspire because he knew that he would have to answer to the Comrade Stalin this evening, treachery from our Allies had caused this meeting, and someone must answer for it, someone always had to answer for it.

Stalin's eyes had lost their humanity ages ago and now his predator like stare fixed upon his often times emotionless Foreign Minister. The irony of the situation was lost on Molotov at the moment or else he would have been struck by the savage nature of the system that he has served for so long. In the Soviet Union, bullying those of a lesser station had become a national pastime. From Stalin on down to the lowliest of NKVD border guards, the intoxicating feeling of power when inflicted on those below can in an instant change as you are called to answer for real or imagined crimes.

How many times had Molotov sat at his desk and struck fear into the hearts of men as his cold exterior and calculating methods had served the often times evil designs of his master. The moment that Molotov read the cable from the Americans about this SS General, he knew his fate would be in the hands of a man without mercy.

Molotov understood Stalin better than most at the table. Comrade Stalin was feeling a greater sense of power and prestige than at any time in his life. The war was being won handily, as Marshal Zhukov and Konev's tanks raced to Berlin, less than sixty miles from the heart of the Nazi regime. The Yalta conference had delivered everything he had wanted. The Americans were leaving, the British were weak, and the French still didn't have a place at the table. And the Poles, well the Poles were posing a minor disturbance, but it was well in hand. Luckily, Russian rulers could draw upon several centuries of experience in controlling difficult Poles.

Comrade Stalin had achieved more than any Czar had ever dreamed and was about to ensure the Soviet Union would dominate European affairs for generations to come. The Soviet Union would have its security and no one would be permitted to violate the Rodinia again, but it was the very nature of this success that caused so much paranoia and anger. Stalin had arrived at this moment by trusting no one, by instituting draconian policies in both war and peace, but he still feared everything he had achieved could be taken from him at any moment. The kulak mentality in Stalin's character was never more evident. A kulak knows that what is his today could be taken from him at any moment and therefore treachery and retribution are behind his thoughts in all things.

Reaching for a glass of water, Molotov noticed his hand trembling and tried to steady it before anyone noticed. Cursing to himself that everything was well in hand until this damn Sunrise operation run by the Americans caused Comrade Stalin to erupt in anger days ago. Everyone in the room remembered the dark days of the 1920 Russo-Polish War and knew Stalin's worse fear was a separate peace between the Western allies and Germany.

Stalin long remembered when Soviet forces held the upper hand and were about to strike the decisive blow in front of Warsaw when disaster struck. Field Marshall Pilsudski led a reserve army that boldly attacked a Red Army force that had overextended its supply lines and nearly annihilated the invading Soviet Army

Near the gates of Berlin, with victory in his grasp, Stalin feared another trap, only this one coming from his erstwhile Allies. Stalin rightly feared a separate peace would allow the Germans to reconstitute their army and send enough reinforcements to hold the Oder River line long enough to deny Berlin to the Soviet Union. Four years of careful and calculated diplomacy appeared to be unraveling as direct evidence existed of collusion between the West and the Nazis.

Molotov trembled inwardly as he remembered Beria had warned them in February after Yalta of revanchist movements in the West led by men who feared the power of the Soviet Union. Molotov waved away the NKVD leader's remarks at the time as being too alarmist. Now he knew the General Secretary would recall each and every word the Foreign Minister had uttered, defending the West against comrade Beria's security concerns.

Josef Stalin's dark eyes narrowed, focused on his Foreign Minister and watched as the man begin to wilt before his eyes. Pointing at Molotov with his pipe, Stalin spoke in a course and gruff voice, "Molotov, what does this Sunrise operation mean by the Americans? Do the Americans take Stalin to be a fool?" speaking louder with each accusation, "Do you think Stalin did not see this coming? I have always said the West can never be trusted. Comrade Beria tried to warn us, but you said they could be trusted. Why would you trust the lies of reactionary imperialists, instead of our own head of foreign intelligence?

Molotov's upper lip perspired. He felt nauseous as Stalin stood above him. Looking at the smug face of Beria, he knew he would have to answer the General Secretary or end up in the Lubyanka this very night to await his fate. Finding the courage to stand and answer Stalin took all of his strength. Molotov knew the real answer could never be said. The truth was that Comrade Stalin tried to humiliate the Western powers, and he may have pushed their current and future enemies together. Someone had to take the blame and the Foreign Minister knew he had to keep his head, accept responsibility and protect himself from Beria.

The monotone voiced Molotov contritely answered, "Comrade Stalin, I agree the talks between the Nazis and the Americans are troubling, but perhaps it is but the work of isolated elements acting independently from the American government. I can't believe President Roosevelt would stab us in the back. Granted, that reactionary Churchill would do anything he thought he could get away with, but not the Americans. Perhaps the Nazis are trying to break up the alliance.

"Regardless, I certainly regret not taking Comrade Beria's advice, Comrade Stalin, but I only wished to counsel you against doing anything that could give the Americans and British an excuse to betray us. I was worried the West would look for reasons to deliberately sabotage the Yalta agreements. I am sorry and swear never to underestimate the recommendations of Comrade Beria again".

Thinking it wouldn't be good enough, Stalin needed to know if some type of collusion was in play even before Yalta. Stalin refused to be outmaneuvered by anyone, least of all by that wily old bastard Churchill or the weak cripple, Roosevelt.

Stalin was not letting his Foreign Minister off the hook that easily. He demanded, "Why have you not delivered protests to the Americans about letting the Germans leave their fronts in Italy and

Germany to fight the Red Army? Why have you not protested this breech of friendship by the Americans?"

Surprising everyone, including himself, Molotov cut off the General Secretary and said, "But Comrade Stalin, why would the Americans and British tell us about this meeting with the Nazis if they were intending to stab us in the back? Wouldn't they have kept the whole thing secret?"

Angry and not wanting to hear anything but utter submission, Stalin responded with disgust, "Molotov, you idiot. What if they only reported what they wanted us to know? What about secret protocols to open up the front in Italy? Why meet in Switzerland, a place that won't recognize the Soviet Union and let observers to meet with this Nazi, Wolff? You had better start coming up with answers and quickly."

The Foreign Minister had seen that look before and he knew Stalin meant business. The other men around the room stared or looked at the ground, none wishing their eyes to gaze upon their struggling colleague. Lavrenti Beria took the moment to make his grand announcement and hopefully end the power of that pinhead Molotov for good.

Watching that neophyte sweat through his wool suit generated much pleasure for the head for the NKVD. He bided his time until the General Secretary was about to blow. The information Beria possessed was enough to poison the mind of his benefactor for years to come. Beria wasn't even sure what Stalin would do when he found out about the bridge over the Rhine. The man's anger knew no bounds, but this time he may go over the edge. It was almost too easy.

Who would have thought agents recruited in the Thirties in both England and America would pay off so handsomely now? Not that it mattered, but in trying to save his country, the German SS man may have done more to ensure its destruction than any other, save Hitler.

Putting on his most grim and official face, Beria stood and asked to be heard. "Comrades, it is far worse than even Comrade Stalin fears."

Stalin angrily cut him off, "What is this you are talking about Beria? How much worse could it be to have our so-called Allies meeting with the Nazis behind our backs?"

With the hint of a grin on his face, Beria turned to his fellow Georgian and said, "Comrade Stalin, just moments before I left for the meeting, I received a very detailed, coded message from our Washington Embassy. This intelligence has been confirmed from two independent sources at the very highest levels and proves beyond a doubt that the Americans are working with the Germans and keeping everything from us.

"The Americans may have told us about this meeting with the SS man, Wolff, but what they failed to tell us was that they made a pact with the devil. The SS man didn't just offer to open the front in Italy, but sabotaged the bridge over the Rhine and gave the bridge to the Americans so they could drive into Berlin unhindered while tens of thousands of brave Red Army soldiers die against the cream of the German army.

Comrades, the Americans were given the bridge to deny the Soviet people Berlin. I believe this Italian business is a ruse. I am afraid we have been betrayed and are alone again to face the full power of the German army."

Beria watched as he saw the shocked looks on everyone's faces. The look of bewilderment Stalin's face was priceless. Quickly that bewilderment changed to pure fury, as the General Secretary let out a roar and pounded the table shattering wine glasses.

Stalin shouted, "The bastards lied to me. You see, Molotov, these are the men you wished to trust. You tell them that the Soviet people will not allow ourselves to be stabbed in the back. Molotov, you tell them that Stalin will make them pay."

The General Secretary's face turned deep red and he became unsteady on his feet, grasping the chair until he collapsed into it. The man who had callously condemned a generation to an early death looked hurt, as if he couldn't believe the man who referred to him as Old Uncle Joe could deceive him. Beria suppressed laughter as the comical scene played out. The head of the NKVD knew this moment would pass and then the only thing on the General Secretary's mind would be revenge. His willing and always trustworthy executioner, Beria, stood ready to push all of the buttons.

Waiting for just the right moment, Beria quietly suggested, "Comrade Stalin, we all understand your anger and look to your strength to protect the Soviet people. Perhaps, rather than confronting the Americans, we could let the imperialists think they have fooled us. Maybe we should merely protest the meeting of this Wolff, especially that they don't want a representative from STAVKA at the meeting. Perhaps Comrade Molotov can tell the Americans that due to losses against the fascists, maybe we won't be able to fight the Japanese. That will scare the hell out of them. Let the Americans shed some blood for a change."

Molotov saw what his rival was moving towards and added, "Yes, Comrade Beria is absolutely correct. We can use their deception to our best interests. The really important thing is now we know conclusively that the Western imperialists can never be trusted again."

Beria thought maybe Molotov wasn't a complete idiot. He knew when to jump in and add his two cents. Beria saw Stalin begin to breathe easier as his two top advisors tried to calm him and plan a way to protect him. Beria finished where Molotov left off. "First and foremost, I have absolute confidence in the Red Army and know we shall capture Berlin no matter what treachery lies before us. With Berlin in hand, we will then dictate the terms of their surrender."

Seeing Stalin understood what Beria was getting at, the NKVD leader continued to steer his master down the path, "Comrade Stalin, Yalta means nothing any more. Now, we will take what we want and punish anyone, whether it be German, Pole, or even the Americans to protect the Rodinia. Then, we will be secure to rebuild our homeland at the expense of our enemies. In the end, this bridge over the Rhine means nothing."

Standing to his feet, Beria poured a glass of vodka, handed it to Stalin and said, "Let us drink, Comrade Stalin. The West is right to fear us, for ours is the way to the future. Victory is within our grasps."

Stalin blankly looked at his executioner, nodded in agreement and thought, *the West will be taught a lesson they won't soon forget. I shall make them come to me and they shall receive nothing.* Feeling his strength returning, the ruler of the Soviet Union took heart from his executioner. *Beria, I can always count on my fellow Georgian.*

He always understood, more so than anyone else, that the master of Russia could never turn his back on his enemies inside or outside the State.

Stalin's doubts slowly evaporated as he saw the opportunity Beria laid out. *Yes, Stalin will go along with this American charade. The only thing that really matters is Berlin. As long as we capture the city and force the Hitlerites to surrender then the Americans mean nothing.*

Standing tall again, Stalin walked over to the map display with up to the moment track of the Red Army advance. Looking over the maps, he clearly saw that his vast army was forming again for the final assault scheduled for the end of April. Lighting his pipe, he stared at the map and pictured Red Army tanks in the streets of Berlin and decided that the time to strike was now. *I won't give the fascists one more moment to dig in their troops, not one more opportunity to move men from the American front.*

Stalin barked, "Voroshilov get Zhukov and Konev on the phone and order them to appear in Moscow within forty eight hours. Also, get Vasilevsky to meet me tomorrow morning with plans to begin an immediate assault on the Oder line. We attack the fascists immediately. The Red Army will complete the destruction of the Germans within the next four weeks or I swear that their families will be counting trees for the next generation. Understood? Now leave me, all of you."

March 17, 1945

U.S. Embassy, Moscow

Ambassador Harriman sat in back of the embassy car and replayed the meeting that just took place. As he looked out the window, he thought, *what a sad city*. Barrage balloons swayed with the breeze, dozens of anti-aircraft positions dotted the city landscape, and evidence of German artillery and air raids were still fresh, as were the tank traps and fighting positions throughout the city.

Shaking his head at the collective siege mentality, the citizens of Moscow and the country as a whole were never in doubt that a war was on and just how close to defeat they were a few years ago. However, Soviets were winning again and with the war coming to a close, the mood was turning uglier by the day.

The day had not gone well and he could feel the tension the moment he walked into Molotov's office. Molotov's normally cold exterior was agitated and more aggressive than Harriman had ever seen him. What was more troublesome was that it wasn't just his accusations, no something behind those eyes suggested something else, he looked almost scared. It is so unlike him to give away anything.

As the car raced towards the embassy sending billows of fresh snow in its wake, Harriman wanted to speak with Kennan; *he always has a better read on these things than me.* Maybe he had heard something from his back channels at State about the half-assed OSS operation in Switzerland Molotov was ranting about. The Soviet Foreign Minister all but accused America of making a side deal with Hitler, himself. Seeing the embassy gates, Harriman breathed a sigh of relief and looked forward to some cognac and a chat with his Soviet expert. Harriman thought as he exited his car, *Kennan better be up to snuff on this one because things are happening too damn fast.*

Fifteen minutes later, the two men sat in the ambassador's office and Harriman began to describe the meeting. Trying to set the scene, Harriman described Molotov's demeanor and tone as well as the actual words used during the meeting. Harriman, still a bit shaken by the turn of events, spoke in a subdued voice, "George, I think we have real problems on this one. Molotov demanded the direct face-to-face discussions between Alexander's staff and Wolff in Bern, Switzerland be broken off immediately unless Soviet representatives were directly included in the talks. The bastard basically accused us of making a side deal with the Nazis and told me to inform Washington that failure to comply with their Soviet ally's wish would bring about a serious reevaluation of U.S./Soviet relations.

"I had enough of his bullshit at that point, so I said American officials were not included in the surrender of Romanian forces at the end of 1944, so we were just following your lead in this regard. You don't see us throwing unfounded accusations around."

Kennan asked, "How did he respond?"

"Molotov got very angry and launched into this diatribe against us, accusing us of allowing German divisions to move east to strengthen German defenses around Berlin. He said that Stalin saw what was happening and this was by design, not by accident. I was floored by such outrageous accusations, so I told him the meeting was ended and I would relay his concerns to the President who would respond as soon as possible."

George Kennan listened intently to every word the ambassador said, and knew immediately something ominous was building. If Harriman was correct about Molotov's reactions, then something must have happened inside the Kremlin to stoke Stalin's paranoia. There must be something more to the OSS operation in Switzerland.

Kennan paused long enough to annoy Harriman who was becoming impatient awaiting some possible explanation to include in a cable to Washington, Kennan searched for just the right connections.

Snapping his finger and pointing at Harriman, Kennan said, "Two things, either something else happened in Bern that the State department has failed to tell us or Stalin is using this Bern incident as an excuse. We have been pushing back pretty hard on this end ever since Yalta. But the one thing I don't know is if this is some political exercise, then why was Molotov so nervous? You have known him longer than me, and I haven't seen him blink during any negotiation I've witnessed, let alone ever really give off any real emotion."

Harriman nodded and added, "Christ, the first time I dealt with him I thought he was a corpse at one point."

Kennan politely smiled, then continued, "First, we relay to Washington the exact words of the meeting. No cleaning up the language. Stettinus needs to see exactly what was said to frame our own reply. Next, we bring in General Deane to verify the military situation and see if Molotov's claims on German troop movements are correct. Maybe we will find out if Old Uncle Joe is getting a bit nervous about who is going to win the race to Berlin after all."

Well into his second glass of cognac, Harriman raised his eyebrows and took a deep breath. He could tell, for all of George's level-headed reasoning, he was concerned too. Harriman wished he could adequately express the intensity of when he looked into Molotov's eyes and saw real anger for the first time. Something changed. *Molotov looked at me as if America had done something underhanded, like we were the bad guys.*

Feeling weary, Harriman turned to George and said, "Fine, you write the cable and I will speak to Deane. Maybe you're right, George, and the Soviets got a bloody nose or something and don't want us to find out, but I have a bad feeling this whole thing is going to blow up before the war's over. I just don't know if we can keep this alliance going until this war ends. I just don't know anymore."

Chapter Fourteen

March 18, 1945

London, The Prime Minister's Office

The head of Great Britain's SIS or Secret Intelligence Service, Sir Stewart Menzies, was annoyed that some absent minded cipher clerk had made him look like a fool in front of the Prime Minister and most of the Defense committee. Desperate, Germans were putting out peace feelers all over Europe, so Menzies had put a low priority on this Sunrise operation headed by the American, Dulles, in Bern and recommended to Field Marshall Alan Brooke to follow Washington's lead and send a military commission from Alexander's command in the Mediterranean to see Wolff and keep everything on the up and up.

The PM was a bit more hopeful, but with the Americans in charge, his operations people gave it a low probability of success.

Thanks to a drunken cipher clerk who misrouted Stevenson's priority one cable from the New York station, he never read about the revelations from Washington's own spymaster, Donovan, concerning the full story behind Sunrise, the bridge at Remagen, the split in the American government, FDR's indecision, anything. *By God that changes everything, and now we get official reaction out of Moscow that is the equivalent of a diplomatic fit and no one had the first clue what the Sovs were going on about. The whole blasted government is fuming with the PM leading the charge. Balls up...another bloody balls up is all I got to say. Now I'll have to eat crow for the whole ruddy meeting.*

Menzies was correct. Churchill wore a dour face and sat chomping on his cigar, looking for explanations for the screw up. Field Marshall Brooke, Chief of the Imperial General Staff, started off by saying, "Well, at least we found out the American crossing was a fraud, Maybe now they can stop their obnoxious gloating. Montgomery's Twenty First Army Group is prepared to launch Operation Varsity and should be ready to kick off in less than a week. The Americans will see what happens during a proper assault crossing of the Rhine, not some bloody cakewalk. Too bad, we can't announce this sham at Remagen in the London Times. It would do the average Tommy well to see the truth."

Churchill angrily said, "Enough of that rubbish. It's bad enough things have hit bottom with the Russians, I won't tolerate any more such talk in regards to the Americans. Understood? Now, Menzies, answer me, how in God's name did we manage to drop the ball on this Wolff business? Your man in New York, Stevenson, knew the whole story behind the American operation, and we don't find out for five days? We cannot afford incompetence at this stage of the game, gentlemen. Has anyone what would happen if Ivan finds out about this little gift from the SS?"

Deputy Prime Minister Clement Attlee, head of the British Labor Party, was always on guard against Churchill's obvious and often belligerent outlook against their Soviet ally. Fearing the ever-unpredictable Prime Minister would attempt to leak the information to create a break with the Soviet Union, he decided to deal with the issue directly. The balding and unassuming Attlee looked more like a clerk at a retail establishment, but underneath his bookish exterior was a man of real determination who aspired to serve as Prime Minister someday after the war.

Speaking directly at Churchill, "Mr. Prime Minister, I would like to stress that however poor the timing of this recent disclosure, we must take heed of the highest level of discretion. Clearly, the Soviet government is becoming increasingly anxious as the war winds to a close, and if this business becomes public or, God forbid, leaks back to the Soviets, I am afraid this would undermine relations with the

Soviets for a generation. Therefore, I must urge everyone at this table to listen to the American insistence against such a leak, and also, warn all concerned that the British people will know who is responsible for such a short sighted decision."

Anthony Eden, the British Foreign Secretary, looked across the table and saw Churchill's face flush at the obvious and unconcealed threat aimed directly at the PM. Eden thought, *if Atlee knew half of what Winston had in the works, he'd have a bloody stroke and call for new elections immediately.*

His people at the Soviet desk at Whitehall were a bit taken aback by the unconcealed anger and clear threat in the Molotov cable. The *Sunrise* operation clearly hit a nerve. Molotov all but accused the West of collaborating with the Germans, awfully strong words to use between allies. The PM mentioned before that Stalin either knows something more about this Sunrise business or else his natural paranoia is really starting to percolate and take root. Either way we have to be on our guard to see how he reacts in the coming days. Winston is very afraid that the Americans will get too nervous and do something silly for fear of affronting their Bolshevik friends.

To his credit, the Prime Minister restrained himself and let Attlee's quiet threat pass, refusing to rise to the bait. Churchill brought the meeting to a quick close. "First, Sir Stewart, enough piling on, it was an unfortunate slip up, but in wartime these things happen. At least Stevenson has the ear of that American, Donovan. Next, I want to assure everyone I will not, under any circumstances, jeopardize our relations with our American cousins by publicizing this awfully tempting information. We will honor the American request to treat this incident purely as a military matter to be handled through Marshall Alexander's command. Hopefully, this Wolff fellow has enough pull to bring this off. We have lost too many good lads fighting in that miserable terrain, anything to end the dreadful conflict, I pray for its deliverance.

"Lastly, although I have great misgivings about the political actions by our Soviet ally, this government will continue to follow both the letter and the spirit of those agreements signed at Yalta. The British people have gloriously fought the Hun to ensure a free Europe, and I will not do anything that endangers the peace, but will do anything to protect our people against further injustice and tyranny. We shall keep the information to ourselves, cooperate with the Americans, and pray that whatever can be done to end this miserable war one day sooner may happen, and happen quickly. Good day."

Churchill finished and stormed out of the room leaving everyone convinced he would keep his mouth shut and not do anything to start trouble. Eden shook his head and, with a bit of a smile, thought, *the old man ought to consider hitting the British stage when this whole thing is over, because I almost believed him this time.*

March 21, 1945

Washington D.C., OSS Headquarters

A simple peace feeler operation coming out of the Bern OSS station was threatening to erupt into a full-scale international incident that could break the wartime alliance. Operation Sunrise had a life all its own and Major General Bill Donovan honestly didn't know where it was headed. Worst of all, the American public didn't know a goddamn thing about the whole mess. The State Department was losing their collective minds about the pending collapse of the United Nations initiative, let alone a complete breakdown in diplomatic relations with the Russians.

Stalin threw down the gauntlet and demanded the negotiations with Wolff end immediately. He accused high rankings members of the American government of not telling President Roosevelt the truth behind the talks. Stalin's cable essentially told the President there were disloyal elements in the American government looking to undermine the entire framework of U.S./Soviet relations and he should not allow himself to be fooled so easily. Even Franklin didn't like that one.

To complicate matters, fresh from Dulles came the next bundle of Wood material. Like the previous batch of information, it came with pictures. It seemed the Reich Foreign Ministry, along with Goebbels Propaganda machine, decided to carefully reproduce in its raw form what happened to a German village after its capture by the Red Army. The official report described the scene as elements of the German 208th Infantry Division recaptured the town of Striegua in the Silesia providence.

As the battle-hardened German soldiers entered the town civilians appeared from cellars, bomb shelters, and attics. As these dazed and shaken survivors emerged from the madness of Soviet occupation, they found evidence of horrific crimes against humanity. More than two hundred of the village's citizens were slaughtered. Most of the dead were women and girls as young as eight. Medical examiners confirmed evidence of rape and most of the dead were mutilated and left in grotesque positions.

The little town of Striegua had the unlucky distinction of housing a small distillery that rear area Russian troops liberated. For the next two weeks an orgy of complete drunkenness and disorder prevailed, as the Russians systematically raped and pillaged the town and refused to allow anyone to escape. One horrifying snapshot of an adult male and possibly his son, found crucified to a barn door upside down caused the OSS man to feel physically ill as he fought back against the bile building in his stomach.

What caused Donovan to react in such disgust was the grisly image in the foreground, because in front of the dead man and boy was a naked woman and two partially clad young girls were apparently raped and then bludgeoned to death as the males in the family were forced to watch in horror and pain.

Next Donovan saw the pictures of a burnt out tank that still had the remains of a torso from two women who appeared to have been chained to the back of the tank and dragged throughout the town on some hellish joyride until destroyed during the counterattack. More pictures of women whose dresses were ripped and showing evidence of burn marks from cigarettes and deep bruises. Each snapshot seemed more unspeakable than the next until he couldn't look anymore.

With hands trembling from rage, Donovan threw the horrible pictures off of his desk and fought against the tears welling up in his eyes. *How could these bastards do such things?* He had allowed himself to forget for a while the earlier pictures Kolbe had sent. *How the hell did I let myself forget? I wonder how many died during the past two weeks* in towns throughout Germany. Goddamnit the Nazis and their SS did horrible things in Russia and deserved to be punished for their crimes at a tribunal, but this? *Raping women, children? Enough.*

Feeling rage building up again, it took several moments for him to get his composure back. Donovan lost all doubts about what had to be done. *How in the hell can we ally ourselves with a government who not only commits these crimes, but actual encourages them?* It wasn't just the work of some isolated units, Donovan had read the leaflets handed out to the Red Army exhorting them to slaughter anything German, men, women, children, it made no difference. *We fought this war to stand up to those murdering bastards in the SS and destroy the Nazi system, not to destroy an entire people.* Americans wouldn't stand for it if they knew what was happening. He knew what he had to do, so he picked up the phone and made the call he should have made two weeks ago.

March 22, 1945

New York Times Building, New York

Murray Bernstein was sweating as he nervously belted out the final few words to the next day's lead story. Bernstein was an old timer who had covered everything from New York politics on the city beat to national and international story lines. At forty-seven, he was too old to want to get shot at anymore, so he let wartime coverage go to the young bucks out to make a name for themselves. He did his time in the trenches and was in no hurry to go back.

Bernstein loved nothing better than to get a hold of a breaking story and reel it in before anyone else got wind of it. So Murray made it a point to know everyone who was anyone in New York and did his best to hook up with all the movers and shakers in D.C. With Roosevelt in office for the past twelve years, a lot of New York big shots moved to Washington and his access just got better and better.

So far he had a good war and perfect for his kind of stories. He caught a dozen profiteers red handed in a Jersey City munitions plant, uncovered disgraceful sanitation conditions in training camps at Fort Dix, sniffed out major kickbacks to union backed by mobsters, and made a lot of people nervous when he reported on the rumors of millions of missing Jews in Nazi occupied Europe. Like any big time reporter, he had more enemies then friends.

A phone call on Sunday evening demanding him to get on a train and meet with one of the most important men in the American government seemed too good to be true. Pulitzers began with unnamed, high-level sources willing to spill the beans on something big. So, he got himself together, and by eleven o'clock the two men were sharing a drink at a rundown Jazz club in one of Washington's less glamorous parts neighborhoods. It took less than fifteen minutes of conversation for Murray to realize he had the biggest story to sweep through town since D-Day.

Bernstein knew Donovan back in the days before the war and the two always got along, but were never chummy. One thing could be said about the ex-Wall Street attorney, he never gave a false tip. If the man said that so and so was dirty or the prosecution beat a confession, anything, his word was always golden. Donovan was a Major General in charge of the biggest hush hush organization in the country's history and he'd just dropped a bomb into Bernstein's lap.

Murray had the story of a lifetime and several frightening pictures to back it up. Even better, the OSS man worked it out so he could get the story past the military censors that were always sticking their noses into everything, looking to kill half the stories generated during the war. The only thing Donovan said, and the thought chilled him, was that under no circumstances was he ever to reveal his source.

With his cold, blue eyes staring at the reporter like daggers, Donovan whispered, "I think you know this thing is bigger than the two of us. I will be able to protect you as long as you keep your mouth shut, but if you let on how high this thing goes, then I can assure you, I'll have your ass in the front wave of the next Marine beach landing so fast, you won't have time to piss your pants.

I want the story to run in two days, exactly two days. If you need any more information, call this number. It will ring through to someone who can always get a hold of me at any time, day or night. Murray, one more thing, just get the story out there and be prepared to write follow-ups. I will feed information as needed. Don't worry, when this thing is over, they'll write a book about this little arrangement and how it started everything. We understand one another?"

Without anything other than a nod, Donovan disappeared into the men's room and Murray grabbed the next train back to Penn Station.

Tomorrow's headline will read in bold print, "**Red Army Massacres the German Town of Striegua**", followed underneath by More than 200 Women Raped and Murdered." The first lines under the headline stated,

> *Confirmed evidence from unnamed sources revealed to this reporter the most extreme examples of organized terror and debauchery since the Crusades. Red Army units captured this quiet Prussian town inhabited by old men, women and children. Dozens of pictures provided to the New York Times show beyond any doubt images of rape, mutilation, and cold-blooded executions of unarmed civilians. During the short-lived Russian occupation, Red Army units gang raped women and children as young as ten years old and then slaughtered them in a series of grotesque manners. The town was ransacked and looted by the undisciplined and rampaging army of the Soviet Union. Although I never thought that I would write this next line during this war, the remaining*

citizens of the town were saved by the brave actions of a counter-attacking German infantry division that pushed through and organized an escape back to German lines.

No other paper in the United States has more openly and consistently opposed the rise of the Nazi regime, and we have proudly chronicled the brave Allied armies fighting to destroy the maniacal regime of Adolph Hitler. But, Americans do NOT make war on children, nor is it our policy to endorse such a barbarous and disgusting affair. In addition, reports coming from the Eastern Front indicate this is but one sad example of dozens of towns looted and raped by the advancing Red Army. It would appear as if the Stalin led government has initiated a grand strategy of revenge against the German people. No doubt, the Nazi government was responsible for horrifying acts of terror and atrocity, mostly carried out by the demented legions of SS. However, this reporter will not let this story be buried for the sake of Allied unity. As more details become available, I will provide additional evidence and recreate the final days of this ill-fated town, apparently one of hundreds of small villages to feel the terror of the advancing Red Army. Perhaps these reports will enable our government to lodge formal complaints against such behavior in future campaigning. The State Department has refused to comment on this affair, but intend to follow up on the facts of the case.

Murray Bernstein's editor, David Burroughs, walked up behind him and grabbed the copy from his hands and asked, "Well, is it ready yet? I don't need to tell you what kind of pull it took to get this thing past the censors, and you probably don't want to know who told me to *run it or else.*"

Murray shrugged his shoulders and smiled, "Well, if your guy is even bigger than my source, then I think right now we are in the business of not exactly printing the news, but creating it. You know as well as I do that shit is going to hit the fan because of this. For Christ's sake though, maybe it should. Did you see those goddamn pictures? You know how I feel about the Nazis after what I found out about their slave labor and concentration camps, but it can't justify what I'm seeing. After we run this thing, every paper in the Western world will try to run this one down and confirm the hell out of it."

As much as he hated the idea of the government using his paper like this, Burroughs resigned himself to it. He looked down at Bernstein and said, "Well, I'll take it down to the print room myself. Tell you what, though, why don't you make yourself scarce for a couple of days, because this time tomorrow, you'll be as big a name as MacArthur for a day or so."

Chapter Fifteen

March 27, 1945

Winchester, Virginia

The OSS owned, black, government issued sedan pulled off the interstate about five miles west of Winchester, VA and continued down a deeply rutted dirt track nearly a mile into the dense Virginia woods. The sedan came to a stop in front of a hunting lodge that resembled a rustic, recently converted farmhouse. The special passenger in the sedan was more than a bit surprised to find a government agency set up in such an out of the way spot. Throughout the course of the war, the OSS expanded rapidly. It seemed that rather than limiting itself to the leftover, pre-war government buildings, Donovan had spread the agency around.

While most of the purely administrative functions were taken care of in the Capital, Donovan's special organization required additional accommodations. The OSS set up shop everywhere from posh New York office buildings to seaside bungalows in Miami to a number of out of the way rural locations. The secretive nature of the OSS led to the leasing of several off-site locations such as the one in Winchester. The Hideaway was being used to perform mission debriefings, hold high-level meetings outside the watchful eyes of both domestic and foreign interested parties, and surprisingly enough, to actually go hunting when time permitted.

This day, Donovan was using the Hideaway for an important meeting to discuss the uproar caused by the leak to the New York Times. Field Marshall Montgomery staged a massive river crossing the day before as British and American forces crossed the Rhine River, but that was pushed back to page three. It seemed everyone, from the Soviet government to Congress to the foreign press, was busy trying to track down and confirm the story..

Nazi Propaganda Minister Joseph Goebbels quickly released statements confirming many of the details from the NYT story. He was only too happy to fan the flames by making the unusual offer to the American government, or, even better, a neutral party, like the

Swiss, to visit the site of the massacre and speak to survivors. Donovan had to admit he hadn't really thought that angle through enough before jumping in with both feet.

Donovan worried about the growing reputation of his agency, in the same way that Hoover obsessed over the public view of the FBI. Donovan knew that if the truth ever got out about OSS involvement, there would be some in town who would look to bury him. He had to admit, with the Nazis reaping a PR bonanza out of the whole thing, it did look rather amateurish.

The Germans sent appeals to the Western Allies asking them to officially reconsider their alliance with the barbarians of the East. Goebbels went even further by describing the current situation as history repeating itself. The Nazi Propaganda Minister positively beamed when he spoke of the great miracle during the Seven Years War in the late eighteenth century, when Russia pulled out of the coalition of nations allied against Prussia and its king, Frederick the Great. Prussia was on the verge of absolute and complete defeat, just like Germany in 1945. Prussia was surrounded on all sides with France advancing from the West, the Austrian Hapsburg Empire moving from the South, and the biggest threat coming from the massive army of the Russian Czarina advancing on Berlin.

Goebbels hoped to encourage the breakdown in relations between the Soviet Union and the Western governments and salvage victory from the brink of defeat, just like what happened two hundred years ago. He beseeched the Christian nations of the world to band together in common cause against the Godless armies of Communism.

Donovan never intended doing anything that would give heart to the Nazis or potentially prolong the war. The story was intended to send a message to the Soviets and wake up the American people. Word had it President Roosevelt, though ailing, wanted someone's head on a platter for the disruption in relations. He even received a less than funny cable from his British contact in New York, William Stevenson. It was simple and direct.

> *Dear William,*
>
> *The next time you wish to get Stalin's attention, do you*
>
> *intend to send a Flying Fortress over the Kremlin? You may want to give it a*
>
> *thought,, for it very well may be slightly less subtle.*
>
> *Good Day,*
>
> *Intrepid.*

At least with Berlin making so much noise, they could probably convince the Russians the leak originated in Berlin and not Washington. Donavan wasn't sure what to do next. The previous night he received an unexpected call from FDR's special advisor,

James Byrnes, who said it was long past time to have a little talk. Donovan first thought he was getting his walking papers, but Byrnes made it clear he required a private location outside of D.C to meet. So with a sigh of relief, Bill set up the meeting at the Hideaway.

At ten in the morning the OSS security team led the distinguished, former Senator from South Carolina into Donovan's office at the Hideaway. Sitting behind a beautiful, old Colonial era desk, Donovan waved his guest into the room and offered a chair. Noticing the way Byrnes looked at the trophy heads on the wall, Donovan began by asking, "Good to see you again Senator, I appreciate your cooperation by making this little excursion into the country. Do you hunt? As you can see, the forests around here are full of some beautiful bucks and even the odd wild boar."

Not entirely thrilled about the overdone arrangements, Byrnes wanted to hint at his displeasure a bit. "I have never been much interested in hunting myself, but I must say that you do have a wonderful collection of beasts hovering over your head, General Donovan."

Getting the not so subtle message, Donovan smiled. So much for trying to give the impression he had everything under control. Byrnes added, "Quite a story in the Times, Mr. Donovan, certainly causing quite the stir."

"Yes sir, I understand that the Soviet government is quite upset."

"No son, I'm talking about folks in Washington. The President, his people, yes sir, there are some angry people in this town, all wondering where that Times reporter got such a good story."

Donovan clenched his jaw and felt his chest tighten thinking, *well, this is it after all*, but not ready to fess up yet. "He sure did, Senator. Problem though is that it could have come from anywhere, from our own people to the Brits, even the Germans, for all we know. My people are working to get to the bottom of it. So, I have to ask, why this meeting and why are we out of town?"

With a twinkle in his eye, Byrne's slyly said, "I seem to recall a meeting not all that long ago when you showed some awfully disturbing pictures, much like what the Times ran on their front page, if I'm not mistaken. You seemed quite worked up about those horrible images, as well you should...shocking pictures. Anyway, it got me thinking. A smart man, such as yourself, may have figured that if good, God fearing Americans knew a bit more about who we are allied with and saw the type of folks they are, then maybe it would put some pressure on those boys in Franklin's cabinet who seem to go out of their way to keep cozying up to the Russians. Now, I'm not saying it was you, but I can see what someone was thinking before they leaked these reports."

Donovan froze at Byrnes' carefully worded accusation, but did not immediately react. Instead, he took his time and said, "Well, Senator, I have to agree. Whoever was behind this story probably was thinking along those lines. You have to give this mystery man some credit, the story certainly got people's attention, now, wouldn't you say?"

Stifling a chuckle, Byrnes liked the man's style. Donovan wasn't going to admit to it and that was fine, but now he knew someone had taken an interest. Byrnes spoke next, "Well, I would say so, Mr. Donovan. Cables are burning up back and forth across the Atlantic and the Russians are having a damn conniption. Stettinius met with the Soviet ambassador Andrei Gromyko yesterday and Gromyko put on quite a show, from what I heard. He was positively livid, demanding an immediate appointment to see the President to express his outrage. He even insisted the government arrest the writer of the story immediately.

"Gromyko read a cable from Molotov that said among other things that it seemed as if we would rather be talking to Nazis instead of killing them. Gromyko added that even if some excesses had transpired in one isolated village, it certainly couldn't compare to the atrocities committed by the Hitlerites against millions of innocent Soviet civilians over the past four years, not to mention the slaughter camps in Poland.

"Stettinius stammered for much of the meeting not knowing how to handle the situation. The Soviet ambassador ended the meeting rather ominously by warning us that Comrade Stalin wants to make clear now that he will tolerate no interference of any kind in the occupation zones liberated by the Red Army. You should advise your President not to push now, it would be most unwise." With that Gromyko walked out and left a much shaken Stettinius behind.

Donovan thought Byrnes seemed to relish telling the story. He asked, "Well, how did the President take it?"

Byrnes replied, "Obviously not well. Franklin called for a small meeting with myself, Harry Hopkins, Stettinius, General Marshall, and Stimson. General Marshall did not offer much of an opinion. He knew these were political matters and stayed out of the fight. But Stettinius, on the other hand, was fit to be tied. He went on for about ten minutes how we have been undermining the Yalta talks by this Sunrise business and now these leaks to the Times over what he termed *unverifiable reports* of Soviet atrocities are about to derail the entire United Nations initiative. He then accused elements in the War Department of making the leak and that sent Stimson through the roof. Stimson is no friend of the Russians, but he was offended at the accusation.

Byrnes then described his contribution to the discussion, "Mr. President, during Major General Donovan's briefing several weeks ago, he indicated that the Soviets were clearly engaging in horrific actions against civilians. I for one believe that the genie is out of the bottle and regardless whoever leaked this information, and this government must be prepared to answer to the American people about our alliance with a regime capable of encouraging such barbarism.

I have been informed this morning that several House and Senate members are preparing a joint-committee on this affair to get to the bottom of these allegations. And sir, it's not just Republicans, more than a few Democrats, especially from the Old South are already on board and looking to hold our feet to the fire on this one. We are going to have to answer to some folks pretty soon."

Exasperated, the Secretary of State cut in and denounced Congress for meddling in his territory. He fumed that foreign relations was an executive function and outside the legislative purview. He said it was a direct slap at the President and an embarrassment to our Russian allies.

While General Marshal and Secretary Stimson looked increasingly uncomfortable about the entire affair, the President looked even worse. Even six months earlier, he would have led a lively debate and relished the idea of taking on Congress over his wartime policy. His closest advisor, Harry Hopkins, looked even worse. His gaunt face and ashen complexion made him a poor choice to protect the administration at a time when Roosevelt needed it most.

Franklin turned to the one man who didn't look to protect his own little fiefdom, but could act strongly to protect the Presidency and bring the war to a successful end. Looking up, with deep, dark bags under his eyes, and in a weak voice asked, "James, I need you to take care of things for us on this one. I know since that meeting in the Crimea things have never been the same with Uncle Joe and us, but we just can't let everything come unglued so near the prize. All this Sunrise business and petty squabbles about the Poles don't mean anything in the long run. Think big. I need to know that all this death meant something. We need to work with them to guarantee the future."

On the verge of passing out, the President motioned to Harry that it was time to leave, but before he left, he said, "I want everyone to listen to James and work with him to keep this partnership moving. Remember, they don't trust us, because they don't understand our system. Sit them down, talk to them, and then they will come around. Good Day, gentlemen."

Byrnes made it clear to Donovan that by directive of the President of the United States, he was now effectively in charge of policy in regards to the Russians and Donovan understood why he asked for the meeting. I'd bet all the whiskey in Ireland Byrnes pushed those Congressional hearings. He'll make damn sure they leak everything and keep this on the front page for a hell of a long time. Every reporter and politician in the country would begin to clamor for even more information, and before you know it we'll be having a good old fashion American political firestorm. What a sneaky old bastard.

Byrnes saw the amazed look in the director of the OSS and felt more than a bit pleased with himself. He decided to bring the meeting to an end. Donovan didn't need to know why he was doing this. Byrnes decided on the return trip from Yalta that something had to be done about these damn Russians. Byrnes looked the man in his eyes and saw nothing but pure evil. Franklin and his people were dead wrong, something had to be done or pretty soon American boys would be locking horns with the Russians, and Byrnes was in the position to make sure America was ready.

Byrnes stood, extended his hand and said, "Major General Donovan, I thank you for your time, sir, and look forward to working with you towards our common goal. Rest assured, I will be doing my part, but you tell your man in Switzerland to make a quick deal with that SS General in Italy. We need to get our boys moving and win this war now."

Looking into Byrnes determined eyes, Donovan nodded in agreement and said, "Senator, I will do everything that I can to make this happen. If all goes well, in two weeks we just might be able to end this war and send Stalin a message he won't soon forget."

Chapter Sixteen

March 27, 1945

Bern, Switzerland

SS General Karl Wolff paced the room. He seethed as he was forced, yet again, to make another trip to Switzerland to deal with the American, Dulles, and British idiots from Field Marshal Alexander's staff at the Allied Mediterranean High Command. Everything had gone to hell since his first contact with the Americans a month ago. One whole month, gone, wasted and all because the fools in Washington, and probably London, didn't know what the hell to do with the opportunity he had presented to the Western Allies. *Ridiculous, holier than thou Americans don't like shaking hands with the SS, fucking children.* Every time Wolff thought how the damn Americans wasted all of his efforts, he wanted to scream.

If any German general ever was handed such a prize and failed to take advantage, he would have been relieved of command within a week. More than three weeks since his engineer rigged the Ludendorff Bridge to remain standing after the charges went off, the Americans were still being held up by a handful of German forces. Instead of racing to Berlin, Eisenhower gets into a city fight in the Ruhr. *How did we lose to these fools?*

That question was easily answered, the Russians. If it wasn't for the damn Bolsheviks, the Americans and English would never have made a successful landing in France and wouldn't have been able to take Europe back for a thousand years. Now he was forced to kowtow to these same people, because without them Germany will be destroyed by the Russians. The irony of it all kept Wolff up at night.

Even worse, the damn Russians have somehow found out about this little enterprise and word had gotten back to Himmler, who was ready to skin me alive.

The German commander in Italy, Field Marshall Kesselring, refused to do anything to weaken his defenses unless he knew he could release divisions for the main fight against the Russians. Smiling, Albert made himself quite clear on that point and refused to lay down his arms and surrender without any assurances from the Americans over what would happen to Berlin and the rest of Germany.

Kesselring is right. How the hell can we deliver a cease fire on the Italian Front unless we know the Americans and British have plans to advance to secure Austria and Bavaria, let alone Berlin? The Americans better grow some balls and fast if they expect to stand up to the Russians or else, Germany will stand in ruins. Looking at his watch, he wondered, *where in the hell is Dulles? Twenty minutes late is past insulting. Bastard.*

Just as Wolff sat on a rather plush chair, the dour faced American, Allen Dulles, walked into the room. Before the head of the OSS mission in Switzerland opened his mouth, General Wolff went at him. The SS man leapt to his feet and moved right in front of Dulles and got into his face. Wolff snarled, "How dare you call me at the last moment, forcing me to rush to Bern, and then make me wait like some chambermaid come to clean your pot. I may have come to you looking for help, but I'll be damned if I will allow you to inflict anymore such indignities. Is that understood, little man?"

Dulles was not used to being talked to like that, let alone in his own house, refused to take the bait. Taking a deep breath to steady himself, Dulles eyed the SS General and calmly said, "I was about to apologize for my late arrival, but I will not be talked to like I'm one of your Jewish slave laborers. Is that understood, Herr General?"

Wolff didn't know if he was more annoyed that Dulles kept him waiting or the fact he wasn't the least bit intimidated when he barked at him. Thinking that if this is the way that people treat general officers of the formerly all-powerful SS, peacetime will be a bitch, *No matter, let's see what the Americans have to say this time.* Hopefully, a reasonable proposal has finally been hashed out and then I can take it to General Kesselring and start this process before the Russians take Berlin and end things themselves.

Dulles poured both a drink. He knew Wolff would need one in a few minutes. Dulles was angry himself after watching what could have been the biggest coup of the war handed away to placate the Russians. The SS man was no angel and probably should be turned over to the Italians for war crimes, but the man was honest with him, at least as honest as one could get in such matters.

Dulles handed the glass of schnapps to the General and took a seat opposite the casually attired German and decided to speak frankly with Wolff. After gently rolling the warm liqueur around in his glass for a moment and then downing a mouthful, Dulles said, "General Wolff, I know that things have not gone as planned or at least as well as you would have hoped when we first met, but both of us underestimated the politics involved here. I should have known better, but most Americans believe that you brought this on yourselves, plus, we have another war in the Pacific to finish."

Turning red with rage, Wolff saw where this was going, and bellowed, "You son of a bitch! I knew it! You have no intention of standing up to those Russian bastards and were just stringing me along while my countrymen are being slaughtered. Hitler was right, you are nothing but a country of shopkeepers, and you'll never have the balls to stand up to the Russians and deep down you know it." Wolff slammed his glass on the table and stormed across the room towards the door.

The SS man moved so fast that the usually unflappable Dulles had difficulty reaching him before he stomped out of his house. Catching up to Wolff, with heavy breath, Dulles said, "Wait, General, wait. You didn't let me finish, for God's sake. Come back to the table. We have come too far, you and I, not to see this thing through to the finish line. Please, come inside."

Wolff pulled back at first, too disgusted with the American to continue, but pulled Dulles' arm away from his shoulder and walked back into the room to at least let the man finish.

This time Dulles brought a bottle of whiskey to the table with two glasses and said, "Look, I know this has not been easy, but you need to hear me out. You know of the stories in the American press about the revelations of Soviet massacres in East Prussia, right? Well, the political pressure that I was leading up to before is now starting to build against the pro-Russian elements in the Roosevelt government, especially the State Department. We are in a much stronger position to act now."

Dulles noted how Wolff seemed to calm by the second shot of good American whiskey as it went down his throat. Dulles continued, "Now, I need you to cooperate with the British staff officers in the next room and arrange the necessary conditions for an armistice to take hold along the Italian Front. Washington has authorized me to tell you that as soon as German forces lay down their weapons, the American Fifth Army plans on storming over the Alps and into Austria.

I assure you that American forces will move as fast as you have ever seen an army move on the march. We hope to enter Vienna in force within seventy-two hours. You have my word that the United States understands the stakes, but I need you to deliver on your end, or else, nothing, and I mean nothing, is going to happen. You have to trust us."

General Wolff stared at the fireplace as the American intelligence officer tried to ease his obvious distrust. Too many weeks of planning, anxiety, and arguing with the Army High Command had taken its toll. Wolff could still feel the warm sensation in his belly left from the strong American spirits. Wolff wished he could get drunk and stay drunk until the war ended, then let those Dagos put him up against a wall and blow his brains out. But not yet, he knew he had to pray the Americans would keep their word. General Vietinghoff was getting ready to take over for Field Marshall Kesselring and he would prefer something in writing.

The Americans may be amateurs, but they weren't stupid. One thing was certain, Vietinghoff was even more willing than Kesselring to negotiate terms with the Americans and this pledge by Dulles would probably be enough if pushed hard enough. *I'll need him to take out the diehards in my own SS special units. Too many are ready to die for Hitler even at the very end.*

With the decision made, Wolff felt stronger and began to put steel back into his spine again. Reaching for the bottle of whiskey, Wolff poured two shot glasses, handed one to Dulles, and spoke with conviction " Dulles, this is damn fine whiskey, I wonder if you will be able to smuggle a bottle or two into whatever camp that you plan to ship me into once I help end this little war in Italy."

Looking at the relieved expression on Dulles face, he could tell that he made the American very happy. Wolff added, "I will convince General Vietinghoff to bring our forces into line, but I will need at least five days or so to have everything ready. I need from you which units and their expected march tables for the advance through the Alps, so I can ensure those road nets have been cleared, bridging in place, etcetera. I don't want to hear that things were held up on account we couldn't fix all the damage your planes created. You made movement a nightmare for my people. Anyway, get that to me within the next forty eight hours and I believe that we have a deal."

Relieved, Dulles downed his shot and placed the empty glass on the table. He thought Wolff was ready to make this happen on his end, and even better, seemed to think he could get the German army to go with him. General Vietinghoff would undoubtedly begin transferring combat troops towards Berlin to fight the Russians, but that was not his concern any longer. The two men shook hands on an agreement that should not only end the war, but stop the Russians cold in their tracks.

Chapter Seventeen

March 28, 1945

SHAEF Headquarters

Versailles, France

After a long morning of working through dozens of memos and cables, General Dwight D. Eisenhower, Supreme Commander of Allied Forces in Europe, decided it was time to take a walk. For nearly three hours he had worked through a series of mundane, but necessary paperwork ranging from infantry replacement problems to shipping schedules, and correspondences from numerous people stateside. However, the cable that just landed on his desk fifteen minutes ago came from his boss, General Marshall, and it was anything but mundane. In fact, it was the biggest decision he would have to make since his order to give the go signal on the eve of the D-Day invasion.

Contrary to popular belief, Eisenhower never saw himself as a political general, more skilled at diplomacy than the battlefield. In fact, he resented being characterized in the media as such. At heart, Ike believed he was nothing more than an American soldier over there to do a job. He just wanted to go home and forget about the whole nightmare. He had become accustomed to the fact that at any given moment since the Allied Expeditionary Forces landed in France, nearly two million soldiers were locked in combat on his direct orders. The burden kept Eisenhower up many a night.

What allowed the former Kansas farm boy to reconcile himself with his chosen profession was that he vowed never to needlessly waste the life of even a single soldier. All his orders were predicated on one thing, how would it help end the war sooner and at the least cost in Allied lives? Everyone on both sides of the Atlantic wanted the additional burden of positioning themselves for the political battle to be waged at the peace table after the war ends.

Ike wasn't naïve about the politics, but American military traditions dictated purely military objectives. Marshall wanted him to start thinking in terms of post-war considerations and the impact of

Soviet and American relations. All Ike wanted was to concentrate on defeating the Nazis and bringing his boys back home.

He had just gotten back to SHAEF Headquarters in Versailles after observing the massive crossing of the Rhine River in Monty's sector two days ago. It was there that the British Prime Minister, Churchill, sought him out about the political firestorm raging between the American, British and the Soviet governments. The damn British were always playing politics. It seemed as if every Brit, from Churchill to Montgomery to the British press, had plagued him to no end since he landed on British shores back in 1942. At this stage in the war, with the British contribution steadily declining while the American forces in Europe were reaching their peak, it was apparent this was an American show. Eisenhower and most of his staff had about had it with anything and everything British.

When Churchill all but demanded Ike to capture as much German territory as possible, especially Berlin, the request landed on deaf ears at SHAEF Headquarters. Churchill acted like Berlin was the only thing that mattered. He ignored the fact that the Russians had started their offensive sooner than anyone had thought possible and were less than fifty miles from the German capital. Allied forces were still more than two hundred miles away and in for a nasty fight in the Ruhr.

The Prime Minister didn't stop there. He wanted to capture everything from Prague to Trieste and completely ignore the agreed stop lines laid down at the Yalta conference. No one could be as insistent as the Prime Minister when trying to make a point, and the man went on for nearly two hours about Russian violations of the Yalta pact, Soviet atrocities in Poland and Germany, and raised the specter of communism sweeping throughout all of Europe.

To make matters worse, Churchill showed Ike the recent cables coming from Moscow accusing the Western Allies of all but collaborating with the Germans. Churchill described the controversy surrounding Operation Sunrise and the secretive work trying to secure the surrender of German forces in Italy.

Eisenhower was shocked at the direct language used by the Soviet government and, to be frank, more than a little angered. He had gone out of his way to extend every courtesy to his Russian ally and never reacted when the same was not extended to American forces in return. Ike knew there had to be more to it than what Churchill let on.

The damn Brits are always playing games and now it looks as if our strongest ally doesn't trust us. Why couldn't Churchill understand I came here and ordered these men to fight and die, not just to get rid of Hitler, but also to bring peace and stability to Europe and now it was all coming apart at the seams?

As Ike walked through the famous gardens of Louis XIV, he thought the gardens spoke more of the nature and character of Europe than anything else. Louis XIV, the most powerful monarch of his time, waged ruinous war for most of his reign, while at the same time constructing one of the most stunning palaces and gardens ever conceived. *Why would a people work so hard at two so contradictory designs, war and beauty?*

His chief of staff, General Bedell Smith, said that the reason the Europeans got so good at building beautiful things is because they were always blowing them up. If for no other reason, this insanity must come to end. Marshall's telegram had to be acted upon and soon.

Just yesterday, General Eisenhower dropped in on General Courtney Hodges First Army Headquarters outside of Remagen. He took the time to speak with Generals Bradley, Patton, Simpson and Hodges about the final direction of the campaign. After crossing the Rhine River, they had a quiet lunch at a German hotel recently liberated and stocked courtesy of the US Army. Eisenhower had pretty well formulated his final offensive, but wanted a chance to touch base with his three key subordinates, especially Bradley.

Patton, as expected wanted to lead Third Army straight into Berlin and personally shoot the bastard. Hodges was noncommittal, waiting to take his cue from his benefactor, Bradley. General Simpson's

Ninth Army was placed along the most direct route and had little opposition to his front. Simpson made it clear, in his quiet way, that he wanted a shot at Berlin.

The head of the 12th Army Group, General Omar Bradley, had come to despise Field Marshal Montgomery and assumed any drive on Berlin would come from the British sector. Therefore, Bradley argued that first the Ruhr would have to be secured before any type of drive Berlin could occur. The Ruhr was Germany's last great industrial complex and was defended by more than three hundred fifty thousand Germans under Field Marshal Model, a man who developed a fierce name for himself fighting on the Eastern Front.

Bradley went on to argue that for Monty just to reach the Elbe River, he had to cross more than fifty miles of lakes, streams, and rivers and would never do it. Bradley reminded everyone about Monty's failure with Operation Market Garden. All those paratroopers wiped out because Monty couldn't move fast enough. General Bradley ended his argument by saying that even if, by chance, a scratch force of Brit and American forces hit Berlin in the back door; they would still probably take a hundred thousand casualties.

Eisenhower remembered Bradley's last words, "A pretty stiff price to pay for a prestige objective, especially when we've got to fall back and let the other fellow takeover." As always, Bradley summed up things in a manner that hit home with Ike. In the end, Eisenhower based his decision not on politics, but on the lives of his men.

While walking back to his office, General Eisenhower read through this morning's cable from Marshall. As was custom from Marshall, the cable wasted few words and got directly to the point. Marshall wrote:

> "With the beginning of the Soviet offensive against the Oder River line, German defense will likely reorient itself to protect the capital of Berlin. The resulting breakup of an integrated German defensive zone in the West will allow American forces to move quickly towards the southeast, as planned, in force. Although, as Supreme commander of Allied Forces final planning remains within your sphere of operations, I want to strongly recommend you ignore recent political overtures from Washington and London and avoid Berlin at all costs. Relations with our Soviet ally are at an all-time low and I don't want to cause irreparable harm to our long- -term relations. We must keep in mind we will continue to need their support in the Pacific against the Japanese.
>
> Further, with the massive Soviet offensive aimed at Berlin, any American or British forces in the area run the risk of clashing with Red Army units unless clear designated zones are established. Review your final campaign objectives and

contact all interested parties concerning your decision for the strategic direction of the Western advance. Keep in mind that First Army forces have already been earmarked for redeployment to the Pacific Theater once hostilities have ended in Europe. Yours is a heavy burden that has been borne well, remain focused on the goal as we approach the finish line. Godspeed, General Marshall."

As Eisenhower entered the hall leading towards his office, he used the final steps to organize his thoughts, preparing to send a dispatch that would likely to be the most controversial decision undertaken thus far. The important thing was that he knew now his boss back home would support him. As a result of Marshall's cable, Ike decided to form one massive, broad front under the command of General Bradley.

The Twelfth Army Group would number nearly one million soldiers and contain the First, Third, and Ninth Armies. The American army would deliberately isolate British forces by taking away most of the US Ninth Army from Montgomery, allowing him to move his units towards the boundaries established at Yalta and not one step further. Ike would shift the axis of attack away from Berlin and move towards Munich and Dresden. Allied forces would surround the Ruhr with Montgomery in the North and a portion of the Ninth Army under Simpson in the South. The rest would move hard and fast to liberate Bavaria and move into portions of Czechoslovakia already agreed to at the Yalta talks. *And if the Italian Front opens up to let American forces meet him in Bavaria, then so much the better.*

To cement his decision, he put together a cable to send directly to Chairman Stalin and make clear his intention to avoid Berlin and ensure a designated stop line would exist between American and Soviet forces. Eisenhower wanted to ensure Stalin knew the British could not steer America into breaking relations. By sending the cable, Ike knew the Brits, and many back home, would scream bloody murder, but the decision was his to make.

Ultimately, it was a military decision and well within his purview as commander-in-chief. Eisenhower wasn't sure who would be angrier, Churchill for going direct to Stalin or Montgomery for taking away American divisions and the chance at the prize of Berlin.

Really, it's better this way. The Russians have earned this. How would Americans feel if we slugged it out with someone and had some other guy sneak in and grab the prize? It just wasn't fair and he hoped Stalin would take this as a symbol of goodwill that the two nations could build upon.

March 30, 1945

Moscow, The Kremlin

Josef Stalin read and reread the cable from the American general, Eisenhower and contemplated what it really meant. The Soviet leader couldn't consider the American offer on its face value. *Why would the Americans deliberately shift their offensive south unless the reactionaries in Washington have some other game to play?*

Might they be considering moves into the Balkans as Churchill always talked about? Well they would have to deal with Tito, and that would be enough to serve them right. The war isn't even over yet, and Tito is already trying to avoid being swallowed up by Red Army liberation forces. The Yugoslavian partisan leader will have to be watched because he would only be too happy to use Western forces to shield Yugoslavia from direct influence from Moscow.

First, the Americans mount this joint operation with that SS bastard in Italy, then the Germans leave a bridge standing over the Rhine to allow the Americans to stab her Soviet ally in the back by stealing Berlin, the rightful prize of the Soviet people. Next we read about the series of lies leaked to the American newspapers trying to taint the victory of the Red Army, such information could only have come from the very highest levels in the American government. Now suddenly the Americans decide to avoid Berlin and instead move into southern Germany. After everything else they have done in recent months, why would they suddenly reverse themselves yet again?

Eisenhower would never have made this declaration unless ordered to do so. No general in the Red Army would conceive even for a moment of making a political decision like this without first being ordered. No, the Americans must take me for an ignorant peasant to think that I will allow myself to be taken in so easily. They must have something else planned, but refused to be fooled again by the West.

The ruler of the Soviet Union walked over to the map display showing the Red Army in the final stages of its advance on Berlin. Bright red arrows moved in two, giant pincer movements both north and south of Berlin. The armies of Zhukov and Konev were competing to earn the honor of capturing the German capital first. After the first full week of the final offensive, severe losses were suffered because the fascists had enough time to construct a strong first line of defense. *But once my Red Army tanks get past their initial defenses, nothing on earth will prevent the final destruction of the city.*

No matter the losses, Zhukov and his generals were finally getting the message they had better get the German capital before the Americans or it would be their heads lost. As always, Stalin understood the fine art of the application of pressure. All men had a breaking point or a soft spot that could be exploited at the right moment. For more than twenty years Stalin had held power by knowing when to push those buttons and, in doing so, he'd made the Soviet Union into the most powerful nation on the planet.

Stalin could see Communism spreading through the world under leadership from Moscow and, with the fascists about to be destroyed, no other world power could threaten the Soviet people. *Once Germany falls, the Red Army will sweep into Manchuria, secure Korea, and as much of Japan as can be taken from the Americans.* Then, Mao and his Communists forces would be able to defeat Chaing and the Chinese Nationalists and secure all the Soviet Union's borders.

Stalin had decided long ago he would outmaneuver the West because the British were weak, like mongrel dogs, and the Americans simply don't have the stomach for a real fight.

Stalin lit another cigarette. He smiled as he reread the cable from Eisenhower one last time before issuing orders to STAVKA, the Soviet General Staff. *Fine, if the Americans want to offer this gift, then we shall take it,* but he would never forget the American stab in the back with those German bastards. Stalin vowed never to trust the West again. He would do as he chose and not allow anyone to threaten his rule, ever again. The first step was Berlin and the final step would be to force the Americans and British off the continent of Europe for good.

Chapter Eighteen

March 30, 1945

London, Prime Minister Churchill's Private Residence

The Prime Minister's voice boomed throughout the room and could be heard by the kitchen staff a floor below. His voice a mixture of frustration and anger, he yelled at Field Marshal Brooke, "Bugger! Who did Eisenhower think he was, contacting the Russians directly without even touching base with us? Brooke, for God's sake, don't we have people on the man's staff to keep tabs on such things? Do you mean to tell me that no one had any inkling he changed the entire framework for the final advance against the Germans?

Montgomery might as well occupy the French Riviera for all the bloody good he's going to do without those Yank divisions operating in his Army Group. I told you that Monty's big mouth would finally get him in trouble with the Americans. So here we are at the end of the road, and His Majesty's Army is being left to hold the flank and give Berlin to the damn Russians."

Churchill had harangued his immediate staff for the past half hour. Having a good old-fashioned fit would probably better describe his diatribe against the Americans this time. Sir Alan Brooke would have enjoyed the irony of the moment if it weren't such disaster. For four years Churchill had been the Americans biggest cheerleader. Now that they had gone ahead and acted like Americans, the old man was going bloody daft.

The irony was lost on the PM because Montgomery had been pleading with Eisenhower ever since the landings in France for one concentrated, massive drive against the Germans. Ike in a rather sadly amusing turn put three whole armies together, but instead of naming Montgomery as the ground forces commander, he shunt him off to the side while General Bradley's Twelfth Army Group would get the lion's share of all supplies and make the final attack against the German Army in the West. Bloody shame, by all rights it should be Monty and Berlin should fall to the British Army, but that's what the PM gets for allowing the war to be taken over by bloody amateurs.

Anthony Eden, Britain's Foreign Secretary was equally taken aback by the American decision. Eisenhower had always been a pretty reasonable chap. Eden couldn't understand why Ike would make a decision he knew would cause a major incident between London and Washington. The Foreign Secretary knew Eisenhower's decision caught much of Washington off guard as well as his English allies.

Poor Ike must be caught up in some power struggle between the State and War Department. Regardless, that cable of his and the change in operational plans is going to have some very real repercussions, I'm bloody sure of it.

Catching Brooke's eye, he nodded to the Chief of the Imperial Staff and gave a look of how long do you think that the old man can keep it up without having a stroke.

Eden knew the decision by Eisenhower was worse than a matter of lost prestige or personal glory. The Prime Minister thought that between the Yanks getting the bridge from the SS chap in Italy and the impending collapse of the Italian Front, the Empire would get Berlin after all and undo the dreadful mistakes at Yalta. With Berlin, Austria, and maybe even Czechoslovakia, Churchill believed the Russian position would be significantly undercut. Short of outright hostilities from Stalin, the West would be able to secure most of Central Europe.

More concerning, Eden feared the PM was apt to do something foolish, like become even more involved with those crazy Poles. Even if by some insane chance that they pulled off killing Stalin, they'd never throw the Soviets out of Poland. *Now the old man will probably want to go full steam ahead on this venture. Why can't Winston just accept the status quo and make do the best that we can. I'm sure that we can eventually convince the Americans to stick around and if we do that then matters need not get so messy.*

Looking at Churchill, Eden could tell the man wouldn't let things lay low. No, everything with him was personal. He couldn't stand to allow that nasty little chap, Stalin, to best him. *I swear that Winston would duel the man to the death if he thought it would work.*

Breathing heavy, Churchill finally calmed down and saw the way that the others were looking at him. *Well bugger them too. I know where this thing is headed, and it'll be too bloody bad for Europe, let alone the Empire.* Disgusted, Churchill waved everyone out of the room, even Eden. *If the man can't get angry over this then what good is he?*

Once everyone left, he picked up a stack of confidential personal files submitted to him by the new man over at MI6, Kim Philby. Sir Menzies had spoken very highly of him, even though his father had gone native while serving the Queen in Arabia. *Imagine giving up the Church of England for pilgrimages to Mecca and praying to Allah five times a day. Besides, what Western man could handle more than one wife without any alcohol? What bloody rubbish.*

Philby had been placed in charge of a new desk at MI6 called Section IX, tasked with organizing activities in the newly liberated countries suffering under the iron fist of the Red Army. Philby was ordered by the head of MI6 several weeks ago after the PM found out about the Polish decision to stage an uprising to begin organizing British officers in the SOE, Special Operations Executive, who could be of service operating within Poland. This Section IX was busy organizing information and agents from every contact with underground groups who fought the Nazis and who would likely contest any Soviet takeover.

Menzies had mentioned that Philby was an industrious fellow and had nearly finished cataloguing every English contact in Eastern Europe, plus the library of old White Russians who would love another crack at the Bolsheviks. The PM spent the next fifteen minutes going over several personnel files trying to find the right sort who could perform the mission and be trusted to keep the utmost discretion in the endeavor. Finally, after narrowing his choice down to three men with excellent war records, Churchill made his decision.

The man Churchill chose was born Mikhail Gorchakov, but went by the name Michael Gordon. Michael was a naturalized British citizen who was the son of White Russian émigrés who escaped during the last hectic days of the civil war. Young Mikhail was named for his great grandfather who commanded Russian forces during the Crimean War. With a great deal of difficulty, Mikhail's father changed his name to a more Angleton version of his proper Russian name.

He was raised in London, sent to the very best public schools, and became an officer in the army of his new adopted country. The young man spoke several languages including German, Polish, and, of course, Russian. He served with distinction in an infantry unit during the 1940 campaign in France, but was later recruited and sent to train as a commando for the SOE.

For four years Gordon smuggled weapons into Poland and German occupied France, participated in dozens of bombing and sabotage campaigns, and established quite a reputation for coolness under fire. He displayed remarkable improvisation skills. What measured most in Churchill's eyes was the fact he blindly hated the Communists for what they had done to his family, He would either get the job done or die trying. *Yes, this boy will do quite nicely, and he will answer only to me.*

The PM did not want Gordon to participate in the attempt, but when the time was right, he would use his high-level contacts to channel information, special weapons if need be, and, most importantly, provide whatever guidance or support necessary to make the attempt succeed. Gordon knew all the key players in the Polish Home Army and especially their special operations chaps. If the venture by the Poles had a chance of success, then they would need as much up to date information and help as possible. Churchill knew this could not atone for his failing at Yalta, and even after a couple months, he was still plagued by a sense of abject failure.

If he couldn't help the Poles publicly and the Americans wouldn't act sensibly, then he had no other choice but to do what he could to make sure that bastard died at the conference. But thinking what would occur if Stalin survived the attempt was enough to chill his soul. If that evil peasant came out of it alive, the Poles would pay a price he could barely conceive. Brushing his dark thoughts aside, the Prime Minster made the call to have Gordon brought in for a quiet, heart to heart chat.

March 31, 1945

Desenzano, Italy

SS Headquarters

General Wolff's aides and orderlies knew better than to interrupt during one of his tirades, but this one seemed far worse than anything they had ever scene. For fifteen minutes the walls shook, not from

Allied bomb attacks, but from the general smashing everything in his office. File drawers were flung, chairs smashed, and one aide swore he heard a yelp from Wolff's favorite German Shepard. They looked at one another and knew something grave must have happened because Wolff loved that dog more than most people.

Finally, the noise subsided and his aide was ordered to bring Major Zimmer to his office immediately. The rest of the staff quietly went back to their duties. No one wanted to be Major Zimmer this morning because the last person that any of them wanted to see was the General in one of his foul moods.

Major Zimmer was found before he had left the headquarters building taken to Wolff's office. The young aide, Ernst, had told him to expect the worst. Zimmer lightly rapped on the General's door. A sullen voice answered for him to come in. Zimmer had expected to find the General in a rage, not a man who looked completely broken, as if his nerves had collapsed. *My God,* Zimmer thought, *he looks like he's just survived a Russian winter.*

General Wolff sat slumped on the floor beside his desk amidst the debris. Coming to attention with a snap of his heels, Zimmer wheeled and gave his commander a parade ground salute. "Herr General, reporting as ordered, sir."

Looking at the young man he had sent on secret negotiations and who had performed so well, all the General could muster was a wave of his hand to come in and sit down.

For a moment Zimmer sat next to Wolff and said nothing, waiting to find out why the General looked so distraught, so defeated. Zimmer feared Germany had surrendered, or worse, Berlin had fallen. The young officer had been kept somewhat in the dark in recent weeks over the continuing talks with the Americans and British. Because he had gotten so intimately involved, Zimmer desperately wanted to find out what was happening. He knew things should have long been set in motion.

General Wolff looked at the young man, dressed immaculately in his black SS uniform. Even after everything that had happened, the boy still seemed to believe in the vision of a greater Germany. Wolff could see it in his eyes. He had performed well for Wolff and knew Dollman could never have pulled off those negotiations with the Americans without him. Zimmer would have had a real future in the Reich but it was not to be.

Those goddamn Americans with all their sentiment and lies had sold him down the river. *I swear if I ever see that bastard Dulles again, I won't bother to use my Lugar, no I will stab him through his fucking heart with my SS dagger. The bastard kept stringing me along the whole time.* Wolff believed he was fed nothing but lies while the Americans waited, never having any intention to make good on their promises. *Even after we gave them the Ludendorff Bridge, they just allowed the damn Russians to devour us piece by piece.*

He held a communiqué, intercepted twenty-four hours ago on the Soviet Front in Hungary. It said the Americans were abandoning the movement on Berlin and, instead, shifting their axis of advance to the southeast. The rest of the intercepted cable was orders from the Soviet High Command to redouble their efforts to beat the Americans into Czechoslovakia and Austria. That did it. The entire scheme to save Germany was at an end, but for one last, probably futile, gesture.

Wolff steadied himself and, considering what he was about to ask of this young man, the least he could do was order him in a manner befitting a German officer, even one who was a former advertising salesman. Fixing his shirt and collar and with a grave expression, said, "Major, I have asked for you because of the great service you have performed in the service of the Fatherland. I want to tell you directly that the Americans have stabbed us in the back. They have decided to allow the Russians to take Berlin. The war is over. We have been defeated and will probably be occupied for the next generation. My life now is coming to an end, either by my own hand or by a firing squad. No matter, my time is done, but I don't want yours to end in such a pointless fashion."

The words slammed into Zimmer like flying glass, the end of the Fatherland. The end of Germany and everything he had believed in since he joined the Hitler Youth before going on into the Young Pioneers Movement and finally becoming an officer in SS, a modern day knight. His family trapped in Potsdam would probably soon come under occupation by the Soviets. His whole life, everything that he held dear snuffed out by the Russians. Why couldn't the Americans see things for what they were? Stalin wouldn't hesitate to squash them next, and then they would slither back across the ocean.

Tears of rage began to well in his eyes as he understood the dream had ended and the Reich was coming to its end. He looked up at his commander and pleaded, "Herr General, I'll do anything you ask, just don't let it end this way for me. Allow me go out to the frontline and die with honor on the battlefield."

Seeing the anguish in his eyes, Wolff felt the boy's pain and knew he was giving the young man a gift, one final chance to act and possibly die with honor in defense of the Fatherland. This son of the Reich would not die by his own hand or sullied by the filthy hands of some Italian peasant with an old rifle. No, he could still serve the Fatherland.

Wolff grasped the boy's shoulder and snarled, "If that's what you wish, then you shall have it. I am sending you along with nearly two hundred hand-picked SS men into hiding. You will lead these men to a series of redoubts and underground caverns stocked with supplies and weapons. This was planned as a last ditch effort years ago by the SS in case of our defeat, but der Fuhrer refused to go along because if Germany were to be defeated then he wanted the entire nation to perish in the attempt.

"A year ago, I took it upon my own authority to order the completion of a number of these bunkers deep in the Thuringian Forests along the Czech border. Now, you are to take these men and go deep underground and avoid all contact with the outside world, no matter what you hear. You are only to strike when I or someone acting on my authority gives you the necessary orders. You are not to waste time blowing up bridges, you are to be Germany's trump card, but this card will be played one, and only one, time. I swear to you, young Zimmer, I will grant your wish. The next time you hear from me, the Americans will find themselves forced into a world of chaos and pain. They will either act to defend civilization from the Russians or die trying."

Major Zimmer settled into a cold stare as he longed for the moment he could make the Americans pay. "Thank you, Mien General. I swear that when you call, my men will be ready to strike in a manner that will chill the American's souls."

Book Two

After six years and nearly forty million lives, the most destructive war in European history finally came to an end on May 8, 1945. In wake of the great conflict, much of Europe had been laid to waste. The cities of Berlin, Warsaw, Dresden, and most of European Russia had been nearly destroyed. From the skies above, it looked as if every village, crossroad, and river had been fought over, leaving behind the shattered remains to be picked over by the lucky few who survived the slaughter. Total war was visited upon soldier and civilian alike for six years, and every man, woman, and child was made to suffer to one degree or another.

In the end, the great conflict which had raged in the air, beneath the oceans, and on land was to pass to a different chapter, a phase in which victor and vanquished alike must fight to claim peace. The remaining great powers, the Soviet Union, United Kingdom, and the United States were left to hash out peace, but much had happened in the months since the last great meeting at Yalta in February 1945. President Franklin Roosevelt died before he was able to see the fruit of victory and was succeeded by a timid and unsure former Senator from Missouri, Harry S. Truman. Winston Churchill still led the British, but found himself struggling to maintain a dying Empire. The war had stolen the last vestiges of vitality and strength from the once great Imperial power. In the East, the Soviet Union, under the leadership of Josef Stalin, emerged as the most powerful country in Europe, if not the world. However, the Soviet Union paid a fearful price as, more than twenty five million Soviet citizens lost their lives in the titanic struggle. Post-war Europe depended on the three nations to chart out a course to rebuild.

Relations among the three allies worsened in the last days of the war. The British believed they were forced to back down to the inevitable and thus reluctantly agreed to the de facto division of Europe. The Americans, under Franklin Roosevelt, were willing to trade away the freedoms of the occupied nations in Eastern Europe for promises of Soviet support in their war in the Pacific against the Empire of Japan. In fact, many Americans looked forward to leaving Europe once again to its own devices and retreat back to Fortress America. Desperate to keep America engaged in European affairs, Churchill secured an agreement with both the Americans and Russians to attend a new peace conference to be held in Potsdam to discuss the future of Europe.

However, leading up to the conference in Potsdam, the Soviet leadership was humiliated before the world. Numerous accusations from the 1939 Katyn Forest Massacre of Polish officers to the rape of Berlin were made public during a special Joint Congressional Committee chaired by an ambitious Congressman from Texas, Lyndon B. Johnson. The Soviets lodged one complaint after another with the new Truman administration and accused America of acting in bad faith. But the new President made it clear that in a democracy Congress was free to investigate whatever it choose. Adding fuel to the fire was Truman's decision to cancel all Lend-Lease supplies the day after the war ended on the counsel of the new Secretary of State, James Byrnes.

Despite the tension, the parties needed to meet and attempt to find enough common ground to establish a long-term peace in Europe. The new order that many hoped would emerge in post-war Europe was clearly in jeopardy, as the wartime alliance of convenience among the "Big Three" was frayed nearly to the point of a complete break. As the American and British delegations prepared for the Potsdam Conference, events were rapidly moving towards a frightening scenario that once again pitted the forces of freedom against the iron fist of tyranny.

Chapter Nineteen

July 12, 1945

Berlin

If it hadn't been for his own near death experiences in the battle of Warsaw, Tadeusz Sobieski would never have believed that a modern city could be so utterly razed to the ground. The city of Berlin, at one time, offered the perfect blend of modern and classic architecture, but today a citizen of Berlin could walk for days and not see a single building that wasn't on the verge of teetering over. Block after block of bombed out rubble and debris littered the sidewalks. Even the ever present Germanic penchant for order could not seem to make a dent in the rubble from the daily bombings of the Allied Air Forces and fifty thousand guns of the invading Red Army.

All that was left to scratch out a living were old men, women, children, and the thousands of maimed and walking wounded. It was for this reason the Polish agent adopted the pathetic identity of a crippled, ex-soldier begging for his next meal. Even a Russian NKVD agent wouldn't bother with the lice infested scarecrow hobbling along, waiting for death to catch up to him. Tadeusz couldn't answer what gave him more pleasure, planning a strike against the Russians or watching the former citizens of the Third Reich on the verge of starvation and utterly defeated. Maybe if he lived past the next five days, he would be able to answer his own question.

His pace was slowed by the double set of worn wooden crutches he used to move down the rubble-strewn streets of Berlin. Tadeusz wore the tattered remains of working man's trousers, patched more than a dozen places with whatever cloth was available. His filthy shirt barely covered his chest and was soaked with sweat as he slowly crossed the Muller Strasse road in the blazing noontime sun of July.

When he came to a corner and saw a group of patrolling Russian soldiers, he held out a tin mess cup and looked up with his one good eye to ask for food or drink. Usually, at least one of the Russians would throw out a piece of black bread to eat or maybe even a ration of Spam.

Ironically, Sobieski thought it seemed the one who was quickest to help usually had a half a dozen stolen watches looted from the remains of German apartments and homes. Maybe they felt slight twinges of guilt and could at least offer crumbs to a pathetic creature who had done his time in the trenches. Men who served in the infantry understood one another. It was the NKVD men who spat on him. They were the dangerous ones and they were the ones he observed to see where they moved and how they examined passing Berliners on their own search for food.

For the past three days, Tadeusz walked up and down every main thoroughfare along the Unter Den Linden, along the banks of the Spree River, and examined every bombed out building and crossroad along the likely path of his target. Soon everything would be in order, he just had to figure out how the hell to make good on their escape.

Tadeusz Sobieski was one of the most dangerous men in the Polish Home Army. What made him appear even more unsettling to many of his own countrymen was At first glance, with his unsettling blond hair and ice blue eyes, he appeared to come right off an SS recruiting poster. But, he had fought with the underground from the moment the Polish government went into exile in 1939. He would never forget the moment when he heard Russians had stabbed his poor country in the back, yet again. He hated all things German and Russian. Perhaps it was fate that Tadeusz now found himself at one of the great crossroads in history and been chosen to be the instrument of his people's revenge.

His grandfather had said it was Poland's fate to be forever on its guard against the Germans from the West and the Russian bear to the East. Tad's very existence was the direct result of Poland's strange history. He grew up in a small farming village outside of Danzig and was raised by his mother and maternal grandfather, who was as proud a Pole as any whoever walked the earth. He grew up without a father because his died during the First World War.

Sobieski's life was destined to be as violent as his conception. A German soldier passing through their little village violently raped Tadeusz's mother. While scrounging for food and drink, the young German soldier saw a pretty Polish farm girl, took her, raped her and nearly beat her to death, but soon met his own fate. Racing in from the fields, his grandfather silently entered the barn and killed his German father with one swing of his sickle and gutted him as one would a pig, but was too late to save his daughter. Three months later upon finding out that his seventeen-year-old daughter was with child, rather than bemoan their fate, his grandfather decided to raise young Tadeusz as his own.

As he grew older and looked more and more German and less like his round faced and plump mother, his grandfather told him the truth and taught him up hate both of Poland's historic enemies. After the First World War, nothing brought the old man more pride then to raise his grandson as a free citizen of an independent Polish nation. After years of abuse and second-class status under the Russian Czars, to be a Pole and free was a blessing to be treasured. Life was good until the German Blitzkrieg of 1939 and nothing would ever be the same again.

Tadeusz was twenty-five and teaching History at the University of Warsaw when he was called up to his reserve regiment and found himself commanding a company of poor reservists like himself who assumed they would have several months to prepare for the German onslaught, as in the last war. Instead, he found himself defending trenches on the outskirts of Warsaw as the fast moving columns of German panzers destroyed all in their path. After three weeks on the front lines, he was devastated to learn his young wife and little girl died when their apartment collapsed during the first round of mass bombings on the Polish capital.

After the ceasefire took hold, rather than go into captivity, Tadeusz escaped to the countryside and joined the newly formed underground Home Army. He vowed to exact revenge for the murder of his family. For the next six years, Sobieski rose in the ranks and became particularly skilled at special operations. Once the Germans began the barbaric practice of executing upwards of ten Poles for every German casualty, the Home Army formed a special unit designed to bring the war to the high-ranking Party officials and SS officers who made policy.

Tadeusz was selected for the Agat detachment whose job was to assassinate the criminals who ruled the Nazi empire in Poland. He mastered the art of demolitions, mechanical ambushes, and wet work up close and personal. Whenever possible, he made it a point to look in their eyes and speak perfect German telling them a half-breed had killed them, one of their own blood was the agent of their death. Tadeusz became cold, ruthless, and much in demand.

The Agat unit later expanded into a more formal military unit and came to be known as the Parasol Battalion. They played a leading role in the Warsaw Uprising. It was this final combat experience that taught Sobieski all he ever wanted to know about killing and death, as his unit fought block by block, through the sewers, inch by inch through the rubble of his once beautiful city. The Germans put down the uprising at a terrible cost and on Hitler's direct orders, they razed the entire city of Warsaw to the ground, one block at a time.

Surviving countless near death experiences, Tadeusz made his way to the countryside and contacted a British liaison team. They were tasked with rearming the Home Army as its tired members recuperated and went underground to operate in smaller units throughout the countryside. Tad found good hunting by ambushing the retreating Germans, but more importantly, he organized a massive resupply effort by stealing literally tons of weapons.

Everything from small arms, MG42 machine guns, panzerfausts, and even a dozen 88mm anti-tank guns, the most deadly in the German arsenal, found their way to hiding places all over Poland. Soon they would be needed as Red Army forces rolled into Poland, causing mayhem and suffering in their wake.

Tad remembered his grandfather's words, *never to trust the Russians*, and he would soon prove to be right. Soon Home Army officers, Catholic priests, or anyone who spoke out against the new occupiers found themselves whisked away by NKVD agents, never to be heard from again.

Tad was prepared to fight the Russians just as he fought the Germans for years. When a high-ranking Polish Home Army officer contacted him to meet the new commander, General Wladyslaw Anders, Tad leapt at the chance. At that meeting he volunteered for the mission. Nearly three months to the day, he found himself on the streets of Berlin, and prepared to attempt what he had thought would be the impossible, suicide more like it. But as stopped at the intersection of the Alt Moabit and the Muller Strasse, he believed, for the first time, that that operation could truly work.

With the intelligence information his friend from the British SOE delivered the night before, he knew this intersection was perfect. NKVD security teams tasked with protecting Stalin had narrowed their choice down to two train stations with the Stettiner Station the most likely choice. The Stettiner station led directly to an intersection less than half a block from a temporary ribbon bridge erected by Soviet engineers to service traffic over the Spree River. It connected to the main road in Berlin, the Unter den Linden. The temporary bridge couldn't handle the same amount of traffic as an intact bridge, so the convoy would be forced to advance at a crawl.

Looking at the remains of a three-story apartment complex overlooking the intersection, Tad surveyed the structure and saw it was perfect for his plan. Turning, he and headed down a side street. He took one more look back and visualized the moment to come, when the most powerful man in the world understood his time was about to come to an end. Tad relished in that one, delicious thought: even a man of pure evil would feel fear at the end. A deadly grin swept over his face, Sobieski thought his grandfather would be proud at this very moment.

July 13, 1945

Ten Miles outside of Warsaw

After two months of non-stop activity and preparation since he was smuggled back to his homeland inside a British submarine, General Wladyslaw Anders, commander of the underground Polish Home Army, could barely keep his eyes open. During the past year, the Home Army used that time to get over the tremendous psychological impact of the failed uprising and, more importantly, recruited thousands of men and women to replace the brave ones who died in Warsaw. He and most of his staff had worked at a feverish pace for the past ten days trying desperately to complete the never-ending preparations of the rebellion

The main problem plaguing Anders' command was that communication to AK cells spread throughout the whole of Poland had become increasingly difficult. His people dared not utter a word over the radio for fear of Russian signal troops intercepting the transmissions and discovering the new AK underground command post. Luckily, the British had been incredibly cooperative and allowed the BBC to make announcements with key words, signaling everything from meetings and resupply efforts to the movement of forces.

As the days rolled forward, Anders had trouble believing the leadership in London was willing to be so bold. So much depended on what would happen in Berlin. If Stalin survived, then hell would be unleashed on his homeland. Either way, the Russians wouldn't just up and leave. But Mikolajczyk was right, cut off the head and the Communists wouldn't know what hit them.

Taking time to sip some tea, Anders reviewed the overall plan again. He had thought it through a thousand times in the past two months, but revisiting the details gave him confidence, or at least hope, in the outcome. The key was the dispersal of his forces throughout the entire country. Unlike Komorowski, Anders had no illusions about the ability of his army to stand up to regular field formations in open battle.

It was not Italy, where he commanded the Polish II Corps and had unending artillery support at his disposal, mountains of supplies, and the luxury of airpower to sweep down and destroy the first hint of opposition. No. The Germans taught the Poles hard lessons. Hit and run attacks and small-scale actions were not the same as operating battalion and regimental type operations. Once the Poles formed attack brigades and exposed themselves, the Nazis slaughtered them in the ruins of Warsaw. Anders had every confidence in his men and women, but refused to use them in set piece engagements.

The new war would be fought on many levels, especially politically, so Anders moved his AK units throughout the entire country. Most of the initial targets would be aimed at his own countrymen, those traitorous Lublin Poles. Nearly every puppet official, especially secret police units, would be targeted in an attempt to take back the countryside and as many small cities and villages as possible. Warsaw would be isolated. Every route coming in and out of the city would be cut off.

Next, Anders planned a series of savage attacks on as many soft targets in the Red Army rear as possible. He could, and would, blow every bridge, crater every roadway, and try to shut down movement across the whole of Poland. He had given his unit commanders standing orders to harass Red Army forces short of full-scale engagements. After fighting the Nazis for six years his people could snipe at officers, attack supply trucks, blow up exposed supply and ammo dumps, and generally, do anything to sap the strength of their oppressors. Ultimately he hoped to convince Polish heavy combat units with tanks and artillery serving in Sebring's Polish army, operating under Russian Red Army command, to turn on the Russians and fight with their Home Army brothers and sisters.

Ironically, as much as he cursed the British for selling out the Poles at Yalta, much of this could never have been accomplished so fast without their support. For reasons Anders couldn't understand, the British government had decided to provide as much intelligence and weapons as his units could smuggle into the country. SOE men had provided priceless intelligence of current Soviet troop dispositions, recent troop movement, and identified numerous exposed supply and communications hubs vulnerable to ambush attacks. Further, the English provided literally tons of high-explosives, satchel charges, and short-range radios for many of his units, and as much captured German small arms and ammo as he could distribute into the Polish countryside. Thankfully, the British put a premium on supplying the Poles with thousands of captured German panzerfausts to add to his own meager stocks. Those deadly, hand held anti-tank rockets would give his men the means to stand up to Soviet tanks and would be a hell of a lot more effective than the Molotov cocktails the Home Army had to use against the Germans in Warsaw.

The British Royal Navy supplied the Poles using submarines to deliver tons of ammunition and equipment. Somehow, the English got someone in the German Kreigsmarine to provide secret entry routes through the belts of thick minefields that the Germans sowed to protect the Polish Baltic coastline from the Russians. British subs never could have attempted a supply effort this extensive without this access.

More importantly, small detachments of Anders soldiers from his former II Corps command were infiltrating into Poland every week to add to his growing Home Army. By placing organized platoons of veteran combat soldiers into the underground army, Anders was growing in confidence that he would be able to hurt the Russians and make them pay a fearsome price in the weeks ahead.

Refusing to allow anything to chance, Anders planned to wage war on as many fronts as possible. He had secretly brought into the country three American journalists who had no idea the story they were about to get. All of them were sons of Polish immigrants and were excited to come back to their native land and report on life under the new regime in Warsaw. *Soon, they shall see with their own eyes the bravery of the Polish people and report on Russian atrocities that will be sure to come.* He feared it might take a river of Polish blood to bring the Americans around, but by God, at least they would be forced to read about it.

As much help as the British had been, the real key was the Americans. Without their open support, Anders feared for the final outcome of this venture. Maybe the new man, Truman, had more stomach for facing up to the Communists. He had barely closed his eyes for a moment before an aide knocked on his door and handed him an urgent dispatch. It read, *"Red Army redeployed a tank brigade to the outskirts of Lodz. The local AK units are asking if there is a change in orders."* Shaking his head and walking to the communication center, General Anders thought, *war better come soon because preparing for it is about to kill me.*

July 14, 1945

Babelsberg, outside of Berlin

Michael Gordon, son of White Russian parents, member of Britain's elite Special Operations Executive, and coordinator of one of the most dangerous missions ever conceived in the hallowed halls of Whitehall, breathed heavily as he tried to run off the tension from the long night's journey back to the British compound. Soviet NKVD agents no longer bothered him after five mornings in a row of running through the woods surrounding Lake Griebnitz, he closed his eyes and felt the wind lash his body as he moved at a rapid pace

This mission was borne from the sense of obligation and purpose of one man, British Prime Minister Winston Churchill. Churchill disregarded the unpleasant fact that discovery of the Empire's support for the revolt could lead to war. He decided the fate of Poland and the honor of Great Britain mandated such a risk. Although raised his entire life in England, Michael's sense of fatalism was very much Russian, and he knew how fraught with danger the mission was for him and his adopted country. But once he met with the British Prime Minister, how could he possibly say no?

As if anyone one could get a word in edge wise, let alone say no to the man. At least he was able to tell his father he had been in the presence of a great man, perhaps a bit mad, but great nonetheless.

His morning run helped him take advantage of the solitude offered by the thickly wooded lakefront and, also, to enjoy the beauty that seemed to have escaped the carnage in evidence throughout the rest of Germany. Somehow he had survived some rather harrowing experiences during the war and hardly relished the idea of playing a leading role in such a dangerous venture.

Lake Griebnitz was once a prime location for Prussian nobles and later rich merchants to come and enjoy the pleasures of the lake yet remain close to Berlin. Because the lakefront homes had managed to survive nearly intact, unlike Berlin proper, and its close proximity to Potsdam, it was chosen to house the three great delegations coming to the Potsdam conference. Plus it was relatively isolated and could be kept secure from any fanatical Nazi partisans looking to disrupt the conference.

Gordon was on the British security team tasked with working with the Russians to ensure a secure site for the conference. Michael later found out that nearly twenty thousand Soviets NKVD agents, soldiers, and diplomatic staff roamed the entire Babelsberg community. Someone couldn't take a leak against a tree without pissing on a poor Russian trying to fit into the local scenery. Anyway, the American and British security teams were completely dwarfed by the Russians who made it clear that the comings and goings of the Western legations would be limited.

The second ranking commander in the SOE, Sir Basil Chesterfield, briefed him while still in London. The operation was so hush-hush that he operated completely outside of normal military channels. Once the general concept of his involvement had been worked out, he was able to make requests for whatever type of intelligence, military, political, anything merely by snapping his fingers. For nearly four weeks, he worked on his own trying to establish everything from planned entry/exit routes to an up to the moment secure channel of communication to feed intelligence to the Poles who would be operating in the city for at least several days or longer in Berlin itself.

The Prime Minister had clearly indicated that, for fear of the Soviets finding out about the Crown's involvement, he was not to directly participate in the actual operation. The Minister also made clear, albeit with some difficulty, that if he were caught, any British government involvement would be denied. He would be branded a fanatical anti-Communist, son of White Russian parents, acting on his own. Although it didn't help him sleep any better, Michael understood why Churchill would have to completely disavow any involvement.

His cover placed him on the detail that was part of the first team of British security agents allowed into the British compound. Quickly he set up a secure space in the former owner's wine cellar to use as his personal base of operations. The former occupants had considerable means and connected the wine cellar into a shallow tunnel that ran to a bomb shelter deep in a grove of trees one eighty meters from the house, which gave excellent cover for his movements. It was, of course, the reason for insisting upon this house, a sticking point the Russians didn't quite understood.

To ensure complete freedom of movement, he stocked several uniforms, ranging from Red Army, NKVD, American military police, plus a wide range of clothing to blend into the seedy world of occupied Berlin. More importantly, his wine cellar held wireless communication equipment and special operations goodies for his Polish friends. All things considered, not a bad set up on fairly short notice, especially when considering that twenty thousand bloody Ivans were poking about and sticking their noses into everything.

Last night Michael had made his third trip deep into the ruins of Berlin to touch base with the Poles. Gordon could not help but be struck again by that Sobieski who was one cool customer, talk about going on with a stiff upper lip. During his work in Poland supplying arms to the Home Army, he had heard of the man, but had never met him.

If the Polish freedom fighter felt fear or at least gave some indication that he was at least a bit unnerved by the whole thing, he never gave one hint of it. The man was focused on the job unlike anyone he had ever seen in his life. In fact, he appeared so focused that his own team members seemed a bit uneasy.

Making his way into Berlin was not easy and took him the better part of six hours, moving mostly at night. Finally, he made contact in a relatively intact basement about three miles from the expected ambush site. Sobieski had brought the other two members of his team. Tadeusz first introduced Aleksandra, a fierce looking, dark haired woman, said to be particularly skilled at seducing her target if need be and then slitting their throat.

Aleksandra lost a child shortly after being raped by an SS officer early in the occupation and decided to use her body to repay the Nazis for their crimes. Her German language skills and ability to interact with Germans in occupied Poland had suitably prepared her for her role in this mission. One other thing in her dossier, her father had been a biathlon champion and taught his daughter the skill of long range shooting. Apparently, Aleksandra didn't want to kill just the Germans she slept with, but wanted to make an impression on the odd Fritz from long distance, as well.

The other team member was a round little man who walked and talked like a soldier, simple, direct. He was a weapons and explosives expert. His dossier clearly indicated a skilled hunter and a very reliable chap who, if put in the right place, at the right time, would not fail to hit his target, no matter the situation. Michael thought he had at least three professionals with years of direct experience, whose nerves would not be a factor. *Good.* Because they would have exactly one chance to get the bastard and even if everything went perfectly, the likelihood of any of them ever making it back to Poland was nearly out of the question.

Michael looked at them in the fading light of the basement, wondering why God allowed good people to be forced into such horrific situations. Trying not to see a schoolteacher, a farmer, and a mother, Michael closed his eyes and instead saw the eyes of three professionals waiting for the tools to make the job happen. Whatever sentiment they once held had long since gone, and Michael was determined to help them succeed, no matter the cost.

Chapter Twenty

March 15, 1945

Casey Jones Flight 101, Western Poland

Major Brent Jones took the stick once they crossed the Elbe River and continued deep into Soviet controlled airspace. It was his fourth Casey Jones mission and he decided it would be his last if he could figure some way to get transferred. He had flown the B-17 Flying Fortress on thirty-five combat missions into Germany and earned one hell of a rep. He brought home a couple planes that were flying wrecks after getting shot by German flak. Somehow, he always brought his bird back to base.

The B-17 was the workhorse of the Eighth Air Force bombing campaign against Germany, but it was being utilized for a very different kind of mission. As he maneuvered his flight of two other Fortresses over the Niesse River in Poland, he began to noticeably sweat under his oxygen mask. He heard from a fellow flyer that the Russians were getting wise to the recon missions and Third Squadron had lost two birds and their crews to Soviet Yak-9s just two days prior.

Ever since his transfer to the top secret Casey Jones wing after the Germans surrendered in May, he couldn't seem to shake the feeling he wasn't going to make it home. He wasn't alone, the rest of the men were becoming jittery as they flew deeper into Poland.

Captain Dan Jensen, Jones' co-pilot, turned to him and said, "This is fucking crazy, Brent, worse than flying missions over Berlin. At least then what the hell we were doing made sense. If I get my ass scattered, I at least would rather be dropping some serious tonnage on those little bastards in Tokyo."

Flipping his intercom on, Major Jones nodded in agreement, but answered, "Look, I don't like this anymore than you or anyone else on this bird, but keep your thoughts to yourself. I don't want the rest of the crew to lose focus before we start our recon run. Got it?"

His co-pilot didn't like it, but he got it. The two men quietly resolved to keep it together for one more time, though easier said than done.

Casey Jones flights were the brainchild of the OSS chief, Major General Donovan. He decided after Yalta that, if his worst fears about the Russians were realized. They better start acquiring as much intelligence as possible. Donovan told his people he wanted everything from oil and gas production, ethnic unrest in the various republics to the size of Stalin's pecker just in case we wanted to embarrass the bastard at the next summit meeting. However, the most important information he needed couldn't be obtained with the resources at his disposal, so he turned to the only organization that had the muscle for the op he was putting together.

Knowing he needed the Army Air Corps' assets for such an ambitious operation, he convinced General Hap Arnold to lend the OSS one hell of a lot of B-17's, not an easy sell. Knowing Arnold felt the Russians had pushed too goddamn hard at Yalta and wanted detailed maps in case the Air Force needed blow those bastards into the Stone Age, Donovan, suggested a marriage of mutual convenience. The OSS needed to map every square inch of occupied Europe for the purpose of infiltrating agents and weapons to support insurgent groups against Soviet control. With Arnold on board, everything fell into place

Playing the bureaucratic game perfectly, Donovan got Arnold to set up a joint Air Force/OSS command in England and began flying missions in March of 1945. With assets in place, the Air Force would be able to compile the most accurate targeting profiles of every Soviet target from the Elbe River to the borders of Russia and the OSS would be able to figure out every possible infiltration route in and out of Soviet control.

Within three months, Casey Jones operations consisted of six squadrons of B-17's along with dedicated fighter squadrons to provide protection for the exposed bombers. Later, the Brits joined in on the fun and added two more squadrons of Lancaster's to make sure they got a piece of the intelligence pie. Neither General Spaatz, the American Air Force commander, nor Air Marshall *Bomber* Harris, his British counterpart, was too pleased with the allocation of resources, but it was a high level security operation and both men were told not to push on this one.

Before too long, American and Russian planes made contact with one another and dozens on both sides were shot down. The Russians weren't stupid. They made it clear that if the Western alliance wanted to intrude on their airspace, then they had better expect casualties. So, an undeclared war in the air raged for several months. The increasingly aggressive recon missions forced the Russians to counter with a shoot on sight policy. While the diplomats prepared for the final peace conference of the war, pilots on all sides were still trying to kill one another.

Major Jones checked his watch and began his descent to ten thousand feet. After about ten minutes he picked up the main rail line leading out of Warsaw towards the German border. He still couldn't figure out why the hell they were bothering doing a photo run on a target grid that must have been one of the first things on the list. All he knew was that he was told he had better find the railroad at exactly seven in the morning and follow the track until he confirmed in detail the freight traffic moving on that line. It sure sounded kind of crazy in the briefing room, but with the sun up and Soviet fighters sure to catch them in the open, it sounded pretty goddamn insane.

Even with promises of several other incursions into the Soviet Zone to pull fighter coverage, Jones didn't feel a bit better about the op.

The photo specialists in the bomb bay radioed up front, "Major, we have conformation of west bound train, approximately two zero miles west of Warsaw. It appears to be a converted troop train, possibly armored, but moving very slowly. Shall I continue taking pictures?"

All Jones could think was, *thank God. Time to go home. We got what we came for, and if the pictures aren't good enough, they can send some other puke up here*. Maintaining radio silence, Jones banked his lead plane and set a course to trace the route of the railroad into Germany and shoot every step of the way until they hit the Oder River. Mission or no mission, he wasn't going to risk his men one mile deeper into Poland if he could help. It was time to head home.

After about five minutes into their return leg home, just when he'd started to breathe easier, he saw two P-51 Mustangs on over watch position go into a steep dive to the left of the B-17 and open up with all six .50 caliber guns. Feeling a rush of adrenaline, Major Jones reacted with a veteran's instinct and began to pull his bird up to get some altitude and looked for cloud cover to hide in. He ordered, "Looks like we got company gentlemen, photo shoot is an abort. Man all guns and open fire at any approaching aircraft. The Mustangs probably scared them off, but keep a close eye out. It's time to get the hell out of Indian Territory."

Grasping the flight controls tightly, he began moving the Fortress to the right and higher in the clouds. Trying to keep calm, he told himself this was just another tussle; the Mustangs would watch his ass and get them home.

Without warning the radio came to life as a one of the fighter pilots broke in and reported, "Flight 101, this is Talon 5 ordering you to make best speed to egress the hell out of here. Talon 4 is down; I repeat Talon 4 is down. There are at least two Soviet air regiments, nearly fifty aircraft on your bearing. Repeat, five zero heading your way, they are all over the damn place. I bagged two already. I just ordered the other four Mustangs to cover your escape. Move fast, now. Get the hell out of here."

Pushing the throttle for its worth, Jones got the B-17 to top speed but it wasn't climbing fast enough.

His co-pilot, Jensen, yelled, "Oh shit," when he heard both the tail gunner and no.4 gunner on the underside of the Fort light em up, and said, "Holy Shit Brent. They must have smoked those Mustangs. Call for help, Goddamnit."

An explosive rumble behind them told Jones all he needed to know. One of the B-17's took a catastrophic hit. Sure, they had made bomb runs ass deep in flak, but rarely had to deal with German fighters, at least never more than a hand full.

Major Brent Jones knew that operations always maintained a strong cap force waiting at the exit point of Soviet airspace. He was under strict orders to only transmit in the open if it was an absolute emergency. *If this doesn't qualify, then the hell with them.* He barked into the radio, "Eagle Ten, Eagle Ten, do you read? Repeat Eagle Ten, this is CJ 101 requiring immediate assist, over. We are under attack by five zero Soviet fighters, Talon flight is down, repeat Talon flight is down."

Closing his eyes for a moment, praying that someone was listening on this net, he was rewarded with "Copy, CJ 101. Head best speed to the coastline. Eagle Ten is responding. Keep it together, CJ 101, help is one the way in fifteen minutes."

Captain Jensen cut in and yelled into the mike, "Fifteen minutes? Are you out of your fucking mind? We are going to be smoked in less than five, Eagle Ten. Do you read? Over."

Jones turned the mike off and told Jensen, "Shut the fuck up and fly the damn plane. Those guys can't get here any faster and you goddamn well know it."

While they were fighting, the last of their escorting Mustangs banked hard left and started tangling with Soviet Lag-5's. The Mustangs were outnumbered four to one and were doing their damnedest to keep the fighters off the B-17's but the Soviet advantage in numbers began to tell. Both pilots, desperate, closed with the remaining B-17 and flew in formation designed to throw as much lead as possible at the likely fighter approach. In the end, it didn't matter. The Soviet fighters caught up with the two remaining converted recon birds and blew both out of the sky.

Frozen in disbelief, Major Jones thought as wind from the shattered Plexiglas swept into the cabin, was how unfair it was he had to die after the war was over. Jones died long before his fiery B-17 plowed into the farmland below and became another casualty in what some of the flyers called the hottest cold war around.

Back at home base in England, communications were monitored throughout the deadly mission. Showing a mix of emotions from anger to bewilderment, the six enlisted men glued to their radio sets reported the blow-by-blow account and plotted every move of the ill-fated flight. Two civilians and one Royal Air Force Air-Vice Marshal listened to the entire exchange and crammed all the notes as fast as they could into their briefcase and left the communications center.

The two civilians were from MI6. The senior man spoke with a typical English penchant for understatement, "Terrible show lads, but at least it confirms the target is on schedule."

Left unsaid was that Major Jones and his whole crew had paid the price to confirm beyond doubt that the train moving west out of Warsaw was in fact carrying the chairman of the Soviet Communist party, Josef Stalin. More than fifty planes covered that train, and no Soviet train rated air cover like that unless they were escorting the big man, himself. The second civilian took the news as well as could be expected and thought, *bloody awful, three bombers and their crews lost just to confirm the movements of one man.*

The two civilians could only imagine what the RAF officer must be thinking, but he couldn't be told the real reason for the mission.

All that mattered was to inform the British team in Babelsberg, that the target was on schedule and the operation was a go. Still, a hell of a way to give the green light, poor blokes had no idea what they were in for.

July 15, 1945

Western Poland, Stalin's Personal Train

Oblivious to the battle raging in the sky, the ruler of the Soviet Union lit another cigarette with his one good hand and stared out the cabin window. Looking at the Polish landscape and seeing fresh evidence of his victorious army, Stalin was flushed with pride and confidence. At every crossroads, on the outskirts of every village and town, and especially at any river crossings, he saw numerous pieces of damaged and destroyed German equipment: everything from powerful German tanks and artillery to the carcass of a burned out Luftwaffe plane laying in the middle of some farmer's field. Nodding to himself, the Soviet leader knew it was the right decision to leave the Kremlin and see the proof of the Soviet victory.

Watching German soldiers labor in the harsh July sun brought a smile, a sense of complete triumph. As the train moved gradually through the countryside, Stalin allowed himself the luxury of enjoying his outing. This meeting of wartime allies was intended to discuss the final decisions on the fate of Germany and the rest of Europe. His allies were about to find that the Soviet Union was no longer interested in playing such games.

Once Stalin found out how his so-called allies attempted to stab the Soviet people in the back, yet again, he decided the time of compromise had long since passed. They would never willingly support the Soviet peoples legitimate security concerns and their actions betrayed their fear of the growing power of the Soviet Union. He could barely wait to sit down with that old imperialist, Churchill, and the new man, Truman. He knew little of the American, but by all reports, he was definitely not half the man Roosevelt was. *He will soon see that I won't allow him to talk to me like he did to poor Molotov.*

The Soviet Ambassador to the United States, Gromyko, said Molotov stammered like a school child when the new American President scolded him. Stalin laughed at the way this Truman fellow actually thought some childish threats would intimidate Stalin. *Yes, my friend you may cut off Lend-Lease without notice like you did in May or plan treachery behind my back, but in the end, America will turn its back and go home. Make your petty threats Mr. President, but by the end of this conference, Europe's destiny shall be mine.*

By this time tomorrow, Stalin thought, *I will be walking amidst the rubble of downtown Berlin and that will give me true pleasure.* He wanted, needed, to smell the death of that city. If what his military commanders said was true, then Berlin died in the fiery manner he had only thought possible in his dreams.

The moment he was apprised of the surrender of the Reich government and the death of Hitler, he knew he had to see for himself. He desperately wished to view the burned out buildings with his own eyes, walk along the avenues of Hitler's capital as conqueror, and stare into the eyes and see the fear of the defeated German survivors. *We will soon see what fine tools these Germans turn out to be. Yes, that would be perfect, the citizens of the former Thousand Year Reich will be forced to labor and rebuild what they destroyed. These Germans will make good tools.* With a slap of his knee, Stalin downed the shot glass of vodka and let out a hearty laugh. Yes, it was going to be a good trip after all.

Later that afternoon, Molotov and Beria were summoned to Stalin's cabin. Both noticed Stalin looked a bit drunk. The Soviet leader always came across more dangerous and menacing after he had been drinking, but this time, surprisingly enough, he appeared to be in high spirits.

Motioning them to enter, "Come in, come in, the both of you", the Soviet leader bellowed.

Placing a fresh bottle of vodka and two glasses in front of his trusted aides, Stalin said, "Now it is time to talk about this meeting with the imperialists, but first I want you to drink a toast to victory. Drink to all the rotting German corpses that we have passed over since we boarded this train. Stalin dreamed of this day. Now Drink."

With that said, the two men, in true Russian tradition, downed their shot glasses and quickly refilled them and drank again. Beria, in particular, enjoyed the little display of peasant behavior. He watched as Stalin downed another glass of vodka. The man's eyes seem to roll back into his head as an animal does prior to eating his prey. *Yes, the great Stalin has the look of a creature about to devour the carcass of Europe.*

Even better, Beria's own position within the Politburo couldn't be stronger after taking Molotov down a peg or two. Plus, after the Red Army victory in Europe, Stalin would look to weed out those officers in the Red Army who appeared too proud or too dangerous. In the end, with new enemies in the West to dangle in front of the Chairman and half a continent to occupy and re-educate, Beria and the NKVD would prove to be quite busy, indeed. Besides, even Stalin couldn't live forever, and with that thought in mind, Beria really did have something to drink to.

Brooding, the General Secretary hobbled over to the map of Europe on the wall and traced with his finger across all of the countries colored in red. The map showed the intended borders for the new map of Europe. Stalin had decided to keep all the territory taken from the Poles in 1939, plus arranged the Soviet Union's new borders to enable Soviet territory to touch all of the occupied countries in Eastern Europe. The Soviet Union would be able to send troops into Poland, Hungary, Czechoslovakia, and Romania whenever it chose. Stalin had long decided to maintain Red Army forces throughout the liberated countries of Eastern Europe to protect against any future dangers from the West, especially Germany, and to establish new, friendly governments under the guidance of Moscow.

Looking at the map again made Stalin feel more at ease. So, he decided to test his Foreign Minister. Stalin asked, "Molotov, how do you think the West will react to our new borders?"

Not sure how Stalin wanted him to respond, Molotov, barely looked up and answered, "Comrade Stalin, the West cannot bargain for what they do not have."

An evil sneer came to Stalin's face, and he said, "Good answer Molotov, you had better be equally convincing at the conference. This whole thing is a sham. You tell them, Molotov, that if they push the Soviet people any further with their demands that Stalin will not sit by like a fool."

Then tapping repeatedly on the map around the Polish capital, he asked Beria, "And what of our rebellious little Poles? Have you established complete control over this miserable country yet?"

Beria immediately answered, "Comrade Stalin, we have smashed the remnants of the Home Army and have seen little of them in the past two months. NKVD controls all of the occupied territories, all known collaborators and capitalists have been rounded up and sent into prison camps or shot."

Pausing for a moment, Stalin listened to his security chief and felt relieved. Thinking he was worrying like some old women. *Beria is right, tonight is for celebration.* As long as he maintained a firm grip in Poland things would be fine. Lifting a tumbler of vodka to his lips, *yes, tomorrow will be a good day indeed.*

Chapter Twenty One

July 16, 1945

USS Augusta, Antwerp, Belgium

Sitting alone in the wardroom of the USS Augusta, President Harry S. Truman looked in the mirror and fought against the doubt and fear creeping into his mind again. The same thought came to him every night of the voyage, how could a man who failed at damn near everything he had ever tried, from farming to haberdashery, ever hope to lead an entire nation in such trying times. There he was, about to sit at the table with the likes of Winston Churchill and Josef Stalin and deep down he believed he had no damn business being in the same room as those great men. Hell, Roosevelt only bothered to even have lunch with him twice.

Truman knew he wasn't exactly FDR's first choice, more than a few papers back home had made that clear enough. Putting a comb through his hair and fixing his glasses, Truman wanted to at least look the part. Never had a man from such humble roots and low self-esteem ever rise to the pinnacle of power. It was a story only possible in America.

Here was a man tasked with leading his nation into the post-war world, and when he looked into the mirror for the final time, all he saw was a simple farmer. Somehow by God's good graces, Harry had risen from small time political county commissioner to U.S. Senator to Vice-President and then God forbid, the President of the United States. Clenching his fists at his side, Truman had to find it within himself and damn quickly to believe that he belonged. With a wink towards the ceiling, the President whispered aloud, "Well, Franklin, you put me here, you better damn well be watching."

A knock at the door brought Truman back to reality and in walked his new Secretary of State, none other than the former Assistant President, James Byrnes. Byrnes had known the junior Senator from Missouri back in their days in the Senate and sat in with him on more than a few poker games that included Majority Leader Sam Rayburn and Arthur Vandenberg among others. With the unfortunate death of

FDR, Truman needed someone he could trust to guide him and to weed out some of Roosevelt's more troublesome New Dealers.

Byrnes very skillfully helped Truman in the early days when he was completely overwhelmed, trying to fill the shoes of an American icon. Byrnes brought Ambassador Harriman over from Moscow early on to begin shaping the new President's views on their Soviet ally. After some straight talk with Harriman, Truman had little patience with the then Secretary of State Stettinius's pro-Soviet policies. Byrnes quickly found himself asked to take over the State Department.

Byrnes understood that much had happened in the closing months of the war and Roosevelt never included Truman in anything of substance while he was still alive. Hell, Truman had to be told about everything from the Manhattan Project to the behind the scenes problems with their Soviet ally. The one thing that Byrnes appreciated about Truman was how the man was always willing to listen but not afraid to jump in once he felt comfortable.

Given enough time and seasoning, Byrnes thought the man could grow into a respectable President. Unfortunately, he didn't have the luxury of time to ease into the position. In two days, Truman had to sit across the table with the likes of Stalin and Churchill, and he was still by no means ready. He had been briefed on all the issues, especially the fallout from Operation Sunrise.

Responding not as a President, but as a former artillery captain, Truman, who had fought with distinction in the First World War, thought any damn thing to end the war sooner should have been looked at as a gift from heaven. The former Senator from South Carolina almost laughed when Truman kept shaking his head and saying he couldn't understand why the Russians weren't happy about an early collapse of the German war effort.

The Secretary of State had to walk Truman through things slowly and explain that once the Russians knew they weren't going to lose the war, post-war considerations and historical territorial ambitions dictated military policy. What was even more effective was when Byrnes brought over Major General Donovan to brief the new President on Soviet atrocities. When he showed the pictures, Truman turned pale and had to look away. The president had a very simple and direct sense of right and wrong and much less willing to cut a deal the way Roosevelt was want to do. Byrnes wanted one last, quick briefing and then to give him a surprise welcome that he hoped would do wonders for the President's confidence.

Impeccably dressed in a charcoal gray, three piece suit and holding a locked leather case under his arm, Byrnes brought the final briefing notes and a few other things for the President to look over. Truman walked over to the door and warmly shook Byrnes' hands, and clearly welcomed the company. Byrnes noticed that the President looked more than a bit uneasy, so he asked, "Mr. President, are you alright? If you don't mind me saying, you look like your stomach is all tied up in a knot."

Truman replied, "Jimmie, I haven't gotten a decent night's sleep since I got on this ship. I suppose it's everything from this big meeting to thinking about our boys still fighting over in Okinawa. I still can't get it through my thick, Missouri skull that all those boys are my responsibility now. It scares me near half to death sometimes."

Using his most exaggerated Southern drawl, Byrnes got right to the point and said, "Look here, Mr. President, far too much is riding on this meeting, so it's time to stop fretting about whether or not you can replace Roosevelt. You can't, the man is dead, and that's that. What you can do is walk into that meeting, head held high. I shouldn't have to tell you this, but Churchill and Stalin aren't sitting across from some failed farmer, but a man representing the most powerful economy in the world.

Let's not forget that old Uncle Joe thinks he has us by the short hairs, but we're going to let him know that the days of pushing Americans around are about to come to an end. Whether or not you believe it, I believe you are just the man to do it, so no more of this *I'm not ready*, cause it's time to step up to the plate."

Chuckling out loud, President Truman broke into a grin and said, "For Christ's sake Jimmie, for a second I thought it was Bess reading me the riot act. That woman can't stand to hear me feel sorry for myself, either."

Visibly relieved, Byrnes moved to the couch and opened up the briefing papers.

Getting back to the point, Byrnes opened with, "Mr. President, the key to the meeting will be to not let Stalin ride herd over us. According to Ambassador Harriman, who will be joining us in Potsdam, and his man, Kennan, the Soviets fully intend to all but colonize the nations of Eastern Europe. Basically, there's not a damn thing we can do except holler about the political rights of the Czechs and the Poles until we are blue in the face. At Yalta, Roosevelt let Stalin think he could waltz in to Poland, Romania, and the rest and have his way there. Now that all those stories about Soviet atrocities have hit the papers, if we come across as weak on communism, the United States will look weak to the whole world and we can't let them do that."

Truman nodded in agreement, "But, Jimmie, can't we tie elections in Poland to some type of economic rebuilding package or something? I hate to think that there isn't a damn thing we can do over there. Is Stalin really that cold hearted?"

"Your damn right he is, and you better not forget it. Stalin just keeps hammering at you in a relentless fashion. The key is Germany. The sooner we build up a democratic Germany to offset the Russians, the better. Plus, we better accept it now that some type of US military presence in Europe will be necessary for a long time to come. I know it won't play well at home, but we can't let the Russians think we are packing up and heading home."

Truman was a student of history, particularly the after effects of the First World War. He always thought that if the United States stayed engaged in the world there probably never would have been another world war. Truman added, "I remember that memo from Kennan in Moscow, describing the way Stalin reacted upon hearing that Franklin had said we would pull out in two years. To be honest, I decided a month ago that I wouldn't be doing my duty to future generations of Americans if I allowed us to just pack up and head home. I won't even tell Churchill, we'll just drop that little bomb at the end of the conference to rattle their cage."

Byrnes liked what he heard so far. It seemed as if Truman was getting his land legs back since they had docked. Byrnes added, "One more thing, Mr. President. Tomorrow is the big test in the desert. If General Groves is right, then in twenty-four hours the United States will possess the most powerful weapon in history and hopefully be able to knock the Japs out of the war and scare the Russians at the same time."

Truman thought about that for a while. He never was too crazy about taking the war to civilians. Somehow, it just didn't seem American to purposely target civilians. *Now I am about to be handed the biggest goddamn bomb in history and be expected to use it. Well, one thing's for sure, at two billion dollars, the damn bombs better work.*

Harry said, "I would rather hint at the bomb with Stalin, myself, rather than try to hold it over his head. I know we're probably never going to be friends, but I really don't think it's wise to push too hard. Let's wait until the end of the conference and hit him with it and see how he reacts. Okay?"

Byrnes arched his shoulders and answered lukewarmly, "It's your call, Mr. President. I just want to make our Russian friends know that we carry a mighty big stick now and not to push us. Anyway, it's just about time to get to the motorcade."

Then, in a surprise Byrnes had planned for some time, President Truman exited the ship to be greeted at the dock by none other than General Dwight Eisenhower. The general offered a warm handshake and friendly grin to make the new President feel welcome. Ike turned to the President and directed him to the convertible waiting to take them the short distance to the surprise. A quick five-minute drive past the massive Allied supply centers and warehouses then, the car came to a stop.

The President's heart all but stopped when they turned the corner and the band struck up "Hail to the Chief". Next, Truman saw the awe inspiring sight of an entire American infantry division turned out in their parade ground best. Waving in the breeze was the divisional flag flying the insignia of the Santa Fe Cross of the 35th Infantry Division, the President's old division from his days in France in the last war.

Eagerly getting out of the car, Truman walked down the avenue, and inspected each battalion. Truman had the chance to look into the eyes of those American boys who risked everything to defeat the Nazis and bring peace once again to Europe. Slowly, marching in step with General Eisenhower, Truman thought about his own days wearing the uniform of his country. Nothing had made him more proud than to have had the opportunity to serve his country, but now to be walking before his old outfit as President of the United States, Truman felt a combination of pride and humility.

Whispering a quiet prayer to himself, he thanked God for seeing these men through the horrors of war and asked for strength to guide him in the days ahead. He hoped he could somehow make a peace worthy of the men standing before him. Truman knew, he owed it both to the living and the dead to do the right thing. As he got to the end of the formation, he turned to Byrnes and said, "Thanks Jimmie, now let's go meet that son of a bitch Stalin and teach him a thing or two."

Chapter Twenty Two

July 16, 1945, 3:00 a.m.

Berlin

Massaging his tired eyes, Michael Gordon tried to reconstruct the events of the past three hours and figure out some way to get back in control of the situation. There he was in the middle of the night wearing a NKVD officer's uniform, blood stained and he stank of sweat and waste from the Berlin sewers. His hands were still shaking a bit as he tried to light a cigarette and prepare himself for what would come next. In seemed as if, in a split second, his little covert operation was about to become the most dangerous paramilitary operation of his career.

Thinking back to the call from the Soviet liaison officer working with the British security component, Gordon shook his head again at how quickly things could come undone. He heard the Yanks use the phrase, SNAFU to describe things when the proverbial shit had hit the fan. Really must say that *Situation Normal, All Fucked Up* bloody well said it all. So, he rocked back and forth, taking quick drags from the fag he'd just lit and tried to calm himself and hope he could reach the Polish agents before was too late.

Feeling a bit cheated after non-stop, dangerous activity for the past week, Gordon planned on spending a very anxious evening with some Russian vodka liberated for this very occasion. Michael never did acquire a taste for British gin, although Jamaican rum went down rather nicely, as he recalled from his public school days. From an operations point of view, everything was done on his end. The big event was on automatic pilot, the Poles had things well in hand and were probably using the cover of night to get into final positions. All in all, his part in one hell of a bloody dangerous operation had gone pretty well according to plan.

Just as he started to unwind a bit, at about eleven thirty, Colonel Grisha of the NKVD changed everything and set in motion the evenings' events that, contrary to orders, made him a very important player if the ambush was going to succeed. Colonel Grisha informed British security that Prime Minister Churchill's planned visit to the burned out remains of the Reichstag for the next morning would have to be pushed back because Comrade Stalin had changed his arrival plans. The NKVD officer told the British team that since it would be unforgivable to place both world leaders at risk at the same time, the British leader would have to adjust his schedule.

When Gordon protested about the last minute change in plans, he inquired if it would be possible for the Soviet leader to come later in the day. The Soviet officer laughed out loud and said that would be quite impossible. Grisha said that he wasn't sure how they did things in England, but in the Soviet Union, one didn't last long if he made such suggestions to Comrade Stalin. Then, offhandedly, the NKVD man added they were having problems of their own because of the foul up at the Stettiner Train Station.

Michael tried desperately not to let on the horror he felt at this news. Colonel Grisha laughed that some engineer was about to start counting trees in Siberia for allowing the pontoon bridge over the Spree River to become too unstable. Grisha didn't mention, of course, that the bridge was intended for only a short- term usage, not to handle the same traffic as the destroyed bridge it replaced. Laughing at the British security officer, Grisha said that morning or afternoon it didn't matter because the damage from Russians shells and British bombs wouldn't look any better in a couple of hours. With that little bit of news passed along, the NKVD man finally left the British security ops center to rearrange their schedule and thought nothing of the visit.

Within moments of Colonel Grisha's exit, Michael ran down to the basement and sent a coded Flash Traffic transmission to SOE headquarters in London. He keyed the radio and simply said, "PM needs new cigars, repeat PM needs new cigars. Over."

The men at the Special Operations Executive Headquarters would know that a major event had transpired and the plan had to be changed, but more significantly Michael did not send the abort signal. So rather than wait for orders to disengage, he shut down communications and decided to immediately go to Berlin and find Sobieski's team.

First, he put on the drab clothes of a Berlin refugee and pocketed his fake identity cards along with the usual food coupons and the like. His papers showed him to be a refugee who lived in the former Reich city of Danzig. Since he didn't have time to take the more circuitous route into the city he had used the past week, he added the uniform of a, NKVD Major over his refugee disguise. Lastly, he armed himself with a Russian Tokarev sidearm, a smaller 25mm caliber pistol, and a SAS stiletto.

Shaking his head, *God help me if I need to use any of these*, because if that were the case, in all likelihood the operation would be blown and his days probably numbered. Pausing for a moment to take a last look in the mirror, he assumed the sneer of an arrogant

NKVD officer and hoped like hell it would be enough to get him through the next couple of hours.

Taking the exit through the wine cellar to the bomb shelter, Michael emerged at the tree line. He spent a minute to let his night vision focus, then, groped towards a partially buried mound covered in fresh shrubberies and tree branches. Thanking the Gods that he took the time to do the job properly, he pulled on a large branch and then cleared the rest of the debris away. Hidden in what had been a small shell crater, Michael pulled off the tarp and saw a well-preserved German motorcycle. He had insisted some mode of transportation be arranged in case an emergency ever called for instant movement.

The British agent pulled out his map case and reviewed the security checkpoints and Soviet outposts surrounding the Babelsberg compound. He decided it had to take the direct route into Berlin proper or he would be far too late and the whole thing would be written off. He put on his goggles and helmet and pushed the bike about two hundred yards up to a trail that would take him to the road heading out of the lake.

As he slowly changed gears and pulled onto the Potsdamer Chausee highway headed northbound, he remembered the only time during the war he had to bluff his way through an operation. He was in Poland and dressed as an SS Captain. He had been delivering captured German weapons to Polish Home Army forces along the Baltic coast. He was surprised by a roving patrol of Gestapo men looking for deserters. Even though he didn't have any current orders giving him access to the fishing village, his identity papers were perfect, but most importantly, he acted the part.

Using heavy makeup to mangle his face with scars, Michael looked like one of the many fierce combat veterans of the Waffen SS who had seen ferocious fighting on the Eastern Front. By physically intimidating the two men and not showing the least amount of fear, the British agent easily passed through the Gestapo's hands. The moment the two Nazi secret policemen stopped him and rudely demanded his papers, his face instantly changed to a mask of barely contained rage. The two Gestapo found themselves confronted by one of the crazies from the Eastern Front who gave the look of a man not only unafraid to die, but to whom killing came second nature.

The older man had seen that look twenty years before in the trenches in Flanders, by men who no longer cared if they lived or died and thus were quite dangerous and not worth the potential harm. Wisely he pulled his younger more eager partner away and merely gave an admonishment to Michael not to stray too far away from his unit.

Gordon willed himself to take command of his emotions and refused to give in to his fears. Besides, he had some beautifully forged documents written on NKVD letterhead giving him access to the center of Berlin, plus the uniform of an NKVD Major that would scare many of the lower echelon in the Red Army. So, he would bank that few would want to contend with Stalin's secret police and possibly end up in some gulag after surviving the war. With that in mind, he revved the engine, took off and hoped to arrive at the Polish rendezvous site by two or so in the morning.

Although the going was slow, after forty-five minutes and two army checkpoints, Michael was starting to feel a bit more confident. He could almost get used to acting so bloody nasty. Imagine, threatening to send that poor Lieutenant's wife to the gulag if he were late. The poor bastard would probably be up half the night. With the wind blowing in his face as he sped up the Potsdamer Chausee, evidence of a massive buildup of Soviet armed forces along the approaches of Stalin's route through the city were impressive. Even at the late hour he saw everything from tanks to artillery pieces being moved along roadways in anticipation of the General Secretary's visit. Luckily, Stalin's visit required so much last minute movement throughout the city, a lone motorcycle traveling at one in the morning was barely noticed.

All was good until he turned off the main thoroughfare and became momentarily confused as he entered the Tempelhof section of the city, just north of the massive former Luftwaffe air complex. The Poles had chosen this section because so much surrounding damage had minimized useable shelter for refugee squatters and they found it would prove less suitable for Red Army garrison forces. Gordon had readily agreed and never ran into any trouble on his previous visits, so his guard was down when he ran right into a small roadblock as he turned the corner on his motorcycle.

The Soviet two-man patrol turned on the jeep's lights and momentarily blinded Michael who tensed up as he brought the bike to a stop. Expecting some Red Army private or maybe a sergeant at most, he was taken aback when he saw it was a NKVD political officer who asked for his papers. He could tell by the look on this man's face that he was all business and wouldn't be bluffed, even by one from his own service.

Using his most commanding voice with a note of impatience, Michael said, "Comrade, I am on State business of the highest order and cannot be held up for one moment. Here are my identification cards, now look at them and let's be done with this."

Refusing to be intimidated, the senior Russian political officer, with expressionless eyes and a frigid manner, took the papers without comment and stepped away from the motorcycle, carefully inspecting the paperwork by flashlight and finally looked up and asked with a note of menace, "Comrade Major Polevoi, sorry to disrupt your travels but I have been given the strictest of instructions, no one under any circumstances is authorized in this zone without the proper papers. Please give me your travel orders for access to the Tempelhof district."

Sensing danger, Michael immediately adopted an indignant tone and, like a true Russian, tried to bully the subordinate officer into letting him through. "How dare you suppose to stop me, little man? I'll have you know that you will be walking the fence at the Kolyma gold fields in Siberia next week if you hold me up for one more second. Is that understood? You, corporal, remove the roadblock and let me through now or do you want to be branded a traitor for helping the fascists? I am on a special mission to hunt down a team of SS fascists said to be operating in the vicinity. Do you know who will be traveling through here tomorrow? Comrade Stalin, that's who, and if anything should happen because of this incident I swear that you will pay dearly, comrades."

The young corporal nearly wet himself, but the NKVD man held his ground and turned to the corporal and said, "Corporal Rykov, if the Major does not hand over his orders you are to put him under arrest immediately, is that understood?" Turning towards Gordon, he added, "If you are part of a special security unit then you should be well aware of standard procedures on this night. So either cooperate or we shall soon see who will answer tonight for their crimes."

Seeing the troublesome, little man would not budge, Michael knew his papers would never pass muster, so he decided to act boldly and convince the stubborn Chekist the error of his ways. In a slow and deliberate manner, he turned off his motorcycle. Both men appeared to relax a bit at this action.

Shaking his head from side to side, Michael sneered, "If that's the way you want to play it, that's just fine with me. When it's time to start packing your winter clothes, comrade, remember I gave you every opportunity to comply here tonight. I hear winter comes early, my friends."

The Soviet political officer suddenly got nervous and thought maybe this man really was who he said, so he took his hand off his holster and moved towards Gordon with his flashlight in hand. As the NKVD man came within arm's length, he reached into his belt. In one, fluid motion, he whipped the SAS blade from his tunic and sliced the political officer's throat.

Before the Red Army corporal heard the gurgling coming from his superiors mouth, Michael pulled out his small caliber handgun equipped with a silencer and shot the sentry in the throat and then once more through his left eye. The poor bastard never knew what hit him.

The political officer was on his knees blood flowing thru his fingers and down his tunic, suffering complete shock. Then in perfect Russian, the last thing the NKVD man would ever hear was whispered by Gordon in his ear, "You would be drinking vodka tonight at the barracks, my stubborn friend, if you just would have let me pass. How does it feel to know that you were right?"

Then switching back to a heavy English accent, Michael added for posterity, "Sleep well, for it's time to see the workers' paradise I hear so much about. Cheerio."

All the condemned NKVD man could think was, *why?* The silencer rang out again and ended things quickly. The night had taken a sudden turn for the worse.

Berlin, 3:30 a.m.

The two Polish assassins stood on either side of the door as they listened with great anticipation at the slowly approaching footsteps. Stefan, the experienced weapons man, was on watch and discovered a lone figure moving through the remains of the apartment complex. Two hard knocks, followed by two softer knocks on the pipe leading to the bedroom alerted the two sleeping Polish Home Army agents. He peered closely through his binoculars at what, at first, had appeared as just another Berliner scavenging for something to eat or to trade on the black market. After closely watching the approaching figure for ten minutes, the Pole's instinct told him something was amiss.

What alerted the experienced, Polish underground fighter was how the person moved towards the entrance of their hideout and seemed to look for something specific. He didn't appear like someone looking to take something and steal off into the night, like so many other hungry Germans. Finally, after alerting Tad and Aleksandra, Stefan moved closer to the ground floor, careful not to make a sound and risk alerting the intruder. The Polish team leader, Tad Sobieski, had moved their hiding spots three times since the team came together the previous week.

Not wanting to take any chances, the newest location offered shelter on the third floor of a nearly demolished apartment complex. The room they shared led directly to an elevator shaft that went down to the basement, an excellent escape route if it proved necessary. More importantly, by setting up shop on the third floor, it gave whoever was on watch an excellent position to spot potential threats.

Stefan gripped the German Lugar pistol tightly as he allowed the interloper to inch towards the exposed hallway leading to their room. The unknown man moved five feet past Stefan when the Polish fighter leapt out behind the man and clasped his strong hands over the intruder's throat and kicked his legs out from under him. The man let out a yelp and began to struggle. Within seconds, Tad burst through the door and pointed a German Schmeisser machine pistol at the prisoner and whispered in German, "Raise your voice and you're a dead man."

Michael Gordon had been unsure if he found the right apartment. With damn near everything leveled to the ground, the usual landmarks proved no help especially at three in the morning. Just when he thought that he saw the right apartment, his life passed before his eyes as a pair of tremendous hands wrapped around his throat so suddenly that he couldn't respond. His first thought was that some hungry Berliner was trying to rob him or worse thought he was a prowler himself, but then he heard the Pole's cold voice and knew that he had found them.

In the darkness of the hallway it was no wonder no one recognized him. With a raspy voice he said, "Sorry to drop in unannounced and all, but would you mind getting your bloody hands off my throat?"

The two Poles instantly knew who they held and nearly collapsed with relief. Both men the mission was over before they even had a chance, that the operation was blown. Quickly, Tad realized it was no social call and deduced something terrible must have happened for the Russian born, British agent to make such a dangerous and unannounced house call.

Helping him off the floor, Tad asked, "Were you followed?"

Shaking his head no, Michael tried to catch his breath and rested against the wall. Even in the dim moonlight, he could see the three anxious faces looking up at him, wondering what in bloody hell he was doing in Berlin. Not wanting to dance around the issue, he started right off by saying, "We have problems. Ivan's changed his route into the city. We have exactly five hours to reconnoiter the new train station, figure out some sort of plan, and find time enough to set a suitable ambush without getting shot.

"One more thing, about forty minutes ago I killed a NKVD officer and a soldier manning a checkpoint six blocks away. I hid the bodies and moved the truck, but I doubt that will last long. So, we got big problems. We have to figure out just what in the hell we can do to stay alive, let alone still try to pull this mission off. I, for one, don't like our chances."

The three Polish Home Army agents were beyond shocked and stared down at Gordon, not knowing what to say or do.

The others in the room instinctively turned to Sobieski, looking to him to say something, to make a decision.

Feeling momentarily overcome with a fatigue and weariness that went beyond words, Tad slowly backed up until he felt the solid plasterboard of the wall and allowed himself to sink to the floor. He had been pushing himself so hard the past couple of weeks that the news hit him worst of all. The ambush site was perfect, the charges had been set, and they had a very real chance to actually perform the unthinkable. *Dear God why now?*

Even worse, he knew everything depended on the success or failure of their operation. General Anders, the Home Army commander, drilled that into him when they met, the one and only time, to decide on the mission. Anders had made it painfully clear that if his team couldn't take out the leadership of the Soviet empire, the uprising would ultimately fail.

With Stalin dead, they believed the Poles would have at least a week to seize control throughout the country before the leadership vacuum was filled and an organized response could be mounted. All the weeks of planning and living on the edge in Soviet occupied Berlin, praying to make it through one more checkpoint, hoping somehow to pull off the impossible seemed for naught.

Every night he remembered the face of his beautiful wife and the angel eyes of his daughter. He did this for them, for the life that was first stolen by the Nazis and then the hope for a future that was taken by the communists. His knuckles turned white as he clenched his fists and began to rise off the floor. He knew even the Englishman was looking at him and wondering what to do.

Knowing he had no other choice, Tad nodded his head, looked at them all and simply said, "It can still be done. It must be done."

With those words, the other three followed Tad into the room, resigned to their fates and prepared to accompany Tad to the gates of hell if need be. Their lives meant nothing, for no matter the risk, Stalin must die.

Sobieski went right to his map case and pulled out a detailed map of the city and turned to the British agent and asked, "Well, I hope my friend that you came with at least some useful information and not just to break the bad news?"

Still in shock from his own experiences that evening, Gordon grimly nodded and moved closer to the map. "You see the Gorlitzer Railway Station, off of the Kopenicker Landstrasse, well, the railway bridge has been completely rebuilt. With the Spree River running on three sides of the station, Soviet security decided that it offered more protection than anything closer to the Unter Den Linden. They are mostly concerned with cordoning off the immediate roadway and are less concerned with some type of standoff weapon. Apparently, Beria wakes up in the night and sees some crazy Fritz with a potato masher or a Lugar up close and personal."

Gordon looked up and saw the two Poles smiling and thought he must have missed something. Only the woman, Aleksandra, remained deathly quiet. She just wanted to be part of the kill and didn't care how it was to be done.

Sobieski knew exactly where this new station was situated and better yet, knew the route the Soviet leader would have to take. He took out a pen and traced out on the map, slowly following the road from the station and circled the spot. He had hobbled around every block within a twelve-block radius of the Reichstag and knew from his notes that the other access road near the Gorlitzer Station was still blocked by the shattered ruins of an apartment complex and concerns of unexploded ordnance around the structure. Looking at his watch it was nearly four a.m., daylight will be coming soon not much time to pull this together.

With avid interest and more than a little professional curiosity, Gordon watched the Polish agents calmly plan their way out of what seemed like a hopeless situation. Feeling that the *where* had been established, the how loomed rather large above it all. He asked, "Mind if I inquire about the whereabouts of the explosives, fuses, and the like that were to be placed at the original ambush site? It would seem to me that we will need things to go boom if we are to make this thing work."

The tired Polish leader grimaced. He was right. They had placed most of their explosive charges at the base of the dilapidated apartment complex near the intersection leading out of Stettiner Station. They had planned to topple the building in front of the motorcade and take out the armored cars from a short distance while everyone was still in shock. It was a good plan that stood a very real chance of working.

Gordon was not familiar with the intersection the Pole circled and asked him to describe it in some detail. Gordon had been involved in more than a few ambushes, himself, while working in occupied France and figured he could be of help.

Trying to remember all the details from his reconnaissance of the city, Tad held a light close to the map and traced his finger as he explained, "The Russians designated several avenues leading into the city as MSR's, or main supply routes. Along these avenues, engineers bulldozed the massive amount of debris from the Allied bombing and Russian shelling to the side of the streets. Nearly the entire length of these MSR's you will find concrete, brick, and steel piled one to two meters high along both sides of the street. The debris is piled high but not packed densely."

Trying to visualize the road net leading from the station, Gordon remembered Red Army formations assembling along the path he had taken the city. If what Sobieski said was true, then the Russians would likely line up on the street side of the piles of debris facing the passing motorcade. Things were starting to click in his head. He asked, "What weapons and explosives do you have you available?"

Tad looked at Stefan who shrugged and spoke to the team leader in Polish. Gordon watched the man. He looked completely nonplussed about the situation.

Tad translated, "We have, at most, enough for three or four charges, not enough for a major explosion, but we do have those dummy bricks to plant them in the debris. Also, we have a trench mortar along with about a dozen high-explosive rounds. Our friend Stefan is particularly deadly with one of those things. I have seen him take out individual trucks in troop convoys. You'd be surprised how accurate one can be if it is properly modified.

"Lastly, other than automatic rifles and a few grenades, we have one more special toy. If you recall I told you about Aleksandra's father, the biathlon champion. Well, his daughter learned to use more than just a hunting rifle the past couple of years. She has brought along a German anti-tank rifle, an accurate rifle that can punch through one full inch of armor out to about three hundred yards. Even if Stalin is driven in an armored personnel carrier, the side plate can easily be destroyed with a well-placed shot from the German AT rifle. Somehow, I have always known it was to be Alexandra in the end who must slay the beast."

Looking at the sleeping woman curled up in the corner of the room, Gordon was filled with a combination of amazement and sadness.

Sobieski smiled as he visualized what was to be done. Taking out a pen and paper, Tad quickly sketched out the rail station and the likely route of the motorcade. He quickly filled in the blanks, adding parallel walls of debris on each side of the street, making notations on both sides of the Spree River, and finally marking four separate X's.

This was his Sistine Chapel, his last great attack, and one that could ignite the beginning of the liberation of his people. Somehow, despite the hardships and the evening's news from the British agent that threatened to wreck everything, the job had to be done. As a former student and teacher of history, Tad knew this one action would be talked about and studied for generations, regardless of the success or failure. Stubborn pride demanded perfection. He knew deep in his soul he would join his beloved wife that day, and he no longer felt afraid.

The others sensed his rising excitement and Gordon spoke up first, "Bugger me, but it looks like we have a plan of action and, from the looks of it, a bloody well beautiful one, at that." Gordon saw the X's and understood each one bordered a rectangular base that would box in the motorcade, the perfect kill box.

Stefan saw it too and slapped Tad on the back and smiled, as he too understood all of the markings. *Yes, keep it simple but deadly my friend.*

The Polish Home Army commando instinctively ducked as he heard sirens and put his finger to his lips. He motioned everyone away from the windows. Gordon felt perspiration run down his back as he remembered what happened just a short time ago. Thinking to himself that he had gotten a bit caught up in the excitement. He forgot the Russians would likely be a bit unhappy once they found out about their missing Chekist.

As the sirens faded, Sobieski pointed to the map again and started to outline the plan, "We will immediately begin preparations and start to move into position. Any last minute questions?"

Gordon loved the simplicity and pure daring of the operation, and desperately wanted in on the kill. Somehow he couldn't bear not playing a role. Grasping Sobieski by the shoulder and with a look of sincere determination, he stated, "You need me today. At least let me try to figure out a way to get you three the hell out of there once it's done."

The Pole respected the English agent even if he didn't fully trust him in the beginning. If their mission succeeded Tad knew much will be owed to this man. Tad spoke gently, "No my friend, I think we both know that this can't go any further. You have done more than enough. You have given us a chance and that will never be forgotten by my people."

The sincerity and gravity in the Pole's voice overwhelmed Gordon, who was near the edge of breaking down from sheer exhaustion. He, too, had pushed himself the past two weeks and the strain was taking its toll. He knew Sobieski was correct, the risk was just too great. The Polish led him to a dirty mattress in the corner of the room. Before Gordon realized it, he felt the soft pillow against his face and warm bedding cover him.

For the first time in years, as sleep overtook him, he prayed. His eyes moistened as he pleaded for the souls of those three brave soldiers as he drifted off into a deep sleep.

Chapter Twenty Three

July 16, 1945, 7:30 a.m.

Potsdam, British Legation

Churchill held the crumpled piece of paper in his hand tightly as he walked back and forth in his room. Usually sleeping well into the morning, the Prime Minister had been up much of the night. Word followed that Gordon had run off into the night to warn the Poles. Only then did the full impact of his decision to support the insane venture take hold. With the dawn of a new day, he could admit the truth and say he was downright terrified. He had always known his backing the Poles in their uprising was a dangerous business. But with the morning sun warming his face, he couldn't say he did it for the Poles. No, he acted because his pride was wounded at Yalta and long ago he decided to lash out in whatever way he could.

The day was upon them and at the chance of disclosure that His Majesty's Government had been directly involved, and still acting to ensure the success of the mad undertaking, he could barely contain his fears. *Dammit, I told the boy to stay out of it. I told him that he couldn't get involved. The government can never acknowledge any connection, but he still chose to throw himself into the fray.*

Standing in front of the mirror, the Prime Minister couldn't help but look up and remember younger eyes staring back at him and saying, "You would have done the same bloody thing, old man." At second glance, Churchill didn't look so young anymore. The man looking back at him was tired and his nerves were about to give. *Have to talk to someone*, so he called for Eden.

Within moments of the call, Foreign Secretary Anthony Eden entered the room. Looking more than a bit harried himself, he wasn't surprised to find the PM in a poor state. Eden had dreaded the trip from the moment they left London, really since the minute Churchill told him of his plan to support the Poles. Eden had always believed that even the slightest chance of disclosure would be so overwhelmingly damaging that the Prime Minister had to be mad as a hatter for even considering it.

Eden could tell Churchill was taking counsel of his fears. In fact, he looked bloody awful, as if he had been up all night. In a rather sullen manner, he greeted the Prime Minster, "Good morning, sir, I trust you spent the night as I did, pacing the floors. Well, any news from our man in Berlin?"

Not in the mood for a lecture, the Prime Minister detected more than a hint of sarcasm in his Foreign Secretary's voice. Churchill grunted back in a raspy voice, "Not yet, but we received a communication intercept about two hours ago. It seems two NKVD men wound up dead while manning a checkpoint near our friends in Berlin." The PM saw Eden's horrified expression and added, "Oh, for God's sake, Anthony, stop looking at me with that *I told you* so face."

Equally annoyed and feeling even more nauseous, Eden's fear raced at high speed as he pictured Soviet security forces capturing their man along with the Poles. *Eventually they would talk, everyone does.* Staring at the Prime Minister with venom in his eyes, Eden felt infuriated at the predicament Winston had placed not just the government but the whole damn country in.

Deciding to no longer spare the PM's feelings, in a shrill voice he exclaimed, "You've gone and done it now, Winston. You know the Americans won't back us if it comes out that we tried to kill old Uncle Joe himself. Then what? The last thing they want is to get involved in some crazy scheme that you bloody well cooked up." The angry words echoed in the room as Churchill stood there and took it.

Starting to get angry, Churchill decided the die had been cast and it was not the time for ruminations of impending doom. No, it was time to think about that brave intrepid fellow, Gordon, who, without hesitation, leapt at the chance to do his duty. Glaring at his Foreign Secretary, Churchill's fire started to come back and he realized that, in the end, even if the plot was foolish and fraught with danger, he was right. He tried to do something and not just give up. *I'll be damned if I will allow myself to be castigated again by this young pup. In the end, I chose to act and if Eden and others can't see it then damn them too.*

The last thing he said to Eden as he pushed past the door and out towards the gardens was, "Anthony, you may despise me at the moment, but whatever happens today, the British people will know that I did what had to be done, for the sake of the Empire, and for Europe and that's how I will sleep tonight. How will you sleep?"

July 16, 1945, 7:30 a.m.

Ten Miles Outside of Berlin

Stalin's personal train had spent the night outside the city limits because Stalin wanted to make a grand entrance into the city in the early morning. Beria arranged for one entire NKVD division to provide absolute security around the train. Foreign Minister Molotov still felt a bit nervous after the strange evening with Stalin, but clearly there was something in the air about this historic moment. To enter a defeated enemy's capital city was a moment to be savored.

Molotov couldn't help but remember his last visit to the Nazi capital early in the war, so long ago when the two had been nominal allies. So much had come to pass, but the Soviet Union emerged victorious and the vanquished must suffer the consequences of such foolhardy leadership.

In the distance Molotov saw evidence of the horrors inflicted upon the Berlin suburbs and surrounding countryside. The Soviet Foreign Minister pictured his beloved Moscow and inwardly shuddered at the thought of it being overrun by Nazi madmen if Hitler's legions had defeated the Red Army. Shaking his head quickly to push away such thoughts, Molotov took one last look out the window and saw the morning sun rising. He knew nothing would mar this day for Comrade Stalin.

Ten minutes later, a longtime member of the Kremlin staff opened Stalin's door and Molotov walked into the rather spacious sleeping car properly provisioned for this special trip. He desperately hoped to find the General Secretary in good spirits and was pleased to find Comrade Stalin not only awake, but also actually smiling.

With a cigarette in one hand and a steaming cup of tea in the other, Stalin waved Molotov over and said, "Good morning, Molotov. You look surprised. Was I that drunk last night?"

Smiling himself, Molotov could only stammer, "Good morning, Comrade Stalin, you look well indeed. What a day, we are going to walk in the ruins of the fascist capital. I still can't believe it myself."

Walking over to the table stacked with sweets and morning pastries, Stalin was positively beaming. Whatever demons confronting him the previous night had obviously been dealt with in the time honored Russian tradition of drowning them in vodka. The only difference was that Stalin was unable to take a morning.

Stalin couldn't help but laugh aloud at his foreign minister's obvious nervous disorder. *How did this man ever last so long serving the Party? Of course today is going to be a great day, why shouldn't it be so. For today I shall see with my own eyes the death of this city.*

He awoke early that morning, just as the sun was rising, and could start to see the shattered skyline of Berlin. Just as the numerous photos from Red Air Force recon missions showed, not a building stood without some type of damage. Rubble was everywhere and traces of smoke from burned out buildings lingered in the air.

Stalin packed his pipe and thought how twice in twenty-five years those people tried to devour the Russians. *Today we see who won in the end.* Stalin hadn't forgotten about the disgraceful peace of Brest-Litovsk when the Germans stole nearly a third of pre-revolutionary Russia. Then the same Germans were allowed by the West to rise again, only stronger and more dangerous than ever.

While his foreign minister watched, he quietly struck a match to light his pipe, stared out the window and relished what he was about to do. He would inhale the stench of death from these people and let them know the power of the Red Army would ensure Germany would never rise again.

Whatever pity the man may have possessed at one time in his life had long since died. Stalin took a perverse satisfaction at reading one report after another chronicling the barbaric actions of his army. Tens of thousands of women raped, homes looted, numerous instances of murder. Stalin understood what the weak people of the West never could, the Germans must feel the boot of their new masters and fear what might happen next. Just like an animal, Germany would suffer beatings from its master. Only then would the Germans be conditioned to serve the interests of Moscow.

Turning away from the window, Stalin motioned for his foreign minister over and said, "I want you to double check with Beria on the security arrangements. I want to leave in forty five minutes. Let's not waste a moment of light."

Starting to feel pretty good himself, Molotov answered in high spirits, "As you say Comrade Stalin, you deserve this moment to last and I will ensure that not a second is wasted." With that, he left the room in a rush, overwhelmed with excitement at the prospects of touring the city with Comrade Stalin.

Puffing on his pipe, Stalin nodded and kept looking out the window. He felt excited for the first time in many years. *Yes, let's not waste one moment.*

July 16, 1945, 8:45a.m.

Downtown Berlin

The once dead city of Berlin came alive with movement. After working at a feverish pace all through the night, tens of thousands of Red Army troops, decked out in their finest uniforms, stood from one end of Berlin to the other. Tanks, self-propelled guns, artillery pieces, all the many weapons of war that were the instruments of the city's destruction were lined up for review by the new master of Europe. In a display that made the May Day parades in Red Square pale by comparison, the citizens of the once proud and all-powerful capital of the Third Reich trembled in the presence of unbridled power.

Most Berliners stayed in their cellars or whatever hiding places they found that gave some protection from the roving Russian hordes who had descended upon them like locusts from some biblical plague for the past two months. Just knowing that Stalin was coming was enough to force more than a few Berliners to finally take their own lives. To have lived through the bombings, then invasion, and finally the hell of occupation, the significance of Stalin walking down the Unter den Linden was clear to all. The nightmare was real and they would likely never awaken from it. To the citizens of Berlin, the devil himself had come to call and most assumed hope had been extinguished for eternity.

Walking along the street amidst the massive show of Soviet force, a wounded Berliner limped along pulling his cart of reasonably well shaped bricks and steel rebar collected from the mounds of destroyed buildings littering the former Reich capital. In a pathetic fashion, the scarecrow of a man used two makeshift crutches and painstakingly hauled the cart of his early morning scavenging with a rope tied around his waist.

Moving at a snail's pace, the dirty German stopped every few yards to scrounge around the enormous pile of debris, hoping to find one more piece of brick or concrete that could be fastened together in some way to build shelter for what was expected to be a winter in hell. He was not the only Berliner up and around that morning and often times men and women came to blows over the pieces of office buildings and apartment houses that once dominated the city. The sad creatures scurrying around the city hardly posed any danger to Stalin or the Red Army occupying Berlin.

The soldiers and NKVD security forces paid little attention to the half-starved creatures trying desperately to survive in a city devoid of any hint of the creature comforts that sustained the Germans through six years of war. Reaching down at another brick, the former soldier pulled the cart in a slightly more deliberate manner than most of his fellow scavengers, but none noticed. His steely eyes darted from face to face, ignoring the others brave enough to go out that day, of all days.

Even though he wore the same lice ridden clothes as the others and smelled of grime and sweat, only one Berliner turned his head and smiled upon hearing the approaching sounds of a train. The man propelling himself forward on crutches that morning looked across the street at the condemned apartment complex and saw all he needed to see. He moved as quickly as he could down the Kopenicker Landstrasse towards the river. Tad Sobieski, the product of a forced union of German and Pole, was about to make history.

At about the same time, Stefan emerged from his hiding spot. On the east side of the Spree River, several shattered German panzers sat on a small rise along a copse of trees overlooking the smashed roadway leading into the city. Using a dried out dike along the Spree River, Stefan moved quickly during the early morning hours and then hid himself in a partially caved in dugout likely made by a scared Volkstrum during the last days of the war.

Using binoculars, he could easily see the rail line parallel to the Kopenicker Landstrasse, leading directly to Gorlitzer Station. For nearly four hours, he watched the comings and goings of thousands of Russian soldiers and security forces as they secured the area. He thought the Russians were much sloppier than the Germans he hunted in his native Poland. Just because the train station was protected on three sides didn't mean danger couldn't threaten the special visitors about to reach the rail station. In typical Russians fashion, they packed men four lines deep along the approaches to the station.

He counted his good luck. The more communist bastards packed into the target area, the easier a target to hit and the more confusion that would ensue. At least he felt better than he had a few hours earlier. Once he made it to his hiding place with the Spree River to his right and the target five hundred yards to his front, everything seemed to fall into place. He was cleaning the barrel of his trusty two-inch mortar, adjusting the sights yet again, when he heard the sound of an approaching train. Stefan immediately emerged from his hole and knew the time had come.

Taking a deep breath, the forty-five year Pole smelled the air and prayed to the souls of his wife and children, begging them to deliver him on this day. Carefully, he pulled out the mortar, attached the base plate, and laid out twelve rounds. He placed six of them to the side. High explosive or smoke rounds were the most common, but the six rounds Stefan isolated were special. The English were very clever. When someone in the Special Operations Executive found that too many of the resistance groups and British agents parachuting into occupied Europe were woefully equipped with inferior weapons, so they decided to do something about it.

SOE weapon specialists developed a two-inch mortar round that made use of the new proximity fuse devised primarily for anti-aircraft guns and later heavy artillery to electronically trigger the shell to shower the target with deadly reams of shrapnel once the round neared the target. This set off an effect almost like a shotgun being fired from about twenty feet above the exposed heads of the target. When used against targets in the open field, the results could be quite deadly.

Unfortunately that capability wasn't completed until nearly the end of the war, but Stefan was about to perform a live field test and see just how deadly the new British toy would perform. With the sound of the coming train getting closer and closer, Stefan surveyed the scene again and knew everything depended on Tad creating the kill box. Without trapping the motorcade, his little mortar wouldn't stand a chance of doing much real damage.

As long as the lightly armored limousines protected Stalin and his lackeys, he would hold and wait to fire his special ammo. *Dear God, please Tad, place those charges well, if that convoy stops and everyone starts leaping from their cars, he will unleash his rain of metal from the sky.*

Elsewhere, Aleksandra had sat high in her perch for more than three hours. Much of the time she thought of her father. Deep down she knew the best part of her died when her father and husband were taken away to the camps. Then her world was forever shattered after that SS bastard raped her, causing her to lose her child. So, she hunted the same Germans just as her father taught so many years before. The poor man never had sons to teach to hunt, so his oldest daughter, who adored him like no other, wanted to please him. Even sitting in a condemned apartment building with the wind caressing her face, warm memories of his huge hand wrapped around her mittens in the middle of winter gave her strength.

Cradling her rifle and cleaning debris around the muzzle, she felt her father's presence and knew he was beside her, guiding her to the end. She thought it was about the ultimate revenge, but as the moment of truth approached, she knew today was really about a yesterday long ago, but still such a apart of her. Today is about another Polish daughter someday holding her father's hand and knowing that he will never leave her. Today is about a hope that there will be a tomorrow.

Seeing the smoke on the horizon, there was no mistaking the armored train approaching the station. What a beautiful weapon, her father would have thought of the German Panzerbuchse anti-tank rifle she cradled in her arms. It had an effective range of three hundred yards and could penetrate an inch of solid armor plate. The weapon was useless against modern tanks, but proved quite deadly when used against light armored cars or personnel carriers.

Burrowed deep in the debris of a half destroyed office building, Aleksandra overlooked the Spree River. The fifth floor had open sights on the first intersection coming out of the train station. Peering through her scope, she knew at this angle she couldn't miss, as long as Tad secured the kill box. If his booby traps failed to explode, then she would have, at best, ten seconds to get off maybe two good aimed shots at the fast moving convoy. Then, it would be dumb luck, and they had come too far for to rely on that.

Using his binoculars, Stefan watched as the armored train slowly crossed the recently rebuilt railroad bridge over the Spree River and finally come to a complete stop in front of the Gorlitzer Station's main platform. With impressive precision, five Mercedes limousines pulled out and parked in front of the enclosed platform and formed a circle. The plan always assumed that targeting the exact limo that Stalin was riding in would prove difficult, and the Poles were correct. NKVD security forces created a manmade wall around the Soviet leader and directed the various high level military and political leaders to their respective cars.

Next, the limos pulled up to the platform, loaded their VIP's and then reformed in a circle. The cars pulled out and drove around the parking lot outside the main entrance, following one another in a circle around the lot. Then, one car after another peeled away and began moving towards the exit. With each car identical, it would be impossible to tell who was in what car.

Two BA-10 armored personnel cars armed with light cannons leapt to the front of the motorcade and two moved to the rear. In a perfectly orchestrated effort, the Soviet security team quickly picked up their charges and, with the motorcade formed up, prepared to move towards the ruins of the Reichstag.

Inside one of the fast, heavily armored Mercedes, Stalin stared out the darkened window in amazement at the unbelievable level of destruction. From the moment his train entered the city limits, Stalin witnessed packs of hungry German refugees milling around outside soup kitchens, others scrounging through the rubble looking for anything of value and he stared in fascination at one collapsed building after another. The Soviet leader could barely wait to actually walk into the streets of the German capital where that madman, Hitler, had walked and survey for himself the completeness of his victory.

Stalin had expected a quick run to the Berlin government district, but found the street leading from the station in terrible condition. He was on ground level and could practically reach out and see the twisted remains of homes and apartments. It was almost too good to be true. Moscow had seen scars from the war from early bombing raids in 1941 to the massive defensive works put up throughout the city in the Fall of 1941, but the Germans never came close enough to visit anything like the ruin he had witnessed thus far.

The one annoying thing bothering the Soviet leader was the huge mound of concrete and bricks piled up along the sides of the roads. It obstructed his view and he did not want to miss observing the defeated remnants of his one-time deadly enemy.

His driver turned left and revealed a sight that was simply staggering, even to Stalin. Up and down the boulevard for as far as he could see, line upon line of Red Army soldiers stood at attention next to their tanks and artillery. He could feel the car slow to enable him to closely inspect his victorious army. Momentarily overcome by the display of both German defeat and Soviet dominance, he rolled his window down and waved his hands out the window.

Security teams throughout the motorcade cursed in tandem as Stalin revealed he was in the fourth car behind Beria, Konev, and Molotov. As his hands emerged from the Mercedes, a roar of cheers and clapping greeted the conqueror of Europe. With an enthusiasm that took Stalin by surprise, his army began waving and yelling adulations to Stalin. Grown men caught up in the moment began to sob as they remembered all that was lost, what was won and the horrific cost.

After years of bitter combat, from the walls of the Kremlin to the siege of Leningrad and through the savagery of Stalingrad, the Red Army soldiers knew the job was done and they had delivered victory. Stalin the Great had come to Berlin to see his victorious Red Army. Soon they would go home to rebuild and start anew.

Even a man such as Stalin couldn't help but be moved by such a spontaneous and heart rendering greeting.

Taking advantage of the Russian reactions to Stalin, Tad Sobieski had plenty of time to climb the fire escape to a second floor apartment that overlooked the intersection. Thanking God the motorcade was moving slowly, Tad tried to remember exactly where he placed the charges. He nervously undid the special radio controlled detonator and quickly assembled the antenna. Although he used a detonator like this once before in Warsaw, he never entirely trusted them.

Nothing like electric wires and a plunger to give some real assurance, but it was too late for second guesses.

Once he snapped the pieces together, he crawled across floor to a spot placing him roughly midway between the four charges below. He prayed none of his fellow scavengers saw anything unusual about the strands of wire sticking out from the mounds on the corner. While appearing to rummage for bricks and the like, Tad was able to dig well into the large piles and place the explosive charge in the middle, but had to leave wire trailing behind to act as an antenna receiver.

With sweat rolling down his cheeks as the sounds from the cheering Russians were getting louder, Tad focused on timing. Everything depended on trapping Stalin at exactly the right point or else the whole thing came apart. His chest tightened as the seconds ticked by one excruciating second at a time, but he closed his eyes and willed himself to slow his breathes and calm himself. Before Tad even realized it that familiar sensation rolled over him as things started moving slow motion, and he felt like a spectator watching himself in a play.

Then it started. Racing ahead of the motorcade, the two BA-10 armored cars moved up the roadway a little too quickly. Tad couldn't believe his luck. The orderly lines of Russian soldiers had completely degenerated as they too began to move to see if they could get a glimpse of the great man as he passed before them. The emotion in the air was infectious as these soldiers starting cheering and bunching together, forcing the motorcade to move even more slowly.

The rest of the motorcade lingered behind as a result and before he had a chance to think about it, he saw his opening flipped the plastic guard over the arm button and pushed the transmit lever. Two seconds passed and then a massive *kaboom* thundered from below, one eruption after another from one end of the intersection to the other. The explosions reverberated through the enclosed area. Smoke and plaster dust covered the entire block. There was pandemonium on the street as the shock of what was happening stunned all present.

Within seconds he could see the two blasts at the front end of the intersection had blasted huge piles of brick and concrete onto the roadway. The motorcade slammed on the breaks and crashed into one another as they drove into the dust. Unfortunately, the blasts at the backend of the procession weren't timed quick enough to prevent the two other armored cars from making it into the kill box. The BA-10's were unharmed, but all around the blast area dozens of bodies littered the road. Wounded survivors and frightened soldiers created pandemonium.

Surveying the scene, Tad watched as the Soviet seized Mercedes tried desperately to move. He knew they were trapped and prayed Stefan and Aleksandra could do their magic. He pulled the flare gun and fired into the sky. Phase two was about to begin. Within seconds of vacating the second floor, he went to his pushcart, hidden under debris at the base of the stairs, and unveiled the false bottom, prepared to apply the coup de grace.

Meanwhile, Stefan had all in readiness as he watched with his binoculars and smiled. He counted one, two, three, four explosions and laughed aloud as he saw the chaos in the Soviet ranks. Next, the flare fired off into the sky, signaling the kill box was secure and to start the fire plan as arranged. He took a moment to center his mass and then shifted the mortar to its firing position. He grabbed a high-explosive round and added to the chaos.

He saw hundreds of Red Army soldiers run towards the trapped motorcade and try desperately to dig through it to save Stalin. Without warning, Stefan's shot soared overhead and exploded right into the middle of the kill box. Although the Pole missed hitting a limo directly, six men trying to dig out the third car were caught in the open and hit from behind. Deadly steel shards laced the sides of the armored limo but did no direct damage.

Before the first round had even landed, Stefan fired again, slightly farther up the column, trying to box them in ever closer. The round landed next to an engineer squad trying to move already wounded comrades out of the way. Stefan kept firing as he walked his rounds from front to back and froze the terrified soldiers and civilians in their tracks. The old Pole kept telling himself he shouldn't be enjoying this so much, but if his life ended moments from then, as he expected, he wanted to laugh one more time. He shouted gloriously loud, "Die you bastards, die!"

Inside the cars, sheer terror reigned, as Stalin and the other VIPS were trapped in crossfire. Stalin went from feeling exhilarated and confident to white with fear. Bracing his good hand around an armrest, he began shouting at the driver to move the car. Before Stalin knew what happened, he was violently slammed forward when the car behind his plowed into the backside of the Soviet leader's car, pinning them against a wall of concrete and debris. He was raging as he and his two security agents repeatedly slammed against the door to no avail. The front grill of the fifth limo had become stuck against the side of Stalin's car, trapping the Soviet leader on both sides.

After about twenty seconds, the thought came to Stalin that he really might not make it through the attempt. All around him he could hear the shrieks from wounded. This was not some film, but real. For a man who had exercised absolute rule over an entire nation for more than twenty years, to suddenly find hinself utterly powerless was too much to bear. He kept screaming for someone to get him out. He started to cry out in terror and threatened the lives of the NKVD men desperately trying to force doors or break the glass.

The whole time explosions rocked the car, shattered glass, and the sounds of firing reverberated throughout the concrete canyon. Both security forces and army veterans searched for the source of the mortar barrage, but couldn't pinpoint the hiding spot. Frantically, all the men could do was try to dig through the rubble a best as they could to get to Comrade Stalin and save him before the fascists finally killed him.

Meanwhile, the third act was about to unfold as Aleksandra tried to get a proper shot off with her anti-tank rifle. The three of them had agreed that the most likely spot for Stalin to be placed was the third car, in the middle of the pack. It took all her power to restrain herself from shooting until she had the perfect shot Tad insisted she wait for. He had been right about everything else and with the chaos she saw below, the leader of this bold enterprise proved correct, yet again. Looking through her sniper scope, she could tell her patience was about to pay off.

Wind began to blow away some of the smoke and dust, at least enough for her to see the cars and the mass of frightened men trapped under Stefan's shells. Seizing the moment and remembering her father's words, she took a deep breath, lined up her target, and slowly squeezed the trigger. She aimed for the back window near the gas tank. In an instant she was rewarded for her accuracy as the 12.7 mm round with a hollowed core of solid tungsten tore through the protected, bulletproof back window and entered the backseat with an explosion of sound.

Before the Foreign Secretary of the Soviet Union, Vyacheslav Molotov realized that the round seared off his arm at the shoulder, the anti-tank round pierced the gas tank causing a catastrophic explosion, lifting the entire limo into the air and then falling back to earth, landing on top of men already wounded in the initial blast.

With tears of joy obscuring her vision, Aleksandra tried to line up her next shot and prayed it no longer mattered, that the man responsible for the second rape of Poland was dead and would harm no more. Shaking her head she said to herself, *now is not the time. Concentrate, kill them all.* She knew she had maybe one or two more shots before they started reacting.

She scanned the mayhem below, but couldn't make out the back end of the kill box because of smoke, so she lined up on the next car she saw. It was the second limo. She calmly took another shot and hit the vehicle, but was forced to fire again before she knew that the car was destroyed.

Across the Spree River, Stefan reached for one of the special VT rounds when he heard the explosion and saw the limo lift up into the air. *Yes, we did it! We got the bastards trapped like dogs.* Although he couldn't see through the smoke, he knew it was time. He could envision the men in those cars assuming they were safe because of the armored protection of the special Mercedes limousines, but seeing one go up in flames, Stefan figured they must be pouring out of the cars.

He adjusted the range of the mortar then let fly one of the rounds and prayed it worked as the English claimed it would. He only wished he could see his handy work with his own eyes. Within seconds of firing his first around, another was dropped into the firing tube.

Meanwhile, five hundred yards away, Red Army soldiers were clamoring up and over the concrete embankments trying to escape the mayhem, while others were trying to get into the chaos to rescue Comrade Stalin.

The men in front heard the swoosh of mortar and tried to take cover, but it was too late. The two-pound warhead was on its downward arc when its electronic fuse triggered the explosion at about twenty-five feet above the heads of the Russian forces. In an instant, cries from dozens filled the air as the shotgun like effect of the proximity fuse round blasted from above in an effect that these men had never experienced. Two more rounds appeared overhead, freezing the men as they searched for overhead protection ignoring the mission to save their leader.

Finally, some enterprising Red Army Major was smart enough to call divisional headquarters for support, armor, anything. The divisional air officer, a Lieutenant Colonel had an idea and picked up the phone.

Within thirty seconds, orders were flashed to security forces throughout the city of a major attack by fascist guerillas. Red Army soldiers by the thousands began to move. More importantly, the air cover flying above Berlin became alerted. Once the train carrying Stalin reached the station, the Soviet escort fighters flew at high altitude in a loose formation, so the air regiment of Lagg and Yak fighters were oblivious to the ambush below.

The moment they received word of the mortar attack, the entire regiment angled the nose of their fighters down and flew for the treetops. The smoke and flames erupting four hundred yards away from the rail station became clear and so they broke formation and began searching for the source of fire.

Just as Stefan loosed his second to last VT round he looked up as he heard the roar of piston engines.

A sharp-eyed veteran pilot in a Yak-9 fighter caught sight of a small puff of smoke across the Spree near the destroyed bridge. The pilot waggled his wings and called for backup. He led a flight of six fighters with guns blazing at the burned out German tanks where the fire seemed to be coming from.

Stefan cursed as they never considered that the damn Russians would come at them from the air. Without bothering to grab his mortar, he moved and ran for all he was worth towards the tree line and cover from the attacking planes. Flame erupted from the wings of the fighters and caused the landscape to explode with fury. He was nearly there when he got clipped through the upper arm. The large caliber 12.7 mm bullets nearly cleaved it off at the bicep. The hit caused him to wheel forward and fall face first in the grass, ten feet away from the safety of the trees.

The rear plane saw him and perfectly lined up his target and struck Stefan in three places. He was thrown back down as a chest wound killed him instantly. The last thing the Polish freedom fighter ever heard was the roar of engines and the sound of a city in chaos. As he closed his eyes for the last time, he tasted blood gurgling in his mouth and choked. His last coherent thought of the green fields of his childhood farm brought a smile to his face.

Tad couldn't believe how fast everything happened. It seemed but seconds before he had blown the charges and set the ambush in motion. He caught himself staring up at the condemned apartment building across the street where Aleksandra was sited. The pandemonium was beyond belief. There must have been five hundred men trapped in the intersection.

With Stefan's mortar barrage spraying death from above, it was unlike anything he had ever experienced. The excitement built as he saw the flash from across the street and then heard the tremendous roar from the catastrophic hit of the anti-tank rifle. Within moments another limo went up in flames. Everything was going their way until he heard the planes.

Across the street, Aleksandra turned to see the diving planes across the river and knew they didn't have much time. Some Red Army soldiers began popping smoke grenades to give cover. They knew that a sniper was out there and this caused Aleksandra to hesitate before firing again. Then an explosion off to her right and one floor below her told her that those BA-10's figured out where the firing was coming from. *Damn.*

Tad heard the guns firing and knew there were still a couple of cars still unharmed. He was back above ground, five storefronts down from his original spot where he had launched the ambush. Hiding in the ruins of a hat shop, he pulled out the reliable German panzerfaust rocket launcher and decided to expose himself to draw fire away from Aleksandra.

He was using a newer version of the powerful German weapon, but was at the extreme range, nearly sixty yards. Looking down at the movement of Russian security forces, he knew it would be impossible to get closer so he decided to take the long shot and hope for the best.

The two BA-10's were firing their 37mm canons at Aleksandra, so Tad carefully lined up the Soviet vehicle that was doing the most firing. He aimed his rocket launcher and was rewarded as the hollow-charged anti-tank round slammed right into the left side armored car. The round easily tore through the thin, steel sides of the Russian vehicle and exited out the other side. The resulting stream of molten plasma caused the rounds inside to cook off and eviscerate three soldiers crouched behind the BA-10 for cover as the armored car ripped apart.

The explosion of the first vehicle jolted the second BA-10 and shrapnel from the explosion blew into the firing ports of the armored car. It crashed into a concrete mound on the far end of the street, immobilizing it. Aleksandra used the time to race down the hallway to a secondary firing position, approximately twenty feet closer to the first limo that suddenly became exposed as the driver tried to drive over the debris mound to the right, but got stuck halfway there.

She saw the occupants emptying out of the vehicle and took the shot. Her shot hit the exposed undercarriage and blew through the interior of the Mercedes and shredded the car. The last man trying to get out was Marshal Konev. Shrapnel shredded his lower extremities and tore off his left hand, leaving him trapped in the burning car.

By that time, Red Air Force fighters had silenced Stefan's mortar so soldiers began moving. Nearly two squads of NKVD security units braved the fire above and made it to Comrade Stalin's car. Tad watched as the first three limos exploded. He then drew fire as soldiers opened up on him. Desperate to finish the job, he crawled as fast as he could to the next room. Automatic weapon fire erupted above him as security units struggled to regain control of the situation.

Aleksandra saw what happened to the BA-10's that were firing on her and thought, *thank you Tad, thank you.* Knowing the chances of escape were almost impossible, she was determined to get those last two cars. She climbed higher in the bombed-out apartment complex. The whole fifth floor erupted as the Soviets wildly sprayed automatic fire into the building trying to cover the last two cars.

Tad found safety behind an old steel radiator and looked out at the street. He saw men piling around the fourth car, trying to push the limo free of the concrete mound where it was trapped. Seeing everyone focusing on the fourth Mercedes, Tad cursed to himself that the bastard must be there. *He's right the hell there, how could we have missed him.*

He heard explosions from below as Russians were throwing grenades trying to blast their way into the building where Tad hid. He knew the last panzerfaust round he had was all that was left if Aleksandra couldn't get the last shots in. He was too far away to get a guaranteed hit, but he knew that if he tried to get closer, he was a dead man. So he stuck his head above the windowpane and looked across at the NKVD troops that had surrounded and nearly freed the two cars.

Desperately, he grabbed the rocket launcher, braved the return fire landing all around him, took aim and fired. Just as he fired the shot at least a half a dozen rounds from soldiers below the window pummeled his body. The rocket soared towards Stalin's car, but missed. Stalin's driver had hit the gas just as the troops made one last tremendous push that separated the two cars. Tad's rocket sailed through the air and landed squarely on top of the last Mercedes whose occupants had long since exited the vehicle. The limo explode as the powerful anti-tank round blew the car into deadly shrapnel that sliced open more than ten soldiers who had just freed Stalin's car.

Inside, Stalin was screaming for all he was worth. His heart was pounding and the last explosion caused him to lose control of his bodily function and he felt urine dripping down his leg. Between the noise of explosions, shrieks from the wounded, and fire from all sides, the Soviet leader became completely undone. He began to convulse in the back and foam appeared on his mouth like some rabid dog.

Aleksandra had just finished climbing the stairs when she heard the big explosion from the anti-tank rocket. She moved to an opening in the wall and saw the remains of the fourth limo. All around the intersection, bodies of the dead and wounded littered the street. She assumed Tad must have seen she was in trouble and tried to take out the last car. She saw movement as the last limo moved at high speed towards a small section of debris that engineers had bravely opened up during all the confusion.

The NKVD driver saw the soldiers jumping up and down and waving him towards the last chance to safety. Pushing the accelerator to the floor, he drove the powerful German car towards the rubble to his front.

Moving quickly herself, Aleksandra pulled out her rifle and fired but her shot went wild as the sounds of approaching planes shocked her senses. The planes must have been radioed to hit the building overlooking the intersection. One flight after another opened up with heavy caliber machine gun rounds and small automatic cannons. The entire structure seemed to come apart before her eyes. Plaster, wood, concrete exploded all around her.

She no longer concerned herself with hitting the last limo, as she curled up into a ball and cried for her father as her entire world seemed to explode. She was choking on the dust when she was hit. Her leg shattered, sending her careening across the room. Then more planes moved on the attack. Before she could capture a last coherent thought, a 20mm round punched through the thin walls of the apartment complex striking the back of her head. All that was left was part of her torso and her prized rifle.

Across the street Red Army soldiers, hastily formed into assault squads, crashed into the hat shop where Tad made his last stand. An experienced sergeant led the way. Still unsure how many were involved in the ambush, he carefully made his way into the gutted room and found the Polish leader's body. Looking down at the still body on the ground, the Russian wasn't surprised to see blond hair and blue eyes with Germanic features. Furious after losing three men in his squad to the fascist bastards, he wheeled and kicked the body hard.

Crouching next to the body, he quickly looked for any evidence of who perpetrated the crime. Expecting to see some type of SS tattoo, he nearly toppled over when he ripped open Tad's tunic. Sewn on his undershirt, bloody and torn, was a small flag. It was the flag of Poland and written in Russian were the words, *'til our last breaths...Freedom.*

Chapter Twenty Four

July 16, 1945, 9:05 a.m.

High above Brandenburg, Germany

A lone British C-54 Constellation transport plane lumbered along, flying lazy eights high in the clouds on the east side of the Elbe River, near Brandenburg. Unlike most transport planes designed to carry heavy loads, this particular plane was in the air at this moment for a very different purpose. British intelligence had mastered the art of SIGNIT, or signal intelligence, during the war and scored numerous victories over their German opponents. The breaking of the Enigma code was but one of many key battles won over the invisible airwaves.

This C-54 was a specially modified plane designed purposely to capture radio signals while in flight. The development of an airborne cipher was important because ground stations often were unable to capture complete transmissions due to atmospheric conditions, line of sight, etcetera. But, by placing sensitive communications equipment on an airborne platform, SIGNIT took a giant step forward.

Flight Argus 101 was tasked with listening to any and all Soviet transmissions coming out of Berlin between the hours of six a.m. and eleven a.m. Flight Commander Arthur Connelly was told, point blank, by the wing commander to break radio silence and report any unusual or important open transmissions immediately to ground control. When Commander Connelly asked if he was listening for any specific messages or any particular frequencies, all he was told by his commander was that he would, bloody well know it, when he heard it.

Not used to getting such cryptic commands, Commander Connelly nonetheless boarded his plane and reached the appropriate altitude and map coordinates right on time, without any mishap or delay.

After about three hours of listening to the typical Soviet chatter over the radio, Connelly's team began picking some open transmissions referring to activity around the Gorlitzer train station in the heart of Berlin. He had been briefed on the arrival schedule of the Soviet leader and tuned his communication equipment to listen to known NKVD frequencies and to the usual Red Army bandwidths. So far everything was going smoothly and he was getting good signals when suddenly one of his crew, a young chap by the name of Miles, franticly waved his hand and motioned for Connelly to come to his radio unit.

The boy's eyes were wide in amazement, as if he couldn't believe what he had just heard. Not wanting to miss anything, Connelly plugged his own headset into the dual port. Within seconds his eyes went wide as Miles stumbled onto some Red Army small unit, probably a battalion radio set. The man was screaming that they were under attack, Comrade Stalin's motorcade was under fire and several cars had already been destroyed.

Quickly deducing why his high-value plane was on this mission, somebody knew something or else his flight wouldn't be hovering that close to Berlin. Another of his crew picked up transmissions from Red Air Force signals, ordering planes to converge on Berlin and to close the air space to all traffic. He took his headset and in a barely restrained voice said, "Inform ground control to send up fighter cover across sector seven to protect our movement back into Allied airspace. Everyone make sure you are getting every bloody word. We will continue listening as best that we can until we are out of range. Understood?"

The next thing everyone heard was Miles blurt out, "All Christ, the big bugger is dead. They just said it over the air sir, Stalin's entire motorcade has been wiped out."

Looking grave, Connelly knew this was exactly what his superior wanted to hear, so he contacted ground control and informed them of unconfirmed reports that the Soviet leader's motorcade had come under fire and was destroyed. All he could think was he had better get his crew back to safety because the Red Air Force would probably be looking to shoot first and ask questions later. The Royal Air Force Commander knew as he felt the plane bank to the left, there was going to be bloody hell to pay somewhere. He hoped it was a coincidence that his bird was there that day and not by design. Because, if it was, God knew what would follow.

July 16, 1945, 9:30 a.m.

Warsaw, Poland

Her name was Maria Lipski and she was known for the special, homemade jelly filled pastries she often brought to the newly established Warsaw Police Barracks in the heart of the city. Maria's brother had been captured by the communists in 1939 and rather than end up in some filthy re-education camp, Joseph became a communist party member and fought against the Germans until severely wounded outside of Vilnius, Lithuania in 1944. During his rehabilitation, he was posted as an aide to a rising Polish party member who eventually became a district police commander under the newly constituted authority of the Lublin Poles in Warsaw.

Maria, on the other hand, spent the previous six years thinking her only brother had died and did everything she could to care for their elderly parents, both of whom later died during the Warsaw uprising in 1944. Once her brother came home from the dead, they embraced and swore never to leave one another again. Joseph was horrified to find out the conditions of his childhood home and city he so loved. His own wartime experiences were difficult to talk about, but when his sister informed him of her own wartime role in the Polish Home Army, he was first shocked and then more proud of her then he ever thought possible.

She told him she had joined an active underground AK cell and provided intelligence on the Nazi animals that occupied Warsaw and fought during the Uprising. Later, her hatred of the Russians for their stab in the back and absolute devotion to the cause of Polish independence led her to rejoin the outlawed Underground Polish Army. She told the story to her brother and when he realized the communists had been almost as responsible for his parents' deaths as were the Germans, he agreed to help and worked as an AK agent within the communist dominated police barracks.

At least twice a week, Maria graced the halls of the Police barracks and doled out her precious pastries to many of the new rulers of Poland. Most rank and file members, as well those of higher rank, knew her by name. More than once, men had come to blows over possession of the last jellyroll left in the box. So on that fine morning, Maria found herself with several large parcels sitting beside her at one of the few operational bakery and cafés left in the city.

She drank her coffee, nervously picked at some sweet bread, and listened with others to the British BBC radio station. She kept furtively looking around at every passing face as she tried desperately to maintain her composure and calm her nerves.

Looking at her watch yet again she anxiously waited for the newsbreak to start and finish with the American Jazz hour that was currently being played. Just as she was pouring some sugar into yet another cup of coffee, the tapping noise of a special bulletin broke into the Louis Armstrong song currently being played.

She held her breath and listened as the English voice spoke.

"This just in to the newsroom, Josef Stalin, leader of the Soviet Union, appears to have been assassinated by fanatical Nazi partisans in the heart of Berlin. Early reports indicate that his motorcade came under intense fire and in the ensuing battle, the entire motorcade was destroyed. The BBC is currently trying to confirm this information and more should be available at the next newsbreak in fifteen minutes. Once again, Josef Stalin is feared dead at the hands of German extremists. More to follow shortly. Thank you."

Maria didn't hear the last few seconds of the broadcast and didn't let out cheers like many of the other patrons. Instead, she calmly picked up her parcels and headed to the police station.

Within ten minutes she arrived at the guardhouse protecting the barracks and rather than delivering the parcels herself, she left them with the guard detail who knew better than to open boxes intended for their superiors. Not wanting to take the chance, Maria made sure to leave a small box with a few juicy treats for the guard detail, so they wouldn't be tempted to open the parcels. Maria told them she had to get home quickly to care for her ailing brother whose wound was acting up and needed her attention, but didn't want to disappoint the men who came to look forward to her little treats.

Maria was several blocks away when the three parcels of goodies were delivered. Her face full of resignation and without a hint of guilt, she barely turned to look when three huge explosions went off one after another. Crowds on the street instantly went to ground or turned to see the black smoke coming from the direction of the Police Barracks.

All three parcels had false bottoms that hid powerful mercury based explosives connected to a timer. Within thirty seconds of one another, the head of the Warsaw Police District, his deputy, and the documents room where all the secret files on Polish Home Army members were kept, were destroyed by the work of one woman.

As she heard the sirens from police cars and fire trucks rush past her down the street to the bombing, Maria Lipski thought, *that was for momma and papa, you bastards.* She then melted into the crowd and began her journey underground, along with her brother, proud to have struck the first blow in the third battle of Warsaw.

July 16th, 10:00 a.m.

Poznan, Poland

The city of Poznan was still in a shambles after having been nearly destroyed by attacking Red Army forces six months before. Hitler had declared Poznan as one of several fortress cities to be defended to the last bullet. Poznan had been an important industrial and communication center in pre-war Poland and was used extensively by the Germans and later the Soviets to support their huge armies. Now the Russians made use of the extensive logistic center where five key railroads converged and a key east-west highway led directly into the heart of Germany.

Poznan not only supported the drive on Berlin, but also now was a key supply point for Soviet occupation forces in Western Poland and into Germany. Everything from Spam to aviation fuel to boots was piled up in huge cantonments throughout the city. Along with the supply units, a rather sizable force of Red Army units set up camp on the outskirts of town. Poznan was a stoutly defended place, essential to the control of both Poland and Germany and thus made one hell of a target.

Polish Home Army District commander, Alexander Komorowski, was determined to make the Soviets feel the sting from the new AK or Home Army. Alexander had been active in the underground ever since the fall of Warsaw nearly six years ago. He had risen steadily in the ranks and commanded an assault battalion during the uprising in 1944. After separating into small cells to recuperate and rearm, and waiting for months to strike back, the moment was now upon them.

He had been infiltrating men and women into Poznan for the past three months, accumulating mountains of intelligence and identifying where the Russians and their Polish lackeys were most vulnerable. Reluctantly, Alexander came to agree with General Anders new tactics, although the idea of staying dormant for so long had been increasingly grating on him and his men. However, once word reached him of the decision by the exiled London government to revolt, he worked himself to the point of near exhaustion.

Pacing inside an underground bunker beneath a half destroyed barn, Komorowski realized the most difficult thing of attaining higher command was the fact that he had to wait in a bunker while his men went out and did the fighting. After stubbing out and lighting yet another cigarette, all things being equal, he thought he'd rather be shot at than stuck in some airless bunker waiting next to the radio.

Meanwhile, inside Poznan, Alexander had separated his command into three dozen small sabotage detachments, six platoon size assault units and two companies of about a hundred men each roaming the countryside, waiting to attack targets of opportunity. He kept two larger more heavily armed task forces hidden in the countryside for the moment. Once the Russians reacted, he would deploy the two heavier detachments as needed.

Within thirty minutes of the BBC announcement, the city of Poznan began to lite up like a Christmas tree. Recently rebuilt railroad and highway bridges exploded in dozens of places as Home Army soldiers attacked in a widespread pattern around the city. In one location, a detachment of Poles in a fishing boat placed underwater explosives around a key railroad support beam. The Pole in charge of the operation stayed behind to detonate the charge and timed it perfectly, just as a large military troop train began to cross the river, sending the train with an entire regiment of armored vehicles and its men careening into the water below.

Elsewhere in the city, mines placed along MSR's or military supply routes began to go off. Demolition teams detonated explosives at more than two dozen major intersections throughout the city and caused absolute mayhem, bringing traffic to a halt within the city. With remarkable timing, dozens of small-scale ambushes erupted against the stopped military traffic. Snipers set up shop and began shooting anyone wearing the red star of the Soviet armed forces. Then, like ghosts, the brave Poles melted back into the city, leaving the shocked Red Army units exasperated and angry.

One special assault platoon led by a pre-war employee of the city's electric company in Poznan infiltrated into the main operations center. With little difficulty, he successfully sabotaged the grids on the main board and caused instant blackouts throughout the city. As it turned out, the former electrical engineer was right when he convinced the District Commander it would be easier to damage the electric generators from the inside rather than trying to attack the well-defended electric plants in a direct assault.

Not only were power lines overloading and blowing out throughout the city, but the main turbines running on diesel fuel overheated and caused permanent damage to the inner workings of the massive generators needed to light the city. The occupiers of Poland would have to try and catch Poles in the dark and, as the Germans could tell them, the Polish Home Army owned the night.

More explosions resounded through the city as two military police barracks were hit by car bombs that nearly brought down one entire structure, causing tremendous damage and injuring more than a hundred policemen. Later, in a bold move, Alexander used two platoons to hit the tank farms brimming with diesel and aviation fuel outside of the city. Supported by a captured German 88mm anti-tank gun, Polish gunners began firing at gas pipelines and huge storage tanks and the men were quickly rewarded with thunderous explosions and towering clouds of black smoke.

In the resulting chaos, the rest of the Poles moved in close under the cover of the mayhem created by the raging fire and attacked fuel trucks, supply units, and anything that could be used to repair the damage. The men watched as wind began to fuel the fire and create a massive blaze that burned for two days.

Alexander wasn't through yet. He made a special point of infiltrating into the city special political action hit squads aimed at taking out as many collaborators and Polish communists as possible. In a brilliantly planned sub-operation, individual houses were stormed, Polish communists acting on orders from Moscow, like the new chief of police who was shot in front of his wife in the middle of his living room, were targeted for liquidation by the AK. Party headquarters in the middle of town was fire bombed.

Any Poles who were known to have worked with the Russians against brother Poles were put to the knife. One particular operation deserved special notice. The NKVD headquarters in Poznan was not huge, but played an important role in coordinating the consolidation of the communist hold on the populace. Rather than simply blowing the place apart, Polish soldiers fought their way into the building and captured seven Soviet security officers, including one full Colonel and shot seventeen others, along with a dozen Poles found working inside the building. Although they lost half a dozen men, they had gained hostages to be used later to bargain for brother AK members.

Finally, Alexander used long-range, stolen Red Army 82mm mortars to attack concentrations of Soviet units looking to counter-attack his forces. Poles along the heights outside the city poured consistent fire onto crossroads and troop barracks to cover the withdrawal of Home Army forces. Unlike in 1944, General Anders refused to get drawn into a city fight. Instead, his forces would collect new weapons from their successful attacks and set up roving ambushes throughout the countryside. Poznan was on fire, many hundreds dead or wounded, but more importantly, the occupiers of Poznan were reminded that the Home Army was still very much alive and hitting back with a vengeance.

Ten Miles North of Warsaw, 1:00 p.m.

After a long night spent in yet another farmhouse, General Anders, commander of all Polish Home Army forces, sat in a darkened bunker, recently prepared for his arrival, and listened as one aide after another came in a rush into his office and read off yet another attack had gone through. To his left, an aide marked green, blue or red on the map to signify actions that either had been complete successes, partial ones, or failures. He had been fixated at the map board all morning and stopped counting once the green stickers reached over two hundred.

All he could think was that each one of those little markers represented his men, fighting on the field of battle yet again to free their native homeland. He tried very hard to maintain a sense of calm for the sake of his young command group, but inside he was brimming with pride and saw the plan developing just as he had imagined.

Each green sticker signified an ammo dump, a police barracks, or a rail yard. His men had taken casualties, but the Home Army struck a major psychological blow against the occupiers of their homeland. God, how he hated the Russians, perhaps even more than he despised Germans. Either way, blood was being spilled throughout the whole of Poland and instead of slugging it out with regular Red Army forces, his men would withdraw and live to fight again. *This will be our way now, until the day I command a real army again.*

Anders took particular pleasure in reading reports of his special action forces who had dealt a severe blow to those Polish communists in bed with the Russians. More than fifty local party bosses and district commanders shot, newly established police forces under siege in two dozen major cities, and in Krakow and Lodz, his AK units actually kidnapped the local communist leaders and planned to hold a trial. Once the London government in exile gave him a free hand to do what was necessary against brother Poles, he decided to lop off, in one fell swoop, as many of the Lublin Poles as possible. At a minimum, he would show the rest of Poland that anyone who gets in bed with Moscow is liable to have his throat slashed or home firebombed.

His attacks against transportation and communication centers would continue unabated throughout the whole campaign. The more Russians spent guarding roads, bridges, telephone exchanges and the like, the less available to hunt his AK fighters. Anders knew Russians and understood how they fought, and why they often won. In a set piece battle, no one was a more dangerous enemy than Russians, as the Germans found out to their dismay. No, Anders knew he could ultimately never win in the end against the Russians, but not losing might just be enough.

As long as he didn't try to hold cities or any permanent defenses, then they had the advantage. Thanks to the British, they had thousands of powerful anti-tank weapons. *We can use hit-and-run tactics, and really hurt them on fields of our choosing. I just have to restrain myself from engaging in anything larger than battalion size operations.* The Soviets would soon start to react and the reprisals would probably be horrific. *But for each Pole shot, we will in turn keep fighting until the West comes around.*

Wiping his sweating brow, he poured himself a cup of cool tea and couldn't help but feel that, with that bastard Stalin dead, his boys might actually be able to pull off the unthinkable. Excited, Anders could feel the blood lust coursing through his veins and thought that Mikolajczyk in London was right, either strike while they were organized and had weapons or prepare to live as slaves for generations to come. Answering his own silent question, Anders shook his head from side-to-side and said aloud, "Never."

Chapter Twenty Five

July 16th, 1:30 p.m.

Berlin, Red Army Headquarters

The men in the room were still shaken at what had transpired. No one, in their wildest imagination, ever could have conceived that someone would actually try to assassinate Stalin. As the Red Army's most successful battlefield commander of the war and senior officer present, Marshal Georgii Konstantinovich Zhukov decided it was time for the Red Army to decisively take charge.

Reports of Stalin's death were being reported all over the airwaves by the West. Rumors had spread like wildfire throughout the city, describing the massacre of Red Army troops trying to defend Stalin.

Between the damn NKVD and Zhukov's own troops, what was left of Berlin was being ransacked in retaliation for this morning's event. Just as he was starting to bring order to the chaos in Berlin, Zhukov was informed of a series of coordinated attacks throughout the length of Poland against Red Army and Polish government forces by the Polish Home Army. The same Home Army the damn Chekists said were wiped out and posed no threat to his troops. The bastards who apparently took part in the attack on Comrade Stalin, by all accounts, were dead, but all of them were wearing the flag of Poland on their chest.

Zhukov was no intelligence officer, but with the day's countrywide uprising, he quickly put two and two together. *Fucking Poles. Who would have thought they would have the balls for it?*

Looking at the scared expressions around the room, everyone was probably thinking the same thing. *What will he do when he awakes? Who will pay for this crime?* Zhukov was a man who feared nothing, not Germans, not Poles, not even Stalin, himself, but the others were about to wet themselves. In Zhukov's mind what happened in Berlin was a political act, but what was happening to their rear in Poland was all military and had to be dealt with quickly. So, he convened the meeting of his staff and those from Stalin's staff who survived the attack.

Zhukov couldn't help but be amused that the person who looked the worst in the room was none other than the little bastard who masterminded the purge of the Red Army in 1937, Beria, head of Soviet security forces. It probably didn't escape his attention that with the NKVD tasked with security, the day's events hardly looked promising for his future within the party, let alone a future that included breathing.

Good, the little bastard.

Pounding his powerful fists on the finished oak conference table, he called the meeting to order and said, "Our dear leader, Comrade Stalin, was nearly assassinated today. Comrade Molotov was murdered as was one of our brother officers, Marshal Konev, plus hundreds more of our brother soldiers were either killed or wounded in this cowardly attack. It is up to us to restore security and punish the guilty for their crimes."

Turning to Stalin's personal physician, Zhukov asked, "Well Doctor, how is the General Secretary doing? Can he be moved and how quickly?"

Dr. Svedlev had been attending to his patient for quite some time and was always amazed at Stalin's constitution for a man his age.

Actually, considering the amazing pressures on the man, the way he drank and ate, Svedlev was amazed that the man was still alive and hadn't already succumbed to a stroke or heart attack.

Outwardly nervous as all eyes turned to him and with a less then confident voice, he answered, "Comrades, I must admit that when I first saw him, I feared the worse, but he is stable, sedated, and has been sleeping comfortably for the past two hours. Although he did not sustain any direct physical injury other than minor cuts and bruises as a result of this treacherous attack, Comrade Stalin was brought to me in a state of complete shock with a dangerously high blood pressure and racing pulse rate. Readings this elevated can result in stroke in a man half his age.

"I recommend complete bed rest and an absolute minimum of stress until he sufficiently recovers. Given time to recuperate, he will physically recover just fine, but the mental and emotional trauma from this attack will likely cause great difficulties." *Talk about stating the obvious, when Stalin wakes God knows who will be left standing.*

Zhukov had been told the all-powerful leader of the Soviet people was stark raving mad once he was pulled from the shattered Mercedes. According to the Red Army doctors who first treated him on the scene, Stalin was screaming incoherently, foaming at the mouth, and smelled of urine. Zhukov knew memories of such things never leave a man, and a man like Stalin needed no more dark thoughts to burden his soul. The commander of the Red Army could only imagine the bloodshed that would follow in the days ahead.

Regardless, Zhukov no longer believed it was safe anywhere in, but transport through Poland was out because of the uprising. With Stalin completely out of touch for the immediate future, the ship of State was, for all intents and purposes, rudderless. No matter who was behind what happened that day, be it Poles, Germans, or even the West, strong measures must be taken, so he gave the orders.

With a grim and determined face, Zhukov spoke in his usual direct and blunt manner, "As of this moment, this conference is over. Send the Western leaders home and inform them that Comrade Stalin is very much alive and will call for another conference once things are back to normal. Next, seal all the borders and cut off the air space to Allied planes over all territory currently occupied by the Red Army. We don't know who is involved at this point, so I don't want any goddamn American or British planes taking pictures of what we are doing. Is that understood?

"Next, I want combat spreads and armed patrols throughout all division and corps areas as of this instant. The fucking Poles may have sold their souls to the fascists and may look to hit us here as well. Lastly, prepare the Sixth and Twelfth Rifle Armies for movement against the Poles." He watched as his military staff took proper notes and prepared to act on their orders.

Zhukov sensed that many in the room wondered what was to happen next, but he had already decided what to do with that problem as well. Zhukov may not have feared him, but didn't want to be around him when he woke up. So, he said, "I have decided to transfer Comrade Stalin onto a Red Air Force specially modified bomber and have him transported back to Moscow, along with the rest of his staff, all under the complete protection of the Red Army's security force. I do not believe that he should remain in what could turn into a combat zone at any time. For his safety, I intend to see him back behind the protective shield of the Kremlin's walls. Don't you agree Comrade Beria? Wouldn't you feel more secure, yourself?"

Communist Party Boss Malenkov, who had arrived late and thankfully missed the morning's ambush, suggested, "Although I do not disagree with Marshall Zhukov's advice, I want to add that Comrade Stalin doesn't like to fly and that he would probably feel most disagreeable to such a plan."

The first and only time Stalin had been in a plane was enroute to the 1943 conference of the Big Three in Tehran. Zhukov gruffly responded, "Normally I would respect Comrade Stalin's wishes, but this is a military necessity. Not only will he be out of harm's way, but also he will have access to better health facilities. Now I need to get back to military matters at once, so arrange to move the Chairman immediately while he is sedated and before he knows it he will awake within the Kremlin. Comrade Beria and other ranking Party members will of course be escorting Comrade Stalin back to the Kremlin. Meeting dismissed."

He stared right at Beria as he watched the man's expression. He probably already knew what would await him back in the Kremlin. *Yes, the sooner we announce to the world that Stalin is, in fact alive, the better, and the sooner I deal with these troublesome Poles the better.*

From a purely military point of view, he couldn't be more than a little bit impressed with the tactics used by the assailants. Beria's security forces were so intent on putting on a show for Stalin and protecting him up close, that they were completely caught by surprise. Zhukov thought this was not the first time his men had died in the war by surprise attacks, but in the end, the Red Army would crush whatever German or Polish partisans were behind this attack, plus exterminate the Polish Home Army once and for all.

July 17, 1945, 9:30a.m.

Potsdam, Germany, British Compound

The feel of the morning sun was invigorating and much needed by British agent Michael Gordon, who was just walking out to grab a smoke in the fresh air after an exhausting meeting with the Prime Minister. On the hillside overlooking the circular driveway, Gordon could see about thirty American security personnel and another three dozen heavily armed British military guardsmen in full combat gear securing the area for the expected arrival of the American President.

Gordon was in a rather bad way. The past forty-eight hours had been the most emotional and stressful, let alone physically exhausting, period in his life. No other operation he had ever participated in could ever come close to what he had just come through. The worse part in the whole Greek tragedy was the fact that after all of the preparation, all of the last minute heroics and risks, the bastard was still alive. Tad's team had almost pulled off the impossible, but somehow, that lucky son of a bitch survived and God only knew what would happen. They all died for nothing.

The Prime Minister debriefed him for two hours the previous night, after his harrowing escape and then again that morning. *What the hell did he bloody well want from me?* It had taken every ounce of luck, plus a good deal of posturing in his NKVD uniform to make it back to the British compound. He couldn't figure out what was worse, sweating through each checkpoint he came to or watching the orgy of violence happening all around him. What he saw visited upon the citizens of Berlin would haunt him for some time to come.

Gordon shook his head as he tried to will away the memories of the past two days. He wished he could forget the faces that haunted him the most, but images of Tad, Stefan, and Aleksandra just wouldn't go away. He was consumed with guilt for not having gone to face their final moments with them, and accept their fate as his own. Somehow, he knew no amount of alcohol would wash away the memories. *God help me, but how can I ever go back home and just forget all of this.* He shook his head, sat down on the warm summer grass, lit another cigarette and let the numbness take over.

Inside the British compound, everyone was involved in the hectic, last minute preparations to vacate the premises and begin the journey back home. Both the American and British staffs were more than a bit surprised at the abrupt orders from the Red Army High Command. For all intents and purposes, the Western Allies were given short notice and expected to leave immediately, without any official contact from the Soviet civilian authorities. Even with the obvious security concerns expressed by the cancellation order, the Potsdam conference should have been bigger than one individual leader, but then again, Josef Stalin was no ordinary leader.

Inside the former German occupants' library, Prime Minister Churchill and Foreign Secretary Eden were discussing the situation. Churchill tried to keep a stiff upper in front of his staff, but Eden knew better. Even though the two men were not on the best terms, Churchill needed Eden's counsel now more than ever. Churchill had been nervously playing with his food for the past five minutes that had been laid out in anticipation of meeting the new American President, Truman. In disgust, he threw the fork down and stormed away from the table and looked out the window to see war clouds rising in the East.

Churchill had spent much of the night before debriefing the boy, Gordon, after his harrowing adventures in Berlin. The Prime Minister was always attracted to stories of cloak and dagger and sat enraptured as he made the young man describe each step coming and going and everything in between. His blood ran hot as he watched the son of White Russian refugees sullenly talk about putting that NKVD officer to the knife and taking out the other poor fellow.

Churchill remembered his own days as a young man in a war zone in South Africa, escaping from a prisoner of war camp, moving for days through enemy territory. He was so proud of this young man for doing the Crown proud by going to the Polish team with the last minute change in plans. The Poles actually almost pulled it off. *Who would have bloody well thought that three months ago?*

He then spent the rest of the night with his military staff and foreign policy advisors on how to respond to the uprising. By all reports so far, the Poles have given Ivan more than a bloody nose. That Anders chap hit hard and fast and then seemed to have melted back into where he had been hiding.

From intercepts captured by off-shore listening posts, the Russians hadn't been able to hit back because the Poles seemed to have picked exactly where they wanted to hit the Soviets and then retreated back to their underground positions. *Really, it's the best thing they can do, but we'll see how long that can last once Stalin starts wreaking havoc on the populace to entice them from their assembly positions.* And as expected, the damned cabinet refused to offer public support for the Poles and, instead, urged only sending some private words of encouragement to the London government in exile.

Churchill didn't expect any better from his people, but what he did want was to meet face-to-face with President Truman before he headed back to the States. Truman's staff would only agree to a quick meeting, not a more formal meeting in London or Brussels as he had requested. They didn't want to send the wrong message to the Soviets, he was informed. *The Americans are nervous and they don't know the half of it.*

Seeing movement to his left, a line of cars began turning into the driveway, so he prepared to meet his new, honored guest. All Churchill could think was he hoped the new American President was a man of conviction and would not flinch in the face of adversity. *Because I fear a new and dark chapter is about to befall Europe.*

President Truman and Secretary of State Byrnes sat quietly in their car and barely spoke the whole trip over to the British compound. Byrnes could tell the former Senator from Missouri was feeling anxious and needed to collect his thoughts while they made the short trip. Like their British cousins, President Truman and the rest of his staff spent a very long night at the American villas overlooking the lakefront, trying to make sense of the previous day's events. The shock from the attack on Stalin was quickly followed up by mixed feelings over the countrywide uprising in Poland.

The attempt on Stalin's life and the Polish business clearly changed a great many things. The President was really beginning to come around after reading a dozen position papers from State Department Soviet experts like Chip Bohlen, George Kennan, and others. He was nearly convinced the Russians could not be trusted and that a hard line had to be taken. Truman had been prepared to negotiate in good faith, but also prepared to tell Stalin to his face, just like he did Molotov, that the American people wouldn't put up with any more funny business in Europe.

The President especially didn't care for Molotov. *But now he's dead*, and Truman felt bad, almost guilty in a way, for reading him the riot act.

This man is going to be difficult to control, Byrnes thought. On the one hand he could be simplistic and straight talking as befitting a simple man brought up on a Midwestern farm. However, once he made up his mind, he could be as stubborn as a Missouri mule. There was very little subtlety to the man and in international affairs that could be dangerous. Unfortunately, diplomacy was not black and white, and too often the basic American principles that served the American people so well domestically, often proved a hindrance on the world scene.

Byrnes could read the mixed feelings all over Truman's face. On the one hand, he applauded the brave Polish attacks to free their country, but on the other, he didn't have the political will to publicly support them, especially since Stalin was almost assassinated. Byrnes tried hard to show off a very nonplussed attitude about everything that was happening, but he could already tell it was going to be pretty damn difficult. *Well, hopefully this meeting with Churchill will go off without any difficulties.*

Ten minutes later, the Americans were quickly ushered into the historic German mansion with little fanfare, as they had requested. President Truman straightened his back and, dressed in a dark gray suit sporting his famous spectacles, he confidently reached out and warmly shook the British Prime Minister's hand. Truman looked the man over closely and was in a bit of awe, even though he tried not to give it away. Churchill greeted the new American President in one of his numerous uniforms, this time a British Army officer's tunic and braided hat. The President saw the slightly drooped shoulders, tired eyes, but also recognized that aura that surrounded the British Bulldog, his sense of history and purpose.

Truman was well aware that one of the reasons Roosevelt and Churchill got along so well was the fact that in America, the Roosevelt family was about as royal or upper class as one finds in the United States. Truman had avidly followed the British legend for more than two decades and to finally meet the man was a bit humbling. He tried to remember what Byrnes had beat into his head, Churchill was not just meeting with a small-time Missouri farmer, but the holder of the office of President of the United States.

On the other side of the handshake, Churchill had always put much stock in his ability to size up a man, a skill particularly important for a politician. Looking the American President over with studied eyes, he smiled broadly and shook the man's hand warmly and with real friendship. Taking a brief second or two to look directly into the man's eyes, Churchill saw something there, a flicker like the man deep down had a strength of character that maybe even he didn't realize.

Releasing his grip, Churchill warmly spoke, "Welcome, Mr. President, I want to extend to you the British people's warmest greetings and heartfelt hope that our two great peoples can continue to work together in this grand alliance. Thank you for taking the time to drop in before we are evicted from our current residence. Terrible days, Mr. President, terrible days indeed, but please, let us move to the study and sit for a while."

President Truman smiled back and said, "Mr. Prime Minister, hell of a thing that happened yesterday. I'm damn glad to meet you face-to-face, but sure wish it was the "Big Three" meeting and not just the two of us. I hope that Stalin pulls through and we can get back on track."

Turning to his Secretary of State, Truman was all business and said, "Looks like we got our work cut out for us Jimmie, why don't we get things on the move and see what the Prime Minister has laid out for us."

Secretary Byrnes was a bit surprised at the confident tone in Truman's voice. He said back," Yes Sir, Mr. President, a full plate indeed."

After nearly an hour of finger food, drinks, and finally a light lunch, the four men had a real chance to get a feel for one another. Churchill and Eden had hoped that their old friend, Harry Hopkins, would have been involved. It was clear now that Truman might be a bit nervous, but he sure as hell was his own man. Eden was particularly impressed with the new American Secretary of State. Byrnes' smooth Southern accent and circumspect demeanor gave off the cool air of a real professional, something the two previous Secretaries, Hull and Stettinus, both sorely lacked.

Churchill also listened to Truman's retelling of the story of his first and only run in with Molotov. The Prime Minister slapped his knee when the tough little American basically told the Soviet diplomat to either tell the truth or go to hell. The two also exchanged war stories about their service in the Great War. Churchill believed that someone who had felt the sting of battle could understand the risks and dangers better than someone who never fired a shot in anger.

As host of their first meeting, Churchill took his cue when the staff removed everything except coffee and tea, plus a wonderful variety of German pastries made for the occasion. The Prime Minister took on a very serious pose and leaned towards his guests and said, "Mr. President, I am afraid that we must get into issues that are facing not just our two great peoples, but the fate about to befall much of Europe. I know that you were not party to the arrangements made at the Yalta conference, but by now, you must surely know that we are faced with a growing crisis. A crisis that I judge will be all the greater once Stalin reacts to recent events.

"Ever since those agreements in Yalta were enacted, our Soviet ally has systematically ignored both the spirit and the letter of those agreements. It would seem that the power of the Red Army now commands all that it touches and I fear that an iron curtain has risen throughout Europe and that the power of Communism will grow with such speed as to threaten the fragile peace that our brave armies have so heroically won on the fields of battle."

Churchill watched as the American President listened to each and every word, but not like a man hearing something for the first time. Sensing that maybe Truman was more receptive than Roosevelt's people, he turned it up a notch and spoke with even more gravity in his voice, "Your great President and my dearly departed friend, I am afraid, and was hopelessly manipulated by Stalin to renounce your historic mission, your grand crusade. The American army came to the shores of Europe to break the chains of bondage and tyranny only to find a new, and perhaps even more terrible, system waiting in the wings.

I, for one, can no longer bear to ignore the actions of our Soviet allies and essentially write off the hopes and dreams for freedom of half the continent. What happened yesterday may have been a crime or perhaps a last ditch effort by some intrepid souls to kill the beast, but we must face the truth that Stalin and his system intends to smother any flicker of hope and freedom for untold millions.

"So the great question before us then is, what shall our two great peoples do now that the brave citizens in Poland have taken up arms and are fighting for their very lives against their oppressor? Can we truly look ourselves in the mirror, let alone face our people, if we abdicate our responsibilities to those principles that sustained our peoples for the past six years of struggle and toil.

I tell you, Mr. President, that the rape of Berlin, the savage attacks against civilians in Poland and Hungary, and the utter contempt for our way of life is no different than the Boche in the First World War and, in fact, as bad as the evils of the Nazis and their sick system of brutality. I ask you now, Mr. President, where do you stand? What shall the great American people do in the face of such evil?"

Churchill's booming voice echoed in the room and then the room became deathly quiet. Churchill hadn't intended on speaking so dramatically, but he didn't know when he would get another chance to make an impression with the new American President. He wanted Truman to understand everything that had been sacrificed, both lives and the wealth of their people, would mean nothing if another tyrant ran roughshod over Europe. All Churchill kept thinking was, what was this man made of? Would he have the backbone to stand on principals or would he back down to the decisions made before him by a man so near death that all he had left were ideals for a different world? Looking at the grimace on Truman's face, he thought, *dear God, I pray that I reached the man.*

He tried to maintain the straight poker face that served him so well in years of backroom Senate card play, but Truman was more moved than he had ever thought possible. He heard several of Churchill's speeches over the years, but to be in the man's presence and speaking directly to him was unlike anything he had ever experienced in his life. Deep down he knew the man was right.

Those Red bastards were no better than the Nazis, that's what Ambassador Harriman, Secretary of the Navy Forrestal, and even Jimmie had been saying for the past three months.

We have been placating and tip-toeing around the sons of bitches for so long that we forgot who we were dealing with and what type of godless system that now occupies most of Europe. Truman knew his recent history and remembered Stalin was the same man who signed a treaty with Hitler and stabbed Poland in the back in 1939. The Communists then invaded Finland, retook the Baltic's, stole parts of Romania, and were content to give the Nazis anything to make sure he could do what they wanted in Eastern Europe. *The only reason we are allies in the first place is the fact that Hitler was an even bigger son of a bitch and double-crossed Stalin and attacked first.*

The two biggest bullies on the block fought it out as far as Truman could see, and the biggest and nastiest bully won. Truman was never all that comfortable back when he was a Senator about all the cozying up to the Russians, but went along with it for the sake of party unity. At this very moment, while he and Churchill were eating pastries and drinking tea, somewhere inside Poland, brave men and women were risking their lives for the same damn thing that Americans fought more than a hundred and fifty years ago against the British Crown.

Men were dying so their children could live free. It's that simple and Roosevelt forgot about that. I may not be ready send American boys over the top, but I'll be damned if I'll just step back allow the Poles to think that they are alone.

After what felt like minutes, President Truman had by this time collected his thoughts and in simple words, said, "I know that I don't speak as well as you Mr. Prime Minister, but let me tell you in simple Missouri talk that I've seen my share of blood spilled and I know that there are few things worth dying over. One of those things is the freedom to wake up in the morning and know that you won't be taken away to some concentration camp for saying the wrong damn thing or because your Jewish or some other such nonsense.

"I reckon that I'm not the man that Roosevelt was to the world, but I'll be damned if I'll sit back and allow brave men and women to die in the cause of freedom on my watch and not come out to support them. I'm not promising anything just yet 'cause we still have a hell of a fight left in the Pacific against the Japs, but as of right this moment, the United States will not allow itself to be bought off in Europe for a helping hand in the Pacific. Does that set your mind at ease, Mr. Prime Minister? Is that what you were looking to hear from me?"

Churchill's face was positively exuberant, while Byrnes was as shocked as anyone present. He was worried that Churchill might try something cute to tweak the nose of the Russians, but it looked as if the Prime Minister made more than a small impression. Always one to look at the political angles, Byrnes was afraid this was going too fast, but another part of him was damn proud. *Hell, I didn't think Truman had it in him. Well, one thing is for sure this is going to make some folks happy, some plum nervous, and take a hell of a lot by surprise.*

Byrnes then watched as Churchill stood and excitedly shook the President's hand and got up to pour drinks for everyone. Churchill could barely hide his pleasure at the way the American President responded, better than he had dared hope.

He was equally taken aback when Truman said, "Now, one last thing, Mr. Prime Minister, before we have to leave. According to Jimmie over here, your people really shouldn't have been all that surprised by what's happening over there in Poland. From our understanding, they have been receiving arms and ammo from British sources for the past three months. Is there anything else that your ally needs to know about?"

Truman delivered this little canned, rehearsed speech from memory. Byrnes wanted to give the President something to surprise their hosts and impress them a bit.

Truman didn't realize how impressed Churchill and Eden were after his little speech, however, they were more than a little taken aback. Both thought that the underground weapons pipeline to Warsaw was a complete operational secret.

Churchill smiled broadly and said, "Mr. President, I must confess that wherever you got your information, they would, in fact, be correct. All I will say in our defense is that we never were told of the exact date of the uprising or the scale of it. We were as surprised as anyone else. Understandably, I am a bit embarrassed to have to speak about it like this, but like I said earlier, the British government was prepared to support actions of liberation by freedom fighters within Europe, even at the risk of offending our friends. You have my sincere apologies."

Truman became quite serious when he responded, "I understand Mr. Prime Minister that you probably weren't sure how we would react, and you would have been right three months ago. But please remember that even though we see things along similar lines, I don't abide folks who play around with the truth. I will be your greatest ally and stand with you through thick and thin, but don't ever hold back on us again, Mr. Prime Minister, and expect us to pull your fat out of the fire."

All Foreign Secretary Eden could think was, *tell them now Winston, tell them now. Churchill read between the lines.* But he decided that it was not the right moment to tell the Americans about their part in in the little action in Berlin. At a minimum, he knew he had an ally in the White House. *Now maybe the Russians won't be so quick to try to roll over us.*

He looked over at the American President again, nodded and thought, he was right, the man had more vigor than he looked. Churchill fought back a little grin, it was the glasses, tough to look fierce wearing glasses.

Chapter Twenty Six

July 17, 1945, 10:45 p.m.

Moscow, The Kremlin

A crowd had gathered in the two outer rooms of his Stalin's bedchamber. Everyone from Stalin's daughter, Svetlana, to the staff of Kremlin physicians, to a whole assembly of political, security, and military men held what at first glance appeared as a kind of vigil. Food was prepared and sat largely untouched, vodka was laid out as was customary, but left largely untouched. Hardly a word was spoken, as if they all feared that he could somehow hear everything that was said.

What if he suddenly awoke and stormed out of the room and pointed a finger at the man drinking vodka or stuffing himself with smoked salmon, all while the "Boss" lays injured and suffering. No one wanted to give the impression that they were anything other then paralyzed at the thought of Stalin being incapacitated or worse.

Grown men who had survived the Revolution, the purges, and even Hitler's invasion waited in the antechamber for what was to come. They all knew that physically, Stalin should be fine, but emotionally, they trembled at what may happen. The man often wasn't predictable to begin with, how were they to predict how he would react after what happened the previous day? Some of the men in the room thought, but dared not even whisper the words, that maybe it would be for the best if he just continued to sleep.

NKVD chief, Beria, was beside himself waiting to find out his fate after the debacle in Berlin. He had seen the man order the death of whole families for lesser crimes than his own sins. As head of security, responsibility for what happened could only fall squarely on his shoulders, and the weight of his crimes had caused Beria to hover near the point of a complete nervous breakdown.

Inside Stalin's bedroom, three nurses and two doctors stood guard over his body, measuring all his vitals. They stood ready to act in an instant in case of any signs of distress suddenly appeared. Finally after more than eight hours, their special patient started to show signs of movement. Both doctors moved closer to the bed to watch carefully if Stalin was coming out of his drug-induced sleep.

Light began to flicker into his eyes and he slowly began to feel unfamiliar sensations. His eyes were heavy and didn't seem to want to stay open. It took tremendous effort, he thought, to keep them open for more than a second or two. He was thirsty, that much he was sure. Patients on oxygen often complain of dry mouth and sinuses.

Where am I? Stalin thought to himself. *Why can't I move?* He was trying to turn on his side, but he felt restraints on his legs and wrists. When he was brought in the night before, the sedative from the flight had worn off and he began pulling at his oxygen mask. So for his own safety, the doctor's decided to restrain him for the time being. Starting to get frustrated, Stalin tried to wipe his eyes, but couldn't get to them because a silk wrapping to keep the light out covered his eyes.

Fear gripped him and he began to wonder. *Where am I? Who has me? The Germans…No, impossible…That bastard Beria?* His pulse jumped as he started to have the beginnings of a panic attack. He was starting to remember what happened. *They tried to kill me,* that much he remembered. He could sense movement in the room, but his hearing was still damaged as a result of the attack. An eardrum ruptured from a nearby exploding shell added to his general sense of disorientation. He began to thrash left and right and called out to be let go.

His seventy-year-old body struggled with the restraints and this forced the nurse to call for help. Stalin could barely hear the doctors telling him to calm down. Then he heard a voice off in the distance that reached out to him like a ray of sunshine. "Father, father, it's okay, it's okay calm yourself. You're home and safe. Release his hands."

His daughter reached out for him and uncovered his eyes. Then he saw that he was back in his own room with his daughter. For the first time in ages, he reached out to her and held her like she was a little girl, as he forgot everything. For one brief moment, the relief he felt allowed him to feel human. Stalin held on to the one thing he knew was real. The one person he knew would never betray him. His little Svetlana was there for him. He knew that he was safe. They held on to one another tightly as the doctors and nurses stood back and let the two have a special moment.

Together they all breathed a sigh of relief because they all rightly feared what would have happened if something had gone wrong. For the moment, Stalin was weak, but he was safe and that's all that mattered.

His doctors closed the room to everyone except Stalin's daughter. After some hot tea and bread dipped in honey, Stalin's strength slowly started to return. After the initial shock of awakening from his long sleep faded, he still felt quite disoriented. He felt bruises along his whole body from frantically slamming into the car door, desperately trying to get out of the trapped car. Ironically, the fact he couldn't budge the door almost certainly saved his life. His ear throbbed and his hands noticeably shook. His doctors' were still quite nervous about his blood pressure, which was now running low again, as the effects of shock were slow to go away.

Along with the pain and discomfort, Stalin's anger began to mount, as he demanded to know what the hell happened and what was being done to fix things. His physician knew they could no longer keep their powerful patient at bay finally, so relented and opened the doors for visitors.

When no one moved to be the first to enter the lion's lair, tension gripped the room when they heard a roar from Stalin's bedroom. "Molotov get in here now, don't keep me waiting any longer. Beria you too, get in here. You both have much to answer for."

His anger swept into the room and froze them like a powerful, icy wind across the steppe. Finally, one man stepped forward, one who held mostly a ceremonial post of little power, but at a minimum, he knew Stalin when he was known as Koba, back in the old days. Marshall Voroshilov marched forward with a stiff back and formal bearing to tell Comrade Stalin what happened and why Molotov wouldn't ever answer his summons again.

Beria inwardly cringed at the sound of Stalin's voice. The words paralyzed him. The man who built an empire of gulags and an organization dedicated to terrorizing its citizens, now trembled at the god-like voice echoing from the bedroom. Thinking, *it can't just end like this,* not after everything he had worked for all those years. All of the lives he had plotted against and destroyed along the way, all of that meant nothing as he knew soon it was to be his time.

Nearly all present turned to him staring, wondering what he would do. Many secretly relished the idea of watching the former, all-powerful leader of the NKVD breakdown before their eyes. Slowly backing up, one step at a time, he just kept shaking his head and muttering, "No, no, I can't, I can't see him yet. Too soon, I, I have to leave. Sorry. I'm so sorry."

Finally, he just turned and ran from the room and excitedly fled through the Kremlin and tried to escape, to leave that place, and especially leave him. He was not destined to go far as a squad of Kremlin soldiers, the famous Taman Guards, secured the NKVD chief and arrested him on direct orders from Marshall Zhukov. Refusing to leave anything to chance, Zhukov had called the commander of the Kremlin guards three hours before and instructed them to detain Beria if he looked to be trying to escape.

Zhukov hoped to, once and for all, pay the Chekists back for the purges of 1937. The military never forgot its humiliation at the hands of the Chekists and fully intended to take control of the situation. Besides, in Zhukov's mind, who better to come to the protection of Comrade Stalin than the victorious forces of the Red Army? A power struggle for the soul of the Party and control of the country had just started in earnest.

Oblivious to the commotion outside the bedroom, Marshal Klimenti Voroshilov, Stalin's oldest comrade from the early days of the Revolution, walked into the room and sadly looked at his old comrade laying in obvious pain on the bed. Voroshilov was shocked at his appearance. Stalin had bruises on both arms, his face was swollen, and he looked very old. It didn't seem possible that they had almost lost him.

Refusing to give in to his emotions, he strode over to the bed and grabbed a piece of bread off the plate and smiled as he said, "How are you doing my old friend? I'd tell you that you looked well, but we both know that you look like the backend of a kulak's mule."

Stalin seemed to smile a bit at Voroshilov's coarse, peasant language, and then asked, "I thought that I asked for Molotov and that little bastard, Beria. Where are they? Did they send you in here to ask for mercy?"

The old marshal looked down at his friend and was alarmed by the look in his eyes. His eyes were glazed over and red with fire and looked as though the pressure was about to make him snap. Voroshilov shook his head and answered in a calming tone, "No, Comrade Stalin, neither Molotov nor Beria called me here to intercede for them. I really just wanted to see you myself, to make sure my old friend is alive and unhurt. You must know we have all been scared that something too dreadful for words had happened, the unthinkable."

Stalin wasn't in the mood to deal with the oldest bootlicker in the Kremlin. Feeling the anger coursing through his veins, he didn't have the patience for this man. *He is lucky I kept him around the Kremlin all these years,* Stalin thought. He tried to dismiss him by saying, "You are wasting my time. You and whoever else is out there should be searching for the traitors who looked to end Stalin's life. Now leave and bring those fools in, now."

Voroshilov saw that Stalin was going to be difficult so he came right out and said, "Comrade Stalin, I regret to say, but Molotov and Marshal Konev are dead and Beria just wet himself and ran off when you called out from the bedroom. Koba, you're lucky to be alive."

Stalin sat up in his bed in shock at the words he had just heard. It didn't seem possible, both Molotov and Marshal Konev dead, but somehow that little weasel, Beria was still alive. It was then he realized how close his own death had come and those memories of fear and panic from that morning rushed back at him. He fell back again against the bed and turned on his side away from his visitor. He suddenly felt his mind reliving those events.

He could remember the first sounds of explosions at the crossroads, the smoke and dust engulfing the car. Next, the terrible sounds of the wounded and then the series of explosions erupting all around him. Panic seized him as he felt again the jarring sensation of the car behind his slamming him into the mountainous pile of debris on the road, trapping him. The tremendous explosions from the cars going up in flames washed over him as his blood pressure suddenly shot through the roof. He instinctively reached for his crotch to see if he lost control again. His fear rose to a climax and then the Stalin of old emerged through the panic.

He roared at Voroshilov, "I want them dead. Beria, the head of Berlin security, the driver of my car, anyone associated with this traitorous conspiracy against Stalin, do you hear me? Dead. I want five thousand Germans in Berlin rounded up and shot and left in the streets as an example for daring to try to kill me. Voroshilov, I want answers and I want them right now."

Starting to regret being the bearer of the news, the old cavalry general decided to try to calm Stalin before he had a stroke. Hands outstretched and motioning for Stalin to calm down, Voroshilov said, "Please, Koba, calm yourself. Everyone involved in this dreadful day will be dealt with, but you need to know something. It wasn't the

Germans; that much we're sure. It was the fucking Poles, if you can believe that."

He watched as his old comrade looked shocked. Obviously, Stalin was as surprised as everyone else that Poles would have the balls for such a desperate action. He continued, "It's worse than you think. Apparently the bandits timed the ambush to coincide with widespread attacks across most of Poland. The Polish Home Army that Beria had been saying was disbanded struck more than three hundred targets, big and small, in every major and minor town in Poland. We have a full-scale uprising on our hands."

Stalin was stunned beyond belief, first to be told that Poles and not Nazis made the assassination attempt, and then to be told the entire country had risen up against the liberators of their country shook Stalin to the core. *How could we have allowed this to happen?* Those goddamn Poles were going to be troublesome, but he never thought for a moment that they represented a real danger. With each passing second, Stalin's fury filled the room. His face turned red as the fear he felt just moments ago was replaced with such rage that Voroshilov turned cold with fear.

Sensing Stalin was losing his grasp of the situation, he said, "It's being handled, don't make yourself sick. Marshal Zhukov has closed the borders and airspace in Germany and ordered reinforcements to attack from army groups east of Berlin. Don't worry, Koba, in two weeks we'll roll over them, shoot a few thousand and be done with them. You'll see everything will work out in the end. The important thing is that you are safe."

Stalin could take no more of this fool, and in a deadly cold voice, He uttered, "Don't worry? I was almost slaughtered on the streets yesterday and now the fucking Poles are staging a massive rebellion. You always were a fool but I kept you around because you amuse me, Voroshilov, but that can be easily taken care of, as you will soon see. I will rid myself of all the fools who let the Party down.

"We look weak to the whole world. Stalin was almost killed by pathetic bandits while thousands of Red Army and NKVD forces stood milling around like sheep. You tell me that there was no conspiracy. Stalin is no fool. I swear to you that I will find out the names of every miserable rat who tried to kill Stalin. Then, we make an example of these miserable Poles. Poles, Poles, Poles, that is all I have heard from everyone ever since Yalta. I am sick to death of them.

"I want them exterminated, anyone who raises arms against the Red Army shall be dealt with, plus their entire families will be arrested and liquidated. I don't care if not single goddamn Pole is left when we're done. Call Berlin and get Zhukov here by tomorrow morning. Tell him that I expect plans on how he will deal with this Polish problem. Now leave me and don't ever come back to the

Kremlin again. Do you understand me? Consider yourself lucky to be alive."

As a shaken Voroshilov entered the room full of frightened men waiting their turn with the boss, everyone heard the ranting coming from the bedroom.

Stalin bellowed, "Traitors all around me. Traitors in the Kremlin, traitors in the West, miserable back-stabbing Poles on our doorstep, none of you can be trusted, only Stalin can be trusted. All of you go home, leave me now."

Trembling with rage, Stalin seethed on his bed and planned revenge on everyone and everything that he could think. He knew he couldn't trust anyone, except maybe Zhukov. *They have all let me down except my Red Army. Starting tomorrow, the Poles will wish they had never been born and just maybe I'll blame the Germans for trying to kill me as well. It'll be a good excuse to burn down what's left of Berlin. Then they will fear me, the Poles, the West, the world.* With that last thought in mind, a tired and depleted Stalin quietly drifted off into a deep sleep.

Chapter Twenty Seven

July 20, 1945

Poznan, Poland

It was late in the evening, nearly ten o'clock, when he felt the light nudge to his ribs. He looked up to see the somewhat sheepish look on his young aide's face. Apparently the young man, really nothing more than a boy of nineteen, had been trying to gently wake him for several minutes, and finally got tired and summed up the courage to shake like hell and finally wake him up. Colonel Alexander Komorowski was feeling every one of his forty-two years and found that even though he had slept the sleep of the dead for the past six hours, he still felt completely exhausted.

Somehow a mug of steaming tea appeared in his hands and without thinking, he began to drink the hot tea rich with honey. Shaking his head, he staggered towards the washbasin at the side of the bed and thrust his head into the middle of the cold water and whipped it up quickly, showering his poor aide with water. Reaching for a towel and another sip of tea, he started to feel a bit more like himself, miserable, but at least conscious.

The Polish Home Army commander had pushed himself hard the past three days and nights. The man's endurance was already legendary, but all men have limits and by late afternoon, Alexander reached his. As he slowly reached under the cot to put his boots on, he knew that, at least thus far, his men had done well.

Traffic in and out of the city was at a standstill, Russian reactions so far had been limited, and the local Polish communists had either been shot or fled with their Russian patrons. Even though his men didn't hold a single permanent defensive position, for all intents and purposes, the Home Army controlled Poznan and the surrounding land for the time being. He hurt them, and he was sure they knew it. He saw the clock on the wall and knew it was time to get reacquainted with the war.

Making his way over to the detailed map of the city and surrounding area, he thought to himself that his boys were really making a fight of it. He smiled as he looked at the Russian troop dispositions on the map and saw two more Soviet divisions appeared to have formed into attack columns south of the city.

Judging by the march table of the Russian forces assembling to attack his forces, Alexander figured now was as good a time as any to hit them. They would be tired after an all-day march, probably a bit sluggish and maybe even arrogant after beating the Germans just a few short months before. Komorowski had adhered to General Anders strategic plan to stage a series of sustained hit and run attacks and fight the Russians on our terms.

So far, he had been right. The one major problem plaguing his forces was resupply. With his units strung out all over the Polish countryside, it was becoming pretty damn difficult to keep his men supplied with everything from bullets to mortar rounds. He got more complaints about ammo distribution than anything else. Finally he exploded and told them to stop bitching and start stealing it from the fucking Russians. So, that's exactly what many of his men started to do. The real godsend so far had been all those captured German panzerfausts. No more throwing Molotov cocktails from ten feet away. Since his men weren't afraid of tanks anymore, the Russians didn't seem like such supermen.

Staring at the map again, he saw the Russians had set up camp along three built up villages off the southern rail line ten miles outside of town. Tracing his fingers along the roads heading north and east, he saw the units he had available in that district and decided to welcome the Russian bastards back to Poland. It was the opportunity he had been waiting for to make use of his only two heavy units. All of the senior commanders and many of the rank and files had fought in the large-scale uprising in Warsaw and were not afraid to pick a fight. In fact, they were chomping at the bit waiting for action orders that hadn't come in the first three days. Well, it appeared they would get their chance.

It took about twenty minutes to sketch out the operational framework for the attack. Noting the time again, he gave the necessary orders and thought it would be a very good night for hunting. *I'll teach those bastards that the AK owns the night.*

Soviet Command Post, Outside of Poznan

The advanced command post for the Twelfth All-Arms Rifle Army established itself in a convent, one of the few buildings left relatively intact after the Red Army captured the city a few months before. The Germans had fought particularly hard to keep this "fortress" city and it took hundreds of Russian siege guns to finally level most of the town leaving it largely destroyed and covered rubble, making movement all the more difficult.

The recent attacks by the Polish Home Army nearly doubled the time allotted to the movement of the Twelfth Rifle Army. It seemed as if every bridge, tunnel, and railroad was destroyed, damaged, or mined. It had taken nearly five battalions of engineers, plus several attached special bridging units to enable the forty thousand strong army to reach their staging areas.

The commander of the Twelfth Rifle Army, Colonel-General Pavel Smironov, was in a foul mood. Marshall Zhukov threatened to strip him of command if he didn't attack at first light and, as the Zhukov put it, "exterminate the Polish criminals within a week or get ready to command a penal battalion."

The commander of the Twelfth Rifle Army was a large, powerful man, with short-cropped black hair and a bulbous nose. He had survived the war and saw heavy combat starting as a commander of an infantry regiment and fought the Germans for four bloody years. His simple peasant features matched his style of command. In the great Russian tradition of sighting the enemy, blasting them with artillery, and then sending in the infantry. Much like Smironov, the system was simple, yet very often, brutally effective.

General Smironov was as tired as everyone else and even at that late hour, nearly twelve midnight, he had only made contact with two of his three corps. He was expected to make a full attack at first light against an unseen enemy. Sweating in the humid summer night, he poured over the intelligence estimates given to him from the former commander of the Poznan military district. Luckily for him, the Poles did the State a favor by sparing the expense of a bullet. He was one of the first casualties during the initial Polish attack. Smironov was self-assured and had every confidence he would avoid his predecessor's fate.

He looked at his general orders again and shook his head. The Russian commander couldn't believe that after killing Germans for four years, finding and squashing a few Poles should be this difficult. He was supposed to move from the south while his counterpart commanding the Sixth Rifle Army moved from the north in a giant pincer operation. With such an overwhelming show of force, they should be able to steamroll the entire region and flush the Poles out of their hiding spots.

In theory, it made sense back in Germany when he was given the orders, but everything that happened since had forced him to revise his estimates of how difficult the operation was going to be. No one knew how many Poles were active in the region and, furthermore, he couldn't steamroll the area if he couldn't move up and down the road. The Poles had mined every road, felled trees, and worse, blew up the Soviet fuel depots along the river. He had enough diesel for his tanks, but barely enough for more than half of his trucks.

Still, with Zhukov breathing down his neck, Smironov felt he could get at least half of his troops into position by the next morning. *Ah, it should be more than enough to remind the Poles who their new masters are now.* With that pleasing thought in mind, he took one last shot of vodka and turned in for the night.

Unbeknownst to the slumbering commander of the Twelfth Rifle Army, Polish Home Army sapper teams were infiltrating his hastily thrown together troop encampments. Komorowski knew his two small battalions of five hundred men each couldn't hope to stand up to the Soviet forces massing in his sector, but he needed to give them something to think about.

Home Army eyes were everywhere throughout Poznan and observers informed the mission commander about Soviet security arrangements. The Soviet commander of the crack 83rd Guards Division had decided to set up his campsite in a giant laager on some farmland off the main highway with his supply units and most of his vehicles and artillery parks in the middle and the nine infantry battalions sequestered on the outside.

Individual units' established local security within their own battalion areas and division headquarters were supposed to be in charge of the inner zone. On paper a textbook example of camp security, but after nearly twenty hours on the road and a breakdown in general discipline and more than two months of peace, the Russian soldiers put out token security elements and bedded down for the night. Besides, they were only pesky Poles, not like they were fighting Germans anymore.

The Polish mission commander kept his men quiet as he continued to observe from the ridgeline overlooking the Soviet encampment. He didn't know whether or not he should be thankful or angered. The communists looked as if they were out on summer maneuvers instead of preparing for combat. Peering through his binoculars, the Pole saw the Russian battalion on the extreme left corner of the laager was only manning a small vehicle checkpoint off the main road. He watched as the guards waved supply trucks by and didn't bother checking anything. Who could blame them? Stragglers came into camp at all hours after a long road march.

Figuring God protects the bold, the Polish commander sketched a plan that would hopefully be as quick as it was simple. So, a half hour later, he led three squads of Russian speaking Polish soldiers dressed in Red Army uniforms.

The small convoy of six Russian, two and half ton trucks all carried the same contents, a dozen barrels of diesel fuel. When the Pole turned off the highway into the Soviet camp, he spoke in halting Russian with an obvious Ukrainian accent and informed the guard detail that he had fuel to deliver and asked to be directed to the divisional supply depot. The Russians were so low in diesel after the long road march that he was welcomed into the encampment and soon found he and his men nearly had the run of the supply area.

Quickly he surveyed the scene and observed how the Soviets had haphazardly piled everything from ammo and fuel to rations in giant piles in the middle of the laager. Much of the supplies were still packed on crates inside the American built trucks, unopened and not even begun to be organized for combat operations scheduled for the next morning. Driving up and down the rows of material, the cool Pole quickly formulated a plan and saw where he could do the most damage.

After about an hour, his men completed their work and drove back out of camp. Even better, they liberated some needed ammunition that would add to the night's carnage.

While the Polish mission commander was operating inside the Soviet camp, other sapper teams were busy mining the access roads leading to the highway and to the ridgeline overlooking the camp. Others squads were moving into position with heavy machine guns ready to rake the camp with fire. It took nearly thirty minutes to get back to his unit's positions along the ridgeline overlooking the Russians.

As the Polish commander looked at his watch for the third time in the past five minutes, he saw it was time. Looking down into the

Soviet camp he counted to himself, and then was rewarded with a brilliant explosion right in the middle of camp. The night sky lit up as an artillery ammo dump exploded in a series of earth shattering explosions.

He watched as several artillery pieces flew through the air as if they were children's toys. Artillery rounds cooked off one after another causing metal shards to fill the air and cut down many dozens of men struggling to escape the deadly fire. Next, he was drawn to another brilliant burst of light and a deafening roar as several other fuel trucks exploded in the night. The Poles smiled at one another and were more than a little impressed with their commander.

They had boldly left individual fuel drums in front of tanks, ammo supply trucks, fuel haulers and the like. Each drum held more than forty gallons of diesel fuel, plus plastic explosives attached to a false bottom on the lid. All of the charges were set to go off one after another throughout the camp. Men were blown to pieces as fire lit up the night sky and shook men out of their sleep. Men already exhausted from the long day's journey were slow to respond and many died as debris rained down on those below.

The next act in the drama began to play out as Polish mortar teams lobbed 82mm explosive rounds right into the middle of the chaos below. Next, the Russians found themselves being hit by a dozen crew served machine guns, mostly captured German MG42 machine guns. Men caught in the open and silhouetted against the burning fires were mowed down by the hundreds. The Poles could barely believe their luck as the Russians were slow to respond and many tried to flee into the night, only to be met by a series of well-orchestrated, small unit ambushes at obvious exit routes outside the camp.

Finally, after about fifteen minutes of mayhem, Russian officers began getting men organized to counter attack the Poles who were obviously holding the heights above the Soviet encampment. Platoon sergeants began pulling men out of their hiding spots and tried to bring some order to the chaos caused by the Poles. Trucks and a few tanks began to motor through camp. They stopped to pick up men as they moved. The small task forces, hastily organized, moved towards the highway only to be stopped by a series of well-placed mines.

Trucks filled with infantry were ripped apart while tanks that hit several mines didn't explode, but men riding the tanks were thrown from their protective rides and flung on either side of the roadway, many wounded or dead. Polish gunners then shifted fire from the camp to those trucks stopped in front of the minefield and raked the trucks from one end to the other.

Things again came to a halt as the Soviet officers panicked and became frustrated at their inability to strike back at their unseen foe. Throughout the engagement, Polish soldiers kept up a sustained fire plan and constantly shifted fire positions. The men were told they would find a target rich environment, and so they kept up the fire until they ran out of ammunition, then melted back into the night.

Meanwhile, one Soviet tank commander organized nearly a full battalion of tanks and decided to get his unit out from under the Polish guns raining fire down on their heads. The Soviet major in command decided to boldly strike at the ridge above and led his forces onto the highway and miraculously didn't lose any tanks to mines or anything else.

Feeling a bit more in control, his rear elements reported Polish fire coming two hundred meters to the right, so he ordered his forces off road and oriented towards the summit above. His forces split along two dirt tracks that moved through the heavily forested hillside to the ridgeline above. Thinking he was about to hit them on both sides and roll the damn Poles up, he was shocked when the night lit up yet again. The clever Poles had left the section of the Russian line open for a deadly purpose.

Hiding in the thick hillside forest anti-tank teams struck the Russian column as it slowly moved up the dirt tracks. The Poles didn't possess any long-range anti-tank guns in this sector so they decided to engage Soviet armor on their terms. The German panzerfausts worked as advertised and the Poles were rewarded with more than a dozen hits as the exploding Russian tanks lit up the night.

The Polish ambush was so sudden and so devastating the Russians began a pell-mell retreat back down the hillside, spraying the forests on both sides with machine gun fire to cover their retreat.

Another four tanks were hit by the Poles who then disappeared back into the forest and deep into the night. Ammunition continued to cook off for the rest of the night from still smoldering ammo dumps, tanks, and burning fuel. The Poles withdrew back to their hiding spots throughout the countryside and left the remains of a Soviet division in utter turmoil.

The sounds of battle roared through the night and woke Colonel-General Smironov out of his vodka induced deep sleep. Off in the distance, nearly seven miles from his makeshift command post, his window lit up as brilliant flashes exploded in the night. Within moments, a distraught young aide rushed into his quarters and handed the General the initial reports, none of which were very encouraging.

Ripping the papers out of the nervous, young staff officer's hands, Smironov stalked out of his room with a barely contained fury. The implications for his command if he failed to begin his sweep operations south of Poznan had been made all too clear to him by Zhukov, himself. Before he had taken one step from his new base of operations, the goddamn Poles snuck up on him and slaughtered one of his Guard divisions while they were sleeping. *How in the hell will I explain this?*

Smironov again was overcome with the feeling that life was so unfair. Instead of enjoying the fruits of victory, he feared he was about to be disgraced because some sneaky Poles wouldn't stand and fight like Germans. So he decided, right then and there, that if Zhukov wanted Poznan, he would give it to him brick by brick. Maybe, just maybe, when he was through with the city, whoever had been taking part in these attacks would find themselves among the casualties. With that thought in mind, he charged into the convent chapel, the temporary operations room, and began to bark orders at his staff and arrange dispositions for the coming counter-attack.

After a half hour of phone calls to his surviving divisional commanders, he went back to his room for an hour or two of sleep. By the next day, the citizens of Poznan would be taught a terrible lesson for daring to raise a hand against their Soviet masters and worse, jeopardizing his career. He had already picked out a dacha along the Black Sea coast. No goddamn Pole was going to deny him what was rightfully his.

Polish Command Post

Reports of the previous night's actions poured into the mobile operations center. The Polish Home Army leader, Colonel Komorowski, couldn't have been more pleased at the way his troops had performed.. He wanted to give the new Russian troops something to think about, at least a proper welcome to Poland, but he never thought his people could really hurt them that much in just one engagement. After the early morning attack, he had already prepared orders for his forces to break into small groups and go underground for the time being.

He had become a real believer in General Anders' grand plan of sustained partisan actions against the Red Army. Now that his brave fighters had delivered a great victory while fighting on their own terms, he didn't want to give the Soviets a convenient target. Plus, as his forces had just proved, they could mass their choosing and inflict major losses when Russian guard was down. Damn, it felt good to have hurt them so bad.

Komorowki's little command group came to a stop on a wooded ridge line about five miles south of Poznan. He was looking for a place to take a piss when he turned suddenly at the first whistling sound coming from the west side of the city. He instinctively ducked low, behind several boulders at the edge of the ridge.

Loud whistles filled the sky as he saw hundreds of smoke trails arching high into the sky, moving west to east in the direction of the exposed villages south of the city. His staff watched as the first series of explosions fell into the town centers with a terrible roar.

A dozen field glasses peered into the targeted villages. They watched in horror as men, women, and children were caught unaware by the Soviet barrage. Most of the citizens of Poznan assumed it was safe to come out because the Home Army wasn't going to make a fight for the city. The Russians had other plans. The Soviets were firing hundreds of Katyusha rockets directly into the villages where the Guard division was hit the night before.

Rockets, unlike tube artillery, fell in random patterns and destroyed home, church, and schoolyard alike. Within minutes a shroud of smoke and dust covered the villages as the impacts of hundreds of rockets devastated the poor Poles caught going about their business.

About ten miles away, orders were relayed to the Twelfth Army Artillery commander to shift fire. With skilled precision, artillery batteries opened up and unleashed hundreds of short and long range guns, ranging from heavy mortars to 152mm howitzers aimed at devastating the Polish landscape. Colonel-General Smironov gave specific instructions that he wanted fire brought to bear along both sides of the highways south of the city and make sure nothing was left standing that would offer defensible positions to contest his early morning drive.

For the next hour he was given a free fire zone and ordered to inflict maximized casualties against the civilian populace to punish them for the criminal attacks against his forces the previous night. The Russian artillery commander and his men needed little motivation. They too were frightened at the ferocity of the Polish attack and enraged at having to risk their lives yet again after such a short peace. If the Poles wanted to risk their necks against his artillery then he would level the entire Polish countryside and turn Poznan into a wasteland.

Colonel-General Smironov watched from an observation tower at the devastation unleashed against the Poles and ordered his remaining divisions to deploy and follow the barrage. He decided the previous night to blast everything in sight, to teach these Poles that the Red Army was not to be taken lightly. He was quite willing to punish the Poles in a manner that would be remembered for a generation. As he was reveling in his battle plan, the drone of engines drew his eyes skyward.

The Red Air Force provided more than two hundred medium bombers in support of his attack. Within minutes they reached the town center and began emptying their bomb loads and unleashed nearly twenty minutes of continuous devastation. Smironov had decided, for the sake of his operations, use of the town center could be minimized as long as the rail lines south of the city were kept open.

Since he didn't need the town, why leave it standing? In a torrent of high-explosives, buildings fell, people died in droves, and the Red Army inflicted a reprisal operation of such magnitude that last night's defeat was quickly forgotten.

Word would spread, and fast, that the Russians would not allow themselves to be victimized by bandits who strike at night. The survivors of this attack would be rounded up and whoever was left alive would talk. Smironov decided he would raze each block if necessary to liberate the city. In two weeks, the Poles would lay down their arms or there would be nothing left to fight for.

On the ridgeline overlooking the city nearly twenty Poles, the architects of the Poznan attack, watched in horror as the deadly lessons inflicted upon the Home Army in Warsaw were repeated for all to see. A chill went down Komorowki's back as he absorbed the brutal lesson the Russian commander just taught him. General Anders had warned all the district commanders to steel themselves for what would follow in the wake of their uprising. The pride they felt just moments before at the wreckage of the Soviet Guards division in the valley below was supplanted by a complete numbness in an instant.

The engines of the departing bombers hung in the air and smoke from the fires in the city created a chilling scene. Many of the men had family in the city, but all had come to terms with their higher duty to Poland. Rather than waste their lives by running into the city in ones and twos like the Russians wanted, they would go to the hills as planned and wait to strike.

Komorowski turned to his staff and somberly said, "This is why we must win. Come, let's move on. Later we will strike back and remind them that we refuse to accept defeat. In two days' time when they start to think that it's safe to piss in the middle of the night, we will hit them again. And then the day after that, we will strike a convoy and then blow up one of their command posts. It will never end for them as long as we maintain our spirits. Never forget, this is a beginning, not an ending, by any means."

Chapter Twenty Eight

July 21, 1945, 10:30 a.m.

Sochaczew, Poland

Michael Zelinski could barely believe his good fortune. Here he was inside Poland with a ringside seat at the only game in town, well at least in the European Theater. As the youngest staff reporter for the New York Times at the Paris bureau, he came in at the tail end of the war and basically hadn't covered a single decent story for the past three months. Since the war ended, he thought it would be back to covering the city beat back in the Bronx.

A week ago his boss called him into the office and asked if he spoke passable Polish. His parents were immigrants who could barely speak a word of English even after ten years in country, so he spoke decent Polish, albeit with a New York accent

His chief said, "Good, here is your press pass and travel documents. Get on the next plane to Poland. A high-level source inside the London Poles embassy leaked that there is a story brewing coming out of Warsaw, and since we got to send somebody and everybody else trying to cover the Potsdam Conference, so guess what, you're it. You up for it, Zelinski or were you looking to go home to momma?"

The Times Bureau Chief had never been all that impressed with Zelinski, and it might turn out to be a chicken shit story anyway. Still, just looking at him, looking greener then green, he had to force himself not to change his mind. Michael was so excited he all but kissed his editor and ran out of the office before he changed his mind.

He was halfway back to his hotel when he realized he hadn't traveled on assignment yet and didn't have the first clue how to get to Poland, but rather than slinking back to the office, he went to his flat and decided to pack first and figure out how to get there later. Laughing to himself as he stood in front of his bathroom mirror starting to shave, he thought, *a real assignment and to Poland no less. Mom and Dad will be so proud.* His next thought came fast, *God, I hope I don't screw this up.*

In a whirlwind week, he went from a comfortable office in Paris to moving at night with a company of Polish Home Army soldiers who were staging a massive uprising against the Russians. Even better, he was the only New York Times reporter in country. The story was his to run with and from what he had seen so far, things were only going to get hotter. He had already observed two major ambushes and various acts of sabotage.

One thing he learned fast was that life in the field was a hell of a lot different than writing copy at a desk in the office. Feeling dirtier than he had ever felt before in his life and sore from sleeping in the field, life on the lines as a combat correspondent was feeling less and less glamorous by the day, not to mention dangerous. The one trait he had yet to pick up was patience, and unfortunately, survival at the front often depended upon knowing when and where to stick your neck out.

Beginning to feel impatient again, he peered up from the entrenched works outside of the town of Sochaczew and looked at the men and few women preparing for the morning's ambush. He stepped on an ammo crate at the base of the trench and tried to look up at the crossroads again for the fifth time in the past half hour. The Poles had dug simple, makeshift firing positions to shoot up the expected Soviet convoy scheduled to cross through the town on the way to Warsaw.

The Poles were equipped with an assortment of mines, small arms, two machine guns, and a few anti-tank rockets. They set up a smart blocking position astride the south side of the road and overlooked the intersection about one hundred and fifty yards to his left. He was looking for dust trails or any indication of the Russians.

He could barely see, so he placed a sand bag on top of the ammo box and was just about to stick his head above the trench for a decent look when all of the sudden he felt the crate give way and as he fell to the ground, he heard a loud voice say, "Hey, dumbass. You trying to get yourself shot?" Landing on his ass, Zelinski knew it was his fairy godmother watching his back again.

Some fairy godmother, the photographer from LIFE magazine was six feet, two inches and cursed worse than any man he had ever known. Considering he grew up in the Bronx, that was saying something. Apparently, the Poles had contacted not just the Times, but also a few other news organizations, including a famous photographer from LIFE magazine. As the Chinese pointed out many years ago, a picture is certainly worth more than a thousand words, and LIFE's photojournalists were considered the best in the business. Probably the most famous of the lot was Paddy O'Rourke, an Irishman who had seen more of the world by the time he turned twenty-five than most people could ever dream about.

After lying about his age, sixteen year-old O'Rourke spent time in the trenches with the Irish Guards Brigade in Flanders in the later stages of the First World War. For some reason he could never come to terms with, Paddy thrived in danger and knew he could never go back to a quiet factory job back in Belfast. So he took some skills he picked up while doing a stint in photoreconnaissance during the war to make a living taking photos of everything from tribal wars in Africa, to the turmoil and famine in China, and later, the horrors of war in Europe.

Post-war Poland was just another hot spot and his reputation confirmed to all in the business that if O'Rourke bothered to show up, then something damn well important was happening. He preferred to work alone on his assignments, primarily because most people, in O'Rourke's mind, were pains in the asses and usually caused more problems than they were worth. He was there in '35 when he caught pictures of dying Ethiopian soldiers gasping for air as they suffered under clouds of mustard gas delivered from Italian planes. He had his camera ready when he tagged along with Serbian resistance partisans, the Chetniks, and made them famous for their daring exploits.

He chilled the world when he followed his hunch that rumors of death camps were anything but. Those shots shocked the world and illustrated man's inhumanity to man in a way few would ever forget.

His work in Poland was no different and he had no intention of playing nursemaid to anyone until he watched the kid pretend he was a real reporter. The first time he saw the boy was when O'Rourke watched him enter the Church the Poles were secretly using to meet the journalists sent to report on their coming action. The kid walked right in, with a camera in hand, went right up to a less then pleased priest and asked if this was the place to meet "them."

The priest looked on incredulously at the obvious American and secretly prayed his countrymen weren't about to rely on this boy to tell their story. Michael's entrance was so obvious and with far too many informants lurking around, the priest just kept shaking his head and finally sent the confused boy down to the bakery for coffee.

More amused than anything, O'Rourke watched the kid sent by the bloody New York Times show up looking like they pulled him out of a high school yearbook office, gave him pen and paper and told him to go find a big story. So, for reasons he didn't entirely understand, he took the kid under his wing, so to speak, and brought him out to follow the actions of a Polish Home Army company he'd hooked up with and followed into active combat with the occupying Red Army.

O'Rourke had to admit the kid was nice as hell, even funny. It was like working with a kid brother, fun at times, but he spent more energy following him around than sniffing out the story. But what the hell, he just couldn't stand by and watch as the kid did damn near everything wrong that can be done in the field. It was almost comical, if it wasn't so damn dangerous, not just to himself, but to the Poles. But, after a week of watching after him, it was beginning to get old. He would start moving around the battlefield solo. Besides, word from his guide was that it was nothing special, just a hit on another Soviet convoy.

The Poles expected some escort, but nothing really heavy. Red Army heavy units mainly were keeping to the main cities, leaving the countryside mostly in the hands of the Poles. O'Rourke saw a rise overlooking things about a half mile back. Maybe he would try to get some wide angle scenes, stay away from his regular close ups. *We'll see what happens.* Paddy knew things wouldn't get interesting until the Russians decided to get serious about reclaiming territory between the major cities. When that happened, he knew he'd get his shots. Until then, he would just bide his time.

Five Miles North of Sochaczew

NKVD Command Post

The activity in the Soviet camp was at a fevered pitch as plans were underway to take direct action against the fascist Poles who had been targeting Red Army supply columns at will for the past two weeks. On direct orders from Moscow, the local NKVD district commanders were ordered to begin direct measures aimed at discouraging the local population from supporting the widespread terror campaign. When Colonel Boris Gudonov received the orders two days before, he decided to act with his customary efficiency.

Ever since his direct action in the small village of Kutno several months ago, Polish Home Army sabotage had fallen dramatically in his sector. More importantly, he had been able to persuade several dozen locals in his district to provide helpful assistance to their fraternal brothers from the Soviet Union, the liberators from Nazi oppression, as Gudonov liked to remind every Pole who had the misfortune to come in contact with him. Of course, his methods of persuasion left a terrible, lasting impression on several of those unlucky to be married to or related to the criminals hiding in the forests and preying on their Socialist brothers.

Several demonstrations had been necessary to convince fathers, sons, wives, and etcetera, to provide the necessary information and be available for further assistance when needed. These unfortunate, dramatic demonstrations were not done without a purpose. They were intended to impress upon the Poles just how far the NKVD was prepared to go to enforce peaceful coexistence in his district.

Several women and two teenage boys had to pay the ultimate price. It would seem the Polish women couldn't stand up to several evenings with Red Army soldiers, especially his little savages from the Central Asian republics. Regardless, those Poles with surviving daughters and wives had proven rather helpful, after all. As Gudonov had always believed, with the proper motivation, men could be made to do nearly anything in the service of the State.

He had been able to compile a rather complete dossier on the suspected local Home Army soldiers and decided now was the time to make the NKVD presence known to the locals in a dramatic fashion, as to encourage further cooperation. He looked down at the trembling man on his knees and shook his head. How many times would it be required to chastise these people until they recognized the Soviet people wouldn't allow such lawlessness? *Imagine, these Poles actually tried to kill Comrade Stalin and expected to get away with it.*

Home Army units staged one successful attack after the other, but now across much of Poland, Soviet reinforcements were pouring into the country and reclaiming districts overrun by Polish rebels.

His dark eyes reminded the Pole of a bird of prey circling its intended victim, waiting to strike, knowing that whatever its eyes focused upon would die in one fell swoop. The widower had two sons and a daughter in local AK units and had just broke down and told this Russian Chekist where the next ambush would be sprung.

Wiping the tears from his eyes, he remembered the previous night being forced to watch as his fourteen year old daughter was first beaten and then raped by two soldiers. Her shrieks of "Daddy, help me, help me," rang in his ears over and over again and would haunt him until his dying day.

When that Russian animal called for his eleven year old twin girls, he broke down and sobbed like a child and told him everything. God help him, but at least his boys and eldest daughter would have rifles in hand when this Russian did whatever it was they were about to do. He couldn't abandon his twins to those swine.

The NKVD Colonel smiled a devilish grin at the Pole and asked in a calm, yet commanding voice, "Well, my friend, I want to ask you one more time, just to be sure. Have told me everything that I need to know? Will that band of criminals hiding in the hills show their faces today? Please keep in mind that your daughter has only spent one evening with my men and will likely survive last night's activities, but I wouldn't be optimistic about her chances after another such night."

He watched as the man wilted before his eyes and seemed to die yet again at the mention of the little blond haired girl being used as a plaything by his soldiers on campaign.

Trembling at the prospect of getting his daughters back, the Pole stiffened on his knees as if he was about to give his parish priest an act of contrition. His voice cried out in anguish as he said, "I swear to you, all I know is that my eldest son told me two days ago that they were going to hit supply convoys coming through our village over the next few days. He said that the crossroads on the west side of town would probably be the most likely ambush site. Please do not hurt my girls anymore, they are innocent."

Gudonov decided to slowly squeeze him like a lemon and said more menacingly, "I do not believe you. How could a father turn on his sons so easily? No. I believe you require additional evidence of my resolve to rid the State of such pests."

He motioned to his aides to bring them in to see their father. The twin girls were in a state of shock and nearly became hysterical when they saw how badly beaten and bruised their father looked.

Ignoring the loud sobbing in the room, Gudonov grabbed the collar of the Pole and pulled him closer and said, "Tell me again, what do your sons have planned for my troops? How many in their little band of criminals? When do they intend to strike? You better start talking little man or my troops will have these girls for dessert tonight. Do you understand me?"

He roared, "Speak! Talk now or I turn them over and you will never see them again!"

The Pole began sobbing uncontrollably and said, "I swear to you that all I know is that my sons are with maybe a hundred men, no more. They are poorly equipped and told me that their job was to avoid attacking any Red Army units except supply units. Dear God, please Colonel, don't hurt my little girls."

The man cried uncontrollably and could barely be understood. Gudonov knew the man had been sufficiently broken and had told him everything. All he really needed to know was how many and where, and this Pole proved useful after all.

Patting the man on the head, he said, "You see, comrade, you must understand that I had to ensure you were telling the truth. I certainly couldn't take the word of a man who had raised his children to defy authority, but now you shall see that I am a fair man. You may take your daughters home tonight after I make an example of your village. If your information is correct, then your family will be resting under your own roof, hopefully preparing the burial of your two sons and daughter. Go now and hold onto your daughters and pray that you told me everything. I will be most upset if you have lied."

With the information the miserable Pole had confirmed, it was time to teach those little Poles a lesson they wouldn't soon forget.

Two Hours Later, outside Sochaczew

O'Rourke found the perfect perch to observe the planned Polish ambush. He started taking a few snapshots of the valley below to give him a good idea of the depth and layout of the land. The more Paddy peered through his camera, the more he thought things looked a little too easy. The Poles were solid troops and had handled themselves surprisingly well so far, but they seemed to be getting a little lax. They really couldn't expect the Russians to sit back forever.

O'Rourke had heard about Red Army forces massing around the city of Poznan well to the west, but there were still decent sized garrisons out there who must be getting more and more pressure on them to start doing something. The LIFE photographer found himself moving from left to right and as he adjusted his lens, he found he could see right into the town center. He watched for a moment as people gathered at a variety of food stalls, store fronts, and for a moment the scene below belayed a sense of normalcy that must have been in short supply the past few years.

Then he heard it off in the distance, the unmistakable sounds of engines, still far off but definitely heading in his direction. The Russians looked to be moving a pretty large sized convoy, judging by the dust plumes rising from the roadway. Still too far to make out individual vehicles, O'Rourke assumed there would be combat vehicles mixed in with the convoy. He continued to watch and thought it strange there didn't appear to be any recon screen in front of the convoy.

As the truck convoy moved closer to the village, it picked up speed in hopes of pushing through any possible ambush. O'Rourke couldn't help but shake his head as he watched the dumb bastards barrel right into a textbook classic ambush. He may not like the Russians any more than he cared for Nazis, but he still hated to see such a waste of life. With that thought in mind, he picked up his camera and focused on the approaching line of trucks as they rapidly moved into the kill zone.

Watching the Poles rapidly position themselves for action, Michael Zelinski was relieved things were about to begin. He found a great spot to observe the action and was thankful that two of the Home Army guys provided some overhead cover for his trench. He was scribbling fast on his notepad and excitedly tried to capture the moment as best as he could. From what he could gather from the Polish officer in command of the ambush, the Russians were coming in dumb again, so this should be violent, quick, and over before they knew what hit them.

He counted about fifteen trucks moving at high speed, maybe more, but he couldn't tell from his vantage point. He could make out several Polish positions and watched as they tensed up in preparation for the action to come. The convoy wasn't being guarded but was moving fast, too fast for this stretch of road. Michael surveyed the scene and almost caught the scared look on the drivers face as the first six trucks blew past the front section of the Polish positions.

Before Michael knew it, the lead truck hit a mine which caught the American built Dodge truck right under its carriage and blasted it about twenty feet to the right of the road. The second truck was moving faster still and tried to plow through the ambush site, but Polish machine gunners opened up with a deadly fire that raked the front end of the convoy apart. Trucks began careening off the road as tires blew out. Two trucks swerved into one another as they tried to avoid the crossfire.

Zelinski, a veteran in his mind after a whole week on the line, actually stuck his head up long enough to catch an important tidbit of information. The trucks that had either blown up or crashed on the side of the road didn't appear to be carrying any supplies. Why would the Soviets send a big, high speed convoy through on the road to Warsaw empty? When the rest of the truck convoy pulled up short and began to turn off road to avoid the Polish ambush, Michael knew something was wrong.

Within seconds, he looked up as he heard a sound that caused his heart to flutter. Piston engines, a lot of them, were coming in low from the east and fast. Polish Home Army soldiers started panicking and desperately ran for cover while he curled up into a ball and went low into his trench and began to pray.

Overlooking the Polish ambush site, O'Rourke thought the same thing as he watched a flight of Red Air Force planes dive out of the sun and line up right on to the very exposed Polish fighting positions. The Poles didn't have any anti-aircraft guns, so the Russians came in low and at a reduced speed to make sure their bombing runs hit right on target. Then the LIFE photographer heard the loud whistling sound of artillery flying in the air, reaching out to the Polish positions on either side of the highway. The Poles were done for from what Paddy could see.

Dammit, he knew things looked too easy. The AK soldiers were still learning and didn't bother to dig decent trenches. They had almost no overhead cover, but if they moved, it would have to be over open ground and they would definitely be slaughtered. He cringed as the first plumes of fire and smoke exploded fifty yards short. The first shot was a ranging round, but the next series of rounds would probably hit right on target.

God help the lad. He won't know what the hell hit him. Dammit, why in the hell did I leave the poor bastard down there on his own? He should have his head examined. Too late, as he watched heavy rounds explode in succession and, more importantly, mark the positions of the Polish fighters even better for the coming air support.

He ducked low as two planes roared overhead and released air-to-ground rockets at the base of the crossroads. More planes followed suit, while the rest began strafing runs.

While O'Rourke was fixated on the heavy shelling and air attack, he failed to notice more than a dozen light tanks and several self-propelled artillery guns along with troop carriers were racing towards the Poles. Like a true professional, he kept taking shots, but inside he was dying as he kept fixating on that kid the Times had no bloody right sending into a combat zone. It was over in ten minutes. The Russians hit hard and fast and the surviving Poles didn't know what hit them. Most of the Poles who were too dazed to fire back were shot where they were found while the rest were killed as they stood their ground.

O'Rourke had seen a lot of action and was very impressed with the speed and power of the Russian attack. Just as he was pulling his stuff together and making sure his press credentials were handy, he used his binoculars and saw that the Russians grabbed a few prisoners after all, three to be exact. He let out a sigh of relief when he saw that one of the three shaken survivors was the kid. He looked dirty and probably pissed his pants twice over, but at least he was alive. Maybe they would get out of this yet.

Colonel Gudonov followed his combined NKVD/Red Army task force and arrived at the crossroads in time to see several prisoners being pulled from the wrecked Polish positions. He stood up high in the commander's cupola of the BA-10 armored reconnaissance vehicle and smiled as he pivoted left to right and saw the burnt out remains of the trucks he had decoyed ahead of his armored units.

He had no intention of giving the Poles a chance to inflict damage on expensive State property, so he decided to use a few German prisoners who had been kind enough to volunteer. Gudonov didn't want to risk the life of a single Red Army soldier, not even ones who were serving in a nearby penal battalion for such a suicide mission. He refused to consider any Poles because they were so damned erratic, and knew they couldn't be relied upon to drive through the crossroads and expose the dug in positions of their countrymen.

Fortunately, with so many Germans handy, it was academic, really. All Gudonov did was to make a small demonstration before a group of fascist POW's before they were sent to their daily work detail. He had ten men pulled at random and shot them in front of the other several hundred Germans who winced in disbelief at the ruthless execution of their fellow countrymen. The NKVD man then made an important announcement that fifteen volunteers would be needed and would be chosen at random. Failure to comply or refusal to follow directions would result in the slaughter of the remaining three hundred men in the work detail. Gudonov knew that Germans, being

Germans, could be relied upon to follow orders when given such simple instructions. Fortunately for the other men, the Germans performed as expected and drove like the wind to set off the Polish ambush as planned.

Once the Poles were in the open, it was a textbook attack as air support and artillery fire destroyed the little band of Poles and his force was able to mop up. Really, all in all, an excellent morning so far. He knew it was time to bring the rest of the day's lesson to an end. With that thought in mind, he ordered the prisoners to be gathered in the town center and directed his task force to seal the approaches to the town. Looking at his watch, Gudonov was pleased because it looked like the day's unpleasantness was moving right along at a nice pace. Perhaps they would make it back to camp by early afternoon.

His mind wandered away from the smoke and death all around him as he remembered the little Polish tart who served breakfast that morning. *Perhaps, she will be convinced to show a little Socialist fraternity in a few hours.* Gudonov thought he probably shouldn't entertain such thoughts, but service to the State should be both a thing of pleasure and pride.

Meanwhile, a much shaken and deeply frightened Michael Zelinski sat on the floor of the Russian truck with his arms bound. He was still quite disoriented from the artillery fire that landed all around him, barely a half hour ago. Thank God for that overhead cover and deep trench the Poles were kind enough to give him. If not, he would certainly have died like the rest.

He felt the truck pick up speed and bounce all over the place as the Russian driver seemed to purposely hit every pot hole for the next five miles until they hit smoother streets in town. The two Polish fighters laying next him were both wounded, one worse than the other, with a nasty stomach wound. As his senses started to come back, Zelinski realized that even though the fog in his head had started to lift a bit, he couldn't hear a damn thing.

What he didn't realize at the time was that a mortar round had landed a scant ten feet away from him early in the bombardment and the concussion damaged his eardrums. He was still too dazed to feel the blood drip out of his ears. Thankfully, his other senses were coming back as he figured he had somehow made it out alive when, by all rights, he should be dead and buried in that trench. From what he could tell the Soviets were driving back to town. Hopefully, once he presented his press credentials, they would let him go and he could get the hell out of Dodge.

After one week of direct combat coverage and a near death experience to boot, Michael Zelinski decided it was high time to get his ass back home to New York City and cover whatever chickenshit story they sent him on, because sticking his neck out for a story was for the freakin' birds.

He felt the truck begin to slow so he tried to check on the two wounded Polish fighters laying next to him, but with his hands tied there was little he could do. Finally, the truck came to a stop and all he could think was, *thank God, it's over now.*

Watching above from a different vantage point, Paddy O'Rourke was getting a real bad feeling where things were headed. It didn't take a genius to figure out the movement of tanks around the perimeter of town was not a good sign. Worse was to come as Soviet soldiers began knocking down locked doors, smashing windows, and causing genuine mayhem throughout the town. The Red Army was angry to a man. Everything from the surprising ferocity of the Polish attacks to the attempted assassination of Comrade Stalin had put the men into an evil mood.

With Colonel Gudonov's junior officers acting as stage managers in the dreadful scenes being played out, the village of Sochaczew would never be the same again. Moving in a systematic fashion, almost as if on a parade ground, Gudonov's men entered each home, place of business, and even church, and forced most of the occupants out, killed others, and kept the pretty ones for their own amusement. The men looted personal possessions, grabbed food and drink, and worked themselves up into a frenzy as the experienced ones knew what was coming.

Working block by block, the Russians were able to gather the majority of the town's citizens in the village square. O'Rourke snapped shot after horrifying shot that would later present an almost blow by blow account of the death of the town. Never in all his experiences around the globe had he witnessed such horrifying brutality. He had seen Hitler's death camps and the horrific images kept him awake at night for weeks, but this was somehow worse.

The Nazis made their death camps into some type of organized and efficient system of mass disposal, no emotions. For the Germans, the camps existed until the purpose of their existence was eliminated; not with the Russians. He watched as the Russians worked themselves up into a real bloodlust, almost as if they thoroughly enjoyed what they were doing. The sounds of shots firing mixed with shrieks of horror as more loved ones were attacked by soldiers who were caught up in age-old hatreds.

Finally, after more than an hour, close to twenty five hundred men, women, and children were huddled together, praying the Russians were through with their punishment and would end the madness. As O'Rourke's long-range camera lens focused on the looks of sheer terror on so many faces, he felt overcome by the pure anger.

Without a doubt these were the most significant photos of his personal career, but all O'Rourke could feel was a deep sense of guilt, being a witness to this mass suffering and not able to do a damn thing. All he kept thinking was that he had to survive and get the photos out to the world. He then observed an armored car move onto the square and from the looks of the way the rest moved in his presence, he assumed the architect of the drama had just arrived. Ten seconds later, he took half a dozen perfect shots of the man whom he decided would be labeled the "Butcher of Soceczew".

Colonel Boris Gudonov didn't know he was about to become famous, not that it would have stopped him. In fact, the idea his actions were to be broadcast to the world would have actually excited him all the more. With his black leather overcoat flapping ominously in the wind, he confidently strode up to the makeshift platform his aides hurriedly put together and spoke directly to the crowd of frightened Poles.

Gudonov motioned for the groveling Polish communist official to grab a bullhorn and translate his message to the crowd. Staring down at the mass of suffering before him, he couldn't help but feel all-powerful. His word was law in this district and one way or another, the Poles would learn to behave.

He pointed to the covered truck with the Home Army prisoners and motioned for it to be driven in front of the townspeople. His aides unceremoniously dumped all three men to the ground. A hush fell over the crowd as Gudonov pointed to the men laying in a heap in front of them. With a powerful voice, Gudonov announced, "I have brought to you the remaining criminals who have disturbed the peace of this district and caused so much needless death of innocent Red Army soldiers."

The translator's voice rang out to the villagers as they remembered Nazi atrocities and knew the day's horrors had not yet come to an end. Gudonov continued, "I have been tasked by Comrade Stalin, himself, to bring order to this region and I shall not rest until each and every brigand lies rotting in the sun. These murderers got what they deserved, as will anyone else who takes up arms against the Red Army. These brigands have taken up arms against their Soviet comrades and did so with the full knowledge and support of the citizens of this town. The Soviet people demand vengeance for their sons murdered by Polish criminals. I intend to bring both justice and peace to this land. Please watch and learn the consequences of resistance to Soviet justice."

The translator finished speaking by the time Gudonov leapt off the podium and marched with a platoon of bodyguards surrounding him. He stopped in front of the three prisoners.

New York Times reporter, Michael Zelinski, tried to listen, but could barely hear a word. Gripped by a paralyzing fear, unlike anything he had ever experienced, he was shaking uncontrollably and tears poured down his face. Zelinski was desperately trying to free his arms so he could show his press credentials and get the hell of there. His credentials and passport were tucked tightly inside his back pocket and he was having a hell of a time getting it out with his two hands bound in front.

He nearly jumped out of his skin when the Soviet officer leapt off the platform and walked towards Zelinski and the two other Home Army soldiers and watched in disbelief as the Russian reached for his sidearm and quickly worked the bolt. Staring at the Russian in horror, Zelinski began yelling in English, "Wait! Wait! I'm an American. I'm an American. I'm a reporter."

In full view of the assembled Polish villagers, NKVD guards lifted the three men to their feet and, without hesitation, Gudonov cocked the hammer and shot the first man in the face sending his lifeless body sprawling to the ground. The second Pole dropped to his knees just as the NKVD man chambered another round and calmly shot the second Pole behind the left ear. Gudonov was concentrating on his last victim and closed himself off to everything around him except the demonstration at hand. This last one was yelling in some foreign language, but he refused to be fooled by such trickery.

Taking a dramatic stance, arm held out fully, and with his Tolkolov pistol extended until the barrel rested against the left side of the Pole's head, he looked to the crowd once more. In those last frantic seconds, Zelinski yanked his right arm free and pulled the NYT press badge out of his back pocket. Caught in an absolute panic, he tried to show that they were making an unbelievable mistake. With a villainous sneer Gudonov looked directly into the filthy Poles eyes and pulled the trigger just as Zelinski whipped his hand free with the passport in full view of his executioner, but it was too late.

The .45 caliber bullet exploded against the left side of his head sending a huge piece of his skull, nearly the size of a man's palm, off to the right and a geyser of blood and brain tissue splattered onto the guard behind him. His press pass flew out of his hands when the gun went off and fell to the ground, landing onto a pool of blood of the poor Pole next to him.

Gudonov looked down at the three men and spat on them in one final act of disgust for the Polish fighters. He always hated Poles. That last one tried to show him some piece of paper as if that would have saved his life. Looking down at the leather wallet, he kicked it with his boot and hoped that his execution had made an impression. Laughing, if that didn't make an impression, what was coming surely would.

Wiping tears of rage from his cheeks, Paddy O'Rourke snapped yet another cartridge of film into his camera and kept shooting. He had lain hidden behind a thickly wooded ridgeline the whole time. He had seen everything from the Polish ambush to the Russian counter-attack to the sack of the town, but he was caught completely unaware by the stark brutality of the execution he had just witnessed.

Each snap of the camera was testament to his own personal responsibility in that boy's death. Even though his eyes were telling him what was going to happen, his mind wouldn't accept he was watching an actual murder of someone he had come to know and like, and it was happening right before his eyes. His job was to capture that horror on film. So when the first Pole was shot, he knew it was over. He captured each moment, reaching out to chronicle the few last seconds of poor Michael's death.

After his body fell to the ground in a heap next to the other two Polish fighters, O'Rourke rolled over on his side and lay there exhausted by everything he had seen. It had been too much. He didn't want to see anything else. He didn't want to shoot another snapshot of a dead boy or burning building or smell the remains of one more battlefield. He just wanted to go home.

He started to move and gather his things when he heard the sounds from below. His stomach knotted up again. Without thinking, checked his camera for film and instinctively began snapping shots below.

Colonel Gudonov judged, by the reaction from the crowd, that his little illustration hit home properly. The looks of fear and contrition he viewed on so many faces differed little from other faces he had seen over the years. These sad people feared for the final act of retribution. A strange paralysis swept the frightened villagers, and for one brief passing moment, Gudonov thought to spare them. *Perhaps, this has been lesson enough. We very well couldn't kill them all, although it would make pacifying things much easier.*

An aide interrupted his thoughts and handed him a radio. Without thinking, Gudonov heard his task force commander's voice, a particularly efficient young officer who spoke matter of frankly, "Comrade Colonel, I am in position. At your command, we shall begin the sweep operation."

Without really thinking, the NKVD officer simply responded, "Affirmative. Begin movement West to East as planned." With that said, whatever doubts he may have had evaporated, then he and his staff began to climb aboard their vehicles and exited the town center.

Eyes turned to the sounds coming from the west end of town, as the boom of tank and howitzer guns began to go off in powerful discharges. Next, the sound of machine gun fire sent the Poles racing like a flock of geese, fleeing down side streets and alleys, most praying to reach the wooded ridgeline outside of town. Tanks were driven through homes and soldiers were shooting at anything that moved. Engineers were laying huge explosive charges throughout the village.

One particularly cruel Soviet tank driver drove his vehicle right through the front doors of the Catholic Church, destroying the vestibule and then added to the destruction when his main tank gun destroyed the alter and much of the interior of the Church. Two priests and a nun were caught in the crossfire inside, trying to secure the ancient relics held inside the Church. Everything from baptismal records to a three hundred year old bible lay scattered around their dead bodies.

Elsewhere, the Soviet forces moved by platoon and destroyed what they could on the run. They quickly moved through the town and caught up with many of the escaping refugees of the horrors visited upon the poor town. Just as hundreds had cleared the other side of town in advance of the tanks, Gudonov sprung the last of his lessons on the Poles. Many were running for their lives and crossing open fields to find security above. It was not to be as the other half of his task force caught many of the Poles in the open and mowed them down like animals.

Finally, after a half-hour, the two forces met on the far side of town and finished what they had begun. Without stopping, the two forces re-combined and moved quickly out of the town's limits. Within minutes, artillery fire began to rain down upon the remains of the town. One series of explosions erupted throughout the town after another and then powerful explosions ripped through the air, as the charges set by the engineers went off.

Gudonov had decided to make sure not a living soul would escape Soviet justice and the town would literally be demolished, block by block. He intended the death of this town should stand as a reminder for all time to honor the Soviet soldiers who had died as a direct result the town's complicity in supporting the rebellion and to remind Poles of the consequences of their actions.

As he watched the death of the town of Sochaczew, all O'Rourke could do was continue clicking his camera and reloading his film. Working like an unfeeling robot, the Irish photographer blocked out what he was bearing witness to, stared through his lens, and silently clicked one picture of death after another. He stayed in that spot well into evening, until the sun had gone down. By then, he had finally run out of film.

One thought, and one thought alone, consumed him, he must get the shots back to his editor as soon as humanly possible. Nothing else in this world mattered anymore, except that. His life meant nothing if he failed to show the world. Looking up to the heavens, he wondered what type of God could have pronounced judgment on that poor town and required so much suffering to be a part of His divine plan.

The only answer, of course, was to do the one thing he was put on this planet to do, show the world evidence of man's inhumanity to man. With that thought in the fore, he put his pack on his shoulders and headed out of town, moving towards the coast. He was going to get the shots out or die in the attempt. He owed the kid that much, at least.

Chapter Twenty Nine

July 24, 1945, 11:30 p.m.

New York City, LIFE Magazine Headquarters

Daniel Baldwin had risen from a simple beat photographer eighteen years ago to the senior editor at LIFE magazine. The war had put a premium on photojournalism because the public desperately wanted to see with their own eyes what the boys were experiencing overseas. Baldwin firmly believed LIFE magazine was performing an essential function for the American people. The country needed to see the scope of devastation in war torn Europe to appreciate just how lucky they were to sit an ocean away from the war's privations.

Baldwin had sent men and a few ballsy women all over the globe to cover everything from the London Blitz and D-Day to the flag rising on Iwo Jima in the Pacific. He had just put to bed the week's current issue with some great shots of Berlin after the Red Army went berserk once word spread about the assassination attempt on Stalin. He had been expecting some shots from O'Rourke over in Poland, but so far, nothing doing. The goddamn New York Times had scooped them last week and had provided the best coverage. He had been hoping to at least have some pictures for this week's edition, but what could he do.

The Russians were clamping down on any Western reporters, especially Americans, so getting the goods out of Warsaw was next to. Chuckling to himself, he thought, *Russians hate bad press coverage worse than the first Roosevelt administration.* However, that week's issue was put to bed and Baldwin had a little ritual that was part good luck and part superstition.

Once the entire magazine had been laid out and set for the presses, he pulled out a bottle of Jamieson Irish Whiskey, poured himself three fingers worth, and tried to pretend he was John Q Public looking at the images for the first time. It didn't always work, but late at night with no one around, he found he could get a real feel for what the average reader was thinking that first moment they saw a new issue. *What the hell it beats heading home to the old lady.*

Daniel was nearly at the bottom of the glass when the phone rang. It was so damned quiet in the deserted office the phone actually scared the hell out of him and he almost knocked over the bottle. *Now that would have been crime*, he thought. Grabbing the phone, he bluntly answered, "Baldwin."

A man with a crisp British accent spoke, "Mr. Baldwin, my name is Stevenson and I work for His Majesty's Government of Great Britain. I am terribly sorry to call so late, but I understand that you are in the process of preparing tomorrow's issue of your excellent magazine. Please correct me if I am mistaken."

More than a bit annoyed at the almost playful tone of the Brit, Baldwin shot back, "So, what's it to you. You got something for me?"

Baldwin didn't trust a soul and always assumed everybody was playing an angle, especially people calling in the dead of night.

"As luck would have it, as a matter of fact, I do have something for you. In fact, one of my men should be moments away from your office about to deliver some very startling photos. I believe you will find them provocative enough to hopefully work them into this week's issue."

"Look, Stevenson, or whatever the hell your name is, stop playing games. If you are who you say you are, then you know we don't mix ourselves up with any governmental agencies. As long as I am editor over here, LIFE magazine will not be used for any type of propaganda for either side. So whoever you are, you better start speaking straight or this conversation will end."

Even more annoying, the British voice on the other line didn't change one iota. He almost seemed to smile at the American's little offering of bravado. "I really must apologize for not being more direct. You see, one of your chaps had some friends in our Foreign Office and used the services of a diplomatic bag to expedite the delivery of, as I mentioned earlier, rather disturbing photos that I have no doubt will generate much interest on your part.

The man's name is O'Rourke and I believe that he does have quite the reputation of, how do you Americans coin the phrase, 'Delivering the Goods.' So please, don't be alarmed at the messenger, we were only the most effective way to deliver the photos. I am sure that you will later thank Mr. O'Rourke for his intrepidness."

The British man on the other line almost laughed at the little play on words. "Call me at the British embassy if you have any further questions, good night Mr. Baldwin and, again, thank you for your time." Then the line went dead. Baldwin downed his shot and took off for the front to desk look for this mysterious parcel.

The forty nine year old Baldwin moved as quickly as his seriously overweight frame would allow, went down the elevator and sped straight towards the security desk. Without a good evening to the long time guard, Baldwin blurted, "Has anyone been here and dropped something off for me, say within the past fifteen minutes?"

The sweating Baldwin startled the aging guard, so he didn't waste any time with small talk. "Yes Sir, Mr. Baldwin, just about to call you when you came a runnin' down and grabbed me just here now. This fellow was dressed mighty fine to be some messenger, but he told me to call you directly, sir, and that's what I was about to do just now."

The watchman handed over the yellow parcel to Baldwin who scooped it up with barely a thank you and ran back towards the elevator. Daniel pushed his floor and refused to open the contents until he was locked inside his office. Chuckling to himself, he realized he was letting this cloak-and-dagger stuff actually get to him, but he had to admit he was more than a little excited. Finally, after about five minutes he got to his desk, swept everything off of it, took his pocketknife out and opened the contents. From what Baldwin could see there was one note, a container used to ship undeveloped film and one other unopened manila folder. He unfolded the note and read the few quick lines. O'Rourke wrote:

Dear Daniel,

I am sorry for the method, but you don't understand what it's like over here. It's pure bloody hell. The Russians are massacring people left and right, and I got it all on bloody print. When you see some of these shots, then you'll understand. Whatever you do, print it all, don't hold back. I have hooked up with another underground group and will send photos out as best that I can. Hope to see you soon and you can buy your brother Irishman a drink, but don't know if there is enough whiskey in all of Ireland to drown out what I've seen. Something bad is building, Danny boy, I can just feel it. Mark my words, this is a beginning, not an end, not by a long shot.

God Bless,

Paddy O'Rourke

O'Rourke and Baldwin went back a lot of years, and Paddy was not easily rattled. Whatever he saw must have shaken the hell out of him. He grabbed the sealed folder and hoped they were already processed shots, so he could see what the hell Paddy was talking about. His knife sliced through the folder, then he reached in and pulled out about twelve photos. He flipped the bundle over and his heart stopped as he saw the first shot. *Jesus Christ.*

In a shot that stunned Baldwin, pictured in the foreground was an evil looking Soviet officer with his service revolver held out straight and caught in the process of shooting some poor bastard in the side of the head. Looking closer, Baldwin saw that O'Rourke caught the shot just as the bullet exited the side of the guy's head and he could see the fountain of blood and a huge chunk of skull, or whatever, flying off the side of the poor bastard's head.

Somehow O'Rourke captured the pure shock and suddenness of the execution. The poor kid's eyes were opened in disbelief at what was happening. Then he saw the kid's hand. Holy shit, the kid wasn't a Pole, but an American. *That's a goddamn press pass that he is showing to that Russian bastard and he still shot him.* He held up the picture again and took the whole shot in and couldn't believe the image that O'Rourke caught on film. A young American reporter executed in a brutal, cold hearted fashion, and all done in front of a crowd of people, no less.

He put the shot down and began looking at the other shots; corpses piled on top of one another in an open field, a tank crashed through the front of a Church, the village burning, and on and on. No wonder Paddy had to get these shots out the safest and fastest way that he could, so he picked up the phone.

Calling down to the pressroom, he got the floor manager. The loud presses drowned out his voice, so Baldwin yelled, "Stop the goddamn presses and I mean now. Hold everything, don't do another single copy. I will be back to you within the hour."

The press operator couldn't believe what the hell he had just heard and shouted back, "Have you lost your goddamn mind? We just started and have got to finish this production run by three in the morning or you can't get the issue out on time. Is that understood? You don't have the pull for this, Baldwin, and you damn well know it. Once it leaves your desk and hits mine, I own it."

"No you listen here, you son of a bitch. If you run one more goddamn copy I swear to Christ that I'll come down there and drop you on your ass. And think for a second, you dumbass, when was the last time I told you to hold a press run, you thickheaded wop? That's right, when Roosevelt died. Well guess what, this is bigger."

With that said, he slammed down the phone and started making calls to get people up and down to the newsroom now. He debated about calling the Times, but decided to hold off until the morning. The reporter in him died hard. He looked down again at the shot of that poor kid and just shook his head. He picked it up again and said aloud, "Just a goddamn kid. When this is over, kid, you are going to be the most famous person shot since the Archduke Ferdinand."

Reaching for the bottle of whiskey, he hoped it would end better than the first one.

Chapter Thirty

July 26, 1945, 10:00 a.m.

The White House

President Harry S. Truman was about as angry as any man to ever sit in the oval office at that moment. The normally composed Truman had had his breakfast interrupted by an aide who handed him the newest issue of LIFE magazine. The President made it a point to take in the weekly news magazines during breakfast in the morning and usually enjoyed the quiet time to get a feel for how the country was taking certain things. His main concern for the moment was how the American public was dealing with war fatigue. Most everyone was complaining now about the need for continued rationing, or getting impatient to find out when their sons or husbands were coming home, and the like.

Truman had just put down the TIME magazine when he saw the front cover of LIFE magazine. Truman froze up inside as the look on the boy's face gripped him like nothing he had seen in years. The caption in large bold-faced print read, 'Soviet **Justice in Occupied Poland: An American Reporter Pays the Ultimate Price'**. He found himself transfixed. He couldn't take his eyes off the cover.

The photo was the most grotesque picture he had ever seen on the cover of any magazine or newspaper in all his life. Right there in black and white, you saw the last instant of the young man's life just as the bullet literally blew out the side of his head. Shaking his head, the President couldn't take his eyes off the stark image of a Soviet officer delivering the death sentence to an American.

Who in the hell did do these goddamn Russians think they are? Sons of bitches every last one of them. Truman was so damned angry that he rolled up the magazine and stormed out into the garden in the back of the White House. He had to think, and he didn't want anyone telling him to calm down.

As he paced back and forth in the Rose garden, he kept rapping the side of his leg with the magazine. Each time the sound kept getting louder and louder, as what happened sank in and made him all the more angry. Without even realizing it, he began to mutter aloud.

The Secret Service agent nearby could make out certain words like, "Sons of bitches... pushed us around too goddamned long...," and, "I'm gonna call the bastard myself."

With that last line, Truman turned and practically raced back to his office. He picked up the phone and called Charlie Ross, his longtime friend and current Press Secretary, and told him to do a favor for him. Hanging up the phone, Truman felt better contemplating what he was going to do and the last thing he wanted was someone to tell him what he could or couldn't say. This time, he wanted Jimmie Byrnes out of the loop.

Trying to calm down a bit, Truman went back to the Oval Office and decided to take a look inside the magazine. Turning to the table of contents first, Truman saw the editors had put together a special, last minute edition that highlighted the widespread Polish uprising against Soviet occupation. The Poles were calling it a war of liberation while the Soviets accused the Poles of being fascist sympathizers and vowed to destroy them. The President flipped the pages and with each picture became more and more disgusted at what he saw.

LIFE dedicated fifteen pages of images and copy to what they called the "Death of Sochaczew". Truman couldn't believe his eyes, thinking these images of Russian atrocities were as terrible as any Nazi or Japanese horror. Page after page of devastation and human misery assaulted the American President. Thinking, *I'll be damned if I'll sit back and let them act like they can get away with this. How in God's name can I face the American people and ever shake hands with those lying bastards?*

Truman knew once the American people saw those images, they wouldn't stand for it. The Germans and the Japanese found out the hard way.

A knock on the door brought into his office Secretary of State, James Byrnes, Bill Donovan, and Secretary Stimson. Sitting with his arms crossed and looking as if he wasn't about to be moved under any circumstances, his inner circle never saw him look so determined. Truman angrily blurted out, "For Christ's sake, who the hell told you people to barge into my office? I don't remember calling a meeting, so you can just go on about your business."

Taken aback by the President's demeanor, Byrnes very respectfully said, "Now, Mr. President, we all saw the pictures, but you just can't decide to go outside channels and contact the Soviet ambassador and summon him to the White House. The Russians embassy said they didn't appreciate the tone of the summons, but

Ambassador Gromyko intends to comply with your request within the hour."

A red faced Truman fired right back, "Jimmie, don't come into this office on this morning and talk to me like that. Your damn right I contacted the ambassador and he better be getting here pretty damn soon and don't look at me that way, because right now I don't give a good goddamn, Jimmie. Did you see that picture? That was an American reporter, doing his job, and he was shot down like an animal, in front of a crowd, no less. I want that son of bitch brought to the United States for a trial and then I want to see him shot! See how they like that."

Truman's face was red and he was practically yelling, "You all can feel free to sit in on the meeting. Don't worry, it'll be a short one. I'll be the one calling him a son of a bitch and if any of you got a problem with that, you don't have to be here."

The men in the room just froze listening to the exchange. Secretary of State Byrnes had been immune to any problems with the President, up to this point at least, and everyone, especially Byrnes, was shocked at just how angry and vehement the President was at the moment. Men who worked in the Roosevelt White House never remembered hearing the former President ever get so angry or yell so loud.

Stimson was more reserved then everyone else in the room, but after looking at those pictures, it brought bad memories of other photos of atrocities he had viewed earlier in the year, except they were inflicted upon Germans.

Trying to calm the President down, the Secretary of War spoke in a respectful tone, "Mr. President, I share your horror at these images and honestly can't fathom how a civilized people could perform such unspeakable crimes. But sir, the Soviets are still officially our ally and have made certain commitments in support of the American war effort in the Pacific. I would urge caution in the exchange. Be strong, but don't burn bridges, sir."

Truman bristled at the attempt to calm him down like he was some kind of rabid dog. Picking up the LIFE magazine, he whirled around from his chair and held it up to the members of his staff. With fire in his eyes, "Don't tell me not to burn bridges, Mr. Secretary. What the hell do you call this? That was somebody's son who was executed to make a point, and now I'm about to make a point of my own. Let's get something straight. I don't want another person trying to calm me down. I'm about to make such a point that Stalin will think twice about ever touching an American again under any circumstances. Is that clear to everyone in this room? There is a family in Manhattan right now, crying their damn eyes out because of those sons of bitches, and I'm not just going to sit back and pretend it didn't happen."

Stimson lowered his eyes as he found he couldn't look at the cover for very long. The President was right that, in the end, it represented some poor mother crying around the kitchen table mourning a boy who was never coming back. Stimson was forced to admit, *maybe this does change everything.*

By all reports, atrocities were being committed on a widespread fashion in both Germany and throughout Poland. A growing chorus in Congress had been calling for the President to condemn the Soviets and, all along, Stimson had to admit that he wanted to hold off. *But now everything is different. By the end of the week, the American public very well may want blood.*

Donovan had been standing back in the conversation letting things ebb and flow and didn't say a word. Just when he felt everyone taking a pause, he decided to jump in and speak his peace. However, he didn't intend to get involved with the issues surrounding the LIFE cover. Instead he had come to the White House for something else entirely and basically ran into Byrnes and Byrnes in the hallway coming in to the office and Byrnes just assumed it was about Poland. He was wrong, Donovan was about to drop another bombshell on this administration.

Somewhat hesitantly, Donovan put his hands out moved them up and down and started slow, "Excuse me, Mr. President, gentlemen, I actually came down for another issue and I am afraid that this will only complicate matters. In fact, I hesitate to even bring it up now, but I don't see how it can wait. Early this morning, OSS agents working in Prague received reports from two very reliable ranking sources, an American listening outpost and the other a highly placed Czech national.

"In twenty-four hours, the Czechoslovakian government under President Benes and Foreign Minister Masyrk are about to demand that all Soviet occupation forces are henceforth forbidden from using Czech territory or airspace to conduct military operations against Poland. Further, they formally announced that they demand that all Soviet forces pullback from occupation duties in their country. President Benes had stated that since there are no more Germans in Czechoslovakia, then there is no need for any Russians. It is expected that he will make a direct appeal to the Western Allies to support this declaration."

The shocked look on the faces staring back at him told Donovan that he had just laid a major policy problem on their collective plate and it had caught everybody by surprise.

Pausing for effect, Donovan looked the President directly in the eyes and, in a deliberate tone, said, "The Czechs have also made it known that failure to comply with the legally constituted government of Czechoslovakia could very well lead to hostilities along the lines of the Polish revolt. Mr. President this is very, very hot stuff.

Gentlemen, once this declaration goes out to the public, it is expected by analysts in my department that Soviet reactions will likely be quite severe, easily along the lines of Soviet reactions against partisan forces in Poland.

Failure to act by the West to support another democratically elected government against an unlawful occupation will be interpreted as weakness and will undermine our position in Europe and possibly prolong the war in the Pacific. Worse, the Japs won't look to negotiate if we are up to our necks in difficulties with the Russians. I suggest we figure out a response strategy and soon."

As Donovan finished his bombshell presentation, he looked over at Secretary Stimson who looked distraught, Byrnes looked surprised and a little unsure of how to respond, and only the President gave a look like he knew exactly how he felt. Truman was a man who had just been given an opportunity to show American resolve, and Donovan thought to himself, *God help us all*.

Breaking the awkward silence, the phone rang and a very tense Truman answered curtly, "Send him in."

Secretary of State Byrnes knew it had to be Gromyko. *Why the hell couldn't he have waited another half hour?* Byrnes had been gradually steering the President towards a more anti-Communist stance over the past several weeks, but Truman looked as though he was ready to pick a fight right here in the Oval Office. As the Soviet ambassador walked in, all he could think was what the hell could he do but try to pull the President back if he started to push too far.

With that thought in mind, he extended his hand and said, "Good Morning, Mr. Ambassador, thank you for being so kind as to come right over. Please sit, you know the others in the room."

The dark haired Gromyko was youngish for such an important post, but the dour faced Russian had steely nerves and never seemed to break a sweat while in negotiations. He was much like the former Foreign Minister, Molotov, and could tell lies all day and not once drop that poker face he perfected over the years. The Soviet Ambassador was not pleased with the sudden summons, but his own intelligence people had informed him of American reactions to reports and photographs coming out of Poland.

He even saw the sensationalized shot on the front cover of a popular weekly magazine and assumed that the American President intended to lodge some protest. Since he had no instructions, he would let the American rant a bit, but wait to see what Moscow wanted until he gave an official answer. *Hopefully this won't take long.*

Gromyko went to shake the President's hand but President Truman never moved from the chair behind his desk, a cool reception indeed. Unused to such a lack of manners in a diplomatic function, Gromyko still refused to take the bait and merely took his seat. The Soviet diplomat did not fail to notice the room was thick with tension, but he brushed off the feeling as the President began.

For a man who had replaced the most significant political figure in American politics of this century, Truman had consciously felt like he was acting in the man's shadows, but, at that moment, the man glaring at the Soviet ambassador wasn't an afterthought on a presidential ticket, he wasn't a man unsure of himself, and he damn sure wasn't thinking to himself whether or not he was the man for the job.

On this morning, Harry S. Truman felt surer of what he was about to do than anything he had ever attempted in his entire public life. That morning, Truman felt more like the real President of the United States than at any moment since he had raised his right hand and swore to uphold and protect the office of the Presidency.

With a snarl on his face, Truman took his worn copy of LIFE magazine and threw it at the Soviet ambassador, "Look at the cover of this magazine and tell me what in the devil are you people thinking? Your government had better have an explanation for the execution of this young man and you had better come up with something acceptable pretty goddamn fast. Is that understood?"

Gromyko's eyes were opened wide in disbelief that a head of state would physically throw something at an ambassador that Truman's words barely registered.

Truman didn't let up, "Take a long hard look at that boy's face and tell me why the American people shouldn't think that you are no better than the damn Nazis."

Rather than wait for an explanation, Truman shot up from his chair and stood over Gromyko and barked, "And before you hand me some piece of diplomatic bullshit, Mr. Ambassador, I want you to understand just how serious this administration feels about not just the execution of an American citizen, but clear evidence of organized genocide being practiced against the Polish people. The American people won't put up with being allied to any country guilty of crimes against humanity. Now answer me! Don't just sit there and pretend you don't understand what I'm getting at. Relations between our two governments are at a precarious point, Mr. Ambassador, have I made myself clear?"

Gromyko was completely taken aback by the ferocious tone of the President. Thus far, the new American President had come off as unsure and seemed to rely heavily on his staff, but this time his most trusted advisors were deathly quiet and Truman was doing all the talking.

Gromyko decided to aggressively come right back at the American, and said, "How dare you talk to a representative of the Soviet people like this? I am not some Filipino house boy that can be barked at by the master of the house. Although we regret the loss of life, the Red Army is merely reacting to the criminal acts of a small band of brigands who are targeting the lawful authorities in Poland. Also, I must remind you that the Soviet government, as a matter of national policy, will not discuss military matters that do not pertain to our current alliance. But I must express shock that the United States could allow itself to fall prey to a cunning propaganda campaign aimed at splitting our great alliance.

"I understand your anger at the death of the American reporter, but how do we know that this man wasn't shot by a Pole wearing a stolen uniform? In fact, Soviet intelligence sources have unearthed a terrible plot by Polish fascists to slaughter this very village and try to blame the brave Red Army in a pathetic attempt to win points in the foreign press. In fact, the United States should be supporting the Soviet people in its fight against fascism in Poland."

Gromyko stood up as he strongly emphasized his last remarks. The Soviet diplomat thought he had made a nice play of his own and turned as he noticed the American Secretary of State, Byrnes, quietly shake his head. Then his eyes moved to the front as the President got to his feet again.

All Truman could think as Gromyko spewed his lies was, *you lying bastard.* Out of a sense of courtesy, he let the man finish, but more so that when it came time to hang him, there would be more than enough rope. *How could these people look at someone who gave his country so much support during the war and just bold face lie to them? Damn if I'll ever understand these people.* He saw Jimmie start to stand, but Truman was quicker and motioned for him to sit down. Donovan's eyes went wide as he could barely believe how tough this old Missouri mule had turned out to be once he got his blood up.

The President slammed his fist on the table and wagged his finger at the Soviet ambassador again and said, "What did I tell you about coming into this office and trying to feed me a line of pure horseshit, Mr. Ambassador? I told you point blank that relations between our two countries are in jeopardy and then you have the audacity to tell me that the Poles slaughtered their own people. What kind of fool do you people take me for?"

Ambassador Gromyko stammered back, "Mr. President, I must protest. I did not come here to be accused of being a liar. You must excuse me…"

Truman moved quick and cut him off before he started for the door. "This meeting isn't over 'til I say it's over. Is that clear, Mr. Ambassador?"

The Soviet diplomat sat back down and looked up into the glaring eyes of the American President and decided to let him finish.

Truman went right back at him. "I am going to make this simple, so simple that not even your government could get it confused. I am holding General Secretary Stalin personally responsible for the death of Michael Zelinski, not to mention those poor innocent Poles. I am instructing you to inform Moscow that we demand, repeat demand, the arrest of the officer in charge of the massacre. He will be tried in the United States and punished according to the U.S. penal code for murder.

"Next, the United States is demanding that independent, neutral observers be allowed into Poland to observe Soviet occupation forces until free and independent elections can be held by the citizens of Poland. We will abide by the results as long they reflect the true will of the people. Lastly, the United States is prepared to work hand in hand with the forces of freedom loving peoples throughout the globe. This country went to war, shed blood, and intended that something good come of it.

"So, Ambassador Gromyko, tell your master in Moscow that this nation will have no other choice than to actively support freedom fighters that refuse to live under the iron thumb of tyranny. Tell your boss that means we will support the Czechs and the Poles if it comes right down to it. I suggest that if your government wishes to participate in the world as a civilized people, you will find no greater friend than the United States of America. However, if you continue down the road that led to ruin for the Nazis and the empire of Japan, you too will be faced by a world united against evil. I hope you reconsider your polices. You may go and contact your government for instructions. This meeting is over."

A flabbergasted Gromyko turned to Secretary Byrnes, who shook his head and so the Russian merely nodded at the President and walked out of the office. As the door closed behind him, all Gromyko could think was, *How will I tell Comrade Stalin?*

The noise from the door closing as the Soviet ambassador left the room hung for a moment, as the President's key advisors sat in complete silence, each contemplating the impact of the interview. Byrnes was utterly dumbfounded. The former Senator from South Carolina had, up to that point, been the President's confidant on all matters, everything from domestic to foreign policy. To be forced to watch what just happened as a mere spectator left the normally composed Byrnes a bit out of sorts.

Secretary of War Stimson sat back in his chair and couldn't help but admire the President for standing up to his own convictions. In all his years of serving government, he never witnessed such a display. Even though, deep down, Stimson knew there were about a dozen different reasons why this meeting probably should have been handled differently, he kept coming back to the thought, *maybe we had to sell our souls to the devil to defeat the Nazis, but not anymore.* The picture of that boy on the cover pushed the President over the edge, and Stimson knew that things were never going to be the same and he hoped the man was up to it.

Donovan was thinking the exact same thing. The head of the OSS believed in his heart the President just gave one of the most significant diplomatic exchanges in American history and probably the most profane. *The Russians are going to go ape shit over our support of the Czechs. It throws out the legitimacy of occupation throughout Europe. It undermines the entire Soviet post-war security framework. They won't stand for that. They can't.*

He looked over at the President who was glaring, just waiting for someone to open his mouth and tell him what a fool he was to start such a brawl. Knowing where it may be heading added a new gravity to the situation, but Donovan long ago decided it was time to confront the Soviets,

Donovan had a feeling that after old Uncle Joe gets a load of today's conversation, we just may see how far the Russians are looking to push this. Either way, Stalin will test Truman's resolve and soon. There is no way that he could back down so easily, then and only then will we see what the President is made of.

Looking up at his advisors, Truman decided to make it quick, get them on board, and start notifying the British and even the French about the change in policy. *Like or not, I just changed things and they will have to get used to it.* "Before anyone says anything, especially you, Jimmie, I know that I stepped all over your territory just now, but it's been a long time in coming and the sooner we dig in our heels the better. No hard feelings, but those pictures changed things forever for me. No turning back now, understood?"

Byrnes always smelled the wind changing better than any political operator in Washington since Lincoln's man, William Seward, a century ago. The Secretary of State stood up and walked over to the President with hand extended and said, "Mr. President, let me be the first to tell you that it took tremendous courage to fire away at the Soviets like that. Who knows, maybe it'll make Stalin think twice before trying anything else in the future. If he doesn't realize that we are serious now, then I am afraid to see what you'll have to do next to get their attention."

That brought a smile to Truman's face and the others in the room smiled as well, breaking the tension in the room. The President answered back, somewhat relieved, "You just have to understand that I can't abide being made a fool, and I think that they have been playing us for fools ever since Yalta, back in February. Back then, no one gave a damn what I thought, but guess what, today, I am in a position to pass along my thoughts."

"Hell, Mr. President, you passed along more than your thoughts, I thought that you were going to give Gromyko a swift kick in the ass on the way out," chimed in Donovan.

Donovan wanted to pass along one important thing from his earlier announcement before things turned too light hearted. "In all seriousness gentlemen, I would like to state for the record that this is the beginning. My analysts are concerned that since the attempt on Stalin's life two weeks ago, he may have become even more paranoid and possibly aggressive. Recent events in Poland seem to bear this out. He won't take what just happened here lying down."

Stimson asked, "Be more specific, do you think that they will back out of commitments in the Far East, or worse?"

Donovan responded right back, "Not necessarily, because he wouldn't have agreed to intervene against the Japanese unless he dearly wanted something in the way of land or else he wouldn't raise a hand to help us. No the key has always been Europe. I expect Stalin to test us, probably in regards to our response to the coming Czechoslovakian proclamation. If we back down early in the game, he will never take what we say seriously and any hope of establishing democratic, friendly regimes in Europe will be lost."

Looking over at the Secretary Of State, Donovan added, "The one thing that I can't answer is how you think this will play on the home front? We better start figuring out a way to start informing the American public over the breakdown in relations."

Byrnes felt a bit better, and spoke with a little more confidence than before, "The way I see things, first we better try to manage how the public responds to these photos, because the story is out now. I imagine that the papers will start resurrecting the old atrocity stories from a few months ago, plus send more folks to Poland and then Czechoslovakia looking for a better scoop. The President must stay ahead on this one. We'll prepare a speech to be read immediately after the Czech declaration. We will make the Soviets out to look like the bastards that they are and not sugarcoat anything. Also, we may want to start leaking a few things today before the Czechs announce tomorrow."

He hesitated for a moment, then in a very ominous voice added, "In addition, I recommend that we announce US demobilization in Europe will be put indefinitely on hold until the current crisis has passed. That will send the proper message, I would think. Either way, we give the Soviets something to really think about. How's that sound Mr. President?"

Smiling as he watched his staff iron out the details, even though the details really didn't matter at the moment, no what did matter was that everyone was on board and they were treating him with more respect than ever before. For the first time, he felt he led them to the decision rather than having them lead him by the nose to where they wanted to go.

Truman said, "That sounds about right boys, I think that I have caused enough trouble for one morning. Figure out the details, I will be back later in the morning, but right now, I have a call to make."

Stimson asked, "Who are you contacting sir, Prime Minister Churchill?"

Shaking his head no, Truman said, "No. I'll be calling a crying mother and father in Manhattan, the Zelinski's need to know that their son's death is going to mean something, somehow. Good day, gentlemen."

Chapter Thirty One

July 28, 1945, 10:00 P.M.

Moscow, The Kremlin

In the twelve days since the attempt on Stalin's life, a great many changes had been in the works. Western observers noted a massive buildup of Red Army military presence throughout Moscow, especially around the Kremlin. Marshal Zhukov replaced the ceremonial Taman Guards Division, with a highly decorated Guards Division to protect the Kremlin.

Comrade Stalin could rest at ease during the night, as he looked out the windows to see war scarred T-34 tanks, anti-aircraft batteries, and the constant movement of roving patrols to prevent any more treachery from endangering the life of the Soviet leader. The victorious Red Army was there to protect Comrade Stalin just as it was tasked to protect Mother Russia and the Revolution.

Hundreds of NKVD officers and their families had already been arrested, tried, and shot for their complicity in the July plot. Polish communists by the hundreds who were working in Moscow, waiting to take over in Warsaw, had already been rounded up, vigorously interrogated, and then dispatched with a bullet to the back of the head. The Red Army needed victims to offer Comrade Stalin peace of mind and the remaining NKVD leadership in Moscow had largely been isolated under direct orders from Zhukov.

The Red Army's own intelligence branch, the GRU, was tasked with pursuing those responsible for the conspiracy against Comrade Stalin and took particular pleasure in arresting, torturing, and then executing Beria both for his role in the military Purges and for his failure in Berlin. Comrade Beria did not die well. His interrogation and execution was filmed for Comrade Stalin's personal viewing delight..

The GRU was able to extract a confession from the former all-powerful head of the NKVD. The Red Army was only too happy to report the extent of Beria's crimes against the State. In less than two short weeks, the Red Army had seen its position grow stronger than any time since the defeat of the White forces during the Revolution under the leadership of War Commissar Trotsky.

Zhukov had long ago decided the Red Army must avenge itself against the NKVD for the purges of the '30's and used Stalin's newfound patronage to assert itself as the ultimate protector of both Mother Russia and the Party. In Zhukov's mind, there was nothing the Red Army couldn't accomplish and with each victory against enemies foreign and domestic, the Red Army's position would be secured for all time.

The night's meeting began late, as was usual for Stalin, and although Stalin could now get around without the need of a cane, he still walked with a pronounced limp. His hands were shakier than most recalled, his hearing still damaged, and he seemed to have aged twenty years in the past two weeks. The one thing that hadn't diminished as a result of the assassination attempt was his anger and the flood of paranoid fantasies that kept him up most nights.

For hours on end, Stalin would think about treachery from within and from without. He refused to take the pills prescribed by his doctors which were supposed to take away the night tremors that plagued him ever since his escape from the deathtrap in Berlin. He didn't trust his own doctors, so when his mind drifted and he found himself trapped in the fiery tomb of that limousine waiting for death to reach out and claim him, only vodka could calm his nerves and eventually induce sleep.

Treachery was everywhere. He could smell it. Deep into the night, those thoughts tormented Stalin and caused him to lose even more peace of mind. Everything had turned against him. The only man that he could trust was Zhukov and Stalin didn't trust him completely, either.

Stalin was in a particularly foul mood tonight. Rumors of a political crisis brewing up in Czechoslovakia had swept through the Kremlin. No one wanted to sit in poor Khrushchev's shoes this evening. *He will have to break the bad news, and that's probably why he looks like death tonight*, thought Zhukov. The Marshal had been spending more time in Moscow as of late trying to coordinate the Polish campaign and trying to maintain relations with Stalin. He glanced around as the others tried to quietly drink their soup when Stalin threw his bowl across the room, shattering the fine china against the wall.

Comrade Stalin's voice erupted against across the table, "Khrushchev, why are you hiding this new treachery of the Czechs from me? Did you think that I would somehow fail to find out about this proclamation? Who do those Czech bastards think they are, trying to dictate to the Soviet people! You had better tell them that Stalin will crush them like the Poles."

A dozen curious eyes looked up and watched how the new Foreign Minister, a man who had served Stalin for many years, would answer. His bald head was already profusely sweating, "Comrade Stalin, that Czech bastard President Benes is trying to take advantage of our troubles in Poland to try and force the Red Army out of Czechoslovakia. This declaration means less than nothing, so we ignore it."

Stalin cut him off quickly, "Of course, we are going to ignore it, you fool." Stalin's rage began to build at the thought of first fucking Poles and now the back-stabbing Czechs. *How dare they presume to force the Red Army out after they liberated their miserable country from the Nazis?*

"Khrushchev, you had better tell them to go to hell. In fact, start rounding up the fascist ringleaders of this conspiracy in their Government, including Benes if necessary. We will make some examples of these Czechs. A couple of thousand should do for starters. Comrade Zhukov will assist you in these matters."

Stalin just sat down again as he felt better at just saying the words, that by merely ordering it done, all shall be made right. Still standing, however, was Foreign Minister Khrushchev, who looked as if he had more to say. Zhukov watched as the new Foreign Minister shifted weight from his left to his right and looked quite tense, as if something worse was to come. What could be wrong, the Czechs would be crushed and that would be that as far as Zhukov was concerned, unless something else was happening.

Stalin saw the same thing.

With a disgusted look on his face, Stalin waved his hand in the air as if he were swatting an annoying fly and bellowed, "Out with it, Nikita. You look ridiculous standing there with that stupid look on your face. I ought to have had my head examined for making you Foreign Minster." Khrushchev bristled at the rebuke, but he summed up the courage and answered the "Boss".

"It's the Americans. Their new President, this Truman, must be a lunatic because he shouted at Gromyko for a half-hour the other day and told him that he was holding you, Comrade Stalin, personally responsible for the death of an American reporter whose execution was captured on film and placed on an American magazine cover. He accused us of committing genocide in Poland and he made clear that he would support any group taking up arms against our occupation.

The Czechs never would have made this announcement unless the Americans told them ahead of time that they would support them. I am afraid, Comrade Stalin, that the Americans have stabbed us in the back yet again. Gromyko said that this Truman hates us and accuses us of all sorts of crimes. He can't be dealt with like Roosevelt. I am afraid that the Americans mean business, Comrade Stalin, and this will only complicate matters in Poland as well. Is that correct, Comrade Zhukov?"

Zhukov could only nod his head as he contemplated operations against the Poles if they were openly supported by the Americans. Zhukov instantly grasped the situation. *You can't fight a war to your rear if you have a more dangerous enemy to your front.* Before he could consider the next logical step, Stalin suddenly went wild with rage.

The tentative words coming from his new Foreign Minister took a moment or so to sink in completely. First, the Americans engaged in a conspiracy to make a deal with the Germans to deny the Soviet people the fruits of victory and then, the same Americans had the fucking balls to hold him responsible for the death of some reporter.

These Americans dare to accuse Stalin of murder. They dare to openly back murderous Poles and fascist Czechs. Do they think that Stalin is so weak that I would run and hide? Is that what they think of Stalin? Stalin will show them then who has the weaker stomach.

In a rage, Stalin's eyes went wide in fury as he became so overcome with emotion that he could barely see straight. Slamming the table, "Stalin will not be talked to like some common criminal. It's all so clear now. It's the Americans who have been behind everything after all, not that old fool in London. This new President wants to encourage first Poles, then Czechs, and probably Germans to rise up against us. He thinks just because his atomic bomb project is successful that we will back down to them, but Stalin does not bend to anyone. Do you hear that, we shall dominate them. They are weak. Why else would they beg us like dogs to help them against the Japanese?"

Looking to calm Stalin before he worked himsef into a stroke, Zhukov jumped in, "Comrade Stalin, I am ordering the Red Army in Czechoslovakia to initiate full martial law immediately. The GRU stands ready to begin arresting the ringleaders as you ordered and begin making public examples of those who seek to encourage lawlessness. Next, I am ordering border checkpoints closed at all points leading into Austria, Germany and Czechoslovakia. The Red Army will show these Americans that we will not be intimidated."

Suddenly feeling light-headed, Stalin slipped back into his chair and listened to his military commander and nodded along. Thinking, *of course he's right*. The West would never openly challenge the Soviet army because to do so was unthinkable. *We would squash them like ants if they ever tried to threaten us. No, Zhukov is right. First we crush the Poles and make examples of these ungrateful Czechs.*

Feeling relieved, Stalin reached for a glassful of vodka and drained the shot glass in one quick pull. Refilling quickly, Stalin started to calm and thought, *the sooner the Red Army destroys these bothersome Poles, the quicker the problem in Czechoslovakia will be dealt with.*

Looking at the other end of the table, Stalin's eyes fell upon the newly appointed head of the NKVD, General Vsevolod Nikolayevich Merkulov. So far, he had escaped any of his predecessors' guilt, but now it was time for the NKVD to serve the State again. Stalin said, "Merkulov, I must know everything about what is happening in London and Washington. Put those spies of yours to work and find out what the imperialists will do next. Don't fail me, Merkulov, or else you'll end up like your former boss. Is that understood?"

The new NKVD man took an almost audible gulp of air and merely nodded assent to Stalin. Stalin refused to be caught off guard again by these Americans. More importantly, Stalin needed more information about the American bomb project. *Maybe they have more bombs then we thought possible and this Truman thinks he can intimidate me. Fine if the Americans want to threaten Stalin, we will see who will suffer in the end.*

July 29, 1945

Outside Munich, Germany

German POW Camp

After surviving the boredom of yet another American interrogation team, SS General Karl Wolff was escorted back to his semi-private home away from home, a converted, aging barracks that dated well before the First Word War. He had already been moved three times in the past eight weeks. It seemed everyone from the British to the Italians and even the Russians wanted to get their hands on him.

To be fair, he thought, as the ranking officer in Italy and second in command of the entire SS, he was still an important figure, or at least notorious. The Italians wanted to shoot him for his role in German reprisal operations in Italy. The Russians wanted him because he was known to be behind the secret negotiations with the Americans.

Luckily for Wolff, the Americans long ago decided they intended to keep a close watch on him, so he was secretly transferred to a special POW camp administered by the American Seventh Army and spent his days answering a barrage of questions. Most evenings he found himself sitting on his cot and smoking American cigarettes to pass the time. He had almost forgotten the aroma of fine Virginia tobacco. By the later stages of the war, it became difficult for even general officers to obtain some of the essentials of life, such as American tobacco and French cognac. The questions were tedious, but he knew that, all in all, things could be worse.

As hosts, the Americans had been more than adequate, but he still felt nothing but contempt for the Americans weak leaders who betrayed him and the German people now suffering under those animals from the East. The problem with Americans, in Wolff's estimation, was that they just didn't have the stomach to act in their own self-interest. They always seemed to need some cause, like children. All in all, it was hard not to like most Americans, although no doubt, he still hated the dour-faced Dulles and the rest of those fools in the OSS who lied to him and made him jump through hoops while the whole time they had no intention of saving Germany.

What had befallen his nation was hard to bear, especially for one who thought that it could have been saved. At least with the information he and his fellow ranking prisoners had been able to put together, the coalition formed to defeat the Nazis seemed to be falling apart. Who would have thought that fucking Poles would have had such balls, and to think that they almost killed the bastard?

Some of Wolff's fellow officers remarked how appropriate it would have been for that animal Stalin to die on the Unter den Linden in Berlin, less than a half-mile from where that other maniac shot himself. Wolff grinned at the thought and expected it would be amusing to watch how this growing crisis played out.

Even though Wolff made light of his present situation, deep down the fatigue, anxiety, and frustration during the final months of the war had taken their toll. The Americans might be protecting him at the moment, but he knew things could change overnight. The goddamn Dagos would love to line him up in front of a firing squad, probably throw a dance and drink wine over his dead body. *Now that's a morbid thought*, he said to himself, this place must really be starting to get to me.

He had just swung his legs over the bed when a knock at the door came and in scurried a familiar face. Dietrich von Hauss, senior aide to General Kesselring, entered his room and motioned to his lips to be quiet. Both men knew the room was probably bugged, so Hauss handed him a slip of paper.

The two men were of the same mind during the final days of the war. Hauss's superior, the former commander of German field forces in Italy, had desperately wanted to turn his divisions in Italy north and attack the Russians outside the gates of Berlin, but was recalled before Wolff's plan backfired. Hauss was the perfect staff officer and had connections throughout the European theater of operations.

The resourceful former General Staff officer had set up a network within the prison camp, plus somehow managed to communicate with other German POW camps in Germany and France. Hauss even knew about certain contingences that had been drawn up as the war deteriorated for the Germans. He even knew of the secret redoubt set up by the SS in the Bavarian mountains. Hauss needed confirmation that something was still active and the only one who could possibly know was Wolff, so after hearing the news, he went to find Wolff without delay.

Wolff's guard went up automatically. Even though Hauss almost certainly didn't pose any immediate danger, nothing was certain anymore. Hauss was one of the diehard nationalist fanatics, not a Nazi, but rabidly anti-Communist. All that he and many ranking German officers dreamed of doing was somehow finding a way to push the Russians out of Germany. Not really in the mood to be bothered, but since Hauss had always been a good officer, he made an exception.

He opened the envelope and read the contents. His eyes looked first quizzical and then opened wide the more he read, until by the end of the paragraph, he knew why Hauss had come. Taking a match, he immediately burned the letter, shook Hauss' hand and motioned for him to give him a minute to digest everything. Somehow, Hauss had confirmed that the Czechs had demanded the Russians leave their country and forbade the Red Army from operating against Polish partisan forces from bases in Czech territory.

What's more, this new American President, angered over recent events in Poland, had stated publicly that they would back the Czech declaration and called for observers and free elections in Poland. As he watched the letter burn, Wolff could barely believe his good fortune. Here it was right in front of him, the perfect opportunity to start a spark.

Wolff tried to imagine Stalin not as the ruler of an empire, but the man left after the attempt on his life and bet he must be a fucking wreck, probably as paranoid as Hitler had been after his own narrow escape. Just one spark ought to do it. He smiled as the flame licked the outer edges and smoldered inside the ashtray. *Yes, all it might take is a spark.*

Turning to Hauss, he pulled him close and whispered, "Thank you, my friend, you have no idea what this means to me. I have one more favor to ask. I need you to get a letter through the American lines to a mutual friend in Bavaria."

Hauss turned to look in his eyes and that moment of recognition made the two veteran officers nod, as both understood the meaning of the request. Hauss whispered back, "In two days' time, your letter shall be delivered. I swear to you."

In a deadly serious voice, barely above a whisper, Wolff added, "You will see, Hauss, that there is still a God left watching over Germany. We will all soon see."

Chapter Thirty Two

August 5, 1945, 4:30 a.m.

Ten Miles North of Pilsen, Czechoslovakia

After an all-night, forced march through thick Czechoslovakian forests, they were nearly in position. Though tired, the men roused themselves for the final approach. After two successive nights of roving ambushes against Soviet occupying forces, the Russians were alert and, more importantly, out in force. Perfect. Operation Loki's initial plan calling for small-scale attacks along the border of the Allied occupation zones worked as intended and the next phase was scheduled to begin within the hour.

Fortunately, the Russians had beefed up their frontline positions within a thousand or so yards opposite their American counterparts far quicker than had been expected and accordingly thinned out their rear areas, leaving behind vulnerable supply depots whose destruction would play the first part in the morning's actions.

.

These three hundred men were the very finest and last surviving soldiers of Hitler's SS, all extremely skilled in small unit combat, most schooled in the bocage in France, the rubble of Stalingrad, and the mountains of Italy. They embodied the Fuhrer's ideal of the perfect Teutonic knights of old. These warriors were determined and utterly ruthless men, who were prepared to perform any act, inflict any harm, and their willingness to die for their cause was without question. They moved with a purpose befitting the last German combat unit active in Europe. Major Zimmer was in command and acting under the direct orders of SS General Karl Wolff.

Zimmer couldn't believe how simple, yet audacious Operation Loki was in concept. Operation Loki took its name from the Norse God of trickery and deceit. *Loki would approve of tonight's plan, for if it succeeds, all hell is about to be unleashed upon an unsuspecting world.*

The Germans had been operating in small units, about squad size, for the past few nights. Zimmer had used the timing of the Czechoslovakian countrywide labor strikes as cover to hit various Russian units in the vicinity northeast of Pilsen. The Russians had recently moved nearly an entire mechanized division to fortify the approaches to the American held Czech city of Pilsen. The strategic crossroads was very important to both the Americans and the Russians. Six key highways and roads all converged at Pilsen and controlled the approaches into the Bavarian region of Germany.

The Americans insisted upon maintaining possession to protect both their German zone of occupation as well as cover the northern approaches to Austria. The Russians had been trying to prevent increasing numbers of Czech civilians from escaping out of their zone and into the American positions in the important city of Pilsen.

Dressed as Czech partisans, the various German patrols had shot up several supply columns, mined several roads, and put just enough pressure on the local Russian commanders to increase readiness without doing any real damage. One thing was clear, with each small attack the Russian response was getting more powerful and swifter. At first, they sent out several small mobile task forces composed of mixed infantry and a few tanks, but the previous night they moved nearly an entire battalion of armor against an ambush staged against a battery of Red Army artillery.

True to the Russian character, the Soviets moved hard and fast without any thought to their flanks, secure in the knowledge that these small attacks posed no real danger to their heavy units. Random artillery was launched against the surrounding forests hoping to flush the suspected Czech partisans out of their hiding spots, while Soviet tank units rode in full display up and down the highways. Zimmer noted how close the Russians moved near the American zone, at one point they came within a three hundred yards of a hidden American observation post.

Zimmer and his three unit commanders agreed that Loki could work. Especially since the Americans were moving more men into defensive positions to augment their own thinly held line. It would seem the Americans were getting more than a little nervous at the activity on the Russian side. Everything was evolving according to plan.

American Positions outside of Pilsen

Captain Marty Bowman commanded a company of mechanized infantry in the Fourth Armored Division's recon battalion. Bowman had served in the 4th Armored ever since the Battle of the Bulge, so he had seen a lot of the war and was happy as hell when the Germans called it kaput back in May. Bowman commanded a motorized detachment of three M8 armored scout cars, three infantry platoons, plus he had two M24 Chaffee light tanks riding shotgun for him. Life had been pretty good for the past few months, but that all changed several days ago.

For the past five days the division commander, Major General Hoge, was inspecting unit positions up and down the security zone set up by division two months ago. Five days before, these outposts were nothing but observation posts, but that all changed when word came down from the man himself, commander of the Third Army, General Patton, to start digging in and begin active patrols along the entire perimeter of the American occupation zone. Word had it the "Old Man" was in an absolute rage over Russian attacks in Poland and the dangerous massing of Soviet armor along the Czech border. No one was going to sucker punch "Old Blood and Guts," so Patton started beefing up American frontline positions throughout the entire Third Army occupation zone.

So, that meant recon men, like Captain Bowman, were tasked with getting a feel for the bad guys on the other side of the line. For the past week, Bowman and his men lived in the field like they were on campaign. Positions were fortified, artillery fire missions were being pre-planned, and nighttime patrols along the edge of the American zones were ordered to begin identifying arriving Russian forces.

To say things were getting a bit tense was an understatement.

More than half of Bowman's men were new draftee's in from the States who made it too late to see any real fighting. At a minimum, Bowman used the heightened tension to begin drilling his new replacements and hopefully get them ready. *Ready for what?* He thought. *What in the hell is happening? The goddamn war was supposed to be over...fucking Russians.*

It was late. He was tired and becoming more disgusted by the moment when he got an excited call on the radio. He had placed two-man listening posts all over his sector and rotated the rest from the three actual fortified fighting positions astride a ridgeline overlooking the valley. The men had been reporting significant movement the past three nights as the Soviets began shifting more forces to the Czech border. He had been tracking more than a dozen incidents of small arms fire, several minor explosions, and at least six artillery strikes, one less than a mile away from his observation post and that was just since his men moved into position last night.

The men were getting jumpier and he didn't know what to tell them other than, "Stay calm and don't do anything stupid."

Then Corporal Johnson over at the number two listening post, two klicks away and with a good view of the main eastbound road into Pilsen, called over the company radio net. "Homeplate, this is

Tucson, repeat this is Tucson. Over."

Reaching over for his radio, Bowman grabbed it and answered, "Homeplate here. Report, over."

"Homeplate, significant movement of tracked vehicles moving across my six. Repeat, fifteen plus tracks, tanks and SP guns."

Bowman asked, "Tucson, repeat heading. Are tracks moving south or west?"

"Homeplate, tracks are moving at high speed, northwest. Repeat, northwest. Will remain in contact with Romeo elements, Tucson out."

"Understood, Homeplate, acknowledges transmission, maintain current over watch posture, over and out."

This was starting to get hairy. Ever since the Russians announced their refusal to recognize the exiled Czech government in London, activity in the Soviet sector had been getting scary. The Russians were getting trigger-happy the past few nights, probably looking to come down hard on any Czech partisan activity.

Bowman was an educated man, nearly done with his degree in History at the University of Delaware when he was called up. He remembered an old professor's lecture about the outbreak of the First

World War. He said it was simply a case of too many men with too many guns, all pointed at one another. Eventually something was going to happen.

Reaching for the field phone, Captain Bowman decided that too many guns were showing up on the other guy's side and not enough on his side of the line. *Time to kick this upstairs.*

Starting to visibly sweat in the humid, early morning air, Bowman wiped the perspiration away from his forehead and hoped it was just the humidity making him sweat and not something else. It sure felt like something hot was going to happen, a hell of a lot sooner than later.

Soviet 32nd Guards Mechanized Divisional Command Post,

North of Pilsen

Major-General Dmitri Danilov, commander of the 32nd Guards Mechanized Division, was becoming increasingly frustrated at the level of partisan activity in his sector. More accurately, his superior at 4th Guards Tank Army had made it clear he had better squash the Czechs, and quickly, so he could begin fortifying his defensive zone along the border or else he'd be assigned to command a supply detachment in Poland. The last thought was sobering because operating in Czechoslovakia was a vacation compared to a command in Poland.

Danilov was a combat veteran and like most of his counterparts, he despised fighting against partisans, too messy. He still had nightmares about operations to pacify Ukrainian partisans left in the wake of the Nazi retreat when he had a rifle regiment back in 1944. Here he was with his own division, a Guards division, no less, and he was forced to confront armed civilians yet again.

The past three nights had seen activity getting worse as the Czechs hit mostly light-skinned vehicles, supply trucks, exposed artillery with no armor or anything vital. The only real problem was how they seemed to be everywhere and nowhere at the same time. He didn't have the manpower to do everything.

Luckily, high command decided this sector must be pacified immediately, so he was given an additional tank brigade, the 22nd Guards Tank. Danilov knew the 22nd Guards commander had a reputation for being utterly ruthless and extremely vigorous in the attack mode, so if the Czechs showed themselves, he man would ride them down like the Cossacks of old. Danilov hoped this powerful brigade would give him sufficient flexibility to be used as a reaction force and allow his engineers time to construct additional defensive positions opposite the Americans.

So he put two of his infantry regiments to work setting up fortified defensive positions opposite the north and westbound highways mirroring American positions outside of Pilsen. He decided to use his own tank regiment along the western approaches with the 22nd Guards to hunt down the partisans astride the rough, heavily forested terrain along the northern highway.

Danilov thought the Czechs didn't pose much of a real threat, but regardless, his men were on alert and that night he would hit back, swiftly and decisively, and hopefully end things in short order.

Army command wouldn't give him another independent brigade any time soon so he decided to make aggressive sweeps along both key roadways. With luck, he would catch the Czechs in the open and end it there and then. Picking up the field phone to give the necessary orders, all he could think was that he had better things to do with his Guards division than hunt down partisans.

Chapter Thirty Three

5:00 a.m., Major Zimmer's Command Post,

North of Pilsen

Major Zimmer looked at his watch yet again and then up at the sky and saw the morning mist shroud the valley, giving perfect cover for the final approach. He grabbed his binoculars and viewed the divisional command post and main supply dump for the Soviet mechanized division. His men had kept the Russians up for much of the night with a series a well-planned running gun battles, nothing major, but enough to keep them active and increasingly frustrated.

Most of the Red Army division he was hunting was busy, by the looks of it, digging fortified positions near the Americans. Perfect. They worked through much of the night, half working on the trenches while the other half stood on alert. *Good, the Russians should be well past the point of exhaustion by now.*

Zimmer smiled as he saw the action develop in his head. The key was how to get the mobile elements of the Russians to react to their attack. By the sounds last night, Captain Kurt Mueller and his men kept the Soviet reaction force busy the previous night. Up and down the northern highway, Zimmer's men listened to sounds of minor running battles focused about five miles north of their current position, barely five hundred yards from the Soviet command post. *With luck, once the attack begins the Soviet commander will think he's been tricked into focusing in the northern sector and hopefully race pell-mell south.*

Taking one last look around at his men, he couldn't help but be impressed by how good they looked in crisp, clean American uniforms. Admittedly, Zimmer felt a bit strange wearing the American GI issue olive green, instead of the normal field gray uniforms of the German army. On closer inspection, not only were his men wearing American uniforms, but they carried perfectly maintained M-1 rifles, M-2 Carbines, Browning Automatic Rifles, and Colt side arms, everything a typical American Ranger company would bring into battle.

Taking his inspiration from the legendary exploits of SS Colonel Otto Skorzeny's Operation Grief during what the Americans called the Battle of the Bulge, General Wolff had long ago decided the key to Operation Loki was for the Russians to believe they were fighting Americans. Skorzeny had dressed several hundred SS English speaking troops in American uniforms and set them loose behind American lines and sowed unbelievable confusion. Zimmer intended to do more than sow confusion. In about five minutes, he planned to touch off a fight that neither the Russians nor the Americans would ever forget.

His men were in place and organized into three assault groups. Zimmer had decided to personally lead a small special assault detachment aimed at attacking the Russian command and supply base. To the south, a larger group, with all of the heavier weapons, was ready to move against the expected Soviet reaction force sure to move down the northern road. A smaller unit was set to stage roving ambushes where needed. Everything depended upon the initial attack. The shock had to be timed just right. Zimmer's most important asset was in place and ready to go into action.

Zimmer's men had disassembled three American 75mm pack howitzer that originally had been used by Yugoslavian partisans until captured by German mountain infantry forces in that bitter struggle. Zimmer's men painstakingly transported them through the dense Czech forests and got them into position to support the attack. The last thing the Russians would expect was to be on the receiving end of real artillery behind their own lines, especially since the Czechs didn't have anything heavier than hand-held grenades.

The American 75mm pack-howitzer was a remarkable weapon that was light enough to be easily broken down into nine main pieces and transported. It was perfect for a partisan force. More importantly, the fourteen-pound round had excellent range and impressive hitting power for such a small gun piece. The Americans were rather clever, Zimmer was forced to admit. He was pleased to be able to make use of their cleverness for his plan.

Major Zimmer's assault force was broken down into three storm trooper sections of a dozen men each. The Russians were using a solid one-story building as their command post along with several smaller, temporary structures that probably served as living quarters or storage facilities, what looked like one of the many pre-war lumber companies in the region. The main structure was about fifty yards off the main road and was situated at the very base of a series of hills overlooking the highway. The building gave excellent overhead cover and protection against anything except direct fire from above.

Two secondary roads or trails cut across the Czech forests connecting the north and eastbound highway. The Russians were using these secondary roads to maintain communications between their divided regiments. Surrounding the Russian command post was several hundred supply troops, a small security detachment, hundreds of supply crates, trucks, and an anti-aircraft battery. The guns would have to be taken out early, but other than that, his men would be able to infiltrate down the thickly wooded hillside and land practically right on top of the unsuspecting Russians.

Taking a last look at the Russian divisional base, Zimmer looked pleased. Most of the Russians were either asleep in their field billets or holed up, completely unaware of the force that had infiltrated all around them. His mission was not just to inflict casualties, but to strike fear into the Russians. The best way was to take out their command structure. Speed was essential, but it was time to let training and experience take over. The men were ready. He was ready and, with one last glance at the pride of Germany surrounding him, he delivered the order in English over his short-range, American field radio, "All elements proceed to Zulu positions and execute Able Golf option immediately."

Before he had finished uttering the last word, he heard the short explosion of air that signaled the first round from the howitzer had left the barrel and was on its way. Zimmer and the rest of the men prayed the Norse God of Trickery, Loki, was in fact looking down on their actions this early morning and would guide them to victory.

The divisional staff of the 32nd Mechanized Division found themselves exhausted after working a very long night. The past week had seen these officers orchestrate a major movement from their main base outside of Prague and engage in building a complicated network of new defenses along the border with the Americans, while at the same time trying to contain a series of partisan attacks breaking out all over their area of operations.

The men were tired, increasingly frustrated, and becoming more than a little belligerent. To a man, they thought these widespread partisan attacks against Soviet occupation forces first in Poland and Czechoslovakia were a direct result of American and English interference. So, instead of enjoying the fruits of victory and the pleasures that even the war torn capital of Czechoslovakia had to offer, the staff of the 32nd Mechanized Division was forced to live out in the field under wartime conditions.

Operations officer Colonel Yuri Rezov had been awake for the past twenty-four hours and was beginning to walk into furniture, he was so tired. He had been pushing the staff pretty damn hard the past few days, and the cable he just received promised to make matters worse. Lighting yet another cigarette, Rezov couldn't believe that Zhukov would order major field maneuvers so soon after the new deployment.

The whole damn 4th Guards Tank Army had equipment and supplies strung out more than a hundred miles. Now they wanted to begin stockpiling everything, including live ammo, for major live fire exercises. As if Red Army soldiers needed any additional practice after killing fascists for four years.

Completely lost in thought, Rezov turned his head sharply when he heard snoring coming from the next room. Bursting into the adjoining office, he barked at his senior aide, "Nikita wake up, damn you. What the hell kind of example are you setting for these young pups they've stuck us with since the war ended?"

His senior aide was slumped on his chair and leaning half off to the side when Rezov kicked the chair out from under him. *Luckily his head broke his fall*, thought Rezov.

The thick headed Ukrainian knew his superior was already angry at him so he wheeled around as fast as he could, jumped to attention and said, "Sorry, sir, must have just nodded off. Exhausted."

Rezov knew he wasn't the only one to fall asleep on the job the past couple of days, but just because the war was technically over, he would not let them go soft. The rest of room came to attention as they waited for the Operations officer to read them the riot act when suddenly windows exploded and lashed the room with flying glass and debris. Two junior officers standing next to the window were shredded by the glass and thrown across the room.

Rezov and the rest of his staff instinctively hit the floor in shock as smoke and the strong smell of cordite hit them. He was just about to stick his head up above the desk when another round impacted on top of the roof. In an instant the room was covered in a cloud of plaster and the remains of the ceiling. Rezov was a veteran of many battles and knew the place was zeroed in. It was time to get the hell out before the whole place went up.

He saw many of his men were already wounded and in need of immediate attention. Whatever the hell was happening, one thing was certain, they were on the receiving end of real artillery fire. No damn Czechs could be doing this, so he pointed at the nearest man he could make out in the smoke, "Boris, start grabbing whatever paperwork you can, make sure the codes are taken. Ivan, organize stretcher teams and get the wounded the hell out of here. Somebody alert General Danilov immediately, put the whole division on alert. Now! Move, Move, Move."

Then he heard another shell begin to fall on their position. He screamed, "Hurry, get down now!" The next thing he heard was a tremendous crash as the shell struck dead on the roof again. He momentarily blacked out as the room became engulfed in smoke and flame, but he found he couldn't move. His body felt an enormous weight crushing the air out from his lungs. He started to scream as he felt the heat from the flames and lost all thoughts except to get out. A wooden support beam had landed on top of him and most of the others in the room were already dead.

As he drifted off into unconsciousness, he heard small arms fire break out in the room. Bullets whizzed by and tore through the air all around him. The last thing he heard before he drifted into the darkness was the guttural sound of a lone German voice and then quickly someone yelled back in English. Blood oozed from more than a dozen punctures, he was losing blood quickly but he thought, *German and then English, how is this possible?* The pain swept him away into sweet oblivion.

Major Zimmer was panting as he led his assault squad through the breech in the wall. Small arms fire and grenades exploded inside as his men quickly moved into what appeared to be the Russian operations room. Paperwork was strewn all over the room. Most of the Russians were dead and the rest were quickly dispatched by a bullet to the back of the head. It was not the time for prisoners, in fact, just the opposite.

Then a tremendous roar shook the structure and caused his men to squat low to the ground. Excellent. Zimmer could tell from the general direction of the blast that his second squad had taken out the ant-aircraft battery parked out front. He had been worried about the firepower those guns could have given the Russians.

A series of small, yet sustained, explosions indicated they must have hit the nearby magazines as the ammo cooked off, sending dangerous small caliber cannon shells all over the nearby field.

Actually, it worked to the Germans advantage as the Russians were forced to keep their heads down while Zimmer's other assault elements moved into position.

The battle-tested SS troops moved quickly and within ten minutes more than two hundred Red Army service troops were either killed where they slept or cut down by a series of well-executed ambushes on men taken completely by surprise.

Throughout the entire engagement, Zimmer's trio of 75mm pack howitzers laid perfectly aimed fire right on top of the Russians, pinning the few security troops turning to stand and fight, but they were quickly able to put an end to organized resistance. Curiously, one structure was left standing. The small cabin containing the Russian communication equipment was left unmolested for the moment, contained but, as yet, unharmed.

Major General Danilov couldn't believe he was still alive. The ground shook as more fire was directed on top of his command. He listened to the unfamiliar sounds of small arms fire raking his poorly defended supply troops. Cursing himself for not posting a larger security detachment, he knew the only reason he was still alive was because he couldn't sleep, so he had decided to take a walk down to the communication building and look for any recent messages from Army command. Now breathing heavily, he tried to reconstruct the past ten minutes and figure out a way to get reinforcements and fast, but the rate of fire was picking up. He was ten feet from the door when the first arty round hit his command post, barely three hundred yards away.

Quickly, more fire rang out and he was about to head for the safety of the cabin. Excitedly, his men clamored for him to get to safety, but he found himself watching a full platoon of soldiers move against his headquarters. There was no doubt in his mind that these were real soldiers and not partisans, not by a long shot. He watched as men dressed in olive green uniforms moved quickly, firing on the run, securing the command post and then began to fan out to the various tents and sleeping quarters.

He crouched behind a sandbag emplacement in front of the cabin. Something was not right. Who the hell could be attacking his men? Lifting his head just above the rim, he tried to listen to the guns firing in the near distance. For a man who fought against German weapons for four years, one doesn't forget the distinct sound of a German rifle or the pulsing rat-a-tat-tat of a MG42 machine gun. No, the sounds were all wrong. Danilov knew these were soldiers, and they weren't Czechs, so who the hell was slaughtering his men?

His heart sank as he heard the voices over the roar of the pandemonium. *English.* Danilov turned pale as he realized he had heard English. Americans. *Dear God, the Americans must have gone mad.* Danilov knew what he had to do, Headquarters must be informed. At that point he moved quickly and made contact with the commander of the 22nd Guards Armored Brigade and ordered him to immediately move his forces towards the command post.

Still in shock, he listened to the screams of his men as, one by one, the Americans captured or neutralized his small command post. Now he understood why Higher Command thought it was so important to build those defensive positions. The Americans had planned to attack all along. Still trying to maintain his composure, he knew he must call Army Headquarters and place the entire Red Army on alert, if possible.

Desperate, his voice excited, he contacted 4th Guards Tank headquarters. A sleepy voice answered. Danilov barked into the phone, "This is Major General Danilov of the 32nd Guards Mechanized Division, get me General Lelyushenko immediately. It's urgent."

Not impressed, the duty officer answered dryly, "The General has given orders not to be disturbed. General Danilov, I'll have him contact you later in the morning."

Nearly turning purple with rage, Danilov could hear machine gun fire moving closer, "Tell the General that we are under attack. The Americans have staged a raid on my divisional command post and inflicted heavy casualties. Now if you don't go and wake the general yourself, in about ten fucking seconds I swear that when I find you, you will be greasing the treads of my tanks. Understood?"

Danilov heard the phone drop in a clatter on the radio and footsteps racing away. Hanging up the phone, he decided to at least try to secure the cabin as best as he could and try to take a few men into the woods and wait for reinforcements to come on the scene.

As he sound of gunfire began to diminish, Major Zimmer took a moment to look through the shattered window of the now devastated Soviet command post and watched as his men moved against the final collection of Russians who holed themselves up at the far end of the base. Reports indicated organized resistance was nearly over except for a hasty perimeter around the Soviet communication hut. The rest were either dead or had run off into the hills and far out of sight.

Even better, the cost had come cheaply, with only three dead and six lightly wounded. This was always thought to be the easiest part of the operation, supply and rear area troops were always soft targets.

His SS commandos, working with absolute precision, effectively sealed off the area and systematically destroyed ammo and fuel supplies. His aide interrupted his thoughts and abruptly handed him the field phone.

"It's Captain Mueller reporting, sir." Mueller's small force was ordered to harass and observe the Russian armored force to the north.

"Major, the Russians just broke contact and mobile elements are heading south at speed towards your position. Over."

All his instincts told him the Russians had taken the bait, but he had to make sure, so he asked, "Is this a general movement or only a small detachment? You must be absolutely clear on this."

"Sir, repeat, major elements of a Russian tank brigade heading towards your sector, more than sixty armored vehicles and dozens of troop transports. Lead elements are no more than seven miles away and moving fast. Over."

Zimmer said, "Make best speed to checkpoint Romeo, good work. Over and out."

Zimmer wheeled about, making sure nothing was lost over the din of battle. He grabbed his aide's tunic, pulled him close and said, "Tell Sergeants Heinz and Adler to set charges and eliminate the Russian holdouts, destroy the whole Russian Signals section and quickly. Next, inform Lieutenant Hochler to initiate the demonstration as planned, but do it quickly. We must be out of here and on the move in ten minutes."

Things would have to move quickly now. Grabbing the short-range radio set, he contacted his main assault force and gave the instructions to prepare to engage. Lastly, his trusty American cannons were ordered to shift fire to the south.

At nearly ninety seven hundred yards, he planned to use every inch of that range to hit what his men were aiming at. Taking one last look at the devastation his force had wrought on the Russians, Zimmer allowed himself a moment of satisfaction because he knew everything was in motion, one way or the other. So far, phase one of Operation Loki was going according to schedule. Time to move.

Once word of the attack on the divisional command post had come through, Colonel Pavel Sobolov, proud commander of the 22nd Guards Armored Brigade, needed little prompting to get his forces on the move. Sobolov's reputation as an up and comer was secured, based on his bold exploits on the battlefield against the fascists and he received his brigade just in time for the final battles around the Hungarian capital of Budapest. The 22nd Guards inflicted severe casualties on elements of an SS division sent to save the last fuel reserves left in the Third Reich. Killing those SS swine was his finest moment of the war.

Sobolov's family lived in Leningrad. He lost both his only sister and dear mother during the nine hundred day siege. The only thing that kept him going was a desire to kill all things German. He drove himself and his men hard, and it paid off time and again on the battlefield. He believed in one thing more than all else, on the battlefield, speed matters more than anything else. So, he developed quite a reputation for aggressiveness and as one the few who weren't afraid to attack with minimal reconnaissance or advance without orders.

During the Budapest campaign, he received accommodations for the two successive nights of forced marches that finally found the German open flank. He personally led the battalion of T-34's that obliterated an entire SS regiment, to a man. His tankers took casualties, but they killed Nazis and won battles, and by the end of the war, winning was all that mattered to the High Command.

With the Red Army fighting the damn Poles, he was stuck tracking down annoying partisans, and Czechs at that. So, when reports of a serious attack on the divisional command post came in, he was only too happy to race to the scene.

With his brigade already road bound, Sobolov knew it wouldn't take long to deploy. His men were tired from the nights' exertions, but a chance to finally hit the bastards would get everyone into high gear. Sobolov sent his third battalion in the lead with the remaining two battalions less than fifteen minutes behind.

Standing in the open hatch of his own T-34/85 as it raced down the Czech roadway, Sobolov saw the rising plumes of dark smoke in the distance. Surprised at the extent of smoke, the Russian Brigade commander grabbed his radio and called the third battalion's commander.

An excited voice got on the phone, "Sir, this is Captain Serov, the major has dismounted already. He had to see for himself. It's a slaughter. Bodies are everywhere."

Sobolov's eyes flared, "What do you mean a slaughter? Get me Grechko now or go find General Danilov, he must be somewhere."

Already quite shaken, Captain Serov finally answered, "I don't think you understand, sir. Danilov's dead. His whole command staff is dead. Can you see the smoke? It's nearly completely black with smoke over here. The bastards piled dozens of bodies on top of one another and lit them on fire. The rest were left where they fell. There are booby traps all over the place. We already lost a dozen men to mines. Explosives demolished two cabins, the main command post is a wreck, plus, I swear, I see large caliber shell holes, seventy-five millimeter or larger. Hurry, see for yourself."

Grimly, the depressed executive officer of the third battalion added, "This was not the work of guerrillas, you'll see."

Sobolov could hear ammo cooking off in the background as Serov spoke. He heard it in his voice. He was rattled and the boy didn't rattle easily. Shell holes, that couldn't be right. Thinking he was missing something, Sobolov decided to act swiftly.

Switching to the general brigade radio net, "We are facing an unknown, well equipped enemy force, so I want full combat drill in place. Grechko, take the lead and secure the command post. Clear the area of any stay behind elements and patrol the heights overlooking the base. I want that whole area secure. Set up roving patrols immediately."

Switching to the brigade wide net, Sobolov ordered, "First and Second battalion move at high speed and make contact with dismounted elements of the 32nd Mechanized defending the approaches to Pilsen. We will run these bastards down and trap them between our two forces. Pavlenko, set up your guns once third battalion has secured the base. I want your guns ready to displace and prepare fire missions along the ridges and hilltops from here to the edge of the American zone if necessary. The rest of you watch out for your flanks, keep a close movement and be careful not to fire on friendlies. Understood? Sobolov out."

The 22nd was a Guards brigade, a ceremonial distinction dating back to the days of the Czar and only just resurrected during the Great Patriotic War, but one taken quite seriously by the men of the 22nd. They were a proud, battle-tested unit, unafraid of combat and had been given a mission. Colonel Sobolov decided to abandon his normal command vehicle and do without interference from Army headquarters. He leapt into his own T-34/85 tank and chose to lead his men into battle against whoever dared to attack fellow Soviet officers in such a cowardly fashion.

If these Czechs, or whoever the hell it was that wanted a battle, then he thought, *battle is exactly what they shall have.* With that thought in mind, he left his headquarters staff behind in the dust and raced south towards Pilsen. Sobolov moved so fast he ignored the waving arms of his screaming junior aide. The aide was trying to deliver urgent information from Army headquarters. He tried to warn Sobolov that as amazing as it sounded, Headquarters just announced that it was the Americans and they may be heading into a trap.

The Soviet tank battalions raced at top speed towards the defensive positions of the now alerted infantry regiments of the 32nd Mechanized Division. The road moving south towards Pilsen was extremely narrow for several kilometers until the thick woods and jagged ridgelines finally give way to an open valley, rich in farmland. The main deployment of the 32nd's two regiments was built up opposite the Americans on either side of the road. From the air, the final stretch of road resembled a giant "Y", as the highway was broken by a deep gully on one side and thick woods to the left.

Waiting in the woods was Zimmer's second in command, a legend in the SS, Major Eric Jaeger. He worked with Otto Skorzeny on more than a dozen special operations, including the daring kidnapping of Mussolini from the Italians back in 1943. With more than one hundred twenty men spread out over nearly a mile of thick forest and broken ridgelines, Jaeger disposed his men in manner intended to inflict a maximum amount of fire in a very concentrated manner.

Jaeger's only complaint was that he would have to make due with the American anti-tank weapon of choice, the 2.36-inch bazooka. He knew they had to maintain their deception, but to have to fight tough Russian tanks with such an inferior weapon made him, and most of his men, more than a bit nervous. The German panzerfausts had nearly double the hitting power, even though the range was better with the American bazooka.

To compensate matters, he was forced to position his forces far closer to the road than he would have preferred. *Bah, what good was range if you can't kill what you aim at?* No matter, orders were orders and to have a mission when one thought everything was lost made up for much.

He organized his men into twenty separate, six man squads, all prepared to act independently as part of the general operational framework hammered out the previous evening. It was a good plan. Simple. Even better, the heavily forested hills would give cover when it came time to disengage. Jaeger thought not only might their mission succeed, but also, who knew, perhaps some would even live to talk about it someday to their grandchildren.

The broken terrain made it impossible for Jaeger to get a good vantage point of the onrushing Soviet tanks moving from the north, but with his American binoculars he could see the dug-in Soviet defensive line opposite the Americans suddenly spring to life as if bracing for action. Excellent. Word of the attack on the command post had finally put the Russians on a general alert. He could see Russian infantry begin moving ammo haulers up to the front line trenches, tents were being broken down, and men were forming up to occupy half-finished positions.

Looking at his watch, he began to worry. The Russian tanks should have been through his position fifteen minutes ago. What if the damn Russians sent one of their now dug-in battalions loose to go hunting in the hills to their rear? Then the whole damn ambush would be blown. Too late to worry, but Zimmer had better be right. Skorzeny would never have tried to do so many tasks independent of one another. In combat it was tough enough to predict a timetable for your own troops, let alone predict the movements of the enemy, even Russians.

Dark smoke to the north was beginning to blow south. Zimmer was a tight-lipped little bastard, but it looked as though they must have really hit them hard to send that much black smoke in the air. Lost in the moment, he was focusing hard on the smoke to the north when he heard the signal. The sound of an artillery round flying over his head towards the Russians brought everybody to attention. The men braced themselves for action. Zimmer's 75mm howitzer shifted fire over their position and began plastering the Soviet infantry units dug down in their trenches. It was only three guns, but with a high rate of fire, the Russians would be hugging the bottom of their trenches for at least the next ten minutes or so.

Then, he heard engines, even better, tank engines for sure and moving fast. His radio squelched twice as his forward observers confirmed that contact was imminent. Up and down the German positions, tough, confident SS men tightly gripped their gun barrels, light machine guns, and especially the unfamiliar American bazookas. Experience had taught them not to fire too soon. Their commander, Jaeger, had picked an excellent ambush spot.

Near the German held tree line, the road curved just enough to force the Russian column to slow down a bit and shift to lower gears to handle the incline and sharp turns. Each man secretly hoped, since they would be firing from elevated positions nearly twenty to thirty feet above the roadway, that the small warhead on the American bazooka would be able to pierce the Soviet tanks and blow through the thinner armor on top. In about thirty seconds they would find out.

The 22nd Armored Brigade's first battalion raced along the Czech highway at high speed, but found they had to slow. The lead tank saw the road narrow as it wound around the hillside. The battalion's twenty-one tanks moved in a tight formation with many of the turrets facing the rear and the open flanks. The men rightly feared an ambush and the first battalion commander, an experienced tanker, ordered his men to brace themselves for action. Just then, the artillery rounds started impacting about two miles away and the Russians, by instinct, sped up to get out of the narrow confines of the enclosed roadway.

Waiting under excellent tree cover, the German commander, Jaeger, watched as the Russians entered the kill zone. He held his breath as he sprung the trap. Pushing the plunger down set off more than a dozen explosions that rained rock and trees hurtling down on top of the Russian armored column. In the next instant, more than twenty bazooka rounds fired at practically the same time.

From one end to the other, American anti-tank rounds rocketed the Red Army column. Tremendous explosions lit the early morning sky as nearly a dozen Russian tanks suffered catastrophic hits and their turrets flew through the air. Men screamed into their radios to either rush forward or back out. Tanks moved off road and found themselves either stuck in the gully to the right or into a deadly minefield sowed along the left side of the road. Three Russian tanks became disabled in a matter of moments and were easily dispatched.

The soldiers of the 22nd were not all caught unaware and many tanks still had plenty of fight left in them. The remaining Russian armor was composed of tough T-34/85's and three giant IS-2 Stalin tanks armed with their 122mm cannons. They fought back with a vengeance. The powerful guns lobbed high-explosive shells into the hillside, hoping to flush out the ambushers. The US built bazookas left a fiery back blast that gave the Russian tankers excellent targets.

The Russians began raking the tree line with machine gun fire and high-explosive cannon shells, trying to cut down the unseen enemy gunners. Unfortunately, for the remaining Soviet tank crews, the road was so cratered with flaming tanks and debris that no matter how accurate the Russian return fire, the Germans were able to keep shifting positions and continue firing from multiple locations.

Within ten furious minutes all of the Russian tanks were either disabled or destroyed, leaving the Czech countryside littered with maimed and dead Russians. Those few tank crews who were able to escape were quickly shot before they had a chance to run away. Throwing his hands in the air and signaling his troops to shift positions, Jaeger was breathing heavy and excited beyond belief. Jaeger could barely believe how great it felt to have delivered such a devastating attack on the Russians. His men literally annihilated an entire Russian tank battalion in a textbook example of a perfect ambush.

After facing boys and old men in the last months of the war, the Russians were just given a deadly lesson of combat against elite German troopers. After hiding in various underground bunkers in the

Bavarian Alps for the better part of the past three months and learning of the absolute horrors inflicted on Germany in the wake of the surrender, Jaeger and the rest of the men were primed for action. After feeling powerless for so long, to be able to inflict revenge on the Russians brought almost physical joy to men known for their strict discipline.

The one thing that surprised Jaeger was, he had to admit, that the American bazookas worked far better than he dared hoped. Next, he got on the radio and speaking in English on an open net, said, "Well done, excellent shooting. Begin general movement to the next position and be on guard and ready for a fight. Section five police the area and lay out your booby traps and then meet up with the main body in ten minutes."

Jaeger then switched channels and called Major Zimmer, "Baker two, confirms first party a success. Making arrangements for our next guests. Recommend you commence starting the music in five minutes." He received one squelch back to confirm message received.

With that said, Jaeger quickly gathered up those remaining in his command. Unfortunately, he lost six killed but had to shoot seven seriously wounded comrades. They understood the risks, those unable to make it out on foot were to be dispatched and left as further evidence of American involvement. Moving on the double, he circled back away from Pilsen and looked to hit the Russians in the ass again. He figured it would be the last thing they would expect.

Colonel Sobolov was traveling with his second battalion when his operations officer finally caught up with him. Driving like hell in a fast moving BA-10 armored car, he personally handed Sobolov the new intelligence alert and current operational orders from 5th Tank Army headquarters. Looking like someone had just struck him, Sobolov couldn't believe what he just read. Was it possible the Americans could have done this? *Why?* What could they possibly look to gain? Quickly his thoughts shifted from why to what he had to do next.

Crumpling the paper up, he was about to throw it on the ground when his radio came to life. He heard sounds of battle explode through the morning air. His first battalion must be under attack. Less than two miles away, he could hear dozens of explosions and saw the dark black smoke that signaled a dead tank. The death of a tank was such a terrible event. Ammo cooking off, burning metal and rubber mixing with the smell of fiery diesel fuel, and the sounds of screaming men turned into human torches was enough to make one vomit. He had seen it all too many times during the war, and it was happening again, to his men, and by the fucking Americans.

He flipped the mike and called out on the first battalion radio net to hold if possible or at least meet up with the second battalion. Next, he ordered his second battalion to deploy for combat and button up. Sobolov wanted to launch some covering artillery fire along the narrow ridges overlooking their approach. He wanted to bring a little fire into the mix to scatter the American ambushers. Moments later, he called his own artillery commander and ordered covering fire be placed along the ridgeline of their approach.

Next, his remaining third battalion was ordered to leave a company of infantry, but for all armored units to hurry to meet up with the second battalion's tanks. Angry at being caught in an ambush, he refused to get inside his own tank and wanted to see what happened to his troops. Standing tall in the turret, he ordered his tank driver to gun the engine and catch up with the 2nd battalion and raced down the road. Immediately, he saw the burned out remains of a dozen tanks. He could see the Americans had mined the sides of the road. His immobilized tanks were proof he was facing a deadly foe.

His lead tanks slowed to a crawl as they tried to navigate through the flaming hulks and rock obstacles covering the road. Two bulldozer engineer tanks started to push the destroyed tanks off the road to clear a narrow lane. Sobolov ordered his units to spray the entire hillside with machine gun fire to keep the Americans occupied and give him a chance to get past the mess.

Looking through his binoculars to see any movement, he was violently thrown back against the turret door and slumped down in the commander's cupola, holding his face. Artillery rounds along with lightweight mortar fire suddenly fell among the Russian forces, sending deadly pieces of shrapnel flying through the air.

Quickly getting his bearings, Sobolov wiped away the blood streaming down his face. He noticed his binoculars must have been blown off his face and he caught some broken glass and metal slivers along the right side of his face. Bleeding from half-a-dozen small cuts, Sobolov ordered his 2nd battalion engineers to move as fast as possible to clear the road. Speaking into the radio, he called out his brigade artillery commander, "Pavlenko, you idiot, you're firing on friendlies, cease fire immediately."

His artillery officer yelled back, "What fire? I haven't unlimbered my ammunition hauler yet. We just started to load our guns." He paused for a second, then said, "The Americans must be dropping on your position to cover their withdrawal. What do you want me to do?"

Thinking quickly, Sobolov called the 32nd Mechanized Division's artillery commander ten miles up the road and requested coordinates on suspected American artillery positions. When the artillery commander hesitated, Sobolov shouted into the radio, "Where is that fire coming from? Start looking and get me those damn coordinates and now."

By the rate of fire, he figured he was being hit by at least a battery of four guns or heavy mortars. With his big tanks stuck in the narrow roadway with flaming Russian tanks blocking the way, if he didn't get some counter-battery fire soon, his brigade would be savaged. Even then, soft skinned troop carriers sent up to scour the high ground were coming under heavy fire. At least his tanks were safe as long as everyone stayed inside the tank, but his infantry would suffer casualties in the meanwhile.

Sobolov desperately tried to keep a handle on things, but between the long night chasing what he thought were Czech bandits to the slaughter at the command post, and then finding his first battalion slaughtered and coming under fire from American guns, it was all just too much. He became alive with fury. All he wanted was to reach out and teach the Americans that the Red Army would not allow these warlike acts to go unpunished. His head was racing and gave a flurry of orders, trying to get control of his unit.

Whatever reason the Americans had for treachery, he intended to pay them back for their cowardly attacks. *They'll find out why the Red Army is to be feared.*

Sobolov began to act erratic as he tried to do too many things at once and became angry. Trying to negotiate the flaming, debris-ridden road while coordinating an attack along the ridgeline was making command of his brigade and the situation became increasingly difficult for Sobolov.

Enemy fire continued to rain down on top of him and Sobolov continued to get desperate calls from his junior officers for support. Then, he received a transmission from the commander of the 32nd Mechanized that observers were reporting puffs of smoke four thousand yards to the southeast, well inside the American lines.

Seizing at once on the transmission, as senior officer on the scene, Sobolov, made an instant decision. Grabbing the radio, he contacted his artillery chief. "Pavlenko, fire mission, now. Get your guns to fire at the two dominant ridgelines on the valley opposite the southernmost Soviet position. Those two terrain features are being used to drop artillery and mortar fire all around us."

"Comrade Colonel, do you mean that you want me to lay fire on the Americans?" Hesitating for a moment, Pavlenko stuttered, "I don't think we can, Colonel. Are you sure?"

Stung by the insolence coming from a man sitting safe in the rear, not in any real danger, Sobolov jumped down the man's throat, "You listen here, Pavlenko, you either start opening fire on the Americans in about five seconds or I swear that you will never live to talk about this conversation. We are being cut down like dogs out in the open, they got us bracketed and I can't maneuver worth a damn. Either blast those ridges or consider yourself under arrest this instant. Is that understood?"

Sobolov's artillery commander knew the Soviet system was quite clear, insubordination could land you in a penal battalion, practically a death sentence. *But what will happen to me if I fire on the Americans and Sobolov is wrong?* Pavlenko thought, *either way, I'm a dead man.* All he could weakly muster was a, "Yes, sir. I'll have a dozen guns in action within two minutes. Please patch me into the 32nd's radio net to direct my fire. I don't want to drop on any friendly if I can help it."

Already angry at the mere hint his orders were being questioned, Sobolov snapped back, "Just do it quickly! And don't worry about High Command, let me worry about the consequences."

With that said, two minutes later flames erupted along the American lines. Worse was to come as edgy Soviet front line troops began opening up on pre-sited American observation posts. The 32nd Mechanized unloaded its own 82mm mortars and 76mm artillery fire onto suspected American positions as more and more troops started adding small arms and long-range machine gun fire.

Within minutes the entire American held Czech valley was swamped with smoke and fire. The Norse God of Trickery was, indeed, looking down on this narrow, lush valley in Czechoslovakia and smiling at the evil wrought on that day.

Chapter Thirty Four

American Defensive Positions

Pilsen, Czechoslovakia

On the American side of the valley, shocked soldiers were digging furiously as artillery fire erupted without warning all around them. Soviet artillery fire cut down a dozen unsuspecting troops caught outside of their bunkers or foxholes. Clearly, the Russians had done a pretty damn good job of sighting American positions prior to the morning's activities, plus the defensive scheme was pretty obvious.

Two main ridgelines opposite the Russian line paralleled the road with the valley, separating the two forces as a built-in, no man's land. To use the valley and the highway leading towards the American held city of Pilsen, the ridgelines had to be secured and the Russians were plastering both American held ridgelines.

Unfortunately, 4th Armored Division Headquarters only saw fit to send recon elements out while the main defensive belt, held by American combat units, were several miles to the rear. Captain Marty Bowman, commander of the cavalry company facing the Soviets, had been sending reports back to Headquarters for the past hour on the unprecedented levels of activity on the Soviet side of the fence.

Evidence of a major battle poured in from all corners as observation posts up and down his company position reported one major incident after the other. Everything from heavy artillery fire to major troop movements, to the obvious manning of the frontline positions caused serious concerns back at Fourth Armored Headquarters.

Instructed to hold his position, Bowman begged to get some aerial support to confirm what the hell was happening on the Soviet side. He got a big negative on air cover, but was told to look for two tank companies moving up to provide backup. Tension was written all over his face as he and his men listened to the sounds of serious combat happening barely a mile away and didn't know what the hell was coming next. Battalion said to start bringing in some of the more exposed observation posts when all hell broke loose.

He had just turned to grab his map case when the first round struck about two hundred yards below him. "Holy shit," Bowman yelled and dove into his dugout. In seconds, the world flashed bright as the heat from exploding shells washed over him, pushing him deep inside the bunker. Landing in successive waves, Soviet 76mm guns had a high rate of fire and could deliver a fourteen-pound high-explosive shell nearly fourteen thousand yards. Bowman lost count of the shells that landed all around him.

Curled up in the bottom of his fighting position, the concussion and explosive force lifted him off the ground repeatedly and shook the insides of the trench. Luckily the Russians shifted fire long enough for him to stop gagging and try to find the radio he dropped when he dove into the hole. Crawling around on his hands and knees, Bowman tried to find the radio but visibility was terrible as smoke covered his immediate front.

As the ground trembled with each explosion, he knew he had to make contact with Battalion HQ and find some way to get his men the hell out of Dodge, and fast. Bowman had been on the receiving end of artillery fire before, but never like this. The Germans never seemed to have enough ammunition for sustained arty strikes, so he was finding it difficult to function.

Breathing heavily, he pulled up the Battalion net and called out, "Echo One, Echo One, this is Homeplate, over. Echo One, we are receiving massive fire from multiple Russian guns. Visibility terrible. Repeat, recon elements taking heavy fire, requesting new orders. Over."

Bowman jumped again from nearby concussion waves as he strained to hear the voice on the other line. "Homeplate, this is Echo One. Repeat message. Did you say you are receiving direct fire? Over."

There was always some rear area pain in the ass that always seemed to ask stupid questions. Fuming, Bowman held the mike up as two more shells landed about a hundred yards over his head. The twin explosions woke the radio operator up over at Battalion and within thirty seconds he was connected to Combat Command B's operations officer. Speaking with a calm, yet commanding, voice, Major Roy Henderson responded, "Okay Captain just stay calm. I can hear the explosions, so I know you are under fire. Keep your head and just tell me exactly what you see. Understood?"

Bowman felt a bit more reassured, "Sir, all hell is breaking loose here. My recon company is taking firing from at least a dozen Russian field pieces, maybe more. Plus, I got Soviet forces on their side of the occupation zone opening up with mortar and machine gun fire. There's one hell of a lot of firepower being laid on my AO, sir. I need to get my people pulled back. What the hell happened? Are we at war, sir?"

Hearing the shock and tension in the boy's voice, Henderson wished he had something useful to say. Hell, he didn't know what the hell was going on either, but he was not going to sit back and let the Russians have a free ride. Not by a long shot. "Captain, you have permission to consolidate your forces and provide whatever defensive measures needed to preserve your unit, including defensive fire. I am ordering those two tank companies coming your way to extradite your men and to be prepared for enemy contact in case we have to shoot our way in and out. I'll contact you myself in fifteen minutes. Good luck, son."

"Thank you, sir. I'll be looking out for those tanks and start pulling back my command to positions along the south ridgeline. Good cover there, sir. Recon out."

Bowman knew he had to get the men in number one and two observation posts out, and soon. They were closest to the Russians, situated at the base of the valley and too damn close to the highway. Until those tanks arrived, his men were too exposed to risk movement out in the open with the arty fire falling all over the place. So, he decided to make the move himself with what he had on hand.

Keying the mike, he ordered the M-8 Greyhounds to mount up for a high speed descent down the road with the M-24 Chaffee light tanks giving back up. With any luck, the M-8's would be in and out before the Russians made any more moves.

Still, Bowman didn't like the idea of exposing those scout cars, they were armored enough to protect against small arms and artillery fragments, but would be in big trouble if Russian tanks showed up. Looking again down into the valley, geysers of dirt and fire lifted off the ground barely fifty yards from his exposed men's positions. *No choice, I have to try something.*

Then he remembered what the Major had said about using his discretion. So, he got the Company's 81mm mortars to start laying a smoke screen down to give those Greyhounds some cover. Pounding the dirt in front of him in frustration, all Bowman could think was, *how can this be happening again?*

Soviet Occupation Zone

Meanwhile Colonel Sobolov's engineers had finally gotten about two thirds of his second battalion through the narrow roadway and out into the open near the defensive positions occupied by the 32nd Mechanized. Delighted at the volume of fire landing throughout the entire American zone, he ordered his third battalion's infantry units to resume clearing the woods along the road that had been such a death trap moments before and make sure the Americans wouldn't get away.

Starting to feel a bit more in control again, he saw the American fire had completely dropped off while Russian guns continued to fire heavy volumes across the valley.

Surprised no more orders had come down from Army Headquarters, Sobolov decided to move his tanks closer to the defending infantry. Suddenly, his radio came to life as he heard on the battalion net, "Smoke screen, six o'clock. We got high-speed movement out of the American lines."

Without his binoculars, he strained to see several vehicles moving at high speed through the light smoke screen being laid across the Czech highway. Deciding not to hesitate and allow the Americans to crash into Soviet lines uncontested, Sobolov ordered his force to split into two elements and move quickly against the American tanks. *We'll see whose tanks go up in flames now.*

Both forces were converging on the same highway at high speed. Sobolov led one column straight down the road while the other half of the battalion moved cross-country over the Czech farmland, masked by a slight dip in the hilly terrain. *They'll move a hell of a lot slower, but with luck we'll catch them right in the flanks.*

As Sobolov came closer, he could see three armored cars, or half-tracks, and two tanks. They were moving fast when the armored cars emerged from the smoke and veered off the main road into a grove of trees to his left.

He was unsure if the Americans saw him first, but no matter. Riding high in the turret, he ordered his gunners to open up at three hundred yards. The Americans had almost made it into the tree line when nearly a dozen shells converged on their targets and caught the last two M-8 armored cars dead center. The powerful 85mm tank shells fired from the T-34's completely gutted the thin side armor and caused the flaming debris to explode amidst the trees. The third M-8 nimbly ducked into the treeline and tried desperately to get away, leaving another half a dozen screaming American soldiers in its wake.

Sobolov's attention was brought back to his front as the American light tanks trailing the scout cars bravely opened fire on his force. The M-24 Chaffee's 75mm cannon was a low muzzle velocity gun and didn't have the punch to crack the tough armored hides of the T-34's. Before they knew it, both American tanks were in flames from the return fire of Sobolov's deadly gunners. The American relief column had been gutted and many of Captain Bowman's recon troopers were trapped on the ground with Russian tanks prowling around the American zone.

Elated at his small victory, Colonel Sobolov decided to sweep the tree line to capture any Americans he could find and bring them back to Headquarters for interrogation. He ordered a platoon of tanks to go find the one American scout car that got away and ordered his remaining tanks to move up the road and patrol closer to the American lines. The Russian commander was so absorbed with giving orders to his spread out battalion that he didn't hear the approach of other tanks.

Without warning, five of his T-34's went up in flames as two American tank companies raced into the valley to counterattack the Russians. Emerging from the rolling smoke screen, American Sherman tanks armed with long-barrel 76mm guns tore into the Russian armor. The unexpected attack knocked the Russians back on their heels but the Shermans and T-34/85's were evenly matched.

The veteran Russian tankers began to maneuver and quickly fired back at the Americans, hitting several in the first volley. Sobolov ordered his units to disengage and draw the Americans towards their own lines, but the American commander decided to push the attack.

With more than half of his tanks hit, Sobolov's desperate force fought back with all the courage they could muster. Still out of range of any anti-tank fire from the Soviet infantry positions, the Americans were about to go in for the kill when fire from their left flank caused a half a dozen Shermans to explode. Sobolov's detached tanks finally emerged from their cross-country movement. They caught the Americans in the left flank and caused the Americans to break off pursuit of Sobolov's battered force. The Americans were clearly caught in a bind. The American tank commander had pursued too aggressively against the Russians and was caught in the open.

In what would be a complete shock to the Russians, the American tank commander ordered, "All elements reorient off road, it's a knife fight, so get in close. Davis, engage the tanks on your nine o'clock and I'll move against the ones to our six. Move fast, one quick sweep, then leap frog back to our own lines. Fire as you move, speed is everything. I'll try to get Regiment and get some air cover. Out."

The remaining fifteen American Shermans split into two elements and crossed into the rolling Czech farmland then drove right into the counterattacking Soviet tanks. Both sides were nearly equal in number, but the bold American move surprised the Russians, who slowed down and moved out of formation, unsure what to do. Sobolov had shifted his remaining command to safety and turned to watch the American maneuver.

In disbelief, he watched as the Americans, in an unheard of move, turned right into his flanking force. Germans would have immediately broke contact but this American commander appeared insane to try a maneuver like this, but he saw his men were unprepared for such a daring counter thrust.

Sobolov soon found, to his dismay, that the American Shermans' turret moved faster than any other tank in the war and could bring devastating fire on a target faster than a T-34. Before he realized it, his flanking force was in real trouble. American tankers, outgunned for much of the war, preferred a close in fight and the Shermans began taking out Russian tanks in ones and twos.

Within ten minutes of hard maneuvering, they began to disengage and retreat back to their own lines, leaving behind the shattered elements of the Soviet flanking force. Sobolov refused to accept defeat and decided to commit the last remaining reserve he possessed, the tanks from his third battalion, who had just come on the scene. Moving at high speed, he decided to lead the counter-attack himself.

With more than twenty tanks under his command, Sobolov believed he could kill the remaining ten tanks left to the American commander, who was now moving at high speed back towards the American lines. As he was nearly in range to the retreating Americans, he heard a roar overhead. Like avenging angels, a flight of eight American P-47 Thunderbolts dove on his exposed Russian tanks. Firing rockets and opening up with .50 caliber machine guns, the American planes destroyed five T-34's in the first pass.

The Soviet tankers began to see for themselves the horror Germans experienced of death from above as the Thunderbolts came back for another pass. Sobolov grabbed the turret mounted 12.7mm machine gun and opened fire into the sky, bringing just enough attention on himself to the lead American pilot.

Within seconds, Sobolov saw the American plane dive and the last thing he felt was the tremendous jarring sensation as a 2.75inch rocket slammed into the turret. The cataclysmic explosion broke his body nearly in half and Sobolov was dead before his body hit the ground.

Luckily, he didn't live long enough to realize that his entire brigade had essentially been annihilated. The retreating Sherman tanks moved at high speed and reached American lines thanks to the timely arrival of the Thunderbolts, leaving behind a valley full of dead and dying tankers from both sides.

Overlooking the battlefield below, Russians and Americans on both sides of the valley stared in disbelief at the horror to their front. Thousands of soldiers in both armies began manning defensive positions waiting for the inevitable counterattack to begin, both sides expecting the other to move in massive numbers. Responding to the falling Soviet artillery fire, American field artillery units began dropping 105 and 155mm fire throughout the Russian defensive lines, adding to the chaos and carnage that both sides suffered that morning. Deadly, long-range artillery duels lasted well into the afternoon until cooler heads eventually prevailed, leaving stunned soldiers and commanders on both sides wondering what the hell happened to start the killing.

Meanwhile, also looking down at the carnage below, were small groups of armed men, but no longer wearing any uniforms. Major

Zimmer ordered his men to shed their American uniforms and hide them in the woods. Breaking out in small squads, the victorious group of SS soldiers worked their way back to the rendezvous point behind American lines. Dressed now as Czechs, they hoped to get back to safety and wait for new orders. Killing Russians was a hard habit to break and most couldn't wait for the next battle.

Zimmer found an excellent observation point and watched transfixed on the tank battle below. Never, in his wildest imagination, could he have envisaged Operation Loki could have worked so well. He had dared to hope his little band of survivors would generate some small unit actions between the two sides, at least implicate the Americans in the attack on the command post, but this was too much to have dreamed.

Lying below him in the now charred fields of the formerly pristine Czech valley were hundreds of dead Americans and Russians. He could still hear commanders from both sides demanding the blood of the other. Blood, real blood, had been shed between the two powers and nothing could ever change that fact.

This was the beginning, he could just feel it. He knew it as he watched, neither side was willing to cut their losses and flee back to their own lines. Both sides refused to give an inch and attacked and counter-attacked with a fury reminiscent of battles he had witnessed on the Eastern Front. Knowing he had overstayed his welcome, he took one last glance at the smoking valley below and, with a tear in his eye, knew that Loki had done it. The last chance of his people may have started that day, and with God's help, the Russians would finally be defeated and his people liberated.

Chapter Thirty Five

August 5, 1945, 10:00am

Frankfurt, Germany, SHAEF Headquarters

The battle raging between American and Soviet tanks in Czechoslovakia set off alerts along the nearly five-hundred mile border zone from Lubeck on the Baltic to American Fifth Army divisions stationed in Austria and Northern Italy. Within thirty minutes of the breakout of hostilities, armies on both sides of the occupation borders in Germany began racing towards the dividing line.

Allied planes took to the skies and began to fly aggressive sweep operations along the border and prepared to defend the skies above the British and American armies. Several dozen aerial dogfights broke out on both sides of the border. Mustangs and Spitfires squared off against Yaks and Lagg fighters in a wild series of encounters in which both sides took casualties.

On the ground, the Soviet Red Army had been operating on an alert status ever since the troubles in Poland. Soviet engineer units had been much further along than their Western counterparts in constructing defensive positions, tank traps, and artillery parks. Red Army divisions began moving swiftly into defensive positions, tanks were gassed and ammo distributed.

While on the other side of the line, British and American divisions, though spread out pretty widely throughout their respective occupation zones, quickly began racing to establish their own hasty defensive positions.

In the American Third Army sector, more ominously, artillery fire rang out from both sides around the Pilsen area and didn't quiet until well into the morning. Heavy guns from the American XII Corps and the Soviet Fourth Guards Tank Army engaged in concentrated artillery duels throughout the morning until ceasefire orders made their way down to individual units. Soldiers and generals on both sides of the border were on guard and both were convinced the other side had fired the first shots.

As a tenuous ceasefire finally took hold, senior commanders on both sides tried to get a handle on events before things spiraled out of control. For the moment, Soviet and Allied armies numbering in the millions squared off against one another, with weapons "cocked and locked" and ready to defend their zones. The Cold War brewing for the previous couple of months had just turned hot.

An exasperated General Eisenhower had decided to play it tough with Patton down in Third Army. "Now, George, calm down a second. We still don't know what the hell happened out there. Now is not the time to lose our heads, too much is at stake and as a senior commander you should know better and if you move one more tank unit to the border, I'll send you back to the States on your keyster. Is that understood?"

He dreaded this call because he knew Patton would be chomping at the bit, looking to hit the Russians hard. *George is dangerous enough to get us into a war that we don't need and one we're not ready for any*way, Ike thought to himself.

Eisenhower was just starting to enjoy his new routine of actually sleeping in on certain mornings and taking the time to enjoy a leisurely breakfast. Since the war had ended, life at SHAEF was hardly boring, especially with recent activities in Poland and Czechoslovakia, but not quite the required eighteen-hour days that he put in for nearly three years during the war.

He had just started dunking some wonderfully flaky German pastries into his sunny side up eggs when a rather somber looking General Bedell Smith, his Chief of Staff, burst into his office. Neither man could believe the reports coming out of Pilsen, but within minutes Ike issued a theater-wide war warning, placed his entire command on alert and ordered combat units to assume a ready defensive posture.

Moments later, he placed a call to General Patton to try to keep a tight leash on his most aggressive and controversial field commander. Patton fanatically hated the Russians and had been complaining about them ever since the war ended, especially with the troubles over in Poland. Ike hated to think George might have been right all along, but deep down, Ike was having his doubts.

Refusing to back down so easily, even from a direct order from his superior, Patton was not going to let this go. Raising his voice, Patton practically roared into the phone, "Goddamnit Ike, don't you tell me that we don't know what those murdering sons of bitches have done this morning. I got more than two dozen Shermans on fire and more than a hundred dead and scores wounded from tank and artillery fire. It was a sucker punch to see if we got any stomach and I'll be goddamned if I'm going to sit back and do nothing.

Just say the word, and I'll be ready in four hours to hit those bastards with two armored divisions and teach those Godless sons of bitches a lesson they won't soon forget. Just don't tie my hands, Ike. I'm begging you. Those are my boys down there lying dead all over place."

Eisenhower had to admit that George was right about one thing, too many dead on both sides to pretend nothing happened. In fact, from preliminary reports, the Russians seemed to have suffered even heavier casualties during the exchange. Surprising himself, in a perverse sort of fashion, it gave Ike some small measure of pleasure.

However, George wasn't backing off, so he had to try a slightly different tack, "Look George, I know how you feel, they are my boys too. They all are my boys and I won't see one more man killed for no good reason, but I can't risk the lives of more men without more information. I swear to you that if the Soviets try anything else, I'll unleash the full power of the Allied Forces on them, especially Third Army. I got calls into the Soviet High Command even as we speak and I guarantee that I will get to the bottom of this."

Still angry, Patton cut him off, "Jesus Christ, Ike, more talk with those bastards won't change a damn thing. A Communist doesn't take a shit without first getting a direct order from the next turd higher in command and you know it. We both met some of those guerrillas in uniform. You think it was an accident that an entire brigade of Russian tanks just happened to find themselves moving into our zone? Bullshit and you know it. Let me go and teach the bastards a lesson.

Twenty-four hours is all I'll need to give them a swift kick in the ass and then I'll be back behind our lines. I swear, just a one day is all I'll need."

Starting to get angry himself, Ike lit a cigarette and inhaled deeply to calm himself, and then took a firm tone, "Now that's enough, George, no more, not another word. You are officially being ordered to maintain a defensive posture only, however, I will allow you to move up some heavy units if you need to counterpunch against any more cross border incursions. At the very least, it ought to give them something to think about, but if I hear that you so much as station a single soldier within the Soviet zone, you will be immediately relieved of command and sent packing just when I may need you the most. So behave, and that's an order. Understood? I will contact you shortly. Be prepared to fly up here for a general conference."

Pausing for a moment, Eisenhower suddenly felt that dark feeling come over him, the way it used to during the dark days of the war. Carrying the burden of command, the power of life and death for so many always weighed heavily on Ike, and the implications of what happened that morning really seemed to hit all at once. In a more melancholic tone, Eisenhower ended the call to Patton more like in the days when Patton was his superior in the early days of the first American Tank Corp.

"George, I have to level with you that, between us, I think you may be right. The Russians don't do a damn thing without planning it out. The damn thing just doesn't make sense. Regardless, keep your head, George, and we will see this thing through, no matter what. Talk to you soon, Ike out."

Not getting a reprieve, General Eisenhower looked up and in walked his Chief of Staff, General Bedell Smith, along with the SHAEF Deputy Commander, British Air Marshall Arthur Tedder. Eisenhower had come to trust the reliable British Royal Air Force officer and was pleased to see him this morning. "Don't tell me if it's more bad news, I'm exhausted after talking to George down at Third Army. I'm afraid he's about to start World War Three all on his own down there."

With his typically clipped British accent and penchant for understatement, Tedder replied, "Haven't you heard, old boy, Patton did start World War Three. The Soviets just announced it on the BBC about ten minutes ago. By the way, are we winning?"

That broke the ice and the three wartime friends started to laugh, and a much-needed one at that. Always one to bring Ike back to reality, General Smith, in his usual gruff manner griped, "I don't know what type of bullshit game the Russians are playing because they just sent a crazy message claiming that an American combat unit attacked their forces ten miles inside their occupation zone. They say they have proof that will be made public that proves our men shot up one of their command posts, shot the divisional staff, and ambushed a tank battalion that came to help. They claim that the only reason one of their units came into the American zone was to counter-attack US forces retreating after making their attacks. George may be crazy, but he ain't nuts. How the hell do you want me to answer?"

Putting both arms behind his head to think for a moment, Eisenhower pondered the meaning behind the message. *What an amazing lie, but why would they go through the trouble?* Still unsure, he turned to Tedder, "They know that we would never attack them in this fashion, no one would ever believe them. Is it possible we have some armed SS fanatics running around trying to cause trouble?"

The British Air Marshall answered, "Intelligence indicates otherwise, sir. I'm afraid some chaps back at MI6 now believe that the "National Redoubt" crisis in April was nothing but misinformation leaked by the Russians in hopes that we would divert forces south and leave Berlin for them. There never was such a thing as a "National Redoubt" of diehard Nazis. We have been quite thorough about securing the entire Bavarian Alps, so I don't see how SS, or anyone for that matter, could stage out of our zone and attack the Russians. Too bloody hard to even think about, I would say."

Smith got diverted as another message was rushed in to the meeting, he blurted out," Holy shit! You're not going to believe this one. The Russians just sent an official complaint claiming that they found American weapons all over the battle site, plus several dead soldiers wearing American uniforms. They demand full disclosure of our activities and warned that the Red Army is giving formal notice that they are declaring an exclusion zone on air, land and sea from Lubeck to Trieste. If any American or British forces are seen approaching the Soviet zone, they will be taken under immediate fire."

A wave of nausea suddenly overcame Eisenhower and his forehead began to perspire. The Russians had just given official notice that they were prepared to initiate hostilities at a moment's notice and, worse, they seem to actually believe Americans started the mess. *This is insanity. What in God's name is going on? Something is not right here.*

Pushing his chair away from his desk, Eisenhower stood and began to walk slowly around the room. Deep in thought, he completely blocked out the presence of both Smith and Tedder as he tried to put himself in the Russian shoes. *The Russians were furious over the Polish uprising more so now with the Czech declaration, but what could possibly motivate them to strike out against American troops and accuse us of having attacked first.*

Granted, the reports coming out of Poland told a story of nearly fanatical resistance coming from the Polish Home Army. The

Russians looked to be reclaiming many of the important industrial centers in Poland, but at a savage price. The Poles still owned the countryside and by the looks of it, the Russians were in for a long winter. Next, the Czechs indicated they would demand the Red Army occupation forces to leave immediately and had staged a countrywide strike in protest, maybe Stalin had gone off the deep end after all.

Air Marshall Tedder broke into his thoughts, "Ike, perhaps we are over thinking this a bit. Clearly Ivan is in a bind. They can't possibly allow Benes and the Czech government in exile in London to force them to leave, so they are manufacturing this crisis. The moment they give in to Czech demands then the whole concept of their occupation throughout all of Eastern Europe comes into question. That's the bloody crux of the matter in Poland. The Poles refuse to acknowledge the Soviet's right to occupy their country.

Let's face it, your "Old Uncle Joe" must be having bloody fits about all this and he isn't one to take things sitting down. Besides, word has it that the Poles came too bloody close for his liking in Berlin. Who knows what the man will do now? For all we know, he may have come completely undone. The one thing he won't do, however, is back down."

His Chief of Staff Smith added, "It's a political question, Ike. Arthur's probably right. Stalin wants us to keep out of Poland and Czechoslovakia, period. This morning was a message, probably more like a warning. All the rest of it is just a bullshit smokescreen. Hell, it was simpler when all we had to do was kill Germans. This peace shit is confusing as hell."

Eisenhower nodded a bit at that one. Still keeping his thoughts to himself, at a minimum he knew conventional wisdom dictated that he order Allied units to beef up their own defensive positions, cancel all leaves, and request Washington to halt any more transfers to the Pacific Theater. More than a quarter of his combat power had already begun the move towards the Pacific or was in the process of being demobilized in Europe and to change those orders would be viewed as a serious escalation.

Ike fully recognized this was a political decision, not just a military one. What really took a hold of him was the fear that the Russians might actually believe America did attack them, *maybe it would be best not to escalate matters. God knows Truman would never directly intervene in Czechoslovakia, let alone Poland, so why up the ante.*

Following that logic, Ike thought if we unilaterally stand down along the border, maybe we can de-escalate the situation before more of his men die. He had said it before that he would not risk the lives of any more American soldiers just to make some political point. If it means we pull back Allied forces and they feel as if they have saved face to forget this whole mess then avoid the threat of general hostilities. That's it. If there's nothing to gain, then risking his soldiers for anything other than victory on a battlefield against the enemy is wasteful and counter to his intentions to bring the boys back home safe and sound.

Turning to General Smith and Air Marshal Tedder, he said, "Gentlemen, I just decided that we will de-escalate this thing and fast. Bedell, I want you to set up a strict air corridor ten miles wide on our side of the border. Absolutely no zone violations will be allowed under any circumstances. You especially make sure General Quesada's TACAIR people know that any pilots looking to push the envelope will find themselves grounded and automatically transferred to the infantry.

"Next, I want to make sure that all my Army and Corps commanders understand that other than preparing for local defense, I will forbid any new fortifications from being erected. I want everyone to return to their original unit areas, except for an extra division down in Twelfth Corp. I think it would only be prudent to get an extra division near Pilsen, but I want the rest of the front to stand down."

Both Smith and Tedder were shocked at Ike's decision. In fact, Tedder assumed that Churchill would order Montgomery to do just the opposite regardless of SHAEF orders.

Eisenhower could clearly see that both men were not exactly enthusiastic about his new orders. "Look, you two, there is nothing to be gained by giving the Soviets any more excuses to continue this bloodshed. They sent us a message, and I refuse to take the bait. I understand that good men died this morning, but the only way to avenge them is by initiating full scale hostilities, and I say it's too high a price to pay and refuse to order it. Understood? Now, let's cut the orders, and fast, and get somebody in here to take down a memo that I want sent to the Russians immediately."

As SACEUR or Supreme Allied Commander in Europe, Ike's decision was final and only a direct order from General Marshall or the President would make him change his mind.

Chapter: Thirty Six

August 5, 1945, 1:30pm

Nuremberg, General Patton's Third Army Headquarters

The old man was in a complete rage that hadn't let up since he was told about the Russian attacks on one of his favorite outfits, the 4th Armored Division. Patton had been in a miserable funk ever since the guns went silent on May 9th. For all intents and purposes, he had fulfilled his destiny and would go down as America's greatest field commander of the war, perhaps any war. Still, he felt haunted by feelings that something was left undone. But, with the first hint of action, America's most flamboyant general came to life.

Like a sprinter hearing the sound of the gun, Patton leapt into action. He stormed into Third Army's Ops Center and started issuing orders to dozens of field units, from individual companies to whole regiments, towards the Pilsen area and then he got Army Air Corps General Weyland's fighter-bombers in the air. Before the engagement ended, he made sure the first thing on the way to Pilsen was a major convoy full of ammo. Patton immediately began planning a major counter-attack. At minimum, Patton thought a penetration of Soviet lines was required just to show the bastards that they could do it.

Everything changed after his conversation with General Eisenhower more than an hour ago, and ever since, Patton was positively left seething. He refused to talk to anyone and ordered everyone out of the room. The staff could hear papers being moved, objects being thrown around the room, and more than a bit of profanity being thrown about. During the course of the war, his immediate staff had listened to Patton curse just about anything and everything that ever ended up in the European Theater, but not even Montgomery caused him to curse like he was cursing about Ike.

Major General Hobart Gay, Third Army's Chief of Staff, sat shaking his head as he held a piece of paper, new orders out of SHAEF, and muttered under his breath, "This is liable to kill him, or worse."

Gay had served under Patton for the entire duration of the war from the moment they hit the beach together in North Africa to the frigid hell on the road to Bastogne and up to the final battles in Czechoslovakia. No one knew Patton better or understood how the man ticked than Gay. He was more worried about what Patton was capable of doing than at any time during the war.

Never seen the general so angry, he may be writing out operation orders to move against the Russians and Ike be damned. Who knows what he will do once I show him the new orders from SHAEF.

Major General Gay, Deputy Chief of Staff Colonel Harkins, and their Intelligence chief, Colonel Oscar Koch, the brain trust of Third Army, wanted to strike back at the Russians as much as the General, but more importantly, they wanted to protect the General from himself. The three of them camped outside his quarters and listened for the General to calm down a bit before presenting the new orders.

Like everyone else in Third Army, these three men were keyed up and ready for action. Patton had selected men who wanted to fight. The men on his staff may not have served directly in the field, but their hard work and diligence was as much a reason for Third Army's success as any field officer. General Patton knew it and trusted these three men like no others.

Colonel Koch had made a name for himself during the war when he predicted the German attack in the Ardennes. Koch was a master at interpreting communication intercepts and putting the pieces together like some giant puzzle. Once the Russians attacked the Poles, Patton ordered Koch to begin evaluating Russian intentions and capabilities opposite Third Army, but ran into problems due to a dearth of Russian language specialists.

Wasting little time, General Patton immediately released two dozen Russian speaking German intelligence and staff officers who served on the Eastern Front to develop decent SIGINT. Koch ordered up whatever intercepts had been received that morning and early afternoon to be read and transcribed on the double. Both armies were transmitting in the open during the engagement and the immediate aftermath. Koch expected to find some clue as to why the Russians attacked the way they did or at least try to piece together what might follow.

Turning to General Gay and Harkins, "The General may be like this for hours. I recommend we try to get some decent options together for him or at least let's figure out some way to prevent the old man from getting into any more trouble."

Harkins added, "Well, what about your Germans, don't they have anything for you yet?"

"The data is still pouring in even as we talk and I still haven't got enough guys who can translate Russian. But my gut tells me that whatever happened this morning, there's more to it."

General Gay agreed. "Oscar, I think that you're right. Those Russians tore into our boys with a vengeance and then kept counter-attacking until nearly the whole damn brigade was wiped out. I can see with Germans, but us? Christ, we were on the same side for the whole war. I think Oscar's right, this wasn't just a skirmish, it was a real battle and our boys gave as good as they got.

Thank God, Weyland had his Thunderbolts on station armed with rockets, or we would have lost another company of tanks or worse. Those up-gunned T-34/85's have got tough hides, and I don't want to even think about going heads on with those monsters, Stalin tanks. Whatever the hell is going on, at least we will not be caught with our britches down again. So, pass the word to all commands that Third Army stays on unofficial alert regardless of official SHAEF orders."

Harkins cut in, "You hear that? While we've been talking, I haven't heard a peep from inside. What say we go in and touch base?"

Gay thought for a minute and added, "Fine, but let me break the news about the new orders from Ike. I don't want him getting all excited again. Got it?"

Expecting to find Patton tense, the three of them were shocked to find the General with his feet up on the desk and a freshly lit cigar in his mouth. Rather than wearing a scowl, the General looked almost, if not quite serene, then at least as relaxed as he could be considering the circumstances. Patton watched with amusement at the looks on his men's faces as they walked in to the room.

Putting his book, down he waved everybody in and said, "What the hell did you expect to find? Christ, you look like I would be lying on the floor with drool coming out of my damn mouth after a stroke or something. Sit."

Koch walked by his desk and noticed the book Patton was reading. *Strange.* Why was the General suddenly reading Douglas Southall Freeman's famous Civil War history of Lee's Lieutenants, volume two? Even more perplexing, why the hell did he look so damn good, almost upbeat, in fact, as he wore a boyish grin that spoke volumes as to what he was really thinking? Usually that grin meant trouble.

Sitting back, Patton looked at his men. He knew they were there to make sure that he hadn't gone off the deep end or to make sure he doesn't do anything too crazy. He thought, *they had reason to be worried.*

He'd be a liar if he didn't admit to be spoiling for a fight ever since the fighting ended back in May. He had been carefully monitoring the Russian buildup in Poland and now in Czechoslovakia. Lord how he admired those brave bastards in Poland fighting the Bolsheviks with everything they had. They were without air cover, tanks, artillery, nothing, and yet they still were killing the commie bastards at every crossroad, every rail junction, and village.

Meanwhile, a bunch of soft, pencil-necked Ivy Leaguers back in Washington were letting them get away with it, pussyfooting around, instead of helping those brave men and women. *Today changed everything, even if no one else has the guts to admit it.* It was time to let the boys know what was on his mind.

"Before anyone else says anything, what's the status along the front?" The use of the word front did not go unnoticed by his staff.

General Gay started off, "General, the ceasefire is still holding, both sides have withdrawn their wounded and dead and ceased artillery attacks for the past two hours. Recon flights have confirmed that the Russians are moving sizeable forces towards the border that much we can verify at the moment. Soon we're going to be blind again. New orders from SHAEF...look at this and you'll see why."

Patton's white eyebrows narrowed as he read SHAEF's new orders, and then he just shook his head in disgust. "Goddamn it, doesn't Ike know that these bastards mean business. If he won't let me attack the sons of bitches, the least he could do was to let us keep track of them from the air. The man's lost his nerve, and that's a fact."

Koch decided to jump in at this point, "General, we have been going through radio transmissions for the past three hours, but nothing concrete has come up yet. However, one thing is clear, this was more than just a test or some probe. They have way too much combat power building up on their side of the line just to fight a few Czech partisans. Whatever the hell happened today, I guarantee they didn't expect us to move so swift with our own armor to push them back. But the way they attacked, it makes me wonder if they may be looking to clear those ridgelines for a straight shot on Pilsen."

Harkins saw where Koch was heading, and nodded in agreement, and added, "Hell, it looks to me that they want to kick us out of Czechoslovakia to make a point. Don't forget we were supposed to hand this part of Czech real-estate over to the Russians after the Potsdam Conference, but that got put on hold for the moment. As long as American forces occupy any part of Czechoslovakia, it'll keep the idea alive that we will support internal revolts against Soviet rule. Makes sense?"

Patton had to hand it to his people, they were thinking on multiple levels, political issues, military, even historical, you name it, but they were missing the main point. Patton burst out, "Bullshit! Let's get one thing straight for the rest of this campaign, those Commie bastards won't be happy until they control all of Europe. It's that simple. The goddamn Russians wouldn't send a squad into our zone let alone an entire tank brigade without a direct order from that murdering bastard in the Kremlin. Trust me, this is just the beginning."

Just thinking about the battles to come sent shivers up and down Patton's spine, while at the same time made him feel more alive than at any time since the guns fell silent. He had been criticized by many as being some kind of warmonger. They were wrong. Patton always believed, from his earliest days, that his destiny for greatness would be found on the fields of battle leading fellow warriors in a desperate battle to victory over some deadly foe. Regardless of his victories over the Nazis, Patton felt deep within his soul that his destiny had yet to be fulfilled.

In the waning days of the war, he became depressed because somehow, he just knew he had been chosen for even greater things, but looked to be denied. Now, on this morning, he understood what had been plaguing him for three months. God had placed him and his Third Army in the right place and at the right time to lead the forces of the Western world against the most deadly and evil foe in history, the godless Bolsheviks. He had to get his men ready for the trials ahead. He swore that no matter how SHAEF tied his hands, his command would be ready for the storm to come.

Adopting the more warlike demeanor his men had seen many times, Patton stood ramrod straight, marched to his desk and pulled out a map. To their collective surprise, it was an old Civil War map that depicted the battle of Gettysburg. Looking close, instantly Koch put it together, *the Freeman book, Gettysburg, and now...*

Slapping the map with his riding crop, "You see that? Does that look familiar to all of you? You see how five roads all led to one place, Gettysburg. Control of Gettysburg would have allowed Lee access to Harrisburg, Philadelphia, or even a quick march back down to Baltimore, and then fall on Washington from the North, where her defenses were negligible. Five roads, keep that in mind when you look at the map of Pilsen and Third Army. We control Pilsen, and you can threaten Prague, or prevent a move against Nuremberg, Munich, or even a march South towards Austria and Vienna, plus, block any reinforcements moving north from Fifth Army.

"Now, Meade was no dummy, but it was an old, smart horse cavalryman, Buford who won the war that day for the North. He pulled back and maintained control of the surrounding ridgelines until Meade could send reinforcements, and let Lee's men get slaughtered as they took on fixed defenses. The only problem was the dumb bastard let Lee get away with the rest of his army. I can tell you right now that I would have ended the war on the northern bank of the Potomac River."

All eyes were suddenly drawn to the door as in walked Brigadier General Conklin along with a German officer, with the rank of general, by the looks of it. General Gay rolled his eyes and shook his head as he thought to himself, *oh Christ what has George gone and done now.*

Walking with an impressive military bearing and the cold eyes of a professional soldier, German General Dr. Franz Baake presented himself to the American commander, Patton. Offering a formal and stiff salute, then in heavily accented English, he said, "How can I be of service Herr General Patton?"

General Baake, a dentist in peacetime, had fought in every major theater of the war, even against the Third Army in France, but he established his reputation fighting the Russians for years on the Eastern Front. He began the war as a reserve First Lieutenant and had risen to command a battalion, then a regiment, a Panzer Brigade, and finally to command the Panzerkorps Feldherrnhalle, who fought until the vicious end outside of Vienna before surrendering.

Over the course of the war, he was awarded the Iron Cross with diamond clusters for distinguished leadership during the battles of

Kursk and the Cherkassy Pocket, and units under his command were credited with nearly five hundred tank kills, including seventy nine personal tank kills; truly a remarkable war record.

Patton had gotten into more than a bit of trouble with Ike over his less than impressive de-Nazification program. Plus, it seemed as if George was a little too friendly with some of his fellow German contemporaries. Ever the student of military warfare, Patton had been debriefing several German generals and colonels, especially armor specialists, to get a feel for Soviet organization, logistics, tactics, etc. General Baake proved a treasure trove of information and Patton knew he was the logical choice to help facilitate his plan.

Coming to attention himself, Patton returned the salute and then told both men to be seated. His engineer officer didn't know what the hell was going on while his staff sat looking worried at what he was about to do, and an unperturbed General Baake was nodding up and down as he looked at the map of what appeared to be the American Civil War era Gettysburg campaign and tried to figure out what this mad American wanted. "Gentlemen, time to get down to business. I'm going to keep things simple and to the point."

Pausing to pull out a map of Third Army operational zone, he continued, "I am going to keep this simple, you see Pilsen on this here map, we own it and I'm not going to give back. Remember, I don't like to pay for the same ground twice. Third Army men bled taking this city, and I'll be damned if Third Army is going to give it back. This morning was a beginning of something big and I don't give two shits what Ike and the rest of SHAEF think. Those bastards are going to be coming across in force, and soon. I don't give a damn what any other command in the American army is about to do, my boys are going to be ready to kick their red asses back to Moscow if they'll let me."

An exasperated General Gay interrupted, "But General, we just got a direct order from SHAEF to stand down our forces…period. How the hell do we get around that?"

Smiling, Patton laughed, "You let me worry about Ike. As for Third Army, we are going on a war footing as of two hours ago. First thing tomorrow, Harkins, you start setting up remedial infantry and armor schools as close to the Czech border as possible. I'd pick Hof and Regensberg to start with, if I were you. I don't give a shit how you do it, but I want to start rotating as many green soldiers as possible to get their training up to Third Army standards. For every unit rotating through these training centers, they go right up to the front lines and then get another one in transit in a constant rotation.

"Next, start moving ammo, spare parts, and gas as far forward as possible. Have Conklin's boys set up small logistic parks, off the beaten paths, use secondary roads but only those with good overhead cover. This way Ike can't accuse us of stockpiling for a major push, but, if the balloon does go up, Third Army will have supplies on hand. Oh yeah, don't forget to set up at least half a dozen maintenance and repair motor pools. If my tanks get hit, I want them back on the battlefield within seventy two hours."

Harkins was writing everything down but had to ask, "General, how in the hell am I supposed to get so much traffic moving without SHAEF figuring out what we're doing? Let's face facts, gentlemen, they are going to be up our asses down here looking for problems."

Good, the boys are thinking, Patton thought. "Good point Harkins, but it'll all make sense in a minute. An hour ago, I decided to rebuild the town of Pilsen and all the surrounding territory from the damage inflicted by Third Army operations this past May. At least, that's the story we're sticking with. To make this thing work, we're going to need a lot of trucks, cement, lumber, hell you name it, doesn't matter. Conklin, you got priority on everything as of this moment."

With a glean in his eyes, Patton next turned to his surprise guest, "General Conklin, I have decided to transfer General Baake and a force of fifteen thousand German POWs currently sitting on their asses in Bavarian POW camps. He will organize these men into fifteen units of a thousand men each, and further broken into ten one hundred and fifty man work details. You will be responsible for supporting our efforts to rebuild Pilsen's defenses. General Baake, do you think that you and your fellow German soldiers can handle your new orders?"

With a look of sheer astonishment mixed with a steely determination in his eyes, General Baake couldn't believe what he had just heard. This crazy American general was actually proposing nothing less than the establishment of a paramilitary organization that can't be used for anything else, other than preparing the battlefield in Pilsen, and hopefully, to fight alongside the Americans the next time the Russians attack.

Without hesitation, General Baake leapt to attention, saluted, and said, "Herr General Patton, I assure you that only the finest soldiers will be chosen. You will find that things are already organized along similar lines in the camps and will enable us to be ready to serve under General Conklin's direction within twenty-four hours. Please, excuse me while I head back to the barracks without delay. There is much to be done."

General Baake excitedly exited the room wearing a grin from ear to ear. He understood exactly what Patton was doing, more importantly, he was determined to pick the very best men for this assignment. If the balloon goes up, as the Americans say, then perhaps his men could serve with enough distinction to take away the stain of the vulgarities of the Nazi regime. Baake and hundreds of like-minded officers would be only too happy to jump at the chance to redeem Germany's honor.

Waiting for the door to close, General Gay jumped to his feet and exclaimed, "Jesus H. Christ, George, have you lost your goddamn mind? Because, I could have sworn that I just watched you create a German infantry division to serve alongside Third Army. Do you know what would happen if this got out? The press will eat you alive and Ike won't have any other choice but to fire you from Third Army this time. Look, you're probably right about the Russians, but this is nuts."

Grasping his riding crop, Patton began pacing the room, trying to find the right words, so his most loyal staffers could understand what was at stake. Finally, he calmed a bit, took a breath, and said, "You really want to know? Well guess what, it's because we need them! The Russians have the biggest goddamned field army in the history of mankind, more than six million veteran soldiers, nearly ten thousand of the best tanks in the world, and a willingness to drown us in their own blood to win. The goddamn Krauts have been fighting Russians for generations and this is their fight as much as ours and I don't give a damn about diplomacy or even about the last war.

I don't know how to break this to you gentlemen, but even when we hold the bastards and we will hold them and make them bleed like they haven't bled since Stalingrad, but even then there's no guarantee what that'll mean if they run through north and central Germany all the way to the Rhine. What I did today is just the beginning. I just hope that Ike and SHAEF eventually understand that without the Germans standing with us, the American Army will be in a world of hurt."

Breathing heavy and all worked up, Patton looked at the faces of his most intimate staff members and waited to see how they were taking it all in. They had to believe it as much as he did or the whole thing would fall on its face. Seeing the determined nods, Patton continued, "General Conklin, you are hereby ordered to begin using those Germans and whatever engineer forces in Third Army to get this battlefield ready. Is that understood? The Russians lost more than three hundred thousand dead when they took Berlin, most of which came during the initial assaults against the prepared, in-depth anti-tank defenses along the Seelow Heights.

"Harkins, I want you to find as many Kraut 75mm and 88mm anti-tank guns that you can scrounge and gunners who know how to use them. Nothing in our inventory can compare to what that gun can do against Russian armor and I like the idea of watching Russian tanks burn at two thousand yards. Conklin your boys will be setting up tank traps, concrete barriers, pillboxes, anything and everything possible to bleed the bastards, and those Germans know how to kill Russians and will work like animals to get the chance again.

"We are going to hold them by the nose around Pilsen and then kick them in the ass just when they think we've had it, and that's when we'll hit them in the flank and drive through them like shit through a goose and we won't stop until every last one of them burns in hell. No turning back gentlemen, history starts today. I swear to you, by all that I hold sacred, that I will lead this army into battle and we will emerge victorious or I will die trying. Now get to work, Third Army is here to stay."

August 5, 1945, 12:30 pm

Berlin Headquarters, Red Army Occupation Forces

Since the untimely death of Marshal Konev, commander of the First Ukrainian Front, in the rubble of Berlin, Marshal Zhukov ordered most of his former competitor's combat units, added to his own, while the rest was sent East to put down the Polish rebellion. With Zhukov's growing power in the wake of the failure of the State Security apparatus to protect Comrade Stalin, his former First Byelorussian Front Headquarters had grown to be the de facto field headquarters of the entire Red Army in Europe.

Stalin had not officially named Zhukov as the commander in chief of the Red Army, technically STAVKA in Moscow still made decisions on the operational use of the Red Army, but ever since the attempt on Stalin's life, things had changed. The Marshal had been on the move for the past forty eight hours visiting the front in Poland and was exhausted by his travels, but his field commanders needed to be shaken up a bit. *These fucking Poles need to be taught a lesson, especially now, more than ever, that the Czechs are now causing troubles around Prague with this damn strike.*

After listening to pleas for more combat units, Zhukov finally decided to transfer another three Mechanized Corps to the Polish Theater and put down the Poles once and for all. No matter how brave, each time the Red Army put heavy units into the field, the Poles were forced to either stand and die or melt into the forests. He wanted Poland pacified in time to set up quiet winter quarters.

Trying to concentrate on a huge stack of messages, he barely noticed as his special armored train gradually came to a halt. Finally, looking out the window, he saw they weren't near a station, but looked to be stopped in the middle of the Polish countryside.

Angered at the delay, he burst through his door just as an aide was rushing to open it. The burly Russian commander barely noticed the man lying on the floor in obvious pain. He barked, "Well, what is it? Why have we stopped?"

His still shaken aide stood up and explained, "Marshal Zhukov, I regret to inform you that, due to communication problems,

Headquarters in Berlin has unsuccessfully been trying to get a hold of you for the past hour. So, they sent a PO-2 light bi-plane from a nearby airbase to fly you directly to Berlin. The pilot handed me this urgent message from your staff."

The message read, "Situation critical, requires your immediate attention. The Americans have infiltrated commando groups into Czechoslovakia and slaughtered the divisional staff of the 32nd Guards Mechanized Division. American weapons and uniforms were collected at the scene. The Americans sent tank units to cover the withdrawal of their commandos and the 22nd Guards Tank brigade countered the American attacks but was destroyed by ambush and direct air and land attacks by American Third Army forces under General Patton.

Both sides inflicted heavy casualties as 4th Guards Tank Army answered with massive artillery barrages and minor counter-attacks along the Pilsen front. The Americans have denied all involvement, but have rushed armed units along the occupation borders in both Germany and Czechoslovakia. We are awaiting your orders so we sent for a plane to fly you back to headquarters."

To a man whose reputation of an iron will and nerves of steel, the news hit like the icy chill of a Siberian winter. Within seconds, his meaty hands crumpled the paper into a ball, threw it aside, and immediately headed towards the plane. An hour later he landed on the outskirts of Berlin, near Potsdam, and called his staff in for an emergency meeting.

His staff knew the Marshal required instant information, better to give a little of what you actually knew rather than wait for the entire picture to show itself. As with most of his meetings, it was short and to the point. His Chief of Staff, Colonel-General Sokolovski oversaw the meeting. With a large map of Czechoslovakia up on the wall, Polenov sketched out the American positions around Pilsen and the Third Army along the Bavarian border.

In ten minutes, a skillfully conducted briefing took place that outlined the attacks on the 32nd command post, the ambush and later tank battle that destroyed the 22nd Guards Brigade, and finally the widespread artillery duel along the entire southern front.

A visibly angry Sokolovski added, "The one thing we are absolutely sure of is that Americans weapons and several dead commandos in American uniforms were left on the scene, not to mention more than two dozen American tanks at the edge of our fortified zone. The Americans opened fire on our forces first during each engagement and they had planes in the air, armed for air-to-ground attacks to cover their withdrawal. The American attack was done skillfully and inflicted heavy casualties. Their tanks were handled particularly well.

"At present, every Red Army unit currently within a hundred miles of the current demarcation line is digging in and building fortifications. Combat patrols have been tripled and movement towards the borders in both Germany and Czechoslovakia has been accelerated. If the Americans decide to hit us again, they will be destroyed by direct fire before they cross the line of departure. The only thing we do not know, Comrade Marshal, is why they attack at all. Other than inflicting some meaningless casualties, nothing was accomplished."

Zhukov listened the entire time, but found himself staring at the map on the wall. Trying to take in every river, stream, hillside, and flatland, Zhukov was already thinking about what might have to be done. *Why they attacked matters less than Sokolovski thinks. No, what really matters is how strong the Americans are and can they hold up to a full attack by the Red Army.* Shaking his head, *I think not.*

Zhukov looked at the angry faces of his staff waiting for him to give them their orders. *Stalin must know by now and will surely want to see him. What should I recommend?* Looking up at the huge wall map, Zhukov envisioned huge red arrows all pointed West. In that instant, he knew what had to be done. Standing up, he started giving orders to his staff and ordered a plane prepared to take him to Moscow tonight.

Chapter Thirty Seven

August 5, 1945, 6:30pm

Washington D.C., The White House

What had started out as a joint meeting of the war cabinet and Joint Chiefs concerning the war in the Pacific, quickly turned into something quite different. Truman had already given the final order to authorize the use of the most powerful weapon ever devised by man and the next morning it would be put to the ultimate test against the Japanese mainland. Hopefully, if successful, the Japanese would come to their senses and forego the necessity of a full-scale invasion.

President Truman relied upon the findings of a committee chaired by Secretary of State Byrnes and composed of civilian, military, and members of the scientific community. Although with some reservations that had been duly noted, and then discounted, Secretary Byrnes recommended the use of the atomic bomb against Japan as the best hope of ending the war.

From the test conducted in the desert of New Mexico, the atomic bomb generated the explosive yield equivalent to nearly twenty thousand tons of TNT, enough, theoretically, to destroy a major city. The military had enough uranium and plutonium to make three bombs and deliver them on target by the middle of August. The first was to be targeted on the port city of Hiroshima. It was hoped the Japanese would not require another demonstration of America's will to win. Thinking long and hard about the implications of the new weapon, Truman finally gave the go ahead.

Still thinking like a Senator from Missouri, Truman worried what the American people would think if the government spent two billion dollars of taxpayers' money and didn't use the damn thing. Anyway, *the bastards started the damn war with their sneak attack on Pearl Harbor, time for them to reap the whirlwind.* Tonight's meeting was to confirm the decision, however events in Europe changed everything.

The military men wore either angry scowls or gaunt expressions of determination, several of the civilians at the table looked nervous while others couldn't wait to sound off against the Russians. For nearly a half-hour, a spirited undisciplined debate took place as the President's advisors argued how to handle the Soviet attacks and several expressed the very real possibility if this was a precursor to a larger general attack and were calling for emergency measures to protect the troops.

Information was still coming in from the field, but the Joint Chiefs were able to piece enough together and delivered the official military briefing on the encounter between the two armies. Army Chief of Staff General Marshall was quick and to the point. He outlined the recent movement of Soviet combat forces to the borders along the demarcation lines in Germany and Czechoslovakia. He discussed the expanding scope of the Polish rebellion and harsher counter-measures employed by the Red Army to suppress the uprising and then led into the sudden outbreak of Czech partisan attacks against Red Army occupation forces in Czechoslovakia.

In a deadly serious voice, General Marshall began the briefing. "Gentlemen, at approximately 0530 hours local time, Red Army units launched a sustained artillery attack upon American forces well within our zone of occupation near the town of Pilsen. When we attempted to pull several observation teams out of harm's way, the Soviets responded by attacking with nearly an entire brigade of tanks. Our initial relief force was annihilated, nearly to the man, but this delaying action was followed by a sharp counter-attack by two companies of Shermans who hit the Russians hard, but suffered heavy casualties themselves. We were able to withdraw back to our defensive lines under the cover of both strong artillery fire and air cover.

"General Eisenhower wisely ordered additional defensive measures, but decided not to enflame the situation by mobilizing Allied forces towards the border areas and restricted overhead flights to avoid any more incidents. As of this hour, a tentative ceasefire is in effect. Both the wounded and the dead have been retrieved and we await orders to decide further action. The situation remains quite fluid and very dangerous, we should remember this as we deliberate policy."

A red-faced President Truman broke into a series of rapid fire questions, "What in the hell are those bastards up to? Could it have been a mistake of some kind? Did we provoke them in any way? General Marshall, is there anything to this crazy notion that we sent commandos over onto their side of the line and attacked first?"

The strain of the situation was written all over the President's face. It was bad enough the man had finally come to the decision to drop a bomb which would probably kill a hundred thousand people in a blink of an eye, but to have this thrown on his plate seemed almost unfair.

Secretary Byrnes saw both traces of indecision and anger in Truman's face. He decided to speak up first, as was his right as senior cabinet officer. Standing up, eyes focused squarely on the President, Byrnes spoke in a slow, deep Southern drawl, "Mr. President, if I may? I want to make this clear to everyone in this room, the Russians can file as many diplomatic protests that they want, but it won't change the fact that we got American boys dead because they want to make a point, keep our noses out of Czechoslovakia. How soon after we publicly backed President Benes request for Soviet occupation forces to leave did they decide to up and attack us? Isn't it obvious that this is an out and out provocation by Stalin aimed at putting a scare into us?"

He took a second to let that sink in for everyone, and then he turned to a figure not usually present at military meetings, FBI Director J. Edgar Hoover. Byrnes addressed the formidable G-man. "I am concerned that, perhaps, there may even be a more troubling matter we need to explore. Mr. Hoover, didn't you send memos to General Groves out in Los Alamos about the possible infiltration of communist agents in the Manhattan Project?"

Hoover, a rabid anti-Communist, took the ball and ran with it. "Absolutely, Mr. Secretary, security has been pretty damn lax with those scientists out there. For the past few months, my G-men have been watching the comings and goings of these people, many of whom came to this country less than three or four years ago. I have a very real concern that some of these individuals have mixed loyalties, especially now that Hitler is defeated. I am afraid to say that it is entirely possible Stalin knows exactly where we stand on the project and has for some time."

Byrnes finished the thought, "That would mean, gentlemen, that Stalin knows we are about to drop the bomb against the Japanese and wants to send us the message that he will not be intimidated."

Admiral Ernest King, Chief of Naval Operations, jumped in and added his thoughts on the matter. King, known for his tough talk and aggressive nature, was not about to let the Soviets sway him from taking the war to a new level against the Japanese. "We own the entire Pacific Ocean. I have already put Third Fleet on alert for possible Soviet moves. We are sending a task force north to shadow their Pacific Fleet and began sending recon flights over the Kamchatka Peninsula to track the Russian buildup along the Chinese border.

Secretary Byrnes, you tell them that, if they think can try anything against American forces operating in the Pacific Theater, they won't have a ship left in their fleet and I'll destroy the only port they have at Vladivostok. The Army may have to take their shit on the ground in Europe, but the United States Navy owns the oceans, so, you tell them hands off my end of the war. Is that understood?"

Secretary of War Stimson was never entirely on board with the decision to drop the bomb on the Japanese, uncivilized in his mind, but agreed to go ahead in hopes of ending the war sooner. He raised a very important concern when he added, "We all can appreciate Admiral King's concerns, but I caution everyone here to be careful how we characterize the Soviets. Notwithstanding what happened today, we are not at war with the Soviet Union. I would further argue that we should be careful not to get ourselves in one."

Stimson words seemed to cause several in the room to take a moment to reflect just what war with the Soviets would mean. Stimson was there in the Oval Office when the President found out about the poor kid who got shot by the Soviets in Poland. As mad as the President was, he should have known better than to tell the Russians to go to hell. Then, he went ahead and publicly backed the Czechs. *What the hell did we expect the Russians to do, just roll over?*

At his age, Stimson wasn't sure if he had another war in him and he wanted to pull the reins back a bit. Stimson also took note that the President looks pretty uneasy at where all this is heading. Stimson thought that cooler heads should prevail and so he continued, "Mr. President might I remind everyone in the room how the Japanese might react if the Russians refuse to tie down their army in China. What if three atomic bombs isn't enough?"

Slapping his hand hard on the long oak table, Admiral King burst out, "Horseshit, Mr. Secretary, I told you six months ago that we didn't need those bastards to invade China. How the hell can the Japs send reinforcements when our navy has completely blockaded their ports? Christ, I got battleships sitting ten miles offshore bombing them point blank and there isn't a goddamn thing they can do about it. The hell with an invasion by the army, we'll starve the little bastards and burn every city in the entire country. A third of their people won't survive the winter, and that's a fact."

As Truman listened to his various military and civilian leaders, he couldn't help but start to really think of the Russians as enemies. Everything from Yalta to the way their army behaved in Germany, then the attacks in Poland, the LIFE magazine pictures, *and now this. Real American kids dead, and for what, to test my resolve, to see if I have enough gumption to stand up to the new bully of Europe?*

Shaking his head, Truman thought *maybe if I could actually meet with Stalin, talk turkey with the man, maybe we could avoid any more unnecessary bloodshed.*

Turning to his Secretary of State, "Hey Jimmie, when's the last time Harriman met with Stalin? You think maybe we could set up a face-to-face, we could straighten things out?"

Disappointed at the president's indecision, Byrnes shook his head, "Sorry, Mr. President, but Ambassador Harriman has asked for interviews with the Soviet General Secretary for the past two weeks, but had been told that for reasons of security, Stalin was taking no visitors under any circumstances."

The OSS chief, William Donovan, saw an opportunity for him to lay out his agency's theory on the situation. Donovan believed this morning's clash was no accident and part of a much more elaborate chess game being played by the Kremlin. Donovan stood to address the room. "Mr. President, if I might add something to Secretary Byrnes analysis. OSS and British intelligence sources believe that Stalin was wounded far more seriously than previously believed to be the case. Since the unsuccessful attempt on his life in Berlin, some rather ominous developments seem to be emerging.

First, the assassination attempt gave the Red Army, under Marshal Zhukov's direction, an historic opportunity to emerge as the new power broker in the Kremlin. The Red Army has taken the lead in the crackdown and assumed responsibility for Stalin's personal security. Also, it appears that the former head of Soviet State Security, Beria, has been either shot or, at least, imprisoned. You see, Mr. President, it's Zhukov's revenge for the purges in 1937, when more than forty thousand professional officers were shot and thousands more imprisoned."

Getting more frustrated by the minute, General Marshall believed Donavan was reaching, so he cut him off. "What you are saying is all conjecture and should not affect the President's desire to reach out to Stalin and look to reduce tensions between the two of us. If anything, it might be rather productive for the two leaders to meet. Once Stalin understands our position on matters, we can come to terms with his security concerns and then he'll just orders his forces to stand down."

Refusing to allow the austere general to intimidate him or get him to back down, Donovan immediately responded. "General you are missing the point. Stalin has always been ruthless and calculating, but word leaking from sources within the Kremlin indicates that he very well may unsound, irrational, and dangerous. Official OSS opinion is that this mornings' clash was no accident. The Soviets want to send a message that our atomic arsenal does not intimidate them.

"I would further argue that armed uprisings in Poland, and now Czechoslovakia, may warrant even stronger measures from Moscow. The Czech declaration that we publicly supported, completely undermines their entire political framework that justifies long-term occupation. Prague is going to be hit and hit hard and soon. We should not discount the possibility that Stalin's paranoia may justify, in his mind, even more aggressive actions against his former allies."

The entire room looked as though an icy cold bucket of reality hit them. Sensing things were at a standstill for the moment, President

Truman stood and everyone stiffened to hear what he was to say. Still hesitant, but knowing it was time to make some decisions, Truman said, "I have decided that we are going ahead as planned with the dropping of the first atomic bomb against the Japanese. I want to know the instant that the planes are in the air and ready to crossover into Japanese airspace. Next, as for the Soviet situation, I back Ike's move for the moment. I agree that we need to combine vigilance with a general de-escalation. Jimmie, send word to the embassy that I want to propose high-level talks between you and whoever their new Foreign Secretary will be. At a minimum, we both get to air things out a bit.

"Gentlemen, first and foremost, we must defeat the Empire of Japan and force their unconditional surrender, the sooner the better. Admiral King, you have full license to press your boys over there and close this thing out, so we can concentrate on the goings on in Europe with the Russians. I appreciate the gravity of the situation and pray that divine Providence will look down on our country and hopefully bring about a peaceful solution… Failing that, gentlemen, we must be prepared for anything, so I will continue to look for your input and counsel. Good day."

With that said, they all had work to do and the office emptied quickly. President Truman motioned for Secretary Byrnes and General Marshall to stay behind. President Truman wanted to speak with Marshall first, "General, I don't know how to say it except to just ask it. If things get to be going from bad to worse, how bad would it be over there if the Russians were to make a move?"

With all of the seriousness the usually taciturn Marshall could muster, he said, "Mr. President, when the Germans attacked us during the Battle of the Bulge, they hit us with a quarter of a million men and nearly fifteen hundred tanks and self-propelled guns, plus two thousand heavy and medium sized artillery pieces. We stopped the Germans because we were able to send in more men, enjoyed complete air supremacy, and had terrain on our side. Even with all of our advantages, the American Army absorbed nearly sixty thousand casualties, a third of whom died."

He paused for a second. The President and his unnecessarily aggressive Secretary of State had to understand the odds against the Allies if it ever came to full-scale war with the Soviets. He continued, "Mr. President, the Russians could attack with more than six million men, ten thousand tanks, seventy thousand guns, and an air force nearly equal in size to our own. The Red Army is organized to fight battles of annihilation. They suffered more casualties in one battle at Stalingrad than we suffered on two fronts throughout the entire war.

Mr. President, pray that the Soviets come to their senses because I don't know if our boys could hold up, war in the East was quite different than one we just fought against the Germans. It would be savage beyond your ability to imagine. Now, if you will excuse me gentlemen, I need to contact General Eisenhower and issue new orders."

Both Truman and Byrnes were left standing to contemplate the chilling words from the most respected military man in the nation.

Chapter Thirty Eight

August 6, 1945, 2:30 am

Moscow

The meeting was being held in Stalin's favorite dacha on the outskirts of Moscow. It was late or early depending on how one looked at it. Even though he managed to catch a few hours of sleep on the plane, Zhukov was exhausted after an extremely long and stressful day. However tired he felt, his place was here with Comrade Stalin and it was his intention to convince the General Secretary to end the German menace and the threat from the West for generations. His Red Army would secure the peace for Mother Russia and ensure no power would ever threaten her again.

The former Czarist hunting lodge had been converted into a veritable fortress. *A fortress,* Zhukov inwardly smiled to himself, *protected by elite Red Army security teams of trained combat soldiers and not parade ground Chekists in uniforms.* It was no small thing to have the duty of guarding Comrade Stalin after the NKVD jealously guarded this honor for so many years.

The reports coming out of Czechoslovakia were conclusive. The Americans clearly attacked and were reinforcing their army near that madman, Patton. The time for talks had long since passed and, from what he surmised by the frantic summons out of the Kremlin, the General Secretary had lost his patience with the West. *Tonight will prove to be historic*, Zhukov thought. Comrade Stalin would demand action and once the Red Army succeeded in driving the Americans and their British lackeys out of Germany, they would leave the continent and never return.

Inside, a rather pale and nervous looking Stalin sat near the fireplace in his bedroom while the others sat in the huge dining room on the other side of the dacha. His doctors had been pleading with him to stop drinking, but the age old Russian remedy of vodka was the only thing that calmed him. Ever since the attempt on his life, Stalin heard things, distant voices, strange echoes in the night, but the nightmares plagued him worse of all.

His damaged eardrums still had not healed and often he had trouble making out what people said around him. So, he either shouted at people or retreated into a shell, pretending to understand what was happening. He had trouble walking, his hearing was failing, and the drugs to control his blood pressure and calm his nerves often made him feel as if he was walking about in a perpetual fog.

Stalin's personal staff and even his most trusted longtime cronies saw the difference in him. Most were more fearful than ever, for one never knew when Comrade Stalin would lash out. Already, three doctors and their families faced exile. He could feel the eyes looking at him, sensing his weakness. *Who among them will be the one to stab me in the back?*

The only one he trusted was Zhukov. Even now Stalin knew Zhukov was coming to help him plan a way to destroy the imperialists, who wanted to destroy him as well. *Soon it will be their time to feel the power of the Soviet Union. Everything will be better once he gets here*, Stalin just knew it.

Fifteen minutes later Zhukov entered the great dining hall where he found Stalin's key advisors stuffing their faces like peasants at the dinner table. Like most real soldiers, he had little time for politicians and bureaucrats. He did take note that the new special envoy for the occupied territories, André Vyshinski, was an interesting addition to Stalin's inner circle. Vyshinski was a Pole by birth, but a committed

Communist from his early student days. He had actually made his mark as a Menshevik in the early days of the Revolution but quickly saw where the wind was turning.

He later earned international scorn as Stalin's Prosecutor General at the numerous Moscow Show Trials and like that other dangerous Pole who founded the Checka, Feliks Dzerzhinsky, he was absolutely committed to the security of the State and would do anything to further the security of the Soviet Union. He may prove useful.

Beside Zhukov was the new Foreign Minister, Khrushchev and one of the relatively new up and comers in the Party, Malenkov, a formidable man Zhukov had been told. Stalin's old cronies, Kagonovich and Voroshilov were back after being banished for two weeks. Zhukov thought the both of them looked like nervous starving kulaks who probably thought their time was up. The Red Army commander found himself drawn to the brutish looking man with a jailer's sinister eyes, the new head of the NKVD, General Merkulov. The new senior Chekist looked surprisingly confident, considering the weakened position of the Security Service.

Luckily for him, he had absolutely no contact, whatsoever, with the debacle in Berlin, so even though he was a part of Beria's Georgian mafia, he was able to emerge relatively intact from the mini-purge that struck his service. No longer worried about the power of the NKVD, Zhukov hoped they would be able to serve the

State in their reduced role. Spies could never fully be trusted, but they could prove useful at times.

Zhukov barely had a chance to sit down when Comrade Stalin made his appearance. Slowly the General Secretary limped to his seat at the head of the table. Most of those seated at the table looked down at their plates or grabbed their glasses to drink, so they wouldn't be found staring at the man. No one wanted to be the one caught looking on with pity, or worse, some in this room secretly enjoyed watching him suffer like this.

Stalin had humiliated the men in this room on numerous occasions, making them dance or pouring food or drink over them for a laugh. Now some inwardly smiled at the man they all feared like no other, who now moved like an old man with haggard eyes and shaky hands.

Like an animal who senses fear or the scent of danger, Stalin knew he must be strong in front of these men. These sniveling toads, who just a month ago shook at his approach, now barely looked up as he entered a room. Stalin could no more trust these men than he could the West. Stalin never expected the imperialists to strike so soon, never thought they would have the balls to hit first, especially the Americans. Looking over at the determined look on Marshal Zhukov's face gave him strength and confidence that the State must be strong and not allow itself to be intimidated by the Americans.

He was just about to begin talking when the emergency red phone rang out. Khrushchev got up from the table and went to answer. Everyone watched as his eyes expressed shock and he asked if they were sure. Gently the new Foreign Minister placed the phone back in its cradle and announced, "Comrades, it's the Americans. They just detonated an atomic device in Japan. Our reports from our embassy in Tokyo indicate that the entire city of Hiroshima has been destroyed." All except the Zhukov expressed looks of shock and fear.

Stalin sat back, clearly unnerved by what he just heard, and then it became clear to him. The timing of everything was so simple a child could see. Fear mixing with anger started to flood through his mind, as the old Stalin, the man of steel started to come out. Even though his right hand was trembling as he spoke, he roared, "Stalin will not be intimidated by their new toy. Don't you fools see, they attacked our forces yesterday and then today dropped their bomb on those little yellow bastards to send us a message? It was the Americans and that Churchill all along who have been behind the goddamn Poles and then told the Czechs try to stab us in the backs. Stalin knows that this is all part of their plan to evict us from Europe, and to deny our people the fruits of victory. Stalin will not back down to their petty threats. They think that they can attack our beloved Red Army because of this new bomb. Never!" Wide-eyed with rage, Stalin was practically foaming at the mouth.

Just then the new NKVD man bravely jumped in, "Comrade Stalin, we have confirmed that the Americans only produced three of these bombs, so they are now down to two. This has been confirmed from sources within their secret Los Alamos base, plus, from our agent in the British Embassy. More importantly, they used up nearly all of their nuclear fuel to construct the uranium-based version, but the Americans have perfected the processing technique to make plutonium atomic bombs. We estimate that the Americans will have another three atomic devices ready by the end of September or at the latest by mid-October. By the end of the year, the Americans will be producing seven to ten per month."

The chief of the NKVD just let everyone in the room learn that the Security Bureau not only still had an important role to play, but that it's services were essential to the defense of the Party and the State. Merkulov looked on quite smugly as this intelligence sobered the room and showed how powerful a threat the Americans were becoming, perhaps even more dangerous than the Nazis, if that were really possible.

It took the fascists millions of men, thousands of tanks and guns to destroy Minsk, Kharkov, Kiev, Leningrad, but now the Americans could do it all with but single air raid and one bomb. Yes, the Americans were quite dangerous indeed.

Refusing to show any signs of weakness or fear, Zhukov's rough voice scornfully replied, "Comrades, this new bomb changes nothing, the Red Army stands ready to defend the Soviet people. If we allow the Americans to intimidate us, we shall never be secure and will be forced to bend to their will."

Foreign Minister Khrushchev hesitantly offered, "What would you have us do, Comrade, the Americans can now destroy whole cities with a wave of their hand? How do we negotiate against that?"

Stalin's eyes were twitching and his face turned a scarlet red, he suddenly smashed the table and burst out, "Stalin has decided that the time for negotiations is over. Marshal Zhukov, you have two months to throw the Americans and the damn British out of Europe before they make any more of their damn bombs. I expect the Red Army to deliver such a blow that the Americans will think twice before threatening the Motherland ever again. I want their armies exterminated.

Vyshinski, you and Merkulov are to begin securing the rear against saboteurs and bandits. Unleash the Mongolians, they'll only be too happy to run rampant in the Polish and Czech countryside. What they don't kill, they'll steal. Khrushchev, contact the Americans and tell them that you want to arrange high-level talks as soon as I am able to travel."

Zhukov was pleased at the opportunity to smash the Americans, take away this new explosive bomb and they were a paper army. He asked, "Comrade Stalin, what would you have us do about the Manchurian buildup? We have transferred nearly a million men, two thousand tanks, everything needed for a full-scale invasion. STAVKA assumed we would have until the end of August, but now with the Americans dropping their bomb so soon, what shall we do?"

Stalin did not hesitate, "You attack in two days with what you have already deployed. We won't allow the Americans to think for a moment that relations have ended between our two countries. Khrushchev, send a cable reiterating our commitment to Allied solidarity, that the Soviet Union fulfills its promises and will tie down the Japanese army in China. Anyway, we have our own designs in Asia. We'll smash the little monkeys."

The men in the room seemed convinced they had chosen the right course, even Stalin seemed relieved to have finally decided to eliminate the West and stand up to the Americans. He stood and raised a glass of vodka, "Comrades, we shall achieve what the Czars, in their wildest dreams, could never hope to achieve. Stalin has done what was said never could be done. World Socialism in our time will be a reality."

With that said everyone downed their glasses and refilled for another toast. Sitting in the shadows, Merkulov had one more juicy plum of information he had wanted to tell everyone, but news of the American atomic attacks changed the whole meeting. He had hoped to merely enflame matters, but it looked too late for that. Maybe he could just turn up the flame a bit. Standing, he said," Comrade Stalin, I have one more piece of intelligence to relay to you."

"Out with it, Merkulov. What is so important?"

"Comrade Stalin, we have just been able to confirm with conclusive evidence that the British were behind the attempt on your life."

Stalin suddenly whipped his head around and focused squarely on Merkulov. Cautiously the NKVD man continued, "You see, Comrade Stalin, we have a highly placed agent in the British Foreign Intelligence Bureau, the MI6, who has been placed in charge of a new anti-Soviet section. He discovered evidence that the son of a former White Russian exile, and now a British spy, was present in Berlin at the time of the assassination attempt. We have not been able to verify if the British actually participated or if they just provided intelligence support. At a minimum, both Western leaders knew of the attempt on your life and probably took an active hand to one degree or another. They must be made to pay the price for their treachery."

Stalin went numb as memories flashed back to Berlin, to the fear. He downed a shot glass of vodka and quickly drank two more.

Merkulov became nervous, maybe he shouldn't have said anything at all. Finally Stalin's eyes flashed again, rising from his chair, he said, "You see, comrades, this is why we still need Chekists. No matter, Comrades, Stalin is still here. Stalin is not going away, and we will destroy the imperialists once and for all."

Feeling some of his old strength return, Stalin raised a glass of sweet Georgian wine and actually seemed to smile as he spoke, "Marshall Zhukov, before the month has ended, you will launch Operation Stalin's Revenge. Marshal Zhukov, crush the imperialists and make the world tremble at our might."

Chapter Thirty Nine

August 9, 1945, 3:30 pm

London, Imperial War Council Meeting

Field Marshal Sir Alan Brooke, Chief of the Imperial General Staff, looked at his pocket watch yet again and was disgusted that even after six years of war, Prime Minister Churchill still couldn't make it to a meeting on time. For what must have been the thousandth time, Brooke shook his head at the notion the world seemed to hold that Churchill was some sort of brilliant warlord, the architect of British victory. *What rubbish? The man caused more problems, wasted more time, and generally made himself more of a nuisance than even the Americans, and that was going quite far, indeed.*

Brooke and the Combined Imperial General Staff were holding an emergency meeting to discuss the buildup of Soviet forces opposite the Twenty First Army Group in Northern Germany. The rapid buildup of Soviet men and weapons was becoming increasingly disconcerting, and Britain's manpower crisis during the last year of the war was very much on everyone's mind. If the Soviet buildup continued without pause, then the situation would become quite intolerable.

Marshal Brooke was cautiously complying with General Eisenhower's decision to maintain current troop dispositions. Field Marshall Montgomery vehemently argued against the American decision and went so far as to contact the Prime Minister directly to inform him that Eisenhower's order jeopardized the security of the British Army in Germany and could lead to total disaster.

Brooke was not one to tolerate an officer, even one as successful as Montgomery, going outside the chain of command. So although he harbored serious concerns, this time, Eisenhower's political arguments were rather persuasive. So for once, Brooke came down squarely on Ike's side and told the British field commander to mind his manners and comply.

Finally the PM arrived and Churchill pushed open the great doors to the ornate meeting room and announced his presence in his usual boisterous manner. Dressed in the uniform of the British Army with his old 21st Lancers insignia showing, Churchill took off his cap and said, "Good day everyone, hope I haven't missed too much. Matters of State, you know. All right, let's get to it. What's Ivan up to today?"

After greetings were exchanged, Brooke stood and said, "Actually, sir, before we discuss operational matters in Europe, I suggest we touch on events in the Pacific. Admiral Cunningham, if you would, please?"

"Mr. Prime Minister, the Americans successfully dropped another atomic bomb on the Japanese city of Nagasaki. This attack, as with the first, left the city in ruins. This second bombing along with the powerful multi-pronged invasion by the Soviet Far East army should make a considerable impression. Additionally, the Americans have deployed their fleet practically off the Japanese coast, and continue to make preparations for a direct assault on the southern Japanese island of Kyushu."

The Prime Minister was pleased to hear that the second bomb type worked as well as the first, so he asked, "Have the little buggers asked for terms yet?"

"Not yet sir, but surprisingly enough, some of our Foreign Office chaps seem to feel the Soviet invasion into Manchuria has made more of an impression on the Japanese than the atomic bomb attacks. Still, at nearly two hundred thousand dead, or so, the Yanks surely must have got them thinking. For all Hirohito knows, Tokyo or Kyoto is next. Still, things would be done with by now if the Americans would drop their insistence upon an unconditional surrender.

The bloody wogs are going to keep fighting until the Yanks give in on that one, at least that's what I've been told. Hate to think what would happen if we have to send any of our chaps along with the Americans to root them out in any direct invasion. Be a bit messy, I would suppose, sir, quite messy indeed. The Yanks have one more of their new bombs left, sir. No word as of yet on their intentions on when they intend to drop the next one. Must say that I hope third times a charm."

Churchill agreed and decided it was time to call President Truman, and convince him to let them have their bloody emperor. He's a figurehead, so is the Queen, but no self-respecting Englishmen would allow the Royals to be dethroned and that's a fact. Americans just don't understand the importance of royalty or an emperor for that matter. The Yanks never understood this and backed themselves into a corner with the bloody Japs.

Sighing loudly, the Prime Minister said, "Has anyone thought to mention to the Americans that we have troubles enough over here without being forced to go at it in Japan?"

Churchill was feeling rather good at the moment all things considered. He had just recently convinced the rival Labor Party leader, Clement Attlee, to postpone scheduled general elections that were to be held in two weeks, he couldn't very well campaign with the bloody Sovs mucking things up. In the end, Attlee was a good man and a dogged opponent, but was willing to place King and Country over party.

Looking at the tense and stoic faces of his war council, clearly events in Germany were having a sobering effect on all of them. Churchill didn't know if he was more unnerved by the fact that the Yanks and the Russians actually came to blows or why the Russians had been so bloody quiet ever since. His Ambassador in Moscow, Stafford Cripps, said not a word has come out of the Soviet Foreign Ministry other than what was announced two days ago.

So far all anyone knew was that the entire Soviet zone was a complete blackout. No information at all coming this way, even radio traffic was way down. The hairs on the back of Churchill's neck had been standing on end for days and he could not shake this nagging feeling that trouble was in the air.

Becoming a bit testy as the meeting dragged on, he asked Marshal Brooke, "What's happening with the Poles?"

"Sir, the Poles have been giving a good account of themselves, but as we have been reporting, the Soviets are conducting massive reprisal operations. Coded signals coming out of Poland report Soviet offensives throughout the Poznan region have been quite successful and that the Russians have re-established rail links with occupation forces in Germany. Poznan is a rather important staging ground and supply depot for the Russian northern army groups, this operation was considered vital to the Soviet position in Germany. However, rail links east of the city are still under threat of Polish Home Army activity.

The Poles seem to be maintaining organized resistance, even though most of the major cities are back under Red Army control. It's the countryside that is the main battleground at the moment. Small unit, hit-and-run attacks seem to be bleeding the Russians."

Admiral Cunningham added, "I would like to officially inform the war council that I have temporarily put on hold all Polish re-supply efforts. The Soviet Red Fleet has dramatically increased its presence in the Baltic and has made our efforts quite challenging, if not nearly impossible. The last delivery was made two days ago, but I would advise against any more such deliveries. We almost lost HMS Valiant on this last run.

I suspended any more such efforts until a political decision has been reached. I would imagine that any direct evidence of British involvement with our Polish friends would be taken rather poorly by the Soviets at this juncture. What will be this government's intentions in regards the Poles?"

Cool silence around the room spoke volumes. No one wanted to admit they would let the Poles down again, yet no one wanted to contemplate what could happen if the Soviets caught the Royal Navy smuggling weapons into Poland. With Soviet forces poised on the occupation borders in Germany, Churchill merely nodded towards the Admiral. The nighttime supply runs to Poles had just gone dry.

Deep down Churchill knew now that he really had gone too far this time. *Damn, why couldn't I have told the bloody Poles to bugger off?*

Then he heard several distant voices pulling him back to reality, "Mr. Prime Minister, Mr. Prime Minister are you all right?"

Blinking his eyes once or twice, Churchill realized he had gone off into a bit of a daze and the others were staring back at him. Rubbing his eyes, he said, "Fine, fine. Everything's quite all right, just a bit peaked is all. Go on with the brief."

A bit unsure whether or not to continue, Marshal Brooke stood again and continued the briefing, "As long as you're alright sir, I will continue. The CIGS agree that the Russian buildup prior to the clash of August 6th was disconcerting enough, but at least we were in a position to track those movements. By the end of the first week in August, intelligence suggests that nearly three million men and seven thousand tanks were being mobilized within twenty miles of the occupation borders. A further two million were in the process of redeploying as a result of the Polish and Czech crises. However since General Eisenhower's decision to curtail recon flights, we find ourselves blind and have not been able to confirm any further troop dispositions or Red Air Force buildups.

"What we do know is that signals intelligence out of Bletchley Park indicates Soviet movements throughout their zone, however radio chatter has been rather disciplined which indicates that Ivan is definitely up to something on their end. Monty wants to remind everyone that his infantry units are still nearly twenty five percent under strength and had never been brought back up to snuff once the war ended.

For the past three months much of Monty's command had been focusing on humanitarian and resettlement operations. At this point, Monty wants to begin pulling units together and try to establish some defensible positions along the border. Also, he requests infantry replacements immediately to bring his combat units up to full strength."

Churchill broke in and said, "Where would the Field Marshal suggest they come from? Need I remind everyone in this room that we were forced to break up two full infantry divisions and two independent armored brigades towards the end of the war? How are we supposed to find the men he needs?"

No one was more aware of the manpower crisis than Brooke and he was quick to respond, "I think that we need to consider his request and quickly, sir, keeping in mind the requirements throughout the Empire as well as the defense of the Home Islands."

Brooke waited for that pronouncement to sink in and wondered how the old man would react. Field Marshal Brooke thought, at this point, all they could really do was play this one smart and pray Stalin remains busy in Poland, but if Ivan does make a play, then all those tens of thousands of British soldiers spread throughout the Empire would be uselessly sitting around while Europe goes up in flames.

Foreign Secretary Eden understood what Brooke was proposing, even if the Prime Minister refused to accept the need. With more than a half a million troops spread from North Africa to Palestine to Iraq, and India, Great Britain must choose and quickly. Eden had been against Churchill's provocations from the beginning and now barely spoke to the man. *So this is what it comes down to, either watch as the Soviets kick us out of Europe and then wait while he makes a play for the Empire or strip the Empire now and make a stand in Europe. Either way, the Empire will never be the same again.*

Churchill looked up at his Foreign Secretary who was giving one of his nasty snide little looks, brimming with judgment and indignation. *Anthony could barely look at me these days. He's probably wondering if I understand what Brooke is trying to tell me.*

The Empire or Europe, those are the stakes, but this time is different. The Yanks are in it right from the beginning. The Empire or Europe? If one goes then the other must follow. If Europe goes then British imperial presence will slowly wither on the vine, and be quietly disposed in the dustbin of history. In the end, Churchill knew that the old English saying, in for a penny, in for a pound applied in this situation.

Standing up and straightening himself out, Churchill looked Brooke right in the eyes and said, "Say no more, Brooke, I know what you are trying to tell me. Whether or not anyone in this room likes it, storm clouds of war are fast approaching and if the Russians come at us, there won't be any Dunkirk's. General Brooke, I hereby order you to immediately redeploy British forces back to the Home Islands for possible employment on the European continent."

Churchill looked around the room at the surprised expressions looking back at him and found himself invigorated just by saying the words and unconsciously his voice began to rise and filled with emotion. "The English people will not back down as this Iron Curtain spreads across all of Europe. We will stand with the Americans and in the end emerge victorious. Brooke, order Monty to begin making preparations to wage a defensive campaign in northern Germany and tell him his reinforcements are on the way. The British Empire will not back down to the Russians any more than it was willing to back down to the Boche. I pray that the Russians come to their senses, but if they continue on this path, then we shall stand like Englishmen and give our due."

Then, to everyone's surprise the room actually started clapping and knocking on the table in response to the speech. Even Eden had to admit that he unconsciously found himself banging the tabletop. *The old wily bastard still hasn't completely lost it*, he thought. *Well, he bloody well got us into this mess, so let's see what he's going to do to get us out.*

Chapter Forty

August 12, 1945

Moscow, Ministry of Defense Building

Once Comrade Stalin made his decision to destroy the imperialists, the entire Red Army went on a war footing, and the Soviet High Command went into full operations mode. The Soviet announced an expanded exclusion zone and the Allied decision to observe a self-imposed ten-mile buffer zone on their side of the lines made movement and concealment much easier. Leaves were canceled, additional reserves were hastily mobilized, and those still recuperating from mild wounds from the last days of the war were called back to active service.

Throughout the entire zone of Soviet occupation in Germany, Czechoslovakia, and Hungary, Soviet tanks, artillery, and men began massing under concealment. The Red Air Force began dispersing into smaller, more compact and defensible airfields. Maintenance crews were working round the clock, bringing aircraft up to readiness, setting up tank farms and armories, plus preparing protected sandbag emplacements to protect their aircraft from Western air attack.

Perhaps even more important than the physical preparations was the organized campaign to prepare the men for a new war, against a new enemy. Political commissars spoke at twice daily session's enflaming the men about the cowardly sneak attack by the Americans on the unsuspecting members of the 32nd Guards Mechanized Division. The soldiers of the Red Army were being told heroic stories of counterattacks by the brave but ill-fated 22nd Guards Tank Brigade who sacrificed itself to throw back the American imperialists and died for the Motherland.

The Americans and their lap dog ally, the English, were the ones who tried to kill Comrade Stalin and responsible for their suffering in Poland and now Czechoslovakia. In blistering talks throughout Red Army camps, hatred of the West was soon to rival even that of the Germans, so the men cleaned their weapons and prepared for the battles to come.

Meanwhile, General Staff officers serving on STAVKA were spending their days and nights poring over every available piece of data on the Western armies. After fighting the Germans for nearly five years, most could quote nearly every aspect of the Nazi war machine, but little was commonly known about their erstwhile allies. The men were confident for no one believed that the Americans or the British could ever hope to defeat the army who defeated the vaunted German Wehrmacht and the dreaded SS.

As staff officers reviewed key battles in the West from North Africa to Normandy to the Battle of the Bulge, none could compare to the titanic struggles that took place in front of Moscow, Stalingrad, Kursk, let alone Berlin. The largest German attack of the war in the West comprised a mere three field armies, barely three hundred thousand men. STAVKA routinely managed combat operations along an active front that was measured in hundreds of kilometers and comprised millions of troops. During the final attack into Germany, Soviet forces numbered nearly three million, with another two million men fighting in Hungary and the Balkans.

To professional staff officers used to compiling operation orders based on numbers and logistics, the numbers said it all, the West couldn't possibly stand a chance without the help of their new super bomb. To men schooled in the operational art, it would only be a matter of when and where to attack, not whether or not the issue would be in doubt. Still, the need for a lightening quick campaign of three to four weeks required significant planning to guarantee success. The days and nights ahead would be long and hard.

General Antonov, Chief of the Soviet General Staff, and Col-General Shtemenko, Chief of Operations, had worked together for nearly three years, planning many of the key offensives which took the Red Army from Stalingrad through the Ukraine, into Poland and finally, the successful invasion and occupation of Eastern Europe. A huge 1:200,000 scale map was laid out on the table and aides continued to update the map as the final outlines for the attack against the West were being sketched out.

Zhukov and the other field commanders were due in at any moment and the final touches were being ironed out on the map display. The detail the staff was able to draw out was impressive. General Shtemenko walked carefully along the outer edges of the map and looked down and could see detailed unit markers down to individual regiments and special assault battalions.

General Antonov entered the room and saw his Operations officer staring at the map, tracing march routes, and checking notes. As always, General Shtemenko could be counted upon to examine each detail, using that brilliant staff officer's eye to anticipate where the breakthrough would occur, when to phase in reinforcements, how to allocate supplies, really to see the battlefield unfold before the first shots were fired.

The field commanders often deride their fellow staff officers, but where would many of these brutes be if it were not for the efforts of men like Shtemenko and his staff? They would be attacking straight ahead, until they either ran into an unanticipated river or out of fuel or any one of a thousand different miscues that staff officers anticipate and plan for. Antonov respected Zhukov, but found him to be too brutish, too willing to absorb prohibitive casualties. *Too bad that Marshal Konev died in Berlin*, Antonov truly believed his intuitive instincts would have made a better choice to lead this massive attack.

Antonov believed the West would prove more difficult than expected, but the correlation of forces certainly favored the Soviet armed forces. With two cups of tea in hand, Antonov moved across the room to his operations officer and smiled, "Well Sergey, are we ready to defeat the Imperialists yet or shall I tell Comrade Stalin that we need to call off the attack?"

With a look on his face that seemed to curse Antonov for even whispering such a thought, Shtemenko confidently said, "Comrade General, please feel free to tell Comrade Stalin that in five weeks he will be able to bathe in the Rhine if he chooses."

Lighting two cigarettes at a time and handing one to his boss, Shtemenko at least looked confident, which was a good sign. Antonov inhaled deeply on the America tobacco that he so loved and looked into the steely eyes of his deputy and asked, "Well can it be done? Will we meet Comrade Stalin's time table of four weeks?"

"Comrade General, with more time, I could practically break it down to the exact date that the Americans and British will lay down their arms and sue for peace, but with only five days of preparation it remains difficult to say."

Sensing by the look on his superior's face that his reply was less than favorable, the Operations officer continued, "Look at the map yourself, the flat terrain in the North dictates everything. The war will be won by holding the Americans at bay in the center and south, and then roll over the British in the North. This wide front attack prevents the Americans from shifting forces to help the weaker British forces on their left flank and once we attain the Rhine River and envelope the Ruhr from the North, the Americans will be forced to either defend their exposed flank or stand and be defeated in detail from their built up positions in the Frankfurt region and in Bavaria.

Regardless, without access to their supply lines originating from Antwerp, their entire position will become untenable within two to three weeks. The British will be forced to fall back and most likely be annihilated on the east bank of the Weser River, at worst the British Twenty First Army Group and whatever American reinforcements who shift to the North will be crushed with their backs to the Rhine River."

"That's all well and fine, but Sergei what about American airpower?" Antonov asked. His worst fears were visions of thousands of Allied warplanes filling the skies and ravaging his long columns of tanks and trucks full of infantry. Once significant portions of the Luftwaffe was forced back to Germany in late 1943 to defend against the Allied air offensive, the Red Army had gotten used to fighting with powerful air support. From 1944 onwards, every major Soviet offensive was supported by hundreds of tank-busting IL-2's and covered by several thousand fighter planes.

Pausing for a second, Shtemenko raised his eyebrows and answered, "We will take losses. At times the losses will be severe, but initial staff analysis suggests that the Red Air Force is large enough to contest for supremacy in the air for at least two weeks, maybe more. In fact, staff studies indicate that we should be able to attain local air superiority in at least two breakthrough sectors for periods of up to four hours or longer. If we are able to do so during the first week of operations, then I feel that we will win. Remember my friend, we don't need air superiority to win the war, while without it, the Americans lose their biggest advantage."

Looking at the map one last time and seeing the four huge red arrows pointing West made Antonov feel better. Nodding to himself, he patted his younger Operations on the shoulder and said, "Sergei, ignore my musings, you're right. The plan is sound and within six weeks from today the Red Army will stand victorious yet again. Let's get the staff together, Zhukov and the others will be arriving in fifteen minutes or so."

Yes, Antonov thought, considering the limited preparation time and the absolute timetable requirements, *this is a good plan and will destroy the Americans and the English and then we can truly have peace. It will be good to retire after the war to a dacha in the South where it is warm and the fishing good. One final campaign and then it will be over.*

Antonov decided to invite only the four field commanders and three or four key staff officers to the meeting. Marshals Rokossovsky, Tolbulkin, and Yeremenko all arrived about the same time. The map display was covered for the moment and refreshments were laid out for all to enjoy. The men exchanged pleasantries and shared their thoughts on the coming operation. All were experienced and successfully commanded entire fronts during the fighting against the Germans. They anxiously waited for Marshal Zhukov to appear.

Finally, a young aide opened the door and in walked Marshal Zhukov looking full of confidence and determination. Zhukov barked loud for everyone to hear, "Antonov, this looks more like some Czarist grand ball than a military conference. You even have a peasant like Tolbulkin holding his teacup like a true noble. What has become of our vaunted Red Army in such a short time?"

Most in the room, not used to Zhukov showing any type of joviality, were taken aback a little. Even if it wasn't all that funny, just to see Zhukov looking upbeat was good for everyone to see, even Antonov smiled and playfully replied, "You're one to talk Georgii Konstantinovich, rumor has it that all the good silver within three hundred miles of Berlin has suddenly vanished without a trace. God, help the French if we ever decide to go to Paris."

The room spontaneously erupted in laughter, all except Zhukov who turned deadly serious, responding with an icy chill in his voice, "Well old friend, do you have a plan that shall take us there?" With that said, everyone knew that friendly banter had ended and the time for business was at hand.

Not wasting any time, Antonov motioned for Col-General Shtemenko, Chief of Operations, to stand and begin the brief. With a wave of his hand, two young captains removed the tarp covering the map table to reveal the plan of attack against the West. Standing tall and in a commanding voice, Shtemenko began, "Comrades, Operation Stalin's Revenge is due to commence at 0300 hours on Sunday, August 26th. As you can see, there are four main troop concentrations, designed to operate from the Baltic coast to the Austrian Alps. Two key factors determined our intent on a wide front advance.

First, the terrain along the North German Plain currently defended by the British and part of the American Ninth Army offers the best avenue for a massive movement of mobile forces. There are few appreciable natural obstacles and those that exist will actually work in our favor as you will soon see. In central Germany and to the south in Bavaria, we see increasingly difficult mountainous and heavily forested regions much more ideal to a defensive campaign. The American First, Third, and Seventh armies defend these regions and are expected to put up a reasonable defense.

"More importantly, the Allied command operated throughout their campaign in Northern Europe without any real strategic or theater reserve. They relied exclusively upon the mobility of the Allied armies to move laterally into and out of the battle zones. The General Staff believe that with most of the Allied combat power focused along the frontier zones, once a breakthrough is initiated against their northern tier, we can prevent any mass movement by engaging the Americans on a wide front. The British forces will be pushed back and eventually defeated, allowing follow-on mobile forces to cross the Rhine, envelope the Ruhr and cut off the supply pipeline originating from Antwerp."

Shtemenko paused for a moment and caught Zhukov completely ignoring the presentation and looked as the Marshal sat transfixed on the map table. The frown on Zhukov's face didn't bode well, but the Chief of Operations decided to continue with the brief. "As you can see, the North German Front under Marshal Rokossovsky will stage from the Mecklenburg region with an axis of advance from Hamburg to Bremen and branching off as one echelon continues towards Antwerp while the main strike force closes on the Ruhr.

Comrade Zhukov commands the largest collection of combat power and has operational control of the Central German Front. His two main mobile strike forces will move through the Gottingen and Fulda Gaps towards Kassel and Cologne while to the south an advance through Fulda to Frankfurt and then he will stage a crossing of the Rhine at Koblenz. Comrade Zhukov will move to envelope the Ruhr and destroy the American First and Ninth armies.

"The First Czechoslovakian Front commanded by Comrade Tolbulkin will stage out of Prague, move on Pilsen and then continue operations towards Nuremberg and ending at Stuttgart. The American Third Army commanded by that madman Patton occupies this front. Comrade Stalin will be particularly interested in our progress in this sector. We have already shifted considerable combat forces into this region, so we expect quick exploitation towards Nuremberg once you clear the American defenses around Pilsen.

Finally, the First Austrian Front under Comrade Yeremenko will stage out of Vienna. You will advance your forces through Linz and Salzburg and aim to capture Munich. Depending on events, you will prepare to advance to the French borders or possibly move south into

Italy as needed and expect the American Seventh and Fifth Armies to oppose this Front. Questions?"

Completely ignoring the Operations Chief, Zhukov was furiously writing on several sheets of paper. Staring at the map, memorizing cities and analyzing the terrain, it came upon him. He didn't like what he saw from the moment he could see the map. His meaty hands quickly sketched out his own operational map and began drawing his own red arrows. Within ten minutes, his map looked quite different than the one on the table. Zhukov was disappointed that Antonov was missing the strategic picture. Speed was of the absolute essence.

Nothing else mattered other than forcing the West to sue for peace and evacuate the continent before their atomic arsenal gave them the strategic advantage. What if the Americans moved like the wind and developed their super bomb faster than the Chekists said they could? What then would happen to his troops if they were caught out in the open against this new weapon? Or worse, what if they threatened to use it against Moscow or even tried to target Comrade Stalin again? No, something had to be done that would split the alliance or sever the head of the weaker force.

With that thought in mind, he stood ramrod and decided to address the General Staff and the various field commanders. "Comrades, I have been listening to the plan you have put together, but I am afraid that we are missing a great opportunity."

The whole room fell quiet as staff and field officer alike wondered what Zhukov would have to say. Marshal Rokossovsky was disgusted. He knew that Zhukov would never allow his command to make the decisive attack. With Antonov's plan, his North German Front would play the most important role in the offensive. Rokossovsky had no doubt that his battle-hardened troops would crush the English and sweep across the Rhine and secure victory for the Rodinia.

Zhukov began, "Comrades, this wide front approach would undoubtedly lead to a great victory if we had the luxury of time. But we don't and you all know the reasons why we have no choice but to plan for a rapid campaign. The Americans and the English only have to hold our forces up at one or more choke points for a week and the entire timetable is lost. If we fail to destroy them within the four weeks that Comrade Stalin has ordered, we run the risk of feeling the fire of this new super bomb that the Americans have developed."

Colonel-General Shtemenko was not happy at the way Zhukov was looking to change things. So he decided to at least make the effort to defend his plan. "Comrade Zhukov, I understand your concerns, but I don't see where the Americans or British can make this stand you are so worried about. The key is to contain the Americans long enough to prevent any units from moving to support Montgomery's forces. If the Central German Front contains the

American First and Ninth Armies or even more likely Comrade achieves a breakthrough, then we win."

Most in the room shrunk from such a confrontation, but Shtemenko had a solid reputation and organized many key offensive during the war, plus he made some good points that even Zhukov couldn't ignore.

Not expecting any opposition, Zhukov's infamous temper flared. "I would expect such talk from a staff officer. The field commanders know that for all of your fancy maps and march timetables, the Germans never cooperated with the plan, why should we expect the Americans to be so accommodating. Speed and more speed is the only thing that guarantees victory. I am prepared to go to Comrade Stalin and absolutely insist upon the changes that I will lay out."

Antonov squeezed his subordinate's arm, shook his head from side-to-side, and told him to stop. The Chief of the General Staff knew Zhukov not only would go to Stalin, but was prepared to destroy any man who had the courage to argue against his plan.

With an air of resignation in his voice, Antonov stood and said, "Okay Comrade, let's hear your changes. I am sure that Shtemenko and the others on my staff are quite interested in your concept. We all agree that speed is of the essence and that anything that can prevent the introduction of such terror weapons from the battlefield must be taken quite seriously. Go on my friend."

Zhukov nodded and began shifting things around on the map table while his peers stood and watched. Immediately seeing he was creating a Second Central German Front, Shtemenko asked, "Comrade Stalin, where are you going to get troops to man this new front? We have already transferred nearly a million troops and tanks as part of the Manchurian invasion. They will never make it back in time."

Knowing this would be a controversial decision, Zhukov looked the Chief of Operations right in the eye and said, "I am stripping divisions from those currently operating in Poland. Plus, I am transferring Bering's Polish Army to the German front. Let's see if our Polish friends are better at killing Americans than they seem to be at killing bandits who roam their countryside. At worst, let the Americans waste their ammunition killing them, it'll save us the trouble later. Plus, I will shift two independent tank corps from my own forces to give extra punch.

"To cover our supply lines, I intend to pull NKVD border divisions to operate as occupation forces in Poland for the duration of the campaign in the West. At a minimum, our Chekist friends should be able to contain the Poles from making too much mischief for the time being, besides, if a few Chekists get their heads blown off by Polish bandits, then so much the better."

Still not entirely sold on the new arrangement, the commander of the North German Front, Marshal Rokossovsky asked, "Is that wise Comrade Zhukov? I don't like the idea of Poles running around my supply lines with guns while I have to face off against the British."

Rokossovsky's comment raised a few eyebrows. The two had been pre-war rivals and went head-to-head on a number of occasions during the war. Rokossovsky and others who suffered during the purges, always secretly hated those like Zhukov who not only somehow escaped the humiliating show trials and imprisonment, but even profited by advancing much faster than they would have prior to the purge.

"You just focus on killing English tanks and you let me worry about your rear area. Anyway, I have decided to place General Chuikov in command of the Second Central German Front. He will make the best of his new command. In fact, don't be surprised if he beats all of us to the Rhine." Chuikov was the Hero of Stalingrad and later commanded the crack Eight Guards Army that spearheaded the drive to capture Berlin. His was a wise choice, widely respected by the men in the room.

Sensing that the others were coming around to his concept, he pointed at the map table and redirected some arrows. "Comrades, by shifting our forces and redirecting our combat power, we have set the stage for a true breakthrough operation. My staff will finalize the new dispositions and then the General Staff will make all of the final arrangements and send the written orders out within twenty-four hours.

Have no doubts comrades, we shall win and guarantee the safety of Comrade Stalin and the Motherland for the next generation. I will personally brief Comrade Stalin this evening." With that said, he grabbed his cap and exited the room, leaving behind two dozen officers fighting for position around the map table to digest what had just been decided.

Chapter Forty One

August 15, 1945, 7:30 p.m.

Frankfurt, SHAEF Headquarters

Excited calls for reinforcements, armed recon missions, and demands for extending the air reconnaissance zone poured into SHAEF night and day. Feeling bone weary from stress filled days and sleepless nights, Ike moved slowly, almost as if in a daze. He had been up for much of the night after a long midnight conversation with General Marshall at the Pentagon. Marshall had been running interference for Eisenhower on the Home front but called to press his protégé for some hard answers.

Ever since the clash of arms between Soviet and American forces more than a week ago, editorial columns and half of Congress were demanding some sort of action, some even called for his resignation. Half the country was scared to death about taking on the Russians while the other half of the country wanted revenge on those godless Commies and send them packing back to Moscow. The country was split right down the middle.

Ike wasn't immune to the criticism. He read the same papers as his boss. He knew what people were saying. Everything felt different this time. Ike always knew in his heart of hearts that we could beat the Germans, but the Russians were a whole different story. His controversial order to stand down on the Allied side of the lines was in hopes of showing the Soviets that we didn't want a fight, that somehow it was a big misunderstanding.

Ike even went so far as to disarm Czech partisans operating out of American occupation zones. His orders were explicit, absolutely no provocations against the Russians under any circumstances, and he swore to send anyone who disobeyed home and broken in ranks.

Back to eighteen hour days, he felt tired and worn down beyond his years. Washing his face with cold water, Ike looked up into the mirror and thought, *if enough of those ungrateful bastards back home want my job, they can have it.* Slowly he lathered his hands and patted his face with icy cold water, trying to wake himself up.

With sad eyes, he wondered if he should show the Russians the ugly mug he saw in the mirror, maybe they would take pity on them and go home. Grabbing a towel, he shook his head and thought, *fat chance.*

How in the hell did this thing get out of hand so fast? At least the reports out of Washington of peace feelers being sent out by the Truman White House, trying to get a handle over recent events may help matters. It seemed as if the new President no more wanted war than anyone else and that made him feel a hell of a lot better at first. Regardless of the disgraceful atrocities meted out by the Russians or their reprisals going on in Poland and now Czechoslovakia, Ike just didn't think it was enough to risk his army.

So he sent back to Washington mounting reports of Soviet troop movements and intelligence reports with estimates of available Red Army personnel and equipment strengths. Ike was making it clear that Washington needed to understand just how strong the Red Army was in the aftermath of the war and how vulnerable the American position was at this time. Even with stopping the transfer of American First Army divisions and support personnel to the Pacific Theater, the balance of forces between the two camps was daunting.

At the height of the war, Ike had nearly three million men under his direct command. But that told only half the story. The American way of war demanded a hell of a lot of support troops for everything from building airstrips, delivering hot chow at the front, USO shows, you name it. Nothing was too good for the men out in the field. The problem translated into a hell of a lot more tail and a lot less tooth.

The combined Allied Armies barely fielded ninety divisions, with two thirds being American. The rest consisting of about twelve under strength British divisions, four Canadian, and the remaining dozen or so Free French forces, most of whom were of dubious value. Even if you throw in another dozen Allied divisions from the Italian theater, it still paled against the six million man Red Army. Ike was scared and he wanted to make sure the hot heads back in Washington were scared too.

After several shots of Canadian Club to calm his nerves, Eisenhower was starting to wake up when an aide came in with a secure phone to talk to his boss. Stubbing out his smoke, Ike put the phone to his ear and said, "Good Morning General, it seems you're in earlier than usual."

General Marshall answered in his usual direct and uncompromising manner, "We have some serious issues with the Japanese in the Pacific, plus everything that's happening on your side of the pond."

Relieved to be discussing any theater of operations other than his own, Ike asked, "Sir, where do things stand with the Japs? I would have thought that two of those damn things would have convinced them to throw in the towel."

Detecting a tone of fatigue in his boss's voice, Ike listened as General Marshall said, "It seems that even with the use of these new weapons, reactionary elements in the Japanese High Command continue to refuse to lay down their arms. It's been almost a week since the last bombing and still no word on surrender. We have no choice but to continue with plans for the direct invasion of the Japanese Home Islands."

"General what about more of these atomic devices…when can we drop another one and show them that we mean business?"

With a note of mild disgust in his voice, Marshall explained, "Actually, there was a bit of screw up on that one, Ike. General Groves and some of his scientists left key bomb assembly components back at Los Alamos. It would seem that some of his group never thought that more than one would be necessary and that three or more would be downright barbaric. We won't be able to drop the next one until the 20th or 21st, but don't worry, Ike, we're going to do everything we can to close the door in the Pacific, so we can turn our attention to Europe and the Russians. Speaking of which, I believe that you and I have some things to discuss,things that should have been dealt with some time ago."

Marshall had become increasingly uneasy at the tone and content of the reports coming out of Ike's headquarters. General Eisenhower had been handpicked by Marshall, chosen over several hundred more senior commanders to lead the American Expeditionary Force to the European Theater of Operations in 1942. Few could actually say that they were friends with General Marshall as his near obsession with maintaining his objectivity prevented him from developing many real friends in the Army.

However with Ike, it evolved into something more akin to a father and eldest son relationship. General Marshall always publicly backed his man at SHAEF, even when privately he may have had to straighten him out over things from time to time. Marshall chose Ike because of his disciplined demeanor and his ability to see through the chaos and make sound judgments.

From the early American setbacks in North Africa to the contentious and tough Italian campaign, and finally to the planning and execution of the D-Day invasion and even through the dark days during the Battle of the Bulge, Eisenhower always maintained his optimism and especially never lost belief in himself as a leader. Marshall knew this man like a father knows a son, just knows when something is not right, and Ike was giving the impression that he may be losing his nerve.

Not one to skirt issues or dance around a problem, General Marshall decided to come right out and deal with things directly. "Ike, I want to be frank with you. I am not satisfied with how you have been handling your command these past two weeks. In my estimation, you have allowed yourself to become paralyzed in the face of the Soviet threat. Every report from your headquarters for the past week has demonstrated to the President that the Soviets pose an unstoppable threat and given the impression that the American Army is not prepared to fulfill its duties.

You even went so far as to recommend to the President that talks should be initiated with the Soviets and that you were prepared to pull out of Czechoslovakia within seventy two hours if need be to prevent further bloodshed. You went too far and you know it. That is a decision to be made by the civilian leadership. We don't make policy. We follow it. Understood?"

The icy cold anger in Marshall's voice was enough to sober him up and fast. Hardly expecting to be chastised at almost one o'clock in the morning, Ike was more than a little taken aback. Ike couldn't understand why Marshall chose now of all times to lecture and rebuke him. Ike couldn't understand how his mentor could see the same facts and figures and disagree with his conclusions. The Soviets had more men, more tanks, more guns, and a willingness to absorb casualties at unheard of levels, levels the American people weren't prepared to accept.

Eisenhower had read the reports from German commanders from the Eastern Front, interviewed several of the more renowned German generals himself, like Generals Heinrici, Guderian, Manstein, and numerous others. Marshall never spoke to these men, never looked them in the eyes, and listened as they told stories of entire divisions being literally swallowed up by a Russian attack.

General von Manstein, who many consider to have been Hitler's most brilliant field commander, told him a story about a battlefield out in the middle of nowhere, some inconsequential village that the Russians recaptured during their 1942 offensive that destroyed the German Sixth Army.

A regiment of German infantry and two companies of panzers held the village. Once the region had been recaptured, General von Manstein flew over the battlefield and all around the village lay evidence of ten separate attacks, and the remains of nearly two full Soviet divisions. Each one came closer and closer to the village, until the inevitable happened and the entire German garrison died to a man.

Ike watched as the veteran German general just shook his head and said, "Once the order has been given, they won't stop until either you have died or they have died. Until you have fought such a foe, you do not know war."

In a shaky voice, Eisenhower answered back, "General, I apologize if you object to my reports, but I feel that it is my duty to impress upon the President and his staff the gravity of the situation. Perhaps I was too forward in my most recent report, but I am certain that our presence in Pilsen is considered to be provocative by the Soviets."

Marshall responded sternly, "You know full well that it is the job of the Joint Chiefs to brief the President and his cabinet concerning the strategic situation. Your job is to provide tactical information and then to follow the orders and directives that have been decided upon by the President. What in God's name has gotten into you Dwight?"

Agitated at the rebuke, Eisenhower fired back, "I'll tell you what's gotten into me, sir. Ever since Churchill and others back in Washington started playing games with the Russians six months ago, you remember that whole "Sunrise" business, the Ludendorff Bridge fiasco, now the Poles, and everything that's followed, well now we stand at the brink of war. I have to be honest General, I don't know what the hell is going to happen over here, but I'm not afraid to tell you that it scares the hell out of me."

About time he finally came out and said it, Marshall thought. A blind man could see it and that's what had him worried. Whatever was going to happen in Europe, Marshall wanted his man, Eisenhower, fully in charge and ready to deal with any eventuality.

With a more friendly tone, Marshall said, "Dwight, I'm not going to kid you and try to tell you that things are going to be alright. Because I think that we both know that although things are awful quiet in the Soviet sector that could change in a heartbeat. Ike, this country owes you a debt of gratitude because you not only defeated the Germans, but also did so at a minimal cost in American lives. That's why I refuse to accept the fact that you have somehow lost your nerve."

"But sir, you don't understand. I can't sleep at night. I'm starting to snap at my staff at the least infraction. All I can think about is how powerful the Red Army is and how ill prepared we are to fight such an enemy. If you and others back in Washington think that I've lost it, well I'm more than willing to step down if need be."

Gripping the phone hard, Marshall stiffened and found himself angry at such defeatism and a lack of moral courage, scolded Ike with a tone verging on disgust," If you keep up this lousy attitude of yours, I will sack you. Not another word along these lines or you will be on the next flight home...in disgrace I might add. Is that understood?"

"But sir, you don't understand it's not self-pity, it's the facts."

Marshall said one word, "Bullshit."

In all of Eisenhower's conversations with Marshall, he had never heard the man curse. It was like hearing a priest swear on the pulpit, it just didn't happen. Marshall allowed the word to linger before he continued, "Now, I want you to tell me, General Eisenhower, right this very second what your command would do if the Soviets attack in force, and I mean right now. Don't tell me that the man I have placed my trust and the man responsible for three million servicemen's lives doesn't have the first clue how he would defend his command in case of war."

Stuttering a bit, Ike blurted out," Airpower, the Soviets never had to fight against the overwhelming firepower we can bring to bear."

"What else?"

"Our divisions have far greater mobility than the Germans ever had at any point during the war. They could never encircle our forces before we could move reserves to plug any holes that would come up. Plus, our Time on Target artillery support would be devastating against any massed movement of Soviet forces."

"Don't let me stop you, General, keep going."

Still a bit uneasy, Ike looked around the room until his eyes found the map on his desk and answered, "Terrain. Other than the North

German Plain, the Russians would have to go up against some pretty tough terrain along the Hartz Mountains, the built up areas east of Frankfurt, and Bavaria has all sorts of wooded landscapes to slow the Russians up, not to mention the Alps."

"What about the men, Ike? It always comes down to the men and the officers leading them into combat. Could you lead them the way you led them against the Germans or should we just lay down and cede everything over to the Russians now?"

Without even thinking, Ike got angry and blurted out, "Hell no! You're damned right my men will fight and you'll have to shoot me before I let you send me back."

Smiling a bit on the other end of the phone, General Marshall was a bit relieved that Ike had started to come around. "Ike, I need to know if you are going to be up to it."

Taking a deep breath, Eisenhower knew his fears hadn't gone away, the Russians still outnumbered them, war could still come at any time, but at least for the moment, he didn't feel the despair of a half hour ago. "General, you have my word that I will do everything humanly possible to prepare this command for whatever the Russians throw at us. Starting tomorrow, I will put my entire command on a higher alert status just short of a war warning and begin preparing defensive zones, strongpoints, and the like. I still intend to maintain the ten-mile exclusion zone. I won't give them an excuse to cross over the lines again, but if they do, I'll make damn sure that we are prepared to meet them with everything we got."

"That's all I needed to hear, Ike. Get some sleep because I have a feeling that you're going to need it."

August 18, 1945, 11:30 pm

Washington D.C., The White House

Dear Bess,

It's late here but I can't seem to sleep much these days. Sure wish that you would have decided to stick around with Margaret, things are kind of glum here. We had a big meeting tonight, all the boys were here, Joint Chiefs, everyone. Jimmie Byrnes and a few others convinced me to drop the last big bomb that we got in hopes of forcing the damn Japs to finally call it quits. As much as I hate the idea of signing the death warrant for another city, I just can't bear the idea of sending anymore American boys to their deaths if I don't have to.

Things are just so damn bad all over the place. We got Stalin up to no good in Europe and the Japs refusing to budge. Something has to give and I finally had to agree with Jimmie that we had a better shot of knocking off the Japs with our last bomb. You have to hand it to Jimmie, he sure is one crafty SOB when he wants to be. He said that the British have been pushing for us to recognize the Japanese emperor as their spiritual leader and not try him as a war criminal. Former Ambassador Grew agrees that if we hit them hard with another bomb and then send them an olive branch at the same time, it could be enough to end things over there.

Boy I sure hope so. Even though it means dropping our unconditional surrender terms, anything would be better than to have to invade a country full of fanatics. The one condition that Jimmie insisted upon was that we bomb Osaka, and threaten to destroy their cultural capital Kyoto next if they refuse to surrender under these new terms. General Arnold, the head of the Army Air Force, said that Osaka was a good choice because it was near enough to Kyoto to see the fireball and mushroom cloud. I guess that would scare the bejesus out of anyone.

Still, talking about it and actually being the one who has to make the final decision, just isn't the same thing. Bess, I pray that the Good Lord who is watching over everything will understand someday that I really didn't have a choice. I wonder if he'll understand. I hope so because I miss you when you leave for a couple of weeks and would hate to spend eternity apart from you.

Anyway, Jimmie says that Stalin finally agreed to set up a high-level meeting with their new Foreign Minister on August 27th in Paris and talking beats fighting any day of the week. Even though you hear all sorts of rumors flying around, it seems as if the truce is still holding up. I gave orders to General Eisenhower to keep a low profile. Maybe if we're lucky we can convince the Japs to give up and then figure out a way to keep Stalin happy in his own backyard. Just maybe everything will work out.

Jimmie keeps telling me not to go soft or to fly off the handle the way I did a couple of weeks ago. I guess he's right, but everything is just so damn complicated and sometimes I see things that are just so evil that it makes my stomach turn. All I want is to bring the boys home and stop this horrible war.

God I wish you were here. I don't care how hot and muggy it gets here in the summer. Give my love to Margaret, tell her to keep practicing her piano and once the war is over I'll be proud to come to her first concert.

Love,

Harry

Chapter Forty Two

August 21, 1945: 8:00 a.m.

Tokyo, Imperial Palace

The six men of the Supreme Council for the Direction of the War held their breaths and hung their heads low as the Emperor entered the Gobunko, or underground bomb shelter beneath the Imperial Palace. Up to this point in the war, the Americans had resisted the obvious urge to target the Emperor and destroy the Imperial Palace Grounds, but army engineers had long ago built a nearly impenetrable bomb shelter befitting a living deity and it was considered to be invulnerable until the Americans introduced an entirely new form of warfare.

Japan was experiencing war in the atomic age. An age where cities could die in a flash of light and all that remained was a towering mushroom cloud blocking out the sun. For a people whose national symbol was the rising sun, the power of this new weapon was not lost on the Japanese people nor the men in the room. That morning, they met at the Emperor's behest to discuss the implications of the latest use of the horrible weapon.

The previous afternoon, at about two o'clock, the ancient port and Japan's second largest city, Osaka was obliterated by an atomic bomb attack. Worse was to come as Foreign Minister Togo announced the previous evening that the Americans had threatened to destroy the Japanese cultural center of Kyoto, the ancestral seat of the Emperor, if Japan refused to surrender its forces and sue for peace.

Swiss diplomats delivered the stern message, but with one significant change. The Americans had decided to quietly guarantee the position of Emperor, and allow Emperor Hirohito to remain as the spiritual leader of the Japanese people, and choose not prosecute him for war crimes.

Togo informed his fellow Council members that they had exactly seventy two hours to agree to the new terms. It would seem that the Americans were prepared to allow Japan to save a certain degree of face, but failing that, were prepared to utterly destroy the Japanese people, one city at a time.

Following the Emperor into the room was the Lord Keeper of the Privy Seal, Marquis Kido. Kido was vehemently against continuation of the war and had counseled his majesty, Emperor Hirohito, to stand up to the militarists who had brought such dishonor and ruin to the people of Japan. Kido, along with Togo, were all that remained from the original cabinet who were present when the decision to bomb Pearl Harbor was made. He had been arguing for several months to agree to terms with the Americans as long as the Imperial throne was preserved, anything short of that would be impossible.

Now that the Americans have finally changed their position, he helped the Emperor prepare for the final confrontation with the Army and Navy. The military caste system had effectively ruled Japan ever since the Meji Restoration in 1870 and was responsible for dozens of assassinations and several threatened coup attempts throughout the Thirties and Forties. If the Emperor failed to obtain the support from the Army and Naval leaders, then his throne would likely be in jeopardy.

Several times in Japanese history an emperor was forced to abdicate or held hostage by a powerful warlord. The samurai caste were very powerful and the idea of surrender was so offensive that many were prepared to continue down the road of national suicide, rather than accept the American terms. Terms which surely included occupation, and to the Imperial officers in command of Japan's armed forces, any sacrifice was worth preventing such a thing. The stain of dishonor couldn't be extinguished for a thousand years.

No, the Emperor was no fool and understood his role was limited, but also understood that a strong willed Emperor could demand obedience. Marquis Kido desperately hoped that the military men would see the necessity of surrender under these new terms. It was no longer their job to defend Japan. They had failed miserably in that capacity. They must be forced to recognize that now their duty was to save what was left of Japan.

The Emperor purposely chose to wear one of his simple, yet ornate ceremonial robes rather than his army or navy uniforms. The experienced members of the Supreme Council understood such symbolism. Hirohito had come to the chamber as Emperor of the Japanese people, not a mere spectator of the war effort as was his custom.

These six men, whose heads now bowed low as the Emperor was seated, Premier Suzuki, Foreign Minister Togo, War Minister, General Anami, Army Chief of Staff, General Umezo, Naval Minister, Admiral Yonai, and the Chief of the Naval General Staff, Admiral Toyoda, ruled every aspect of the war effort. For men whose entire lives, their very existence was guided by certain unyielding absolutes, to accept that they had failed his Majesty was unimaginable, yet that was the reason for the meeting. For months, the Council was deadlocked on the final direction of the war. Three were for peace and three were prepared to institute the climactic Ketsu-Go battle plan.

Ketsu-Go could roughly be translated as the Decisive Operations Plan or the final Homeland Defense Plan. Working together, the Army and the Navy prepared to drown the Americans in blood as they came to invade the Home Islands. Thousands of man-hours had been spent in the past year, building beach and inland defenses, combat divisions were being raised at a rate far faster than American estimates, and finally, massive numbers of special attack units of every form were being raised and trained.

If the Americans dared to invade the Japanese Home Islands they would be met by a Divine Wind of Kamikaze forces such as they had never dreamed, never even in their worst nightmares. By pooling resources, nearly twelve thousand planes were being readied for suicide attacks, thousands of baka bombs and kaiten torpedoes were being built and hidden for the day of Ketsu-Go.

These special devices were steered to their targets by men whose sole meaning in life was to die gloriously for the Emperor, yet each death in his name made this same Emperor wince in pain. Emperor Hirohito believed it was time to stop the madness and save His people from the horrors that the Americans were prepared to inflict upon them.

General Anami rose to speak first as was his right for meetings of the Supreme Council, but the Emperor stood and waved at the General to sit. The normally fierce General Anami had no choice but to bow his head and sit with the rest of them.

The naturally quiet and taciturn Hirohito began in a solemn tone, "With this third atomic bomb attack, the Americans have demonstrated that they are prepared to burn all of our great cities to the ground, and we are defenseless to prevent this from happening again and again. I cannot bear the thought of my beautiful Kyoto being reduced to ashes. Therefore, I ask the Supreme Council for one final meeting to decide the fate of our people.

Now with American ships off our coasts, their fleet of bombers raining death from above, and the near certainty that all our great cities will be destroyed, you must decide now on the continuation of the war or acceptance of the terms that they have offered.

"I am prepared to listen with heavy heart as the fate of our people and the twenty six hundred year dynasty may yet be saved. Let us remember that today we are not discussing the honor of the Japanese people, but its very existence. All that we cherish will be annihilated if we fail."

Several in the room were nearly moved to tears as the forty-four year old Hirohito who spoke as the living embodiment of the Japanese people. To men whose own deaths held no fear for them, a worse fate would be to insult or fail to honor his Majesty on this most solemn of moments. With a nod to General Anami, the Emperor intended to hear from the most trusted men in the land and then in the end, ask for them to vote their conscience.

General Anami rose from his seat, bowed toward the Emperor, and began his last attempt to convince His Majesty that the decisive battle was approaching and they should persevere until the end. Hoping to play on the relationship that Anami developed with the Emperor when he was the royal military liaison in the Thirties, Anami was determined to undermine the weak-minded fools filling the Emperor's mind with defeatism.

The General Staff agreed that the Ketsu-Go defense plan for Kyushu would inflict such horrendous casualties on the Americans that they would be forced to the negotiating table and hold off on the final invasion against the main Japanese island of Honshu. In Anami's mind, something more important than the fate of the Japanese people was at stake.

What was truly important was the need to convince the Emperor that to allow Americans to occupy the Home islands would lead to the undermining of all things that made Japan unique in world history. Anami and the purists believed that once foreigners came to act as occupation forces, Japanese culture would forever be changed and held hostage to a new set of beliefs determined by Americans, a people without any sense of spirit. This he was determined to stop.

The fierce looking War Minister stood before the Emperor, bowed, and offered up his impassioned reasoning for favoring Ketsu-Go. "Your Majesty and fellow Council members, I agree that this is a most terrible time, but I refuse to accept that we are defenseless and must accede to the arrogant demands of the Americans. We have been preparing for the past year for the Ketsu-Go plan. The people are ready to offer their lives in sacrifice so that we should not have to submit to these criminal threats."

Becoming impatient, Premier Suzuki had heard all of the same arguments from Anami for the past six months. Even now the man refused to accept defeat. Suzuki was an admiral and had won distinction as a young captain of torpedo boats during the Russo-Japanese war in 1905. He was old and frail, but his mind was still able and he refused to sit back and let this go on indefinitely.

Cutting the War Minister off, "General Anami, the Americans have used their new atomic weapon three times now. This last time, our second largest city was destroyed and nearly one hundred and twenty thousand dead and countless more injured. Let me ask you General, what if the Americans decide to drop their super bombs on your vaunted defenses of the Ketsu-Go plan? How many thousands of troops would die with but a single bomb?"

Anami's mouth opened in fury at being cut off and was about to answer as another voice of dissent joined in when Marquis Kido asked, "General, also, we mustn't forget the Russians. The Kwantung Army is being overrun and our forces are in retreat throughout Manchuria. How do you suppose to defeat the Americans and this new threat coming from Korea and eventually from the North towards Hokkaido? A blind man can see that we will be defeated, and if the Russians assault these shores, they will never leave. At least with the Americans, they can be reasoned with."

Barely able to restrain his anger, Admiral Toyoda absolutely agreed with General Anami that the only honorable solution was authorizing the Ketsu-Go plan and make the Americans earn their victory, not hand it to them. Coming to his fellow officer's support, he sneered at Kido, "What do you know of the Russians, Kido? Even as we speak, the Americans and the Russians are fighting over the spoils of war in Germany. If anything, the longer we resist, the better deal we can make. Why be so quick to lie down like dogs to the Americans."

Foreign Minister Togo saw a clear opening and turned to face the Emperor as he spoke, "While Admiral Toyoda is correct about the situation in Europe, he ignores the opportunities opened by such a break between the Americans and the Russians. The Americans will need strong allies to confront the power of the Soviets. Would we not be a powerful instrument to counter Soviet influence in China?

I would much rather negotiate a peace with the Americans because Kido is correct about one key truth, once the Soviets come to our shores, they will never leave and then what would happen to our people? History has demonstrated that while the Americans can be terrible enemies, they can also be powerful friends."

These last words sent a chill through the room. For all of the talk of drowning the Americans in their own blood, the mere suggestion that their current mortal enemy could eventually treat Japan as a potential friend seemed ludicrous at first, but only at first.

Naval Minister, Admiral Yonai, felt humiliated as his once vaunted Japanese Imperial Navy, who ruled the Pacific a short time ago, must now watch as American Battleships pummel the defenseless coastlines. Three years before, an American Carrier Battle Group wouldn't have dared come within one thousand miles of the Home Islands, but now carrier-borne aircraft flew above Japan's skies with complete impunity.

Yonai knew a foe that couldn't be defeated and understood better than most at the table that Japan's long-term best interests lay with the West. If the Russians were to succeed in destroying Japanese influence in China and then convert China's masses to communism, Japan had better have a powerful ally, for he couldn't think of a more nightmarish scenario.

So with humility borne out of already accepting the stain of defeat, Admiral Yonai bravely stood up to his other military chiefs and declared, "As difficult as it is for me to accept, I am afraid that Togo and Kido are correct in their assessment. The terms the Americans offer us today allow us to build upon the spiritual guidance of the Emperor and provide the seeds for Japan's ultimate salvation. As powerful as the Americans appear to be, the Russians are greater in numbers and more powerful on land than the Americans could ever hope to be. They will need allies in the future."

Pausing for a moment to allow his words have their effect, then in a deadly serious voice, Yonai said, "We may choose to commit national suicide today and salvage a certain degree of honor, but what then. Maybe the Americans leave us to the Russians or even the Chinese to finish us off in our weakened state. I say No! Make peace today knowing that when conflict between the two giants sitting bestride the world happens, it is the Americans who will need us and then we can extract the conditions we require to sustain and rebuild our country."

The discussion raged for the next two hours, but neither side was willing to budge. As Emperor Hirohito listened, the words of Togo and Admiral Yonai made more and more sense. He was deeply saddened that the other military men in the room refused to open their minds and try to find some other solution other than national seppuku or ritual suicide.

For months, he had sat back and allowed this tie to continue as was custom, but no longer. In days of old, even a weak Emperor could issue an Imperial Command. Such a pronouncement could be ignored by a powerful warlord or Shogun, but done so at his own peril. Such a final Imperial decision was often called the Voice of the Crane. Today, this very moment, the crane would be heard again, this time to save a nation.

With complete realization of the significance of the moment, Hirohito rose from his seat and with a serene tone spoke to his War Council, "The time for talk is long past. I had hoped that the realities of the war would be more apparent to some in this room, but three of you remain wedded to your beliefs. I for one can no longer bear the suffering of our people in silence. How many millions will be lost in my name? No more. On behalf of my people, I have decided to bear the unbearable and accept the American proposal."

Some expected such an announcement, but to hear the Emperor make a pronouncement literally sucked the air out of the humid chamber. Kido inwardly smiled and secretly thanked Buddha for granting the Emperor his strength. Emperor Hirohito cleared his parched voice and then continued, "Foreign Minister Togo, you are to immediately, at the conclusion of this meeting, inform the Swiss intermediaries to contact the Americans with our acceptance. We will await their instructions and the specifics of the terms of occupation.

General Anami, I understand that this decision falls heavily upon you, since yours will be the responsibility to arrange the laying down of arms and preventing any officer from resisting this decision. You have served me and the Japanese people well throughout the war. There is no dishonor in accepting the inevitable. I beg of you to maintain yourself in the coming days, do not give in to tradition for we know not what the Americans will ask or enforce. Your assistance and strength will enable me to persevere and act honorably on behalf of our people."

Knowing that he had no choice, General Anami barely had the strength to whisper, "Yes, you're Majesty. It shall be done."

Realizing the degree of control that General Anami was trying to desperately maintain, Hirohito said one more thing, "General, although we are laying down our arms against the Americans, I feel honor bound to continue the war against the Russians. Minister Togo will NOT accept any terms that requires surrender to the Russians. You are ordered to maintain your armies in the field in China and Korea and fight to the last man to protect our northern islands of Sakhalin and the Kuriles. In fact, I wish you to immediately begin releasing formations from Kyushu and Honshu to confront the Russians and stop them from endangering the Home Islands. Is that understood, General?"

Realizing that he had been given a perfect opportunity to restore the Army's honor, General Anami stood from his chair, walked towards the Emperor, then went to his knees in complete submission but with tears streaming down his face, "Thank you, your Majesty. I must go now and prepare your Imperial forces to obey your commands."

The others bowed their heads and closed their eyes as the Emperor left them to follow his instructions to perform the unthinkable. The Empire of Japan had, for all intents and purposes, come to an end. These men were left with heavy hearts knowing they had failed the Emperor, but also with a burning desire that they could regain their honor against the Soviets.

Chapter Forty Three

August 22, 1945, 11:30 pm

Tuszyn, Poland (ten miles south of Lodz)

It was late, the stars were out and he could hear hundreds of his men scurrying around in the dark. Ambush teams were moving to nighttime positions, supplies were being prepared to move to the next command post, and somehow his men maintained their spirit in the face of unbelievable adversity.

After two months of relentless fighting, they were reduced to moving in the dark. The Russians owned the daylight, but at night, his men could still hurt them. A convoy here, a small armored column there, mortar attacks on Russian barracks, assassinations of Polish traitors, his men just refused to give in.

It was a miracle they were still alive, let alone still fighting. His brave Home Army soldiers had been standing up to the most powerful army in the world, alone for the past two months, and he was tired, more tired than he ever dreamed he could feel. General Anders, commander of the Polish Home Army, refused to give up the fight. He knew that as long as his people stayed in the field, then hopes of a reborn Poland remained alive.

A student of history, he remembered his readings from the American Revolution two hundred years ago. George Washington's leadership taught him the most important and single guiding lesson that he clung to throughout this struggle. *It doesn't matter how many battles you lose, as long as you win the final battle.*

As long as he kept his forces in the field, as long as he continued to attack and hurt them, then the cause was still alive. He had watched as the Russians inflicted unspeakable acts of reprisal against Polish civilians, smelled the burning soot of flesh and village alike as Soviet anti-partisan sweeps roamed the countryside. Reports of young and old alike being shot like animals or whole city blocks reduced to rubble for the crimes of the Home Army. Still, through it all, in a fashion that humbled him, the Polish people endured.

On nights like tonight, the emotional toll of command seemed to hit him worse. Wiping the nighttime sweat off his forehead, he wondered, *what makes our people have the strength to endure.* Just as he began to drift off, he mouthed a quiet prayer, "Dear God, don't let this all be in vain. Give me the strength to continue to lead these brave men and women until the end."

After a couple of hours of sound sleep, his Chief of Staff, Colonel Anton Starzewski, shook his cot violently to get him moving. Starzewski's youthful face grinned as he said, "It doesn't bode well if our fearless leader can't even get his ass out of bed in the morning. What will the men say?"

Too tired and sore to knock the grin off his young aide's face, Anders wiped the sleep out of his eyes and reached for a steaming mug of tea, the smell alone was enough to start waking him up. Still a bit grouchy, Anders grumbled, "What now Anton, you know that I haven't been sleeping well these days?"

"General, I have urgent news from Warsaw. We received confirmation last night concerning the massive and sudden troop movements we have seen for the past week or so. Our man working inside the Lublin government has said that the Russians are massing their forces for a move against the Americans and English in Germany. They are rapidly pulling their combat formations out of

Poland and transferring nearly a dozen NKVD border guard divisions even now as we speak.

"It would seem that the business between the Russians and Americans in Czechoslovakia was much worse then was reported. I can barely believe it, but it does explain the Russians pulling two whole Rifle Corps away from Krakow and all of the rail traffic moving west towards Germany. I don't know what to think of it, that everything changes. We can kill these NKVD border guards a hell of a lot easier than regular Soviet tank formations."

Momentarily stunned, Anders held his right hand and index finger up and motioned for his aide to be quiet. He stood from the cot and began walking around the room in his bare feet thinking about the possibilities. What does this mean for the rebellion? Do the Americans know yet? What can we do to attack the rail hubs? Or should we lay low, lick our wounds and let the Americans jump into the fight for a change?

Suddenly a shiver ran up his spine, as he understood why Stalin was making the attack. Once the Americans and the English are gone, they'll never come back. The Russians would never allow another D-Day like landing in Europe and the Americans probably wouldn't have the stomach. Then Stalin could turn back on the rebellious Poles, Czechs, and whoever else that he chose, at his leisure. *Dear God, if the Russians succeed, then all hope is lost.*

Seconds after that awful thought entered his mind he yelled aloud, "NO! I will not give in to such thoughts!"

Starzewski had served with Anders throughout the Italian campaign and knew enough to watch his boss stomp and curse, get quiet, think some more, and then start cursing again. He watched as his commander put on his boots and officer's tunic then stormed out of his quarters and headed over to the Operations tent. He could already tell that the old man had made probably a half a dozen decisions and was ready to start barking orders. He followed right behind, ready to make things happen.

As the humid August morning hit him, he couldn't help but think everything suddenly made sense now. The Russians changed their entire tempo of operations about ten days ago. Instead of massive sweeps into the countryside, they were pulling their mobile groups back and fortifying communication and rail hubs. Anders thought it was supply issues, but now he understood the reason for this operational shift of forces. Now everything had changed…now he knew what needed to be done.

First and foremost, he absolutely must get word to General Eisenhower or Field Marshal Montgomery as soon as possible. If their man in Warsaw was correct and the Russians catch the Western armies by surprise, then all hope would be forever dashed for the people of Poland. Just the thought of his son and grandson growing up in a society where it wouldl probably be a crime to be proud to be a Pole was just too much to bear. He couldn't allow it. He wouldn't allow it.

No longer needing tea, Anders felt alive with energy and renewed hope because along with the danger there was also opportunity in this Russian attack. With his small staff around him, he started, "Anton, we can't send this information out over the radio. The Russians may have compromised our codes for all we know. This is too important, besides the British and the Americans would never believe us. So you will immediately send three different teams whose mission is to reach the commands of Montgomery, Eisenhower, or Patton. We will use ground, air, and water transport in hopes that at least one will make it through in time. The members of these teams must be the very best and inform them that failure is not an option. Is that understood?

"Next, I want every block of explosives that we have in our inventory broken down and parceled out immediately. We are about to go on an immediate sabotage offensive against the Russian military supply routes. I want bridges blown up, pontoon bridges under constant harassing fire, railroads, tunnels, barges, anything carrying military equipment and supplies to be attacked and then attacked again. I want all rail and road traffic to come to a standstill, and I want it done within the next seventy two hours."

One of his Operations officers blurted out, "But sir, that doesn't seem possible. We can barely move during daylight and must rely on the cover of night to move anything heavier then a rifle, let alone heavy supplies. Maybe we could reposition our forces in about a week or so and stage operations against Soviet units near Poznan or maybe even Warsaw, but certainly not across the country. It's too risky, sir."

His operations deputy nearly swallowed his tongue when he saw the look Anders gave him. The Home Army commander roared, "Everyone in this command listen here and now. The battle that will win back Warsaw begins in a hundred different fields and streams across the country. We either bring to a halt all military supplies and reinforcements moving against the Americans and English or Poland will cease to exist. Every train trestle that is blown, every container full of ammo and food means one less thing for the Russian war machine to throw at our Allies. If we help them win, then they will help us win.

"The moment those Russian tanks cross that border, then everything changes in a blink of an eye. We will no longer be alone. We will have allies in this fight. Now I don't trust the British and never have, but if we help the Americans, then I believe they will see this thing through.

So, I don't care if you have to steal Russian uniforms and enough trucks to move our men around the country, under their noses if need be. I want communication wires and telephone lines cut. I don't want to read reports of a railroad blown up in one place. I want a stretch of line hit in five places. Then I want you to shoot the engineers sent to repair the lines. Act now gentlemen, be bold. I will not tolerate excuses from anyone for the rest of this campaign."

Stopping for a moment to look at his men, he saw hope in their eyes for the first time in ages, so he said one last thing, more subdued, but in no less intense a voice, "I don't know what else to say, gentlemen, except that when history is written about these dark days what we do today, this very moment will determine who will write our history, Poles or Russians and if the Russians get to write the history, my brothers, then we will have seen the end of Mother Poland. We can't allow that to happen. I pledge to you that I will give my dying breath to Poland, as I know that you will all do your duty. God bless."

With that said, the meeting ended and the Polish camp went into overdrive. The key was getting those men to make contact with the Americans, everything depended upon taking away the element of surprise or God help the Americans and English, for they would receive a baptism of fire that would shake the very heavens.

August 23, 1945, 11:00am

Nuremberg, Third Army Headquarters

Laid out on a huge tactical display map, US Third Army unit dispositions were starting to shape up. With only three corps to defend the critical approaches leading into Bavaria, General Patton placed Major General "Bulldog" Walker's XX Corp around the Hof Corridor, VIII Corps under Major General Middleton, covered the approaches south of Regensberg to Pausau, but the most critical position centered on the city of Pilsen and its five critical roads was held by Major General Irwin's XII Corp. There was no doubt in Patton's mind that the battle for Bavaria meant holding this strategic Czech city or else Third Army would be split and defeated in detail.

Every morning, Patton received a report from Third Army's Chief of Engineers detailing the status of the multiple fortified belts of defenses being secretly built along the approaches to Pilsen. So, he further beefed up Major General Leroy Irwin's XII Corps even though he had three crack divisions, the 26th Infantry, the 90th Infantry, and the best tank outfit in Third Army, the fearsome 4th Armored Division.

Over the past two weeks, Patton transferred five engineer battalions, six heavy anti-aircraft battalions armed with long-ranged 90mm guns, three independent Hellcat anti-tank battalions, and two independent tank regiments. As for firepower, more than two thirds of Third Army's heavy artillery battalions, mostly self-propelled 155's, eight inch howitzers, and as many 4.2-inch heavy mortar batteries as he could find, were being sent to support the XII Corp. He intended to set up a ring of fire around the town and if the Russians so much as stuck their tongue out at them, he could blow their asses away in a heartbeat.

After a week of reading the reports, Patton decided to order his driver, Sergeant Meeks, to make a surprise visit to view things himself. He was about ten miles south of Pilsen when he started to see what he had damn well expected. Major General Irwin was using the cover of darkness to move the mountain of supplies, cement, reinforced rebar, trench digging engineer equipment, everything needed to protect his men from Russian artillery and make Pilsen impossible to take by storm. Patton watched with his practiced eye and could tell that this Corps was being well led and clearly was operating on a wartime footing.

During the last days of the war, Irwin replaced one of Third Army's old-timers, Major General Manton Eddy. Eddy was an outstanding infantry division commander and Corps commander. He led the 9th Infantry Division in North Africa and during the early days of the Normandy campaign. He then was promoted to command the XII Corp and did so with distinction throughout the rest of the campaign, but had to go back to the States because of a bad ticker.

Major General Irwin commanded the 5th Infantry Division through the better part of the fighting. He was serious, smart, and an aggressive commander who knew how to keep Patton happy, and that wasn't easy.

Patton could tell Irwin had his men ready, his jeep was stopped three times leading up to the city. Good, he didn't want any goddamned communists running around taking snapshots. He threatened to put any MP in the brig for the duration if they radioed ahead and warned the next checkpoint. He wanted to surprise the men, especially to see what his Germans were up to. That General Baake was a hard man. Tough son of a bitch, that's why Patton chose him for the mission. *Not only will he work his men until they nearly keel over, but the bastard is willing to have his men fight to the very last to remove the stain of Germany's dishonor for the excesses of the Nazis.*

Finally after another two hours of stops and starts, General Patton roamed wide and far within the perimeter. Each step of the way, he took out his own map and marked the various tank traps, minefields, trench lines, and gun emplacements. Smiling as he traced his finger along one of the six rivers and streams that converged around Pilsen, he said aloud," You nasty son of a bitch."

He saw they were making particular good use out of the river lines. Each potential crossing was being dug out with tank traps, camouflaged bunkers were being erected, bridges were primed with explosives, and fighting positions on the other side of the river were being prepared, all to kill the Russians in droves.

It was really coming together, another week and he felt confident that XII Corp could hold against a major attack. Seeing what he needed to see, he called for Irwin, his division commanders, and General Baake to report immediately.

Before heading over to the XII Corps Command Post, he decided to check out the area that worried him, the vulnerable left flank. The American position made use of the Mize River that unfortunately was really more like a stream by this point. He was worried about getting flanked and encircled on this end of the line. Irwin had placed Combat Command A of the 4th Armored to cover the approaches, but with almost no natural defensive terrain, this was going to be trouble and he knew it. It was here that he ran into a startled General Baake on the way to the meeting.

Immediately coming to attention, Baake saluted and said, "Herr General."

Returning the stiff and correct German salute, Patton eyeballed him and was impressed again. To see a German General, a former medical physician no less, covered in dirt and grime from his own labors directing his men in the field was impressive. Patton grinned as he said, "Goddamned but you're mess, General. What the hell have you and your men been up to?"

He was momentarily embarrassed to be seen without his proper uniform and covered in mud from the field, but then he saw the strange American grinning.

"General Baake, you must really be looking forward to killing Russians again to be out there yourself playing in the mud. So, what are you doing to fortify this side of the line to send those Russian bastards to the hereafter?"

Still finding it very difficult to deal with these peculiar Americans, especially Patton, Baake hesitated before answering. All of the intelligence reports on Patton during the war were correct. The man was a bit mad, brilliant perhaps, possessing a real grasp of the battlefield and an inspired leader of men, but at times Baake hadn't a clue what the man would say next.

In a very serious tone, Baake responded, "General Patton, as you must have ascertained already, this part of the line is easily the weakest. No depth, the river is low, and completely flat, plus, there are good roads once you make the river crossing, and with relatively wide open farmland on either side. This is where the Russians will look to make their breakthrough. Luckily, since this terrain describes nearly the entire Russian steppe, my men know how to prepare to defend the area."

Patton cut him off, "Knowing where they will hit us is one thing, but stopping it is another."

Not used to being interrupted during a briefing, General Baake hesitated and then continued, "Yes Herr General, stopping a determined Russian attack was never easy. The key is to prevent the Russians from infiltrating your positions with sappers prior to the attack. So, as you can see, on the map my men have been creeping closer and closer to the Russian lines each night, laying overlapping minefields. Your mines aren't as good as the ones we used, but we are mixing a very dense field of anti-personnel and anti-tank mines, covering three full belts out to five miles from the river line. If they move in force, we'll be alerted and can start killing them with artillery before they even approach the riverbed.

"Once they breach the minefields and make it to the river, and General Patton, please remember if they choose to attack at this point on the line, no matter how many mines we lay, they will eventually breach the minefield. The Soviets are prepared to lose a division just during the approach phase.

My men have been digging hull down tank positions, two zigzag trench lines with concrete dug out bunkers and all covered with more mines. Most importantly, we have encased in concrete dozens of anti-tank gun emplacements, including eight 88mm anti-tank guns to completely sweep the field of supporting tanks.

They will know that you are there, but it won't matter once they launch the attack. Most importantly, we left three distinct openings in the minefields and trench zone to allow for mobile elements to counterattack the Russians once they have made their penetrations. Please keep in mind, General Patton, never allow the Russians to establish a bridgehead. Even if all you have is an armored tank company, launch the counter-attack, never allow them to grab a finger hold or they will never let up."

Baake finished his brief, could see the American commander was suitably impressed but what he could not bring himself to say was that these Americans truly had no idea what is in store for them. The Russians were going to hit these Americans harder than they have ever been attacked before and Baake still could not make up his mind if these Americans could hold in the face of the nightmare to come.

All Patton could think was that this son of bitch knew his business. Putting him in command of this German unit was the smartest thing he had done yet. Saluting the German General, he turned on his heels and motored out to Irwin's Headquarters. For the next two hours, he went over details of the defense until he was satisfied and the men primed.

Most were standoffish about having a former enemy walking amongst them, but after a week and a half of watching the Germans professionally go about their business, they learned to respect them and knew that if they did their job then it made XII Corps job easier.

Patton kept things straight and to the point, now was not the time for one of Patton's time honored kick them in the ass speeches. Now was the time to prepare, and the men were getting ready and making do with what they had. Even though some units were composed of a third to half of newcomers, he had just enough veterans to make things work.

Come one way or another, if those Russians bastards decided to come at him, he'd give them a kick in the ass that they'd feel all the way back to Moscow. There was no doubt that Irwin had his XII Corps ready to go at it with the Russians. He almost felt sorry for the Godless bastards.

Pleased with his nights work, Patton decided to take time out for a civilized lunch and perhaps go for a ride on one of those beautiful Lipizzaner stallions he had brought up from Salzburg. With everything that had been going on, a nice ride would help him relax and take some of the pressure off.

Patton thought, *once a man served in the horse cavalry, you just couldn't take away your love and affection for the powerful four-*

legged creatures...feeling the power around your legs, the wind in your face as prepare to launch yourself across an open field like in the days of old. Nothing like it, tanks are the future, but armored warfare just doesn't have the romance or nobility of the old cavalry.

Lost in thought for a moment, he barely looked up when his Chief of Intelligence, Colonel Oscar Koch came into his office. He was one of three men who had permission to barge in day or night. The man looked like hell. Koch and his intelligence specialists had been putting in eighteen and twenty hour days trying to piece together Soviet intentions and capabilities. Pretty tall order once Eisenhower kept in place that insane order against over flights.

The Russians were maintaining excellent radio discipline, short bursts, almost nothing broadcast in the open until last night. That was all Koch needed to put two and two together. Colonel Koch was probably the only man in the entire American Army who got it right about the German attack in the Bulge. Patton trusted him as he trusted no other.

Without any formalities, Koch blurted out, "Sir, for the past week I have been sending Czech partisans across the lines with instructions to get me something, anything to present to SHAEF headquarters to convince them that the Russians were coming. We have been hearing movement all along the entire frontier.

I have even been talking informally to friends up in Monty's 21st Army Group and the American 1st Army. Everyone is saying the same thing. There is movement all over the damn place, but no radio traffic. Rumors are running up and down the line, but Ike is squashing anything unless we get something hard."

Not liking the look on Koch's face, Patton suddenly felt as if they were going to have less time to prepare than was originally planned. "Well, what the hell is Ike doing about it? Is Monty or Bradley saying anything or am I the only crazy bastard in charge?"

Weary from fatigue, Koch struggled to continue, "I think one of my guys hit on something last night. They picked up radio chatter between a Soviet engineer brigade and a unit that we confirmed is the Fourth Guards Tank Army Headquarters. By the sound of the transmission, a young officer confirmed that all of the bridging equipment was nearly delivered and would be ready within two days. The response from 4th Guards Tank Headquarters was "Good that will give you another twenty four hours to move to the crossing site."

The transmission ended when another voice cut in that called both men idiots and told them to stop transmitting in the clear. The implications are clear, so I did one more thing that I hope you will back me on. I sent one of my guys up in a Piper Cub and told him to catch the Soviet lines at first light. Now I know that SHAEF threatened court martial if anyone tried something like this, but I'm afraid that a court martial is going to be the least of our problems."

Koch was hesitating and Patton blurted out, "Christ, will you stop stammering and spill the beans. What the hell did your guy see?"

Looking Patton right in the eyes, the intelligence officer just shook his head and told his boss, "Not a damn thing."

"What the hell does that mean? Goddamnit, I'm too tired to play guessing games. Did you see tanks, infantry, artillery, what?"

"That's just it sir, except for what's been deployed to their front lines, as far as I can see, hardly anything has changed except the obvious. My guy said he saw evidence of tank tracks all over the place. The wet ground was soft from the morning mist, and he said that he saw tracks and deep ruts along dirt tracks and secondary unpaved roads leading to the heavy forest cover off the main roads. For an hour before first light, he just kept flying high, turned his engine off and drifted, trying to hear movement, anything.

"He said it was the eeriest damn feeling he ever felt. He says that they are there, deep in the hills, waiting to make a move, but he was damned if he could see evidence of a single tank out in the open. My officer said he hasn't seen that many tank tracks since the Bulge. By all rights, he should have seen something, but with the Russians, nothing means something.

The Red Army was able to secure tactical surprise against the Germans in nearly every main battle. No one is better at hiding movement and massing of forces under cover than the Russians. The German officers that I have interviewed said the worst feeling in the entire world is to feel that your command is secure and then they come almost out of thin air. More battles were lost by shock at the point of contact than anything else."

Letting that little piece of evidence sink in, Koch hit Patton with the final piece of information. "General, I did my very best to put together a picture of how the Russian Army deployed its forces in Hungary and Czechoslovakia at the end of the war. Factoring in redeployments, casualties, consolidation of forces, etc., I estimate that when the Russians go on the offensive, and at this point, I expect contact within the next seventy-two to ninety-six hours...perhaps sooner.

"Between the Hof corridor through Pilsen and down to Passau, the Soviets can throw nearly twelve full armies, three of which could be tank armies. Third Army is looking at being hit by more than one million troops and nearly two thousand tanks and self-propelled guns. The intelligence on the bridging equipment says it all, sir. You don't need pontoon bridges if you're sitting on the defensive. I think we need to accelerate preparations for contact, General. We need another a week or so...two days just isn't enough time to get ready."

Patton kept focusing on the map and couldn't take his eyes off Pilsen. The numbers were just staggering. One million troops with all those tanks pointed right at his men, and all of it had to pass through Pilsen or the roads it commanded. He knew that Koch's intelligence was a little thin, but it didn't matter. The Russians were coming, he could feel it in his bones. Starting to get himself and the rest of his staff ready for war, he excitedly grabbed his holster and ivory handled pistols when the phone rang out.

The two men froze, but refusing to give in to his worst fears, Patton reached out and grabbed the phone, "Patton here."

For a split second he was relieved when he heard Ike's Chief of Staff, Bedell Smith. That ended in two seconds as Smith roared on the phone, "George, are you out of your cotton picking mind? What are you some type of lunatic? Now you answer me and answer me right the hell now. Do you have a bunch of goddamn Nazis building fortifications around Pilsen under some Nazi general? Because if it's true, you better pack your goddamn bags now, you're going home in disgrace."

Never liking the son of a bitch, Patton knew when he was caught and decided that Smith could come on down and kiss his ass because, one way or the other, the Russians were about to start World War III.

Refusing to back down, Patton cursed right back. "Maybe I am some type of lunatic, but when the Russians come crashing over the lines, I'll be the only son of a bitch smart enough to have built up enough fortifications to stop the bastards. So when you and Ike are packing your bags and running off to Paris, I'll be down here in Czechoslovakia, killing Russians."

Smith never liked Patton, either, and never could understand why Ike stood by him all these years. Waiting for an opportunity to finally get rid of Patton, Smith yelled through the phone, "You listen here, you over-rated pain in the ass, the Russians aren't going anywhere unless you provoke them. Ike is trying to avoid a war, not start one, you foolhardy bastard."

Waiting for the opening, Patton revealed his trump card, "You think so, well, Bedell, my intelligence boys down here believe they have enough hard evidence on hand to prove that the Russians are about to attack us and pretty damn soon. I'm going to send my intelligence chief, Colonel Koch, to go meet with some of your own people up at SHAEF and prove you wrong. If it will make you any happier, Bedell, if the Russians haven't attacked in a week, you can come down here and kick me in the ass yourself."

"That won't be necessary George. Ike warned you, he practically begged you not go off and be yourself, but you just couldn't help it, could you? You are hereby ordered to report to SHAEF Headquarters by 0900 hours tomorrow morning to answer to Ike. One piece of advice, pack your bags because if the Russians need a sacrificial lamb to calm things down, Ike's ready to hand them your head. That's all."

With that said, the phone clicked off and Patton was left standing there dumbstruck that Smith and Ike would go so far. He couldn't believe that with a war eminent he was about to be thrown off the continent. *It just can't be.*

Koch was alarmed and asked, "Sir, are you alright? When does General Smith want me to leave?"

Still somewhat in shock, Patton just shook his head and said, "They don't want you, Koch, and damn well don't want to hear what you've got to say. They want me and they want to nail my ass to the doghouse for one last time, the blind bastards."

Then, as Patton's expression went from shock to pure rage, he slammed his desk, kicked the chair across the room and bellowed, "I'll tell you Koch, this time they won't take me away from my destiny! This will be the ultimate battle of the Twentieth Century and they think they can take this away from me. I won't have it. They'll have to shoot me first before I leave my command, so by God, Koch, you and Harkins are going with me tomorrow and you better be right. We're going to show those bastards that I had the smarts and the balls to prepare this command for the biggest battle in American history while they have been sitting around with their hands up their asses."

Chapter Forty Four

August 24, 1945, 10:30 a.m.

Tokyo Bay, aboard the Battleship USS Missouri

It had been a grand morning, a morning that many had thought would never come. As of ten o'clock in the morning the former Empire of Japan and the United States officially, and with great ceremony, ended the war in the Pacific. In a struggle that was as fearsome as any the United States had ever fought, the two very different peoples agreed to come to terms as Japan accepted the inevitable.

For the tens of thousands of American boys who never expected to live out the year and for the hundreds of thousands, perhaps millions of Japanese soldiers and civilians who would surely have died during Operation Downfall, peace brought a glimmer of hope and special thanks for sparing them any more horrors from this war.

As a result of the Emperor's decision to surrender to American forces, as of twelve o'clock, American occupation forces were due to arrive and begin landing on the Japanese Islands. General MacArthur was named Military Governor or de facto ruler of Japan as all civil matters now became the responsibility of US occupation forces.

Always looking ahead, MacArthur had already decided to orchestrate a massive allocation of food and re-establish social and medical services to the defeated Japanese people. Flying over the burnt out cities of Tokyo, Kokura, and especially the still burning city of Osaka, even MacArthur was left speechless by the sheer extent of the destruction.

Although he was as determined an enemy of the Japanese Imperial Army as any, MacArthur never felt the degree of pure hatred that many in the American Army and Navy felt towards their Japanese counterparts. After spending so much of his life in Asia, MacArthur always felt he had certain insight into the Japanese mind and an appreciation for their culture that few Americans understood.

Now that Japan was defeated, MacArthur's true intentions came to the fore. Looking out of the porthole at the destruction of the

Tokyo Bay dockyards, he believed that the sooner Japan could stand on its own two feet, the sooner the United States would have a bulwark against the threat of Communism in Asia.

Two days ago MacArthur was prepared to kill every Japanese soldier, seamen, and civilian if need be to end the war, now he was equally prepared to make use of these brave and hardy people in the fight to come. For like Patton in Europe, MacArthur believed that the day of reckoning against the Bolshevik menace originating from Moscow was nearly upon them.

Arriving exactly on time, Admiral Chester Nimitz, commander of the U.S. Pacific Fleet, entered the ship's wardroom to meet with his Army counterpart. Tall and lanky and with hair so blond that it was almost pure white, the level headed architect of the defeat of the Japanese Navy extended his hand to the new ruler of Japan. The two men did not so much as dislike one another, but more distrusted the intentions of the other man.

The Army and Navy carried their own internecine war for four years concerning which service should dictate the direction of the war. The Navy generally had its way, but as the land battles grew larger and the Japanese Navy became a non-factor, the Army and Army Air Force came to supersede the Navy in the final days of the war.

Although the Navy intended to play a role in the occupation of Japan, both men understood that the Army, by nature of its mission, would naturally play the key role. As a result, General MacArthur called the meeting because, with war clouds in Europe brewing, the Russian factor had to be dealt with, and quickly.

Washington was pushing MacArthur to accelerate the surrender of Japanese forces on the mainland of Asia as a gesture of goodwill to the Russians. Not having very much respect for the new man in the White House, MacArthur found him to be nowhere near the man of his predecessor. MacArthur was very much against this idea, so he wanted to enlist the cooperation of the Navy.

The Russian offensive in Manchuria had turned out to be significantly larger than his staff had projected. The Soviet Red Army had deployed more than one and a half million men, twenty five hundred tanks, four thousand planes, and additionally massed all of its growing Pacific Naval Fleet for what appeared to be preparations for an amphibious move against the Japanese Island of Hokkaido.

The speed and power of the Soviet advance had impressed the Americans, but what concerned MacArthur most were the political implications for Nationalist China. That much combat power could be used to assert the will of Moscow against a weakened Chinese

Nationalist regime and essentially shut out American influence from the continent.

After initial pleasantries were exchanged, the General motioned for the two to sit. He insisted the two meet alone and in the end that was the best choice. Admiral Nimitz was always on his guard against MacArthur, he was unlike any other American he had ever really known. Nimitz detested the arrogance of the man, and most of his staff for that matter, but there was no questioning the man's personal bravery. The man's exploits on the battlefield during the First World War were legendary. Though many in the Navy maintained grudges against MacArthur for what many felt was his failure to hold the Philippines.

Regardless, his handling of the New Guinea campaign and later multi-pronged invasion of the Philippine Islands were masterful. Staring at the Army icon for a moment, Nimitz thought, *what the hell, if I can make peace with the Japs, I should at least be able to sit down at the same table with this arrogant bastard.*

MacArthur began, "Admiral, thank you for agreeing to meet with me today, of all days. Our country has come a long way since the dark days of 1941, but the Japanese are as utterly a defeated a people as any that I have ever seen. I believe the devastation that your Naval forces and our brave Army troops on the air and on the ground visited upon these people will sufficiently awe this nation and teach them never to raise a hand against the United States ever again."

Nimitz responded, "General, I have to agree. Just flying over the burned out remains of Tokyo, let alone Hiroshima or Nagasaki, I don't believe that we'll see any trouble from these people ever again. We just have to protect ourselves against the diehards. A couple of my squadrons took out another secret Kamikaze base that looked to be getting ready to launch a final attack. Make sure your boys on the ground are ready for anything."

Unable to resist a little dig, Nimitz added," You know General, I'll have my Marines around in case you run into any trouble. The Jap civilians are scared to death of my Marines. Their propaganda have been saying for years that the Marines are going to come to rape their daughters and burn their villages to ground."

Not taking the bait, "Thank you, Admiral, but that shouldn't prove necessary. I do believe that with the official pronouncement by the Emperor over the radio the other day, we will find a populace in utter awe of our forces, Army and Marine alike. But that's not why I wanted to meet with you today."

Taking a moment to pull a map out of his briefcase, MacArthur laid out the most recent estimates of Russian advance throughout Manchuria and Korea. "Admiral Nimitz, we need to discuss the

Russian threat to our interests in the Pacific. I am curious as to the views of the Navy to the Russian buildup."

Studying the map very carefully and taking notice of the Russian invasion into Manchuria, Nimitz had already ordered his staff to start tracking Soviet forces, aircraft, naval vessels. He was duly impressed with the details of the extent of the Soviet land forces, but he really wasn't worried about the Soviet Navy. As Admiral Halsey put it the other day, "He'd sink every goddamn Russian tin can in about two minutes once he got the word."

However, Nimitz was more concerned about securing the Chinese ports and especially those in Korea than anything else. Admiral King from the Joint Staffs had already ordered him to start preparations to seize Pusan at the tip of Korea just to show the Russians we could. Still, as large as the American Navy was in the Pacific, the Red Army was a powerful instrument, not to be underestimated. It appeared from MacArthur's tone that he was equally concerned.

Nodding his head and tracing the extent of the Russian advance in the past week, he looked up and said, "General, it looks like the Russians ran through the Japanese Army pretty damn easy. Are the Japs still fighting?"

"Yes, Japanese commander of the Kwantung Army in Manchuria and Korea has refused all orders to surrender to the Russians and has indicated that they will fight to the last man if need be. The Russians are pressuring Washington to cooperate against the Japanese forces on the mainland, and it looks as if the current occupant of the White House has readily caved to the Russian demands."

"An order from Washington, General, is exactly that, if I'm not mistaken. Your newfound occupation authority over the Japanese does not seem, to me, to allow you to ignore direct orders from Washington. I would be very careful, General."

Suddenly very uneasy, Nimitz wondered what MacArthur was hoping to accomplish. Regardless of the Russian threat, the United States was treaty bound to the Soviets. The General was treading on very thin ice and Nimitz did not want the Navy caught in the crossfire.

Nimitz asked," General MacArthur, if I may be frank, why did you call this meeting and what exactly are you proposing?"

Sensing resistance, MacArthur decided to disclose his fears about the Russians and the concern for China. "Admiral Nimitz, it is my belief that the Russians are trying to take advantage of the current crisis in Europe between our two countries and are attempting to mount a campaign aimed at undermining our long-term interests in the region. The Communist threat looms large in Europe, but it is equally dangerous here in Asia.

Need I remind you that Mao Tse-tung and his Chinese Communists spent much of the war fighting against the brave Nationalists Chinese armies instead of dedicating themselves to the defeat of the Japanese. The Communists can't be trusted, no matter what the politicians in Washington may think."

Still nervous about the nature of the conversation, Nimitz added, "General MacArthur, however much I agree with your concerns over the looming political crisis in Asia, I am afraid that the Navy is more accustomed to taking orders than giving them to Washington. If you want to coordinate over flight, reconnaissance operations, and the like, I am all for it, but anything else is above my pay grade."

Calmly, MacArthur slowly pulled tobacco out of its pouch, filled his corncob pipe and began to puff lightly on it. Then, dramatically, he stood up and with a dignified air about him, he spoke, "Admiral, I am going to take the responsibility upon myself and allow the Japanese to continue their defense against the Russians. In fact, I have already decided to encourage the Japanese by allowing re-supply efforts to get underway across the Korean straits, and soon I intend to allow troops and airpower.

"Now before you say anything, I want you to consider the importance of seizing control of the Chinese ports. The longer Soviet forces are engaged with the Japanese forces on land, the greater the likelihood that our Army and Marine forces can secure Chinese ports and make contact with Chiang's Nationalist troops. Once political control reverts back to a strong central government in Peking under Nationalist control, we can withdraw our forces at Washington's leisure.

The Army and Navy must act as one in this operation or else we run the risk of delay and being forced to acquiesce to Soviet control of Manchuria, Korea, and their likely movement towards installing another puppet regime. If we hesitate, then it shall be too late."

Somewhat annoyed, Nimitz found himself nearly captivated by the man. It was uncanny the way he spoke with such authority. *No wonder his staff doesn't just work for him, they hero-worship him.* Nimitz had stood up to him on a number of occasions, but today, the s.o.b. made a hell of a lot of sense. With the Japs reeling back on their heels, the window of opportunity to seize the ports was rapidly closing. Thinking that not only was it in the Navy's best interest, but also the country's, Nimitz decided to play this by the book.

Rising from his seat in a somewhat less dramatic fashion, as was his style, he moved over to MacArthur and said," General, I will send word back to Admiral King but I suspect that I already know what he will say. The Navy will cooperate but this must be done quickly and quietly. I refuse to allow the United States Navy to be drawn into some type of political battle between you and Washington. Is that clear? I don't care what you think of President Truman, as far as I am concerned, he is the commander-in-chief, period.

However, I will inform Washington that to accelerate the surrender of Japanese forces on the Chinese and Korean mainland, armed landings will occur within three days to secure port facilities under the auspices of transferring Japanese forces back to the Home Islands. Whatever deals you work out with the Japanese high command is yours to make, leave the navy out of it.

"Next, no US ship will be party to any re-supply efforts or troop movements, but will provide escort if necessary. If a single incident gets back to me about some suicide attack or anything that puts my sailors and marines at risk, I will shut the whole thing down. Lastly, I will send Admiral Spruance with elements of the Fifth Fleet to begin screening the Russian naval presence, and begin maneuvers towards Vladivostok to shake them up for a change. I assure you that the United States Navy will make its presence known to our Russian friends. Do you find these conditions acceptable?"

Refusing to allow the Navy man the merest hint that he was fazed by the conditional support, MacArthur extended his hand and said, "Admiral Nimitz, not only can I abide by your suggestions, I would say that we are very much of the same mind. By coordinating our forces, we will stand up to the Bolsheviks without directly confronting them…yet."

The General was probably correct that acting now, America's position in this part of world would be a whole hell of a lot more secure. Returning the General's handshake he was about to say something when MacArthur cut in, "Just be aware of one thing Admiral, if Stalin chooses to make a fight out of it, which he very well may, we shall find ourselves in the fight of our lives. If they seek to test the mettle of the United States Army, we shall offer battle until either they are destroyed or my army is destroyed.

I hope the Navy will prepare itself for such a possibility as I intend to stand with my command. There will be no PT boats whisking me away in the middle of night, Admiral. If the Communists challenge our forces, I will lead them until the very end."

With that last chilling thought said, MacArthur donned his cap, saluted Nimitz and briskly walked out the door. The look in MacArthur's eyes sent a chill up Nimitz's back. All he could think was that the man's preparing himself for something, God help us all if it comes to be.

Chapter Forty Five

August 24, 1945, 9:30p.m.

Soviet Occupied Germany

From the Baltic coast to the forests of Saxony, the buildup of Red Army forces continued without pause. Division upon division of men and equipment massed along the border region waiting for their final orders. The sustained Russian buildup of defensive fortifications along the border seemed to keep Allied forces focused on what was in front of them. All the while, massive movements were taking place to the rear.

Between the Allied and Soviet outposts there existed a no-man's zone, and ever since the clash of arms in early August, soldiers on both sides were more inclined to shoot first and ask questions later. Taking advantage of the declared state of emergency after the attempt on Stalin's life, the Red Army had already moved substantial amounts of combat power to the forward areas. Most of the current movement focused upon shifting the specialists, assault engineers, reconnaissance battalions, intelligence teams, and all of the war material needed for the initial breech operations closer to the border.

This was the veteran army that had defeated the vaunted German Wehrmacht. Infiltration teams identified American and English units, captured German officers were forced to reveal as much as possible about the defensive works erected before the end of the war, and General Staff officers poured over every detail, identifying every possible key piece of terrain, water crossing sites, the secondary road network, everything needed to smash the Imperialists.

Working under intense pressure, staff officers kept telling themselves that these were the same men who destroyed the German Sixth Army at Stalingrad, the same who crushed the Nazis at the Battle of Kursk and then went on to one smashing victory after another, until this same army stormed and reduced to rubble the final stronghold of Berlin.

After four years of war, this army was composed of survivors who knew war, understood their profession, and went about their duties with single-minded determination. In the end, the plan was simple, direct, and overpowering. The West would be crushed and the Red Army would stand triumphant.

Now that most of the first echelon forces were nearing their respective jump-off points, the men were restricted to mostly night movement. Engineers worked around the clock preparing pontoon bridges, hundreds of miles of communication wire was laid, radar installations were being emplaced, anti-aircraft positions were being dug-out, and supply trains labored to establish massive, well-camouflaged ammo and fuel depots.

However, with Lend-Lease ended, some Quartermasters noted dwindling spare parts, commo gear was being not as plentiful, and even the supply of Spam was running short. Some whispered this had better be a quick campaign or things could get grim.

The Red Air Force was nearly as important for the coming battle as the Red Army, and so they too worked feverishly and stood down for one final massive maintenance overhaul. Ammunition belts were fed into their planes, bombs were readied, and flight crews studied reconnaissance reports, reviewed target lists, and pilots bragged about who was going to bag the most Americans.

No one would admit that the chances of defeating the Allied Air Force would be nearly impossible. The Red Air Force knew it would take unprecedented causalities, but it, too, was ready to perform its duty for the Motherland.

Back on the ground, last minute maintenance was performed on thousands of Soviet tanks and self-propelled anti-tank guns. Tank treads were replaced whenever possible, lubricants were brought up to field manual standards, guns were re-sighted, and drums of diesel fuel were attached to the backs of many of the tanks. Artillery and rocket batteries sprouted up all over the place.

Respecting Allied airpower, artillery officers sited hundreds of small batteries all over the German countryside, rather than the one or two massive artillery parks used against the Germans. Red Army artillery commanders stood ready to deliver a volume of fire that the Americans and English had never experienced.

Lastly, the preparations for the infantry were the simplest and yet most difficult of all. There were no machines to attend to, no bridges or lines to lay, the only thing that could be done was to prepare oneself for the terror of battle. In the end, no matter how many tanks, guns, or airplanes, it was always the Red Army infantry units forced to brave enemy fire and come face-to-face and capture the objective.

This war would not be won until these tired and battered men stood up to the new enemy of the State and destroyed them as well. Then, and only then, could they go back to their fields and factories and rebuild their lives. Many would not make it through this battle, but then again, most never thought they would survive the war against the Nazi invaders. So, in the end, most took the opportunity to sleep, eat, and rest their minds, for when the order comes to attack, they would be ready as always.

The Soviet General Staff was amazed that the element of surprise was still holding up. Even though the Americans continued to adhere to their own reconnaissance ban, the High Command maintained absolute noise and light discipline during the evening hours. The key to achieving strategic surprise would depend on the next twenty-four to thirty-six hours.

With each yard closer to the border, the Red Army grew stronger while the Americans and English grew weaker. Each moment the Western armies slept in their comfortable billets in their quaint German cottages and were not out in the field constructing bunkers and anti-tank ditches brought Stalin's army closer to its goal, strategic surprise.

Refusing to take chances, draconian security measures were taken against those German civilians unfortunate enough to live within thirty miles of the border. For the past week, trains arrived at night carrying war material and returned East with boxcars filled with weeping German women, children, and the old. NKVD security teams executed suspected subversives caught wondering near troop concentrations or anyone who could endanger the operational security of the Soviet buildup.

Soon it would no longer matter, because within the next thirty-six hours, the final campaign to liberate Europe and destroy the last remaining threat to the Soviet Union would begin. And so, while the West slept, the Red Army moved quietly and with a purpose that would reveal itself to the Americans and English in two short days.

August 25, 1945, 1:30 a.m.

Flying West over Poland

The transport plane carrying Marshal Zhukov was a converted bomber whose designers spent more time on payload and range than comfort or insulation from the constant drum of the propellers. Shifting position for what felt like the hundredth time, Zhukov sat up in disgust and tried to shake off how tired he felt at the moment.

Here he was, a little more than twenty-four hours before the massive attack against the Americans and English was due to commence, and instead of being tucked away in his field headquarters getting some much needed sleep, he was flying over Poland on his way back from an impromptu briefing in Moscow.

Angry at the waste of valuable time, he spat on the ground at the fools running things, including Comrade Stalin. Even though Zhukov was confident about the coming campaign, they couldn't conceive of the amazing complexity and details required to move millions of men and thousands of tons of supplies to the point of decision. Worse, some think themselves military strategists, always making their little suggestions. *The Red Army needs no suggestions. We smashed the Germans and we will smash the Western armies.*

Still, a command to appear before Comrade Stalin could not be taken lightly, so he traveled more than a thousand miles for one final briefing.

After traveling the better part of the late afternoon, his plane landed and a government car whisked him away to the Kremlin. As he drove past the heavy security put in place more than two months ago, Zhukov understood the importance of his newfound relationship with the ruler of the Soviet Union and refused to jeopardize it.

Also, Zhukov was quite mindful of the fact that Stalin was in poor health and with the NKVD weakened as a result of Beria's failings, the Red Army very well may be the single most powerful institution left in the Soviet Union. As the de facto commander of the Red Army, his role in the future leadership of the country would forever be sealed by victory over the Americans and English.

Zhukov was determined that not only the standing of the Red Army, but also his own position must remain paramount. Secretly, he admitted to himself that with the NKVD, a shell of its former self, a victorious Zhukov may very well find himself with an opportunity to do something that even a year ago would have been inconceivable. Never known as a political general, Zhukov knew he was delving into a world that was very different from that of the field of battle.

Perhaps, Comrade Stalin may find himself so incapacitated from his wounds that he would finally succumb in a fashion not so different from his predecessor, Comrade Lenin. Lenin, too, was quite ill and under constant medical care until he found himself under the thumb of the man who would eventually put him out of his misery, or so the story went. Only the Red Army would have the necessary prestige to keep the country and the new empire together.

As he walked through rooms once dominated by the Romanovs, Zhukov's final thought before he entered the meeting was perhaps he could get used to life away from the battlefield if surrounded by so many splendors. Shaking his head, *no, not yet…mustn't allow myself to lose focus, first we must smash the Americans and then the future will take care of itself.*

Walking into the middle of the discussion, Zhukov was dressed in his field uniform rather than his more official Marshal's parade ground clothes. Rugged and powerful, Zhukov couldn't have been more imposing, the very symbol of the Red Army. The first thing he noticed was the unsettling look on Comrade Stalin's face. The man looked horrible, somewhat stronger, but his eyes suggested that he hadn't slept in days.

Coming to full attention, he moved closer to Stalin and said, "Greetings, Comrade Stalin, you look much better. Glad to see that you're ready to watch as we smash the Imperialists."

The pain medication and blood pressure pills were taking their effect on the General Secretary, especially when they were being washed down with vodka. His hands still shook a bit from the tremors, but his eyes had fire in them. Reaching for his favorite general's hands, Stalin stood with difficulty to greet Zhukov. Stalin said, "Zhukov, good of you to come. I needed you here to tell these idiots that we mustn't fear the Americans or their bombs. You won't let the Motherland down, will you, Marshal Zhukov? These women here try to fill my mind with doubts. Tell me now, how long will it take to crush these traitorous backstabbers."

Zhukov's face never wavered for a moment, he looked Stalin right in the eyes and said, "Comrade Stalin, I assure you that within four to six weeks, the Americans and the British will have been taught a lesson that their people will not soon forget."

Turning to the rest of the toadies and staff personnel in the room, Zhukov's voice deepened and he said, "Whoever here fears the Americans and their bombs insults the honor of the Red Army and the brave Soviet people. Listen, Comrades, as I show you how we will crush them." Zhukov watched as Stalin took strength from his determined words, and Zhukov went on to set up his map display and brief the assembled leadership.

Those present at the meeting were Foreign Minister Khrushchev, Chief of Heavy Industry Malenkov, the NKVD man Merkulov, Kagonovich, Voroshilov, and several members of the Soviet General Staff. They watched with rapt attention as the Red Army's premier field commander briefed them in detail on the coming operations. Zhukov watched as Stalin studied the map display and nodded his head, as he seemed to grasp the operational framework for the attack.

Zhukov ended by saying, "Comrades, the Americans and English forces at times will put up determined resistance, but we will emerge victorious. We have shifted so much combat power forward opposite of their lines that when we attack it will be likened to a tidal wave. Our troops are battle hardened and ready to serve the Motherland once again on Comrade Stalin's behalf."

Turning to Stalin and looking direct in his soulless eyes, Zhukov said, "Comrade Stalin, I give you my absolute vow that the Red Army shall do its duty and you shall have your revenge on those traitors."

Stalin paused for a moment and finally asked, "Marshal Zhukov, what happens if the Americans figure out that we are about to attack them?"

"Comrade Stalin, it is already too late. There is no way that the Americans and English could make the necessary preparations or shift enough forces towards the front lines within the next twenty four to forty eight hours. We have amassed more than five million troops and thousands of tanks and guns within fifty miles of the front lines.

The Americans and British barely have two and a half million soldiers and they are spread out throughout France, Germany, and Italy. Plus, Comrades, they are soft. While our men survived by eating Spam every day, they ate ice cream. They will sting us, but not stop us."

Voroshilov was not considered to be much of a military man these days, but he still sat in the inner circle with Stalin. The old Marshal asked, "But what of their airpower? The Americans destroyed German tanks, guns, even whole cities with their attack aircraft. What good is all of these men if they cannot reach the battlefield?"

Zhukov thought, *at least all the vodka the man drinks hasn't completely made him brain dead yet.* American airpower was the one great variable that worried him. Zhukov and his staff had a very low opinion of American infantry and the American tankers with their under gunned Sherman tanks caused him little concern. Even though studies by the General Staff indicated the Red Air Force would be able to contest for control of the skies, Zhukov had many doubts.

Shaking his head up and down and with a bit of a grimace, he answered, "Marshal Voroshilov, you are right to consider the power of the American and English forces in the air. It is their greatest strength by far. However, unlike the Germans, the Red Air Force is quite strong and we intend strike a mighty blow in the opening hours of the offensive. We will take losses, comrades, in the air and on the ground from their planes, but in the end, we will be washing our feet in the Rhine while their air force retreats back to England." By the looks on their faces, he knew it was a good answer.

And so it went on like this for the next hour, one question after the other. After exhausting all of their questions, Stalin stood from his seat and walked over to Zhukov and led him out of the room. Clearly uneasy with the move, Zhukov did his best to help brace the limping ruler of the Kremlin. Stalin wanted to sneak away from his many enemies. He knew they all secretly enjoyed watching him suffer. Stalin could barely hear what was being said, but he could read what was going through their devious minds. He knew that Malenkov and Khrushchev and the others couldn't wait for the day when they could seize power.

Stalin knew that by crushing the Americans in one fell swoop, his position would be secure and Zhukov would guarantee the security of his rule and oversee the new Soviet empire. Zhukov was the one man he could trust. Stalin remembered it was Zhukov who took control of events when the NKVD let him down.

So, he stopped and motioned for the two of them to sit on a couch in the hallway. Unsure what to expect, Zhukov merely asked, "Comrade Stalin, you should be husbanding your strength, not wasting any effort by seeing me to the door. You need your rest."

With trembling hand, Stalin patted Zhukov on the knee and spoke with genuine sincerity, "Georgii Konstantinovich, I wanted a word before you left. There is nothing but a nest of vipers in that room, all waiting for me to have a stroke. You and I should talk before you go off to finish the Americans."

Zhukov couldn't shake the feeling that he felt as if he were talking to a real human being. Zhukov said," Comrade Stalin, nonsense, you have nothing to fear from anyone. Remember it was the failings of Beria for the debacle in Berlin, not some conspiracy against you."

"You trust too easily, Georgii, but if you say that I have nothing to fear, then I trust you. Just don't fail me or the State. The State does not tolerate failure, Georgii, you know that."

Zhukov's eyes betrayed him for a moment, as he watched the old Stalin shine through for a moment. Uncomfortable with those last chilling words, Zhukov stood and said, "I must leave, Comrade Stalin, if I am to attend to the many last minute details for the attack. All I can say is that no matter what happens, I will do my duty for the Motherland and in the end we shall smash them." With that said, he turned and left for the airport.

Zhukov tried to shake off Stalin's parting words. Despite his wounds, Stalin still managed to come across as menacing, even chilling. Hearing those words again, "The State does not tolerate failure...,"

Thinking back to that animal, Beria, Zhukov had to admit one failure was all it took to destroy someone who once appeared all-powerful.

Angry at himself for allowing such thoughts at this late moment, he pulled a vodka filled flask out and decided to drink and pass the time reading the file outlining a proposed NKVD operation. Automatically distrusting anything originating from Merkulov, he took a strong pull on the flask and read on. After about ten minutes of reading he had to admit that if they could pull it off, it would sure as hell help.

Still, the very nature of the operation seemed too underhanded for the conventional military man in Zhukov. Plus, he didn't want anything to raise the stock of the NKVD in the ruling circles in the Kremlin. After several more drinks from the flask, the hum of the propellers started to make Zhukov drowsy.

As he closed his eyes, he envisioned a huge map display with unit markings and huge red arrows pointing west. He knew the plan, the march tables, the re-enforcement schedules, everything. In his mind, he watched the steady advance of the red tide engulf the defending Western forces. Soon Operation Stalin's Revenge would be remembered as his greatest triumph. As he drifted off to sleep, he thought no one would remember the Chekists and their Operation Red Spark.

Chapter Forty Six

August 25, 1945, 8:30 a.m.

Hamburg, Headquarters of the British XII Corps

Field Marshal Sir Bernard Montgomery was a man on a mission. For the past week he sat in his headquarters on the outskirts of Dortmund in the German Ruhr, and he listened as his staff continued to report significant movement of Soviet forces on their side of the demarcation line. In the past five days alone, there were more than three dozen reports of Soviet aircraft violating British airspace in the vicinity of Hamburg and Hanover, plus the disturbing fact that the bloody Soviets went off the airwaves about ten days ago.

The only thing his Signals people could come up with were short transmissions, but without any rhyme or reason to them. The occasional German refugees that made the harrowing journey past the line of Russian outposts spoke of huge numbers of Russians building up on the other side of the Elbe River. Usually, Montgomery paid little heed to such first-hand reports, as it had been his experience that civilians rarely have anything of interest or use to add, but when added up with everything else that seemed in the works, it was making things feel quite a bit dicey.

Never could trust the Russians, Montgomery always thought of them as a rather cheeky people, lie right to your face. The commander of the British Second Army, General Miles Dempsey was becoming increasingly agitated himself and already issued orders to all commands within fifty miles of the Soviet occupation zone to begin preparing fortified defensive zones.

Very quietly, ammo dumps were being opened, fuel depots established along supply routes, and a general heightened alert status for British units in Second Army. *Not like Dempsey to jump the gun*, so Monty decided nothing like seeing things for himself to get a feel for the situation.

Montgomery had been chafing at the bit ever since the clash of arms between American and Russian forces. As a commander who understood how to handle men on the battlefield, the after-action reports were quite disquieting. The Yanks and the Russians really had at it by all reports. Casualties were quite nasty for some supposed border incident. Why would the Soviets keep counter-attacking if the Yanks pulled back?

To a man who liked to keep a tidy battlefield, the whole action was far too emotional, especially the Russians. Granted the Poles and Czechs were making waves but there was still no reason to waste a good brigade's worth of troops.

More troubling were the orders coming from Ike's headquarters. The British Field Marshal had always felt that Eisenhower was in over his head, possessing absolutely no feel for the battlefield. Even so, he never expected such passive reactions, considering American forces were the ones who had been hit by the Soviet fire. Only a direct order from his superior, Marshal Alan Brooke, to stand down his own forces and make no moves to either reinforce or construct new fortifications, kept him from responding to the Soviet provocations.

But after a week of constant reports of imminent danger, he decided that Ike be damned. So he left his headquarters and decided to inspect his most exposed command, covering the approaches to Hamburg, the XII Corp under Lt. General Ritchie and put things in order.

Love him or hate him, and most felt one way or the other, the average British "Tommy" loved the man. Monty's reputation of husbanding his forces, massing his combat power, and preparing the battlefield so as to achieve complete supremacy prior to battle saved the lives of countless British soldiers. For men who grew up on the horror stories from their fathers and uncles who served under the notorious General Haig during the First World War, such discretion was welcomed. Haig knowingly threw his forces into the teeth of German entrenched positions again and again, without regard to losses.

The words Passchendaele, the Somme, and countless other foolhardy attacks killed hundreds of thousands of British soldiers and Montgomery, who was severely wounded himself, refused to waste his soldiers needlessly.

Most American commanders especially Patton and Bradley came to loathe Monty and all but accused him of being too timid on the battlefield. Montgomery in turn believed the Americans to be amateurs at best on the battlefield and the war effort would have been best served if all those wonderfully hardy American lads would have been parceled out to serve under British officers under his direct command.

Regardless, Montgomery was a consummate professional who knew his troops, was a tenacious opponent, and utterly unflappable in times of chaos. He decided to have a look himself and then make whatever decisions to protect his command that he felt necessary. If the bloody Russians were going to have a go at it, then he'd be damned if his men were going to be caught with their britches down.

After about two hours of motoring around the 53rd Welsh Infantry Division defending the northern approaches to Hamburg, Montgomery was not pleased at all. Like all field grade officers, Montgomery could do a field inspection and tell within a few short hours whether or not a unit was ready or if the defensive layout would hold up. In this case, he was less than pleased with either at the moment.

For the past four months, the 53rd Welsh and every other Allied unit was organized as occupiers, not preparing for battle. Artillery positions were exposed, hardly any ammunition was stocked near the guns, his tank units hadn't fired from their tubes in months, and what defenses were in evidence were those left by the bloody Germans after he captured the city back in April.

The only thing his forces looked to have done was to help clear the streets, repair bridges, and help the staggering number of refugees moving through the city. Even with Dempsey's call to begin preparing defensive positions, the men were still moving at a peacetime pace.

With a disgusted sneer on his face, he pointed to the collapsed line of trenches in the distance and said with barely held contempt, "General Ross, this simply will not due. What in blazes have your people been doing other than running soup kitchens and consorting with German prostitutes? For God's sake man, maybe you haven't heard, but we've got Ivan massing their forces about thirty kilometers from this very spot and your command is in utter disarray. What do you have to say for yourself?"

General Ross stammered a bit at the rebuke, then answered sharply, "Field Marshal Montgomery, General Dempsey never mentioned that we were on an official war footing and I don't recall receiving a single command from 21st Army group, either, for that matter."

"Don't try to be clever, Ross. It doesn't suit you. If Ivan comes over the top tomorrow, half your command won't last two hours on this battlefield and you bloody well know it."

General Ritchie just stood there listening as one of his officers took it on the chin, knowing full well that Montgomery was going to blast him later. Ross is right about one thing, Ritchie thought, the British system does not encourage the type of initiative that Montgomery was taking him to task for, and Monty knew it.

Turning to have a better look at an anti-tank ditch that had been half filled in last week by engineers looking to prepare prime farmland for planting, an aide interrupted with a cable. Reading quickly, Ritchie's eyebrows narrowed and then his eyes went wide as he understood the implications.

Taking a breath, he tapped the Field Marshal on the shoulder and said, "Excuse me sir, but really I must have a word."

"Now is not the time to save your man from embarrassment. If you had been doing your job properly, then I wouldn't have to."

Ignoring the rebuke and Monty's ugly sneer, Ritchie blurted out, "Sir, my staff has just informed me that we have someone back at headquarters that has some rather ticklish information. Perhaps we should cut things short here, sir, and see to this immediately."

Already angry by everything he had seen this morning, Monty was about to blast the both of them when Ritchie cut him off again. "SIR, I really must insist. Look, my chief of staff just sent this urgent dispatch. They found a Pole, sir, from the Home Army. The man had made a rather harrowing journey. He apparently commandeered a small crop dusting plane and flew over the Russian lines and landed within our zone last night. Poor fellow, plane got shot up and he was severely wounded as a result, but the man all but crawled through the night to get us this information. It seems that this chap has some rather pressing news to go to so much trouble."

Pausing for a moment, barely believing it himself, Ritchie continued, "Sir, the man had pictures, maps, and official papers from the Home Army commander, General Anders, all of which indicate that Ivan is about to launch a full-scale offensive, perhaps as early as tomorrow morning. My intelligence chap has already vetted the man through contacts with the London Poles, sir. I know this will have to be kicked upstairs, but I really think we would all be best served if we moved at once and speak to the man, just to be sure."

Not easily silenced, Field Marshal Montgomery just stood there staring at his subordinate. General Ritchie was a solid officer, had a bad go of it back in the North African desert. Rommel gave the man fits and a few black eyes awhile back, but the man came back and commanded the British XII Corps with some distinction ever since the Normandy invasion. As shocked as Monty felt, Ritchie looked nearly paralyzed with the awesome implications for his command.

Slowly nodding his head as he reread the dispatch from Ritchie's Chief of Staff, Monty shook off the initial shock and, in the very finest English tradition and offered up a stiff upper lip look and immediately went about issuing orders. Within fifteen minutes the entire 53rd Welsh Infantry Division went on full alert and the rest of

Twenty First Army Group soon followed and was placed on alert one status.

RAF planes were immediately scrambled and seen mounting patrols overhead. British units throughout northern Germany started filling their fuel tanks, live ammo was distributed, and men started reporting back to their battalions for full deployment. Refusing to waste one bloody second, Monty decided to assume the worst. If this was some bloody bluff, then this would turn out to be the biggest drill the British Army had run since the end of the war. All he knew was that if Ivan were looking to cross the Elbe River, then he would do his best to give him a bloody nose.

Still, Monty wasn't blind to the realities facing his command. Most of his forces were utterly unprepared for a major engagement. Looking at the map again, he made one crucial decision; he ordered the entire First Canadian Army along with the Polish Armored Division to pullback and begin constructing a defensive line to cover the Weser River crossings.

Doing the math, Montgomery had already decided the British Second Army with the VIII, XII, and XXX Corps would cover the main approaches and pray they could hold them up long enough for the Yanks to send reinforcements. If the Yanks were unable to redeploy in time, then fortifications along that Weser line would be absolutely crucial.

As the lorry came to a halt, his last thought was to get on a secure line and tell Eisenhower everything. Refusing to give counsel to his fears, Montgomery decided at that very moment to take personal command of the forward battle. Every instinct that Montgomery possessed told him that this would be the field of decision. With a black pen, Montgomery made a large circle which encompassed the cities of Hamburg, Hanover, and Bremen, everything between the Elbe River and the Weser.

The British Army would make its stand here and go toe-to-toe with Ivan, leaving no doubt that His Majesty's forces would do their duty for King and Country.

August 25, 1945, 9:45 a.m.

Frankfurt, SHAEF Headquarters

Sitting in a sparsely furnished office in the basement of the wartime IG Farben Corporate headquarters, General Patton and his two main aides, Colonels Koch and Harkins, waited impatiently for their so–called day in court. The three of them had been waiting outside General Eisenhower's conference room since 8:30 sharp, so as to be ready for their nine a.m. appointment.

Patton looked like hell. Koch looked over at the old man who barely slept a wink all night. The three of them drove thru the night to make the appointment and hopefully find some way to get to Ike before General Smith crucified them all. Nothing doing, as Smith made sure Patton and his men were persona non-gratis at SHAEF Headquarters.

In fact, the few who at least talked to Koch or Harkins spent more time asking where they think they will get posted once Patton packs his bags and heads to the States. Koch brought with him every single scrap of information that he and his team had put together in the past two weeks, while Harkins decided to take personal responsibility for explaining the use of German POW's in and around the Pilsen fortified zone. He had already decided that if they would accept his head on the platter, he was ready to give it to protect his benefactor.

General Patton's emotions were swirling out of control as he ventured from pure rage to quiet depression and back again. Koch felt the general still couldn't believe that Ike would really pull the trigger this time. They all knew Patton was in and out of the doghouse more than all the other generals in the European Theater of Operations put together, but he also was the best combat commander in the US Army.

Koch refused to believe that Ike would force him out, but the general was clearly nervous as hell. Worse, it was past nine, almost nine fifteen when some staff officer told them to move to the basement until General Eisenhower called for them.

So, they continued to wait. Finally, having run out of what little patience he possessed, Patton pounded on the adjoining door to the next office and bellowed, "Smith, you goddamn pussy footed coward, if you're in there come the hell out and get this over with, you son-of-a bitch."

Patton grabbed the door handle, tried twisting it, but to no avail. So then he started kicking the door and pounding on it so hard that Harkins finally jumped up and tried to pull the General away. Patton barked, "Harkins get the hell away from me. If that bastard won't let me in there, then, goddamn it, he's got listen to me through the door. You hear me, you chicken shit, Smith?"

"General, we don't even know if he's behind the door, and if he is, then you can be sure that this won't help matters."

Stopping short of kicking the door again, Patton put his hands out in mock surrender, and said, "Goddamnit Harkins, the next time I start making an ass out of myself, you have permission to shoot me. Right now, they'd probably give you a medal. Why don't they just come on down and get it over with?"

The three of them sat for the next twenty minutes in near silence. All Patton could think was what would happen to his beloved Third

Army if the shit hit the fan and he was relieved of command. Patton loved Third Army and couldn't bear the thought of his imminent disgrace.

Then, breaking the silence, a latch moved and in walked General Eisenhower. The three of them snapped to attention and waited for the Supreme Commander to put them at ease. Ike looked deadly serious. He didn't say a word as he walked right over to Patton and stood in front of him.

Eisenhower was all business, he looked Patton up and down and asked, "George, I'm going to ask you one thing and you better tell me the whole truth. Did you disobey a direct order and began to fortify the area around Pilsen? I want a yes or no out of you."

Sensing that Ike was not in the mood for one ounce of bullshit, Patton stood completely ramrod at attention and answered, "You're goddamn right I did."

Not hesitating for a second, Ike followed with, "While you were disobeying a direct order, did you also organize and put to work a quasi-military formation of German POW's to help with this construction?"

Knowing he was on pretty thin ice with this one, all Patton could do was nod his head up and down, and say, "Yes, sir. It seemed at the time to be the best way to prepare the battlefield. I decided to make do with what resources I had on hand."

"You know this could end your career, George. Why?"

Without hesitation, Patton blurted out, "Because those Red bastards aren't going to stop until they control all of Europe and I can't bear the thought of Third Army soldiers dying because I didn't have the balls to disobey a direct order."

Afraid that he went too far, Patton closed his eyes and bit his tongue. Grim faced, Ike moved closer to Patton and asked in a deadly serious voice, "If the Russians come across tomorrow, could you hold?"

Without missing a beat, Patton said," If those Commie sons of bitches look to attack Third Army, I'll personally kick their Asses all the way back to Moscow, if you'll let me." His eyes starting to moisten up a bit, Patton's high pitched voice broke a bit as he asked," Will you let me, Ike? Can I keep Third Army?"

Pausing for what seemed an eternity to Patton, Ike thought about the firestorm that let loose when word of Montgomery's call hit SHAEF barely an hour ago. Under intense pressure from his Chief of Staff, General Smith, Ike was prepared to cashier Patton and send him home for his outright insubordination.

Ike knew he had done everything possible to maintain relations with the Soviets, and for the past three weeks, Allied forces stood down across the demarcation line. Ike refused to authorize a single provocative act, no recon incursions, no massing troops near the border, no fortifying the border, nothing, all in hopes that whatever was happening could somehow be de-escalated.

Monty's call this morning ended those hopes, and if the Polish agent was, in fact, telling the truth, then the bulk of the Soviet Army would have been allowed to mass in such overwhelming numbers that they could overrun most of Ike's forward positions, causing massive casualties. *Damn them.*

Ike felt like a fool. All along George and others had been right, but in the end, he had a job to do. So after a series of quick phone calls with Montgomery and Bradley, he ordered the mobilization of all Allied forces in the European Theater.

Allied tactical air forces immediately began patrolling along the forward edge of the border zone with armed recon missions into the Soviet zone planned for later in the morning. Ike was going to find out what was on the other side, one way or the other. Still, Ike didn't know how in the hell he was going to get his forces ready on such short notice.

He shuddered at the thought of what would have happened if this Pole never showed up, and the Russians were able to hit his command without a hint of warning. It would have been utter chaos, a catastrophe in the making. Remembering the disparity in forces, Ike thought it still might be.

General Eisenhower decided the moment he got word from Monty that now was not the time to be without one of his key commanders. Patton may be a pain in the ass in peacetime, but in the days to come, Ike knew he would probably need Patton like never before. Without a doubt, if the Russians came at them in full force, it would be the largest military battle the American Army will have ever seen. *If Patton and Third Army can slow them down or better yet stop them cold around Pilsen, it may help buy enough time to absorb the hammer blows sure to fall up North against the Brits.*

Finally, after an eternity, Ike said, "George not only can you keep Third Army, but we're probably going to need your boys more than ever…those defenses around Pilsen better hold or else God knows what will happen."

Feeling absolutely elated, Patton couldn't believe what the hell just happened. Ike drew this out so much that he thought for sure his ass was gone. "Jesus Christ, Ike, what the hell happened to make you save my ass from that son of a bitch Smith?"

Raising his eyebrows in a way that spoke volumes, Patton instantly picked up on his former subordinate's body language and asked, "So, I'm not so damn crazy, am I? When are they going to hit us?"

Not in the mood for any "I told you so," Ike grunted, and told the story of the documents found on the Polish Home Army courier and how they came to Field Marshal Montgomery's attention. "George, worst case scenario has the Russians hitting our lines within the next forty-eight hours. We're simply not prepared. So I need you to get back down to Third Army and place your command on war footing. Further orders and intelligence will be sent as they come through. Any questions?"

Feeling more like himself, Patton straightened out his uniform and started moving around the office, visualizing the coming battle. What to do was obvious, "Ike, hit the bastards now when they are at their most vulnerable. Now's not the time for half-measures. We should hit them right this second with every goddamn plane and artillery shell within range. If we can disrupt their initial assault forces, we can buy some time."

"Now hold it a minute, George. Don't be so damned quick to start firing off orders to me. You were just about to get yourself fired fifteen minutes ago. Let me make this clear to you, you are not authorized to fire so much as a spitball at the Russians. If this Pole is wrong, and we attack them with full force, then it will be our fault that the war started. You know that I can't risk that, the President would never approve it."

Forgetting himself, Patton couldn't believe Ike was still playing politics instead of acting like a commander. "Are you out of your mind, Ike! You gave the bastards a free ride for the past three weeks. At least let's hit the sons of bitches where we can do the most damage. If you wait until they have attacked, then you've given up our best chance to attrit the hell out of their first echelon forces."

Not liking the way Patton came back at him, Ike squared his shoulders and tersely commanded, "George, you are hereby instructed to return to Third Army this instant and put Third Army's defensive campaign into operation. You will be informed directly from me when, or if, you can initiate offensive operations against Soviet forces. SHAEF reserves the right to make that decision, not you. Is that understood?"

Patton knew Ike wouldn't budge, so rather than waste time, he put his hand out and shook Ike's hand and said, "Ike, thanks for not firing my ass. Third Army will do everything we can to hold the line and then kick them in the ass. I just hope like hell we get a couple more days or the first seventy-two hours will be the worst three days in the history of the American Army. Remember Ike, no matter what happens, don't lose your nerve. If we can absorb the first punch, then we got a chance to beat the bastards."

Chapter Forty Seven

August 25, 1945, 1:30 PM

Wiesbaden, Germany

General Bradley's Twelfth Army Group Headquarters

It was a little over three and a half hours since the imminent hostilities alert came in from SHAEF Headquarters, and already things appeared quite chaotic. The telephone exchange was flooded with calls from excited Corp and Division commanders looking for orders. What started as a few dozen exchanges by high-ranking officers quickly turned into a flood of regimental and battalion grade officers looking for everything from intelligence to supplies.

Frantic staff officers of the Twelfth Army Group had little in the way of firm contingency plans set up and had to keep putting off increasingly angry requests for some kind of information or deployment orders. Other than plans for localized defense, no one had ordered the staff to seriously prepare a defensive plan for a theater wide attack by the Soviet Union. When the shit hit the fan earlier in the month, most Corp and Division commanders followed Ike's orders to the letter. Some enterprising commanders did their best to start accumulating supplies, fuel, and instituted accelerated training schedules for the new troops, but that was about it.

The emergency alert had an unreal quality to it. Not a single Corp command in the American First or Ninth Army was even remotely ready to form a continuous defensive line. Units were spread out all over the United States occupation zone. It didn't take a three star general to figure out that it could take as much as three days just to completely rearrange the two armies and set up a continuous defensive line.

Already rumors were spreading that Russian fifth columns were lurking behind every bush and treetop. More than a dozen units reported seeing Russian tanks moving towards American lines. Jumpy anti-aircraft gunners reported firing on Soviet planes, but unfortunately, the actual result was two downed Allied airmen and another three planes shot the hell up. For professional staff officers, this was hardly an auspicious beginning.

At least Patton in Bavaria, with his Third Army, looked somewhat ready to receive an attack, but that did little good for the dozens of American divisions strung out all over the rest of Germany. Patton's operations people were already transmitting Third Army unit dispositions, reinforcement schedule, and supply situation.

Bradley couldn't help but shake his head at his old boss. No wonder Patton almost got sacked, by the looks of these maps George must have been working his troops day and night for the past three weeks. *Christ, the crazy bastard already has minefields laid out, concrete bunkers in place, anti-tank ditches. The Russians won't know what hit them.*

Taking his glasses off for a moment, Bradley thought it's a good thing one of his armies has their zone in order, because preliminary numbers about the possible size of the Soviet offensive capability was enough to send a chill through his tired bones. Deciding that every minute counted, he ordered his staff to prepare operational movement orders, giving his divisional commanders wide latitude in establishing defensive positions. He planned on sending more detailed orders later in the afternoon.

Bradley called an emergency conference to begin coordinating a defense. First Army commander, Lt. General Courtney Hodges, and Ninth Army commander, Lt. General Simpson, were ordered to meet at two o'clock at Twelfth Army Headquarters with all of their respective Corp commanders and key staff people. They were going to get a handle on things or there would be hell to pay. All everyone knew was that, as tense as many felt, it could be worse. There could have been no warning at all. The very thought was enough to scare the bejesus out of anyone.

First Army officers and staff arrived first as they were closest to Bradley's headquarters. Their commander, General Courtney Hodges, was an infantry soldier all the way. He joined up as an enlisted man in 1904, later got a commission and won the Distinguished Service Cross during the First World War while serving in the Fifth Infantry Division. He was known prior to the war as a small-unit tactics man who made his mark as commander of the Army's Infantry School at Fort Benning. Bradley chose him because they had similar philosophies and he had a reputation as a solid performer who did not rock the boat.

However, many believed that his handling of First Army was less than stellar throughout the campaign. His units were unprepared to fight the Germans in the bocage of Normandy. He gutted half a dozen good divisions with plodding attacks into the Huertegan Forest in the Autumn of 1944, and got caught with his pants down during the Battle of the Bulge. By the end of the war, Hodges looked quite old and worn down.

Although Hodges couldn't compare with the more flamboyant Patton, Bradley stood by his man. Quickly pulled back from a scheduled redeployment to the Pacific Theater once things started heating up with the Soviets, Hodges spent the month initiating a serious training program throughout First Army to bring new, green soldiers, just in country, up to snuff. The man did what he did best and that was teaching soldiers to fight.

The Ninth Army commander, Lieutenant General William Simpson, or Big Simp, was tall and lanky and had a long face that seemed even longer as a result of his shaved head. Simpson was as quiet as he was effective. After graduating from West Point, he served with distinction as a battalion commander during the Meuse-Argonne Offensive during the First World War. He later went through all of the key command schools, and rose up to command a stateside Army Corp and later oversaw the Fourth Army, which was largely a training formation. For his expert handling of each succeeding command, Simpson was awarded the prestigious command of the Ninth Army six weeks into the Normandy campaign.

General Simpson's Ninth Army served under Montgomery for much of the campaign but also served under Bradley's Twelfth Army Group off and on during the later stages of the war. The only time he complained was when Monty refused to allow his Ninth Army any share of the assault on the Rhine in March. All Simpson did was kill Germans with little fanfare and with a great appreciation of the need to protect his soldiers from unnecessary casualties. Simpson kept a cool head in a crisis and, in the days ahead, Bradley would count upon the big lanky Texan to keep his army under control.

By quarter past two, most of the general officers and their staffs had arrived for the briefing. The mood was grim. Many were frustrated at the lack of information and would rather have been back with their divisions and corps, but without a framework, it would have led to more chaos. Not a single shot had been fired, yet many already looked worse for the wear. They had all read the reports, talked to German POWS, and knew the tremendous capabilities of the Red Army.

The Soviets had managed to create, perhaps, the most powerful land army in the history of mankind and defeated, in an epic battle, the deadly Nazi war machine. The Russians, for all intents and purposes, rewrote the German blitzkrieg strategies and applied them on scale that devastated the German Army.

Now, this same army was massing in force and if the rumors were true, ready to unleash the full power of the Red Army against the Western Allies. Those units closest to the Russians were the most exposed and most in need of some type of operational orders designed to absorb the initial blows. The veteran combat commanders assembled knew that without much in the way of fortified barriers, it wouldn't take much to find gaping holes to attack into the American rear areas. Exposed units were going to have to hold the line under tremendous pressure, some until the last man.

Most were surprised when General Bradley walked up to the podium to start the briefing. Bradley felt these men needed to hear from the horses' mouth, so to speak. Bradley was known as the "GI General". Although not regarded as a brilliant tactician, Ike counted upon his steady nerve and professional demeanor throughout the European campaign.

Bradley was no Patton, and no one expected some rousing speech. These men wanted information and orders most of all, whatever inspiration that would be needed would have to be found in each man in the days to come. Huge map displays were set up for everyone to view while, at the same time, written op orders were being handed out to all the principals in the room.

Bradley started, "Gentlemen, as you are all aware, General Eisenhower declared a formal emergency and ordered the entire European command to go on official war footing. At 0930 hours this morning, we received confirmation of an impending Soviet attack aimed at expelling the American and British armies out of Germany and off the continent for good. I called this meeting to brief you on how we are going to stop them, and have no doubt, gentlemen, we will stop them."

Several of the officers called out confirming Bradley's words, but now was not the time for false bravado. Bradley stared everyone down. "The American Army will be tested in the comings days. We all will be tested and your men will be looking to you to provide leadership. I don't want to hear one damn thing about what should have been done or what could have been done. We may have less than twenty fours to prepare our commands, so the decisions we make now are crucial. Ike has already ordered a series of armed reconnaissance missions for later this afternoon, so we should be getting better intelligence in the next three hours. Any questions?"

No surprise the first man to stand and offer up a question was the commander of the VII Corps, Major General Lightning Joe Collins. Many considered him the best American Corps commander in Europe. His unit was quite exposed and if the Russians came, his men would bear the initial blows. "Sir, I request permission to begin immediate artillery attacks across the border against suspected Soviet assembly sites."

Quickly General Bradley answered, "Permission denied, Joe. Ike has ordered all Allied forces to assume a defensive posture and to provide no pretext for the Soviets to attack. Look, if somehow all the intelligence data is wrong, then the last thing we want to do is to provoke the Soviets. But don't worry, call it a gut call, I suspect we're all going to get our chance to shoot at Russians before this whole thing is over."

Frustrated at the answer, Collins fired back, "What about preparing roads, bridges, trees and the like for demolition?"

Bradley answered, "Those divisions in the forward areas are expected to begin a crash program to defend your command. Minefields, patrols, and whatever preparations needed to fortify your positions are hereby ordered."

Another outspoken Corps commander, this time from the Ninth Army stood to speak. Major General Matthew Ridgeway, commander of the XVIII Airborne Corps, was younger than most but made a fearsome reputation throughout the war. Cutting right to the chase, he asked, "General Bradley, has there been any formal arrangement made with our English neighbors to the north as to how to tie together our defenses? The British are pretty exposed up there. They are understrength to begin with, plus they are defending the flattest terrain in Germany. Can we count on Monty to hold his end up?"

There was no love lost between Bradley and Montgomery. Hell, there was no love lost between the American and British armies, but there was a grudging respect. Drawing off this respect, Bradley got a little annoyed and responded, "Matt, you just worry about your end, Ike will figure a way to tie in with Monty on your flank. Keep in mind, there is nowhere for the Brits to go. Look at the map, there won't be any Dunkirk's on this one…for any of us for that matter. They will either hold or they will be destroyed in detail."

General Ridgeway was not entirely happy with Bradley's response. Ridgeway wanted concrete answers, and soon, because he had been studying this situation for the past three weeks and thought the numbers just didn't add up. If the Russians brought to bear what they are capable, then he couldn't see how the British forces could possibly hold them up for more than five days at best.

His XVIII Corp anchored the line just south of Hanover, and if Russian forces broke through British defenses, then his command could be taken in the rear. Shaking his head, he had a very bad feeling about what was to come. Unconsciously touching the grenades attached to his combat field jacket, he wondered if he was going to have to have the opportunity to use them himself.

General Bradley could feel the tension rising in the room. The men wanted answers and fast. To a man, they wanted t get back to their commands as fast as possible and start getting ready for the fighting to come. Sensing that taking any more questions would only prolong things and probably end up being counterproductive, Bradley decided to quickly lay out the deployment scheme.

"Gentlemen, time is short, so I will get right down to it. Although information is sketchy and will probably remain so for some time to come, this is what we must be prepared to stop. As you are all aware, the Red Army can field as many as six million soldiers, with upwards of ten thousand tanks and self-propelled guns, and supported by tens of thousands of light to heavy caliber guns and howitzers. This army is huge, hits hard and moves fast. We believe they will attack on a wide front, with an ultimate goal to capture Antwerp and to cross the Rhine River in force.

"After his fight with the Russians in July, General Patton's Third Army already began constructing defensive works centered around the communication hub of Pilsen in Czechoslovakia and anchored his defenses to cover the approaches to Bavaria. Third Army has good terrain and will slow the Russians down enough to give us breathing room or, at least, so I've been told. Ike told me that he's already promised Patton another front cover shot on Time Magazine if he holds out for two weeks. We all know with Georgie that all but guarantees he'll hold."

That little bit of levity brought some much needed nervous laughter from the assembled officers who all knew Patton's reputation as a media hog. As in any army, there is a great deal of rivalry, especially between the First and Third, but *if Patton's men can hold down south, the officers of the First Army wouldn't give a damn how much press he gets if it gives them a chance to set up their own defenses.*

Shaking his head to clear his thoughts, he realized he paused for far longer than he thought and whatever laughter was in the room had long since passed. Closing his eyes, he knew these men didn't just want some type of direction. They needed it, and he needed to feel like he did something to get them ready for what was to come.

Clenching his fists, he snapped back to attentions and said, "Gentlemen I apologize for the delay. I think that in the days to come, we're all going to have moments where we get lost in our own thoughts, even fears. Whether we like it or not, the Russians are probably coming and the American Army has to find some way to stop them. This enemy will be like nothing we have ever faced before. More powerful and unrelenting than the Nazis and they won't stop coming until we utterly defeat them. We will all face decisions in the coming days which will try our souls. Men will be sacrificed. Units will be lost."

To make his point felt, he forcefully added, "That's right, I said units, as in whole units. We all read action reports about fighting on the Eastern Front. The Germans lost tens of thousands of men in any given week during Russian offensives. We must steel ourselves for the battles to come."

Sensing his words were having the intended effect, Bradley continued, "Make them pay for each yard that they take. Don't give up any terrain cheaply. Once you have a strong position, give them hell until the last possible moment and only then move back to the next prepared line. Counter-attack at the first opportunity to keep them off guard. Remember they took unbelievable losses during the war and have reached the end of their manpower reserves. They need to win and win fast. Each day we hold the line, means another day that they are weaker and brings us closer to stopping them. You will all do your best that much I know. I just pray that our best will be good enough. May God bless you and your men and give us all the strength to defeat our enemies and secure the peace."

Bradley then adjourned the meeting, but wanted to speak with Courtney and Simp. Pulling his two senior commanders aside, Bradley asked what they thought. Both Simpson and Hodges were on the quiet side and waited for the other to answer their boss.

Finally, General Simpson answered, "Well Brad, you sure paint a hell of a bleak picture. I have to tell you that my boys just aren't ready yet. Hell, maybe if we had a week, even five days, then I could say that we could really give them hell, but I just don't know."

General Hodges echoed the point, "Brad, Simp is right. If the Russians come across within the next seventy two hours, I'm afraid they will catch units on the move and just tear the hell out of them."

Simpson added, "Courtney, you're lucky partner. At least, you got some decent terrain to cover. I got fifty miles of open terrain from south of Hanover to the Hartz Mountains to cover. The Russians aren't stupid. If they get mobile forces through this gap, they can get to the Weser and either take the Brits to the north or come at your left flank. All I know is that we better get control of the air and damn fast. If we can begin to attrite them from the air, it ought to slow them down a bit. Matt was right, we need to start hitting them now with everything we've got while they are still moving towards their final assembly areas."

Nodding in agreement, Hodges didn't envy his counterpart in Ninth Army. Worse, Hodges figured it wouldn't be too long before Ninth Army would pass to Montgomery's command. Hodges hated Montgomery and wouldn't ever serve under him again after the way he acted during the Bulge. *Now it'll be his turn to feel his oats in the fire. See how he likes it.*

Bradley listened to his two commanders and worked out a general phase line of first and secondary battle lines. General Bradley said, "Look I don't know how else to say it other than you two have to hold the initial attack in check until I can get enough reserves in place to prevent any major breakthroughs. In three days, I'll have elements of Gerow's Fifteenth Army moving to back the both of you up and plug any gaps that come up."

Reaching out his hand to both men and with a look of determined resolve, all Bradley said, "Do your best and give them hell."

August 25, 1945, 11:30 pm

Wolfsburg, Germany

Colonel-General Pavel Semenovich Rybalko, commander of the Third Guards Tank Army, listened to the sounds of unfamiliar aircraft engines overhead and knew the element of surprise had been lost. General Rybalko was widely considered the premier Soviet tank commander of the war. For Rybalko, speed and daring was everything on the battlefield.

He had served under Marshal Konev during the last stages of the war and Rybalko came to respect the First Ukrainian Front Commander for his understanding of the proper use of armored forces. Rybalko cared little for the more brutish command style of Zhukov, who was often times more inclined to run over his enemies instead of moving around them.

Rybalko believed Konev would be missed during the days ahead. Nevertheless, because of his reputation, Rybalko was given the honor of leading his command on one of the key projected breakthrough routes. His objective was to secure the southern hinge of the encirclement operation south of Hanover. Intelligence indicated a mixed force of British and newly arriving American forces would be opposing his attack. In his mind, it mattered little if he came up against either Western force.

Rybalko knew if his men could defeat the SS in their powerful Panther and Tiger tanks, then his tankers would roll over the Americans with their under gunned Shermans opposing him. Earlier in the evening, at the last staff meeting prior to the assault, he slammed the map table hard and yelled, "SPEED, SPEED, and more SPEED!" His men knew that, to Rybalko, speed meant everything and he planned to hit the Americans and English so fast they wouldn't know what hit them.

Walking over to a tank park, near some of his follow-up brigades, Rybalko couldn't help but rub down the thick steel hull of one of the newly arriving heavy tanks, the new JS-II, Stalin tanks. This monster weighed forty-six tons, had a 122mm gun and almost five inches of solid armor to protect the crew. *Oh yes*, he thought, *while my nimble T-34's roam the enemy flanks, I will send you right up the middle, blasting anything that moves.*

In Rybalko's mind, the correlation of forces were clear. He could bring to bear an enormous amount of combat power at the place of his choosing and there was precious little the Western armies could do to stop him. As a child of the Russian steppe, he understood the need for quick mobility always aimed at keeping your enemy unsteady and unsure of the next attack. Never let them breathe and never attack the same way twice.

Rybalko was a thinker in an army known for its bloody victories. He had no intention of defeating the Americans and English by gutting his command. No. He was going to outmaneuver them at each turn. They didn't have the manpower to cover all the ground he could cover, let alone stop him. What he really wished, though, was that the element of surprise would have held but twelve more hours. Those twelve hours could have meant an extra fifty kilometers tomorrow, *but what's done is done*, he thought.

He remembered the final map exercises earlier in the afternoon when everyone looked up to the skies and saw more than a dozen American fighter planes sweeping the sky. After enjoying complete operational security for the past three weeks, such a sight caught all of them by surprise. Some took it as a bad omen, but Rybalko quickly ended such talk. Still, he found himself staring up high as the battle was joined by a regiment of Soviet fighters flying top cover over the still hidden Soviet forces.

In a wild melee that lasted ten minutes, Rybalko's staff watched transfixed as two dozen planes fell from the skies. They were disappointed that half a dozen Americans escaped back to their own lines and disturbed that apparently the Americans shot down nearly eighteen Red Air Force planes during the quick engagement.

Even worse was the smell of burning diesel fuel and towering plume of black smoke signaling the American fighter-bombers must have hit a forward fuel dump. To a man, they all feared the Allied Air Force. The Americans on the ground held no fear for men who faced off against the best the Germans could hit them with, but death from above was a different matter altogether.

Bringing them back to reality, Rybalko made it clear to all that no matter the Allies discovery, the Red Army had achieved as close to strategic surprise as possible. The Allied armies were strung throughout their occupation zones, not manning built up defenses. The Soviets had gassed up tanks loaded with full ammo racks, artillery batteries with stocks of high-explosive shells ready to sunder the lines.

Red Army reconnaissance patrols dressed as German refugees observed every major crossing site and major unit from the Weser to the Elbe. Targets were pre-registered and, considering the accelerated preparation time, Rybalko couldn't be happier with what he saw.

They went over the Oker River line breach operations one more time and reviewed the march tables for the exploitation forces that will break out of the bridgehead. He could see the looks on the men's faces as their confidence grew with each movement on the map table. It all seemed so clear. Like dominoes, each Soviet move was designed to generate a likely response that was countered and then defeated until the plan played out in all its simplicity and daring.

Yes, Rybalko thought as he walked through the night, *we will crush them.* Small arms fire breaking out in the night caused him some small concern. Roving allied patrols stumbling onto his engineer and assault forces as they neared their jump off points couldn't be avoided. You couldn't hide this many men for this long and expect to stay invisible forever.

Deciding that he needed a few quick hours of shut eye, he abruptly turned around and headed for his command tent, ignoring the growing sound of fire in the distance. *Let them try to stop me and all they'll see is my tank treads as I rumble to the Rhine.*

Chapter Forty Eight

August 26, 1945, 2:00 am

Frankfurt, SHAEF Headquarters

Attention: Eyes Only General Marshall

From: General Eisenhower

Subject: War Warning

Please inform the President that hostilities now appear to be imminent. Documents brought in by the Polish Home Army agent have been confirmed. It is estimated that the Soviet offensive is timed to hit on a Sunday morning and will likely commence within the next three hours. As a result, I authorized deep penetration armed recon flights that were sanctioned to return fire if fired upon. After a series of running air battles and at the cost of nearly thirty Allied planes, we have been able to confirm the Red Army has massed its forces on a massive scale and are in the final preparations for an assault against both the American and British occupation zones.

Allied ground units have been on alert and on the move for the past fourteen hours and emergency defensive measures have been enacted. Defensive positions are being readied, but expect extremely high casualties at the point of initial contact. SHAEF is preparing for the worst. Third Army appears in solid shape, Ninth Army is setting up blocking positions to the south of Monty's Twenty First Army Group, and Hodges First Army has good terrain to defend and should be available to reinforce Ninth Army as needed. General Simpson's forces will be the most exposed American command at the outset of hostilities. Allied forces are racing towards the border area and makeshift defenses are being readied to repel the invasion.

Please request from the President the immediate recall of all military personnel from demobilization schedules and begin immediate reinforcements of both men and material, especially the new heavy M26 Pershing tank and massive amounts of artillery ammunition. I intend to authorize deep strike attacks by Allied Air Forces into Soviet controlled territory, up to but not including the Soviet border and have released all Allied ground commanders to declare free fire zones in their respective sectors. Allied artillery is now in action hitting Russian crossing sites and troop concentrations.

Allied tactical air units are preparing to launch massive ground attacks at first light.

Please prepare the President...the situation is grave and will likely get much worse before it gets better. I await your orders.

Respectfully,

General Dwight Eisenhower

Made in the USA
Middletown, DE
06 March 2023

26290017R00433